RESCUING ALLY PART 2

Guardian Hostage Rescue Specialists: Charlie Team`
Book 8

ELLIE MASTERS

MASTER OF ROMANTIC SUSPENSE

JEM Publishing

Dedication

This book is dedicated to my one and only—my amazing and wonderful husband.

Without your care and support, my writing would not have made it this far.

You pushed me when I needed to be pushed.

You supported me when I felt discouraged.

You believed in me when I didn't believe in myself.

If it weren't for you, this book never would have come to life.

Also by Ellie Masters

The LIGHTER SIDE

Ellie Masters is the lighter side of the Jet & Ellie Masters writing duo! You will find Contemporary Romance, Military Romance, Romantic Suspense, Billionaire Romance, and Rock Star Romance in Ellie's Works.

YOU CAN FIND ELLIE'S BOOKS HERE:

ELLIEMASTERS.COM/BOOKS

Shop Ellie Masters Romantic Suspense and Steamy Contemporary Romance by series.

Angel Fire Rock Romance

Guardian HRS: Alpha Team

Guardian HRS: Bravo Team

Guardian HRS: Charlie Team

Guardian HRS: Delta Team

Cerberus Personal Security

The LaRouge Triplets

The One I Want Series

Angel's Peak Series

Billionaire Boy's Club

The Lovers

Changing Roles

SUGGESTED READING ORDER

START HERE

Rockstar Romance

The Angel Fire Rock Romance Series

EACH BOOK IN THIS SERIES CAN BE READ AS A STANDALONE AND IS ABOUT A DIFFERENT COUPLE WITH AN HEA.

IT IS RECOMMENDED THEY ARE READ IN ORDER.

Heart's Insanity

Ashes to New

Heart's Desire

Heart's Collide

Hearts Divided

Hearts Entwined

Forest's FALL

Hearts The Last Beat

CONTINUE HERE...

Military Romance

Guardian Hostage Rescue Specialists

Rescuing Melissa

(Get a FREE copy of Rescuing Melissa

when you join Ellie's Newsletter)

Alpha Team

Rescuing Zoe

Rescuing Moira

Rescuing Eve

Rescuing Lily

Rescuing Jinx

Rescuing Maria

Bravo Team

Rescuing Angie

Rescuing Isabelle

Rescuing Carmen

Rescuing Rosalie

Rescuing Kaye

Cara's Protector

Rescuing Barbi

Charlie Team

Rescuing Rebel

Rescuing Stitch

Rescuing Mia

Jenna's Protector

Rescuing Sophia

Rescuing Malia

Rescuing Ally (Part 1)

Rescuing Ally (Part 2)

Delta Team

Rescuing Ember

Rescuing Aria

STANDALONES IN THE GUARDIAN HOSTAGE RESCUE

SERIES YOU CAN READ ANYTIME

Military Romance

Guardian Personal Protection Specialists

Sybil's Protector

Lyra's Protector

Angel's Peak Series

Steamy Instalove Small Town

EACH BOOK IN THIS SERIES CAN BE READ AS A STANDALONE AND IS ABOUT A DIFFERENT COUPLE WITH AN HEA.

SNOWED IN WITH THE MOUNTAIN DOCTOR

Rescued by the Mountain Guide

Stranded with the Resort Owner

Matched with the Small-Town Chef

Trapped with the Forest Ranger

Snowbound with the Vineyard Owner

Reunited with the Hometown Hero

Colliding with the Coffee Shop Owner

Falling for the Firefighter

Wrecked with the Reclusive Author

Tangled with the Single Dad

Whirlwinded by the Helicopter Pilot

Sheltered by the Veterinarian

Bound by the Sheriff

The One I Want Series
(Small Town, Military Heroes)

By Jet & Ellie Masters

Each book in this series can be read as a standalone and is about a different couple with an HEA.

Saving Abby

Saving Ariel

Saving Brie

Saving Cate

Saving Dani

Saving Jen

The LaRouge Triplets

Asher

Brody

Cage

Billionaire Romance

Billionaire Boys Club

Hawke

Richard

Contemporary Romance

Cocky Captain

Romantic Suspense

Each book is a standalone novel.

The Starling

The Swan

~AND~

Science Fiction

Ellie Masters writing as L.A. Warren

Vendel Rising: a Science Fiction Serialized Novel

If you enjoyed this book by Ellie Masters, the LIGHTER SIDE of the Jet & Ellie writing duo, and aren't afraid of edgier writing, you might enjoy reading BDSM themed books written by Jet, the DARKER SIDE of the Masters' Writing Team.

The DARKER SIDE

Jet Masters is the darker side of the Jet & Ellie writing duo!

Romantic Suspense

Changing Roles Series:

THIS SERIES MUST BE READ IN ORDER.

Command Me

Control Me

Collar Me

Embracing FATE

Seizing FATE

Accepting FATE

HOT READS

A STANDALONE NOVEL.

Down the Rabbit Hole

Light BDSM Romance

The Ties that Bind

HOT READS

Becoming His Series

Dark Captive Romance

To My Readers

This book is a work of fiction. It does not exist in the real world and should not be construed as reality. As in most romantic fiction, I've taken liberties. I've compressed the romance into a sliver of time. I've allowed these characters to develop strong bonds of trust over a matter of days.

This does not happen in real life where you, my amazing readers, live. Take more time in your romance and learn who you're giving a piece of your heart to. I urge you to move with caution. Always protect yourself.

Grab the First Book in The Guardian Hostage Rescue Specialists Series for Free

https://elliemasters.com/RescuingMelissa

ONE

The Empty Apartment

HANK

THE MEETING RUNS LONG.

Three damn hours of grim faces and bad news delivered under fluorescent lights that buzz just loud enough to irritate. Forest lays it out, Mitzy supports with live drone feeds and intercepted chatter, but the message is clear even before CJ drives the final nail in.

Malfor is back. Bolder. Smarter.

And targeting us.

"The ambush in San Diego was targeted," Forest says. His voice is gravel, low and certain. "They weren't after the asset. They wanted Alpha team."

Alpha team walked into a trap in San Diego. Routine extraction turned hostile in under ninety seconds. One operative wounded. Civilians nearly compromised. The attackers left behind zero trace—but they wore Sentinel insignia under their gear. A direct strike against Guardian HRS.

A message.

Malfor's resurfaced, and he's making moves. Big ones.

We hear it loud and clear.

But there's nothing concrete. No new locations. No new names. Just whispers in the dark and the echo of too many unanswered questions.

By the time we're dismissed, my skin's tight with tension and my jaw's wired shut. We need intel.

Movement. Action.

But there's none of that yet.

We walk out of the bullpen into the humid night air, tension still riding high. Muscles tight. Minds wired.

So we do the only thing we can: we regroup.

"Still time to crash the girls' sleepover." Gabe elbows me as we step out of the bullpen. "That scoreboard's gathering dust."

"Only one name on that board, and that's not fair." Blake snorts.

"Yeah," Walt mutters, shooting a glance at Gabe. "Some of us would've liked a shot before deployment."

Rigel stretches his arms overhead, cracking his neck. "Pretty sure Ally's tally needs a penalty. Two-on-one? Not exactly fair odds."

"Hey, we play the hand we're dealt." Gabe doesn't bother hiding his grin.

"You want points on the board, you earn them," I add, casual as ever, and loving the fact that there's no way Ally's going to lose on that leaderboard. Gabe and I are *very generous* lovers.

Laughter sparks like a match. Easy. Familiar. Laced with heat and the promise of something to chase.

Walt jerks a thumb toward the motor pool. "Golf carts?"

Ethan's grin is pure mischief. "Last one there does tomorrow's gear checks for the whole damn team."

"Pack your patience," Rigel says, already jogging. "I'm not going down easy."

We explode toward the carts like overgrown teenagers with

too much testosterone and not enough adult supervision. Blake shoves Walt sideways and vaults into the driver's seat. Ethan slides in behind Rigel. Gabe and I are dead last.

The engines hum to life, and in seconds, we're tearing across the compound like we own the night.

"You're driving like a rookie," I shout at Gabe over the roar as we lurch forward.

We tear after the others, wind slashing across our faces, gravel biting the wheels. Ahead, Rigel and Ethan swerve, cutting tight around the maintenance shed. Blake and Walt are already veering toward the staff housing shortcut.

The six of us—Charlie team—charging toward Jenna's apartment like we're about to breach Heaven's gates. Wind in our faces. Laughter in our throats.

Gabe floors it.

The engine snarls, and we surge forward.

I brace as we bounce over a pothole, gaining. Fast.

Up ahead, Blake's cart skids wide, trying to block Rigel's path. Ethan flips him off mid-turn.

"Left!" I yell.

Gabe yanks the wheel, and we shoot through a gap between the two carts, narrowly missing Blake's back bumper. Walt whoops behind us, the sound swallowed by wind and the crackle of tires on gravel.

The trees blur in our periphery—tall, dark sentinels flashing past in streaks of shadow and moonlight.

We're neck and neck by the time Jenna's building appears.

Gabe hits the brakes hard, skidding into a perfect slide. We may have started last, but that's definitely a win.

Everyone piles out laughing, breathless, adrenaline still firing through our veins.

"You clipped us at the finish," Rigel says, brushing dust from his shirt.

"Clipped you? We flew past." Gabe grins.

"Dream on," Walt mutters. "And gear checks? That's all yours, Ethan."

"Like hell," Ethan fires back, pointing at the dirt smudged across Gabe's front tire. "He cheated the inside line."

"Still got the job done," Gabe says, climbing out. "That's what matters."

We head toward the building together, still laughing, the good-natured ribbing rolling easily between us.

Overgrown kids with scars, bonded by fire, forged in chaos, and racing to the women who've somehow made warriors like us believe in something more.

We pile into the lift. Someone makes a crack about Walt's snoring. Gabe jabs back with a story that has Blake snorting.

The elevator ride up is filled with banter, half-laughed threats, and silent anticipation. When the doors open, I step into the hallway, and silence slams into me like a freight train.

The air. Too still.

The hall. Too quiet.

The kind of quiet that isn't empty. It *screams*.

Gabe freezes beside me. The others follow, the weight of silence smothering every joke, every grin.

Ethan's arm shoots out, halting Walt. Rigel's gaze sweeps the corridor.

No sounds bleed into the hallway. No laughter. No music. Just a vacuum.

Hollow.

My hand drifts toward my sidearm without thought. Gabe tenses beside me.

Ethan falls in behind, face hardening. Rigel scans the hallway, a subtle shift in stance. Blake's smile fades. Walt's jaw ticks.

We know this feeling.

Combat silence.

Then we see it.

Jenna's door.

Hanging off its hinges. Splintered. Bent inward.

The frame hanging half-on, half-off its hinges. A spiderweb of bullet holes stitched across the wood. One wine glass lies outside the threshold, shattered, red soaking into the rug like blood.

Tactical formation. No words needed.

Ethan takes the left. Blake and Walt flank right. Rigel covers the rear. Gabe and I go for breach.

I push what's left of the door open with the muzzle of my Glock.

My stomach drops.

Hell greets us.

Furniture overturned. Blood smears the floor like someone dragged a body—maybe more than one. Bullet holes pockmark the walls. Glass crunches underfoot, glittering like ice in the scattered light.

The air reeks of cordite, gas, blood, and sweat. And beneath it … Something heartbreakingly domestic.

Garlic. Pasta. Wine.

They were having dinner.

The food's still on the table. Plates half-full. A bottle is knocked over, bleeding red across the floorboards.

My throat closes as I move deeper. Wine glasses on the counter. A paused movie. One of the kids' drawings is still taped to the fridge. The kind of night you never think will end in violence.

And blood. So much blood.

Long, wet smears across the cream carpet. Palm-sized splashes across the wall. A chair shattered in the corner like someone tried to throw it—tried and failed.

Gabe steps deeper inside, weapon raised, eyes tracking the

destruction. "Clear right."

"Clear left," Ethan calls.

Then I see Max.

Jenna's German Shepherd sprawled in the wreckage, unmoving. He lies on his side near the hallway, motionless. A dart protrudes from his thick neck, fur soaked dark around the edges. I drop to one knee. My fingers search.

"Alive," I grit. "Tranqed. Not shot. Pulse is there."

Relief buzzes through me, sharp and shallow.

"Hallway's got defensive spatter," Rigel reports from behind me. "Someone fought back. And hard."

"Overturned table used as a barricade," Blake says. "They tried to hold them off."

"Three sets of drag trails," Walt adds. "They didn't walk out of here. They were carried."

The others sweep through behind us. Silent now. Controlled.

Rigel appears from the kitchen, holding up a bent brass lamp. "Improvised weapon. The base is cracked. Someone got a hit in."

"They fought hard." Blake kneels beside a shattered lamp.

And lost.

Rage hits like a freight train.

I force it back.

Not now. Focus.

"Calling it in." Ethan pulls out his phone. "Mitzy, we need footage. Now."

"Of what?" Mitzy's voice crackles through, confused.

"Jenna's apartment."

"What am I looking for?"

"Security breach. Multiple assailants. Multiple …" His voice catches. "Multiple hostages taken."

A sharp intake of breath across the line. Then steel replaces shock. "On it. Pulling feeds. Getting you everything from the last four hours."

Wine glasses. A half-finished movie is paused on the TV. A stuffed bunny sits under the table.

Zephyr's.

God no. Not the kids.

I move toward Jenna's bedroom, mind parsing the layout, the angles, the tactics. The closet door is ajar. The faint red glow of the panic room lock is lit.

"Someone's inside," I call. "Panic room's sealed."

"It's Gabe. The rest of the Charlie team is with me." Gabe presses the intercom hidden in the closet. "Open up."

No response.

"It's Hank." I lean in. "You're safe now. They're gone."

"Gabe? Hank? Is it really you?" A soft voice sounds from the other side of the door.

"Yes."

A beat. Then a soft click. The door hisses open.

Sophia stands tall, pale but alert, a sidearm steady in her grip. Behind her, Violet holds Zephyr and Luke, their eyes wide with terror.

They're safe.

The only ones.

And that's when it slams home—hard and brutal.

Everyone else is gone.

The panic cracks inside me, molten and vicious, but I hold the line.

"Sophia," I say tightly, "what happened? We need to know everything."

"Harrison," she spits the name like poison. "He showed up with documents. Claimed they were from Ally's dad for her to sign. Max knew something was wrong. He started growling before the door even opened. Then everything exploded."

She's trembling. Trying not to.

"Sophia?" Blake races down the hallway toward us. His face crumples with relief when he sees her alive.

He gathers Sophia and Luke into his arms, crushing them against his chest. Sophia breaks then, a sob tearing from her throat as Luke buries his face against Blake's neck. The boy's small shoulders shake with silent tears.

Ethan pushes past me, his usual composure cracking as he spots Violet and Zephyr. He crosses the distance in three long strides, gathering them both into a protective embrace. Zephyr's tiny hand clutches the front of his tactical vest, her face streaked with tears.

"Tell us everything," Ethan says, his voice gentle but urgent.

Sophia takes a deep breath and straightens her spine. Her hand finds Blake's, squeezing once before she steps forward to face us all.

"He pulled a gun."

"Who?" Ethan asks.

"Harrison. Max attacked. Jenna disarmed him, but then a team came in—flashbangs, gas, tactical sweep. Full black-ops extraction. No kill shots. Just tranquilizer darts."

"They wanted them alive," Gabe mutters.

"Rebel got us to the panic room. The last thing I saw—" Sophia swallows hard. "Was Harrison, bleeding, standing over Ally like he didn't feel a thing."

"Did they say anything?" I ask.

"No. But there was a symbol on their gear."

"Let me guess. Chinese characters?"

"It was Sentinel," Sophia confirms, her eyes haunted. She'd recognize it anywhere—she spent years under Malfor's control. "I saw it on their tactical vests when they breached."

"Malfor." Gabe's voice is quiet, lethal.

The room spins with that word.

The broken furniture.

The blood.

The open wine bottle.

The silence.

We failed them.

We all did.

I clench my jaw hard enough to hurt.

Mitzy's voice cracks through Ethan's phone. "I've got footage. Security feeds from the hallway and the exterior of the building. They didn't try to hide their faces or wipe the video."

Ethan gathers us around his phone, the screen casting blue light across our grim faces as the footage plays.

It's Harrison.

Robert Collins's head of security.

Leading a tactical team straight to Jenna's door.

Professional. Precise. Military-grade gear. Gas masks. Tranq rifles.

"Timestamp?" I ask.

"Ninety minutes after you left for the meeting."

It was a distraction.

The mission. The briefing. All of it.

To get us out of the way.

The feed switches to the hallway. Women being dragged out, unconscious. Ally. Jenna. Mia. Rebel. Malia.

Gabe's face hardens, comprehension dawning in his eyes. "This wasn't about intel or assets," he says, voice cold. "Malfor went after what matters most. He took our women." His fists clench at his sides, knuckles white. "A direct attack. Personal."

Ethan starts barking orders: "We need to get Max stabilized. Blake and Walt, secure the perimeter. Hank and Gabe, sweep the building. Mitzy, we need every feed you can give us."

Gabe moves beside me. His face is stone.

Charlie team locks eyes. One by one. No need for speeches.

This is war.

They took our women.
And now?
We're going after them.
The rage is white hot now. Purposeful.
Relentless.
We're bringing the war to Malfor's doorstep.

TWO

Survivors' Account

GABE

THE KIDS ARE THE WORST PART.

Luke's eyes are vacant—a thousand-yard stare on a five-year-old face. He hasn't made a sound since we found them. Just clutches his stuffed dinosaur with white knuckles and burrows deeper into Sophia's side whenever someone moves too fast.

Zephyr's different—won't stop crying. Silent tears track down her cheeks, and she hiccups when Violet tries to soothe her. The crying strips you raw because there's no tantrum in it. Just pure, distilled fear.

And I want to fucking kill someone for putting tears in Zephyr's pretty eyes and that vacant stare in Luke's.

Techies swarm Jenna's apartment, cataloging blood spatter and retrieving tranq darts. The scene's gone clinical—evidence markers dotting the wreckage like toxic yellow flowers. Max is on a stretcher, still unconscious but stable. Carter crouches beside him, hand resting on the dog's flank, his face carved from stone.

He hasn't said a word since we told him about Jenna. Not a goddamn sound. Just nodded once, jaw so tight I thought I heard something crack, then went straight to Max.

The hollow look in Carter's eyes—it's worse than if he'd broken down. This ain't no storm. It's the calm before something apocalyptic.

I pace the perimeter, calculating blast radius, entry points, tactical advantage—the shit that keeps my brain from short-circuiting.

Five steps. Turn. Five steps. Turn. Repeat.

"Sophia." I stop mid-circuit. My voice comes out rougher than intended. I dial it back. "We need everything you can remember. Every detail."

Blake gives me a warning look—*Back off, she's traumatized*—but Sophia straightens, steel in her spine despite the tremor in her hands.

"It was Harrison." The name is acid on her tongue. "It all happened so fast. He was at the door, claiming he had documents from Ally's father."

She strokes Luke's hair mechanically as she speaks. The boy doesn't stir.

"Max knew something was wrong right away. Started growling before Jenna even opened the door." Her eyes go distant, replaying the memory. "When she cracked it open, Harrison reached for something inside his jacket. Max just—exploded. Went straight for his arm."

"Good boy," I mutter. Mental note: steak dinner for that dog when he wakes up.

"Then everything happened at once." Sophia swallows hard. "Harrison screamed. Dropped a gun. Jenna shouted 'Gun!' and dove for it. His men outside started moving. Rebel yelled for me to get the kids to the safe room."

Her hands tremble. Blake covers them with his own.

"That's when I grabbed Luke and Zephyr. The last thing I saw was men in tactical gear rushing through the doorway and Jenna raising Harrison's gun. Then there was gunfire, glass breaking … I got the kids to the panic room like Stitch taught us."

"So you didn't see what happened to Ally? The others?" Hank asks, materializing beside me. His voice is too controlled.

Dangerous.

Sophia shakes her head. "No. Once we were in the panic room, we could hear everything—the fighting, the shots, someone screaming. Then—silence." Her voice breaks. "When it went quiet, we waited, like Stitch taught us. We stayed hidden until you came."

"You did exactly right," I tell her, the words scraping against my throat. "You saved the kids."

"The bastards had a plan all along," I snarl. The magnitude of Harrison's betrayal is staggering—the man's been Robert Collins's head of security for decades. He watched Ally grow up.

Protected her.

And now?

I've never wanted to unmake someone as badly as I want to unmake Harrison.

"We need to see what happened after Sophia got to the safe room," Hank says to Ethan, his voice flat. Deadly.

Ethan plugs a tablet into the wall display. The apartment's security feed fills the screen—multiple angles, high-definition clarity, but views are limited to the hall.

It's an incomplete picture.

I analyze it with a technician's eye—cataloging weapons, tactics, vulnerabilities. The team moves like pros, but there's something—*off*.

"Stop," I say at one frame. "Go back fifteen seconds."

Ethan rewinds.

"There…" I point. "Gas deployment pattern. That's Guardian protocol. See the formation? The way they stack? That's our standard breach procedure."

The weight of this sinks in.

"These aren't random mercenaries," Hank says, following my thought. "Someone's feeding Malfor our playbook."

"Or he's got more moles," I mutter.

The footage continues. We watch Harrison enter first, the smooth deception as he approaches the door. The moment Max lunges, exactly as Sophia described. The gun falling. Then chaos erupts.

The hallway camera catches glimpses through the doorway—flashes of movement, Max latched onto Harrison's arm, Jenna diving for the fallen weapon, then gunfire.

As the team floods in, we see what Sophia couldn't. Rebel grabs a kitchen knife from the counter and slashes at the first operative to reach her, opening his arm from wrist to elbow. Malia flips the heavy dining table for cover. Ally—my chest tightens—swings a brass lamp at an attacker's ribs. The impact drops him.

"Fuck," Walt breathes as we watch the assault continue. "That's Trac-tech equipment. Ghost-class thermal. Government contract only."

"And look at the build on the two at the back," I add. "Similar profile to Sentinel operatives. Same stance, same kit configuration." I can't be certain—Kazakhstan was a blur of smoke and blood and explosions—but the physical signature feels familiar. Like a scar you recognize by shape, not sight.

The footage captures what happens next. Gas canisters roll across the floor. Max collapses from a tranquilizer dart. Jenna fires until her gun empties, then swings it like a club before succumbing to the gas. Rebel takes a dart to the shoulder, yanks it out, and keeps fighting until a second one drops her. Mia and Malia fall to the gas.

Then Harrison reappears, blood streaming down his arm, his

face a mask of fury as he stands over Ally. He extracts something from his tactical vest—a syringe.

"What's he giving her?" Blake asks.

"Something specialized," I reply, demolitions training kicking in as I analyze the delivery mechanism. "Not a standard tranq. Look at the delivery system—that's a pressure injector. High-velocity deployment. Military grade."

The rest of the feed shows the extraction. Women dragged through the hallway, unconscious. The elevator security camera captures them loading Ally, Jenna, Rebel, Malia, and Mia into what appear to be large equipment cases. Then they move to the roof.

"The roof?" Blake's brows tug together. "What the fuck?"

"Mitzy," Ethan barks into his comm. "We need rooftop footage. Now."

Her voice crackles back, "Working on it. Roof cameras were compromised, but I've got fragments from the perimeter sweep."

The screen flickers, switches to a grainy night-vision feed. At first, it's just static darkness, then movement. Shadows against the sky, whirring blades cutting the air.

"What the hell," Rigel breathes.

Drones. Not surveillance models. Not the little quadcopters used for recon. These are military-grade transport drones, featuring heavy lift capacity, near-silent operation, and massive payload potential. Six of them hover above the roof like mechanical vultures.

"They used drones for extraction?" Walt's disbelief mirrors my own. "That's—"

"Brilliant," I cut in, mind already calculating lift capacities, flight ranges, and acoustic signatures. "High-risk, but fucking brilliant. Low radar profile, especially at night. No heat signature like a chopper. Virtually invisible to perimeter security. Relatively silent."

The footage shows figures loading the equipment cases, which hold our women, onto harness systems beneath each drone. Then they rise and vanish into the night sky.

Hank's face transforms as he absorbs every frame. His eyes go glacier-cold. His jaw locks. His breathing slows to a predator's patience. The mask slips into place—the one I recognize from our darkest ops. Our worst recoveries.

This is Hank at his most lethal.

"Timestamps," he says. "Cross-reference with perimeter breach alerts."

"Already calculating," Ethan responds, fingers flying. "They had a sixty-eight-minute head start before we arrived."

"Sixty-eight minutes, fifteen seconds and counting," I correct automatically, my brain already mapping distances, potential extraction routes. "We need Mitzy to run calculations on probable range and capabilities of these things."

Mitzy's voice cuts in through the comm. "I've tracked the initial flight path. They headed west, out over the ocean. Lost them after about three miles offshore."

"Ocean extraction," Hank mutters. "That means a vessel."

"Rendezvous with a ship," I agree, connecting the dots. "The drones don't have the range for a full extraction, just the initial phase. Could be anything waiting out there—yacht, fishing trawler, cargo vessel."

"Checking maritime traffic now," Mitzy reports, the clatter of her keyboard audible through the comm. "Four commercial vessels passed within the projected flight path window. Cross-referencing against satellite imagery to identify any vessels running dark."

I'm running mental calculations—drone flight endurance, ocean currents, shipping lanes—when Forest's voice cuts through the chaos. The Guardian HRS founder looms in the doorway, his face weathered granite as he surveys the destruction.

"Stitch is missing too," he says without preamble, each word precisely measured. "Her apartment was hit simultaneously. Professional. Clinical. Same approach."

The air stills around us. Stitch—Malfor's prodigy, until he sold her out and left her to rot in federal prison. The woman Mitzy recruited for her incomparable skills as a hacker.

"Full lockdown," Forest orders. "All operations suspended. All personnel are confined to quarters or duty stations. Sigma protocols are active."

Sigma protocols. Our nuclear option. The glass-breaking contingency for when Guardian HRS itself has been compromised.

Ethan steps forward. "Our team—"

"Is missing five civilians and one essential operative under our direct protection," Forest finishes, steel in every syllable. "I'm well aware, Ethan. This is now a Category 1 recovery operation."

Category 1. No restrictions. No rules of engagement.

Forest's eyes lock with each of us in turn. "Whatever you need. Whoever you need." His gaze settles on Hank. "You have full operational autonomy. Find them."

"And Malfor?" I ask.

Forest's expression doesn't change. "Bring me his head or don't come back."

He doesn't wait for acknowledgment. None needed.

"Mitzy's running traces now," Forest continues. "CJ and Sam are activating international assets. We're calling in every marker ever owed."

I'm barely listening, my mind already calculating. Sixty-eight minutes, forty seconds. Every second burns, acid eating through my control.

Flight trajectories over open water. Vessel interception points. Drone battery life versus payload weight. The weather conditions over the Pacific tonight. I map it all, trying to predict where they'd take six heavily guarded women.

Where they'd take Ally.

My chest constricts thinking about her—unconscious, at Harrison's mercy. The specialized injection. Malfor's particular interest is in her brain and her research. The fact that he's tried to capture her twice before.

And succeeded, this time.

I catch my reflection in a broken mirror—I barely recognize the face staring back. Eyes like blown glass. Jaw rigid. Something feral is lurking beneath the surface.

I know this feeling. I've used it before.

The rage builds, familiar and dangerous. A tightly controlled explosion is waiting for detonation. The kind that, properly channeled, lets me do the unthinkable. The kind that lets me move mountains or tear men apart with my bare hands.

The kind that lets me hunt the most dangerous men alive through the darkest corners of the earth.

The kind that will bring Ally back to us.

Hank catches my eye across the room, and the same savage calculation is reflected there. His fury runs cold where mine burns hot, but the destination is identical.

We're going to kill Malfor.

THREE

In Transit

ALLY

I'm awake, but I don't open my eyes.

Not yet.

Years of my father's security training kicks in—assess before revealing consciousness. Gather intel. Create advantage.

That and the experience of two prior kidnappings. They always say the third one's the charm. Whoever "*they*" are, they can eat shit. I can't believe this is happening again.

Fortunately, I've developed a few skills after kidnappings one and two.

The chemical burn of the gas lingers in my lungs, each breath scraping raw tissue. My mouth tastes like pennies and ash. Sedative aftereffects drag at my limbs, but my mind is clearing, cataloging sensations.

The floor vibrates beneath my cheek, rhythmic and mechanical. It's an engine—an aircraft, not a vehicle—the hum is too consistent, and the air pressure is subtly wrong. My wrists burn where zip ties cut into skin, already swollen and angry. Someone bound my ankles too.

There is no slack to exploit.

I crack my eyelids a millimeter, letting in slivers of dim light. Cargo hold. Military grade. Bench seating along the walls. No windows. The air reeks of fuel, metal, and blood.

Jenna lies nearest to me, her face a topography of bruises flowering purple and black. Her breathing is shallow but steady. One eye is swollen shut. Dried blood crusts her hairline. But her chest rises and falls.

Rebel is motionless beside her, right arm bent unnaturally. Compound fracture, my brain supplies clinically. Her skin has a gray undertone. She fought the hardest. The damage reflects it.

Malia's slumped against the wall, hair matted with something dark. Still unconscious. Mia curls beside her, awake but pretending not to be—just like me. Smart girl. Her fingers twitch slightly. Counting seconds, maybe. Mapping time.

Then—a figure I don't expect.

Stitch.

The shock drives a nail of ice through my calculated calm. Her presence rewrites everything I thought I understood. Stitch —Malfor's former protégé, abandoned to federal prison when she failed him. The woman who knows his systems inside out, who has been helping Guardian HRS dismantle his networks piece by piece.

Footsteps approach—measured, unhurried. The familiar cadence freezes my blood.

Harrison.

The man who's been part of my life since childhood. Who taught me self-defense when I was twelve. Who rushed me to the hospital when I broke my arm at fourteen. Who my father trusted above all others.

Who sold us out.

"I know you're awake, Miss Collins."

His voice is the same measured and professional tone he's

used all my life, as if he didn't just betray everything and everyone. Like, he isn't currently transporting us to a monster.

I open my eyes fully, abandoning the pretense. There's no point now.

"Harrison." My voice is sandpaper, throat raw from the gas. "Enjoy that promotion to Judas? What does thirty pieces of silver buy these days?"

He doesn't react to the barb. Just stands there in his tactical gear, right arm bandaged where Max tore into him. Good dog. Hope it gets infected.

"You're taking the situation rather well," he notes, clinical, detached. "The others weren't so composed when they woke up."

When they woke up? All the others are asleep. Or sedated. Shit, am I the last to regain consciousness?

"That's because I'm imagining all the ways Hank and Gabe are going to tear you apart," I reply, pushing myself to a sitting position. The motion sends daggers of pain through my skull, but I refuse to wince. "Piece by piece. Nerve by nerve. They're very creative."

Something flickers in his eyes—not fear, exactly. Awareness, maybe. Good. He should be afraid. They're coming, and there's nowhere on earth he can hide from what they'll do when they find him.

"Your men at Guardian HRS think they're untouchable," he says, moving to check Rebel's restraints. "We'll see how they feel when we break them."

I track his movements, cataloging details. His injured arm. How he favors his left side. The blood loss has left him slightly pale. There are three other operatives in the cargo hold—all armed, all watching.

Weak points. Vulnerabilities.

Data for later.

"Why?" The question burns out of me before I can stop it. "Why betray us? My father trusted you. I trusted you."

He straightens, something almost like regret crossing his features before the mask slides back into place.

"Your father's not the only one with resources, Miss Collins. Not the only one with reach." He gestures to the cargo hold, to us—women bound and broken. "And this? This is just the beginning."

"Beginning of what?" I push, needing information more than comfort. "Malfor's revenge tour? Is that what you signed up for? Being an errand boy to a sociopath?"

His jaw tightens—a tell I've known since childhood. I've struck a nerve.

"Malfor sees the bigger picture," Harrison replies, voice even. "This isn't about revenge. It's about balance. Correction." He looks at each of us in turn. "All of you are tied to Guardian HRS. To Charlie team. The perfect leverage."

"You're using us as bait." The realization crystallizes in my mind. "To draw them out."

"Among other things." His smile doesn't reach his eyes. "Your value extends beyond mere bait, Miss Collins. Your research has —*applications*. And Malfor has plans for it."

Ice spreads through my veins. My quantum containment research. The fusion reactor modifications I smuggled out of Kazakhstan. He wants more than revenge; he wants my brain.

"Where are we going?" I struggle to keep fear from my voice.

"Somewhere secure. Somewhere, your Guardian friends won't find you until we want them to."

"Sophia? Violet? The children?" The words scrape raw on the way out.

"They weren't part of the extraction. Should've been." For the first time, Harrison hesitates. "That's—a failure I'll have to answer for."

Relief crashes through me, followed immediately by calculation. If they're not here, they must have reached the panic room. They're alive. Protected. And they can tell Guardian HRS everything they saw.

Another thought grips me—hope wrapped in dread.

"And Max?"

Harrison's hand drifts unconsciously to his bandaged arm. "Sedated. Not dead."

I almost smile, visceral satisfaction warming me for a brief moment. Good. Carter would kill this man himself if they killed his dog.

"You made a mistake." I lean forward despite the pain it sends through my shoulders. "You think you know the Guardians. You think you know what they're capable of, but you have no idea what happens when you take someone they love."

"I know exactly what they're capable of." His voice hardens. "I've studied them for months. Every move. Every weakness." He gestures around the cargo hold. "And now I have six of those weaknesses right here."

"Why Stitch?" I challenge, nodding toward the unconscious woman.

Something passes across Harrison's face—confirmation.

"Malfor doesn't forget betrayal."

"Neither do I." The words emerge like bullets. "And neither will my father. You know what he'll do to find me. What resources he'll deploy."

For a heartbeat, uncertainty shadows his features. Then it's gone.

"Robert Collins is a businessman," he dismisses. "When the time comes, he'll make the practical choice."

"You don't know him at all," I say softly, certainty burning like wildfire. "Not if you believe that."

Harrison checks his watch, visibly done with this conversation. "We reach the rendezvous in thirty minutes. I suggest you prepare yourself, Miss Collins. It's going to be a very long and arduous journey."

I close my eyes, drawing deep on everything I've learned from Hank and Gabe. From their training sessions. From their protection.

From their love.

The rational part of my brain knows our chances are microscopic. Six bound women against armed operatives, and a madman waiting at the destination.

But I refuse to be helpless.

I think about quantum entanglement—my research, my life's work. Particles that once connected remain connected, no matter the distance separating them. Change one, and the other changes instantly. A bond that transcends physical space.

Like me, Hank, and Gabe.

Connected. Entangled. Inseparable.

Distance doesn't matter.

Malfor doesn't matter.

Harrison doesn't matter.

They will find me.

Find us.

That's not blind hope or faith—it's inevitable.

We are Charlie's Angels, and we'll do whatever it takes to survive until they come.

FOUR

The Transport Container

ALLY

THE AIRCRAFT SHUDDERS TO A VIOLENT STOP, AND MY BODY SLAMS forward against the restraints, cutting into my wrists. The engines that have been my constant companion for what feels like hours finally spin down, their mechanical whine replaced by harsh voices barking commands in rapid-fire Spanish.

I've been conscious for most of the flight, cataloging every sound, every vibration, every shift in air pressure that might tell me where we're going. But the sedatives still cling to my thoughts like fog, making everything feel distant and wrong.

The cargo ramp drops with a hydraulic hiss, and tropical sunlight sears through the opening like a surge of gold. The heat hits instantly—wet, thick, oppressive in a way that makes California's warmth feel like air conditioning. After hours in the aircraft's climate-controlled cabin, the humidity is disorienting enough to make my head swim.

Armed men board with the efficiency of people who've done this many times before. No insignia on their tactical gear. No identifying marks. Just the purposeful movements that scream professional military training. One of them gestures toward us with the barrel of his rifle.

"Out," he says in accented English. "Now."

My legs are cement when they haul me upright. The zip ties around my ankles have cut off circulation for hours, and pins and needles shoot through my feet as blood flow returns. Every muscle in my body protests as I'm yanked toward the ramp, my shoulder screaming from wherever I landed wrong during the initial takedown at Jenna's apartment.

Around me, the others are being dragged out with the same rough treatment. Jenna's limping badly, favoring her left leg, and there's a cut on her forehead that's crusted with dried blood. Mia's shirt is torn at the shoulder, revealing angry purple bruises underneath, and her hair is matted with dark blood from what looks like a head wound. But it's Rebel who makes my stomach clench—her right arm hangs at an unnatural angle, broken, and her face has gone gray with pain.

I stumble down the ramp, blinking against the glare, trying to process our surroundings through the haze of heat and disorientation. The air is dead still—no breeze to cut through the oppressive humidity that makes every breath feel like drowning. It reeks of jet fuel and rotting vegetation, with an underlying metallic tang that could be blood or rust.

Stitch moves beside me, and even bound and injured, her eyes sweep our surroundings.

We're on a small airstrip carved out of dense jungle, the kind of place that doesn't appear on any civilian maps. Palm trees press close to the runway's edges, and beyond them, razor wire-topped walls stretch into the green.

The airstrip is completely enclosed by those walls, with only one visible gate leading to what appears to be a road that vanishes into the jungle. No tower. No communications equipment I can see. No signs of civilization beyond this isolated facility.

One of the guards shoves Malia forward when she doesn't move fast enough, and she flinches away from his touch. The sound she makes—half fear, half anger—cuts through the tropical air like broken glass.

They herd us across the scorching tarmac toward a matte-black container truck parked near the airstrip's edge. No markings. No license plates. No identifying features beyond its obvious purpose as a mobile prison.

As we get closer, more details of our surroundings emerge. The walls surrounding the compound are at least fifteen feet high, topped with multiple rows of razor wire. Guard towers are positioned at regular intervals, though I can't see if they're manned from this angle. The jungle beyond looks impenetrable —the kind of dense tropical vegetation that could hide a person for days or swallow them completely.

No signs of rescue.

No friendly faces.

No indication that anyone even knows where we are.

One of the guards hits a remote, and the truck's rear doors hiss open. The interior is exactly what I expected—empty metal walls, welded bench plates along the sides, mesh ventilation panels near the ceiling. A mobile holding cell designed for human cargo.

They load us hard and fast, like we're equipment being moved between facilities. When Jenna hits the metal floor wrong, she cries out sharply, the sound echoing off the container walls.

Stitch immediately shifts as much as her restraints allow, maneuvering closer to check on her. "She's okay," she says, voice steady despite everything. "Breathe, Jenna. Just breathe."

The doors slam shut with finality that makes my chest tight.

Total darkness swallows us for a moment before red emergency lights flicker on, casting everything in a hellish glow that makes the injuries on our faces look worse than they probably are.

The heat builds immediately inside the metal container. No windows. No air circulation beyond those small mesh panels. Only the sound of six women breathing raggedly and the faint hum of whatever machinery keeps those emergency lights running.

"Everyone okay?" Jenna's voice cuts through the heavy air.

"Broken arm," Rebel says through gritted teeth, cradling her injured limb against her body. "But I can still move my fingers."

Stitch shifts closer to examine her. "Can you feel this?" She touches Rebel's fingertips gently.

"Yeah. Hurts like hell, but there's circulation."

"Mia?" Jenna calls softly.

"Head's pounding." Mia's voice is thick, and when she turns toward the red light, I can see the dark stain matting her hair. "Vision's okay, though. No nausea. Probably not a concussion."

"Malia?"

"Bruised ribs. Nothing broken." Her voice shakes slightly. "Just scared."

All eyes turn to me, and I realize they're waiting for my assessment. "Dislocated shoulder, I think. Zip tie burns. But functional."

The simple act of checking on each other, of confirming we're all still here and still fighting, steadies something inside me. We're hurt, but we're together. That has to count for something.

"Anyone got a plan? Because I'd love to hear one." Rebel's voice is rough with pain and something harder.

"Unless it involves snapping zip ties with our minds, not yet." Malia's response is a choked laugh that borders on hysteria.

I test my bindings again, systematically probing for any weakness or slack. Nothing. They're professional-grade restraints, applied by people who know what they're doing.

I shift my position to ease the pressure building in my thighs, where the plastic cuts into my circulation.

"They need us alive," I whisper, as much to convince myself as the others. "That's something."

"As leverage against Charlie team," Stitch says, her eyes finding mine in the red-tinted darkness. Her expression is harder than I've ever seen it. "A way to hit them where it hurts most."

She's right. This isn't just about my research, though that's certainly part of it. Harrison's betrayal, the coordinated assault, the professional extraction—it's designed to hit Charlie team where they're most vulnerable.

Through us.

But for Stitch, this is something else entirely. Malfor was her mentor. He taught her everything she knows about hacking and systems infiltration. She was his protégé until she got caught breaking into NSA servers, and he disappeared, leaving her to face federal prison alone.

This is personal revenge wrapped in tactical strategy.

Silence falls over the container, broken only by the truck's engine turning over and the slight vibration as we begin to move. And in that silence, with the weight of Stitch's words settling over us, I realize something that makes my blood run cold.

This isn't just a capture. This isn't even the beginning of whatever Malfor has planned.

This is stage one of something much, much worse.

The truck picks up speed, carrying us away from the airstrip and deeper into whatever hell Malfor has prepared. The engine growls as we climb what feels like a winding road, the vehicle swaying slightly with each turn.

My wrists burn where the zip ties cut into swollen flesh. My shoulder throbs in rhythm with my heartbeat. And somewhere in the back of my mind, the part of me that's always calculating probabilities starts running scenarios.

None of them end well.

But I'm still thinking. Still planning. Still fighting.

And as long as I can do that, there's hope.

Even if I can't see it yet.

FIVE

Island Arrival & Courtyard Collaring

ALLY

THE TRUCK LURCHES TO A VIOLENT STOP, AND THE SCREECH OF brakes cuts through my awareness like a blade. The hiss of hydraulics follows—doors unlocking. My stomach clenches.

I've lost all track of time. The sedatives still drag at the edges of my mind, making everything feel underwater and wrong, but I'm alert enough to catalog what matters. We're on solid ground. Based on the salt-heavy humidity seeping through the open doors, we're somewhere coastal.

Blinding-white light floods the cargo space, and harsh voices bark commands in what sounds like Spanish mixed with accents I can't place. My eyes water, pupils contracting painfully as shadows move against the glare—more armed figures in tactical gear gesturing for us to move.

"*¡Vámonos!* Now! Out!"

My legs are cement blocks when I try to stand. The zip ties have cut off circulation for hours, and pins and needles shoot through my feet as blood flows back. I stumble into Rebel, who's pale as death but upright, her good arm braced against the truck wall for support.

"Easy," she murmurs, steadying me with her uninjured hand. Her broken arm hangs at an unnatural angle, and white-hot pain flickers across her features every time she moves.

Jenna moves ahead of us. Her swollen eye has opened enough to function, and I watch her make mental notes of everything—guard positions, equipment, potential weaknesses.

We're herded across a narrow concrete dock that reeks of fish and diesel fuel. The ocean stretches endlessly in all directions, a nauseating shade of green blue under the harsh tropical sun. No land is visible on the horizon. No aircraft contrails in the sky. Just water and sky and the growing certainty that we're completely isolated.

At the end of the dock, a military-style RIB waits, its twin outboard engines idling with barely contained power. The boat looks like it could outrun anything on this water—if we had anywhere to run to.

Another team of operatives in black tactical gear waves us aboard. Their weapons stay trained on us, but there's no shouting. No unnecessary movement. Just the quiet professionalism of people who know their prey is already caught.

The boat launches before we're properly seated, and I grab the bench beside me as we accelerate across the choppy water. The engines roar, drowning out any possibility of conversation, which is probably the point.

I count islands as we speed past—or try to. Small volcanic outcroppings covered in jungle vegetation. Nothing that looks inhabited. Nothing that looks like it has an airstrip or communications equipment. Just endless tropical wilderness scattered across an ocean that could be anywhere from the Pacific to the Caribbean.

Twenty minutes pass before land emerges from the heat haze ahead. This island is different—larger, more jagged, with steep cliffs rising directly from the water. Dense jungle covers every surface, but as we approach, there are structures hidden in the green. Concrete. Metal. The hard edges of human habitation carved into the wilderness.

A weathered dock extends from a small cove, and beyond it, a road cuts up through the vegetation toward what looks like a compound perched on the hillside. Razor wire glints in the sunlight along the perimeter fencing.

Another truck waits at the end of the dock—same model as before, same black tint on the windows, same sense of inevitability. They transfer us with the same silent efficiency, and we're moving again before I can fully process our new surroundings.

The road winds upward through increasingly dense jungle. Through the truck's small rear window, I glimpse the terrain—lush, wild, humid enough to make breathing feel like drowning.

The island isn't just isolated.

It's designed to be inescapable.

When the truck finally stops again, the heat hits me like a physical blow. Thick, oppressive, carrying scents of flowering plants and something else—something metallic and wrong.

We're inside the compound now. High concrete walls topped with razor wire stretch in every direction, broken only by guard towers and surveillance equipment. The courtyard we're standing in is large enough for a helicopter to land, paved in weathered stone that radiates heat even through my shoes.

And there, waiting in the center like he's been expecting us, is a man I've never seen in person, but immediately recognize.

Malfor.

He's smaller than I expected—average height, unremarkable build, the kind of person who could disappear in any crowd. But his eyes are what stop my breath. Cold, calculating, and completely focused on us with the intensity of a scientist studying specimens.

No guards flank him. No weapons visible. Just that detached

smile that somehow manages to be more terrifying than all of Harrison's threats combined.

"Welcome," he says, his voice smooth and cultured with a slight accent I can't place, "to the heart of my operation."

The words hit me like ice water. This is it. This is where he's been planning everything—hidden away from satellites and surveillance, surrounded by enough ocean to swallow any rescue attempt.

Behind me, the others shift restlessly. Malia makes a small sound that might be terror or rage. Mia's breathing has gone shallow and quick. Even Jenna's composure shows cracks.

"I know this isn't the reunion some of you were expecting," Malfor continues, his gaze lingering on Stitch with something that might be amusement. "But I believe in completing unfinished business."

He moves to a black case sitting on a concrete ledge and opens it. Inside, nestled in custom foam, are six objects that make my blood freeze.

Collars.

They're sleek, matte black, obviously high-tech. Each one bristles with small components—electronics, sensors, maybe transmitters. The kind of sophisticated control device that a man like Malfor would consider elegant.

"Let's make this official." He lifts the first collar from its casing.

He steps toward us himself, taking his time, and I realize with growing horror that he's going to do this personally. Not delegating to guards or subordinates. This is important enough to him that he wants to handle it himself.

"Don't touch me," Rebel snarls as he approaches her first, but her broken arm makes resistance meaningless.

He fastens the collar around her throat with the careful attention of someone adjusting jewelry, his fingers brushing aside her hair to make minor adjustments to the fit.

"Perfect," he murmurs, then looks directly into her eyes. "You have such fire. I'm looking forward to seeing how long it lasts."

One by one, he moves down the line. Malia tries to pull away, but the guards move forward just enough to discourage resistance. Mia stands rigid as stone, her biochemist's mind probably cataloging every detail of the device being locked around her neck. Jenna's jaw is set in furious lines, but she keeps still, calculating, waiting for better odds.

When he reaches Stitch, his smile deepens.

"My dear protégé." There's genuine affection in his voice that makes my skin crawl. "You've learned so much since our time together. All those Guardian systems you've been helping them understand. All those secrets you've shared." He adjusts her collar with particular care. "You're going to help me again. Whether you want to or not."

Stitch's eyes are pure hatred, but she doesn't speak.

Finally, he reaches me.

"Miss Collins …" he says, and his attention feels like being dissected. "The brilliant quantum physicist. The woman who nearly destroyed my reactor with such—elegant sabotage." He lifts the last collar, examining it in the harsh sunlight. "Do you know what these devices are capable of?"

I force myself to meet his gaze. "Control mechanisms. Probably a neural interface, given the component configuration. Designed to inflict pain as a compliance tool."

"Very good." He steps behind me, his fingers brush my neck as he lifts my hair.

The collar is surprisingly light as it settles around my throat, but I can feel the weight of its implications. The soft click as it locks is as final as a prison door.

"This is not just decoration," he says, stepping back to admire his work. "This is compliance. Cooperation. The beginning of a new phase in our relationship."

He moves to the center of the courtyard, lifting a small remote from the case. It's deceptively simple—black, compact, with a single red button prominently displayed.

"I believe in demonstration over explanation," he says conversationally. "So let's see how synchronized you are."

The question in his voice is rhetorical. His finger hovers over the button, and I have exactly enough time to realize what's about to happen before—

Pain explodes through my nervous system like molten metal poured directly into my spine. Every muscle locks simultaneously—my back arcs, my jaw clamps shut, my vision goes white at the edges. The world disappears except for the sensation of being torn apart from the inside out.

Around me, I hear screaming—mine, theirs, impossible to distinguish individual voices. We hit the ground, bodies convulsing against the hot stone.

It lasts maybe five seconds. Maybe five hours. Time becomes meaningless when every nerve ending is on fire.

When it stops, I'm flat on my back, staring up at a too-blue sky, bile burning in my throat. My muscles are liquid. My heart pounds so hard I can see it in my peripheral vision.

"That," Malfor says, his voice floating down from what seems like a great distance, "is level three. There are seven levels available on these devices. Level seven will stop your heart."

I try to speak and discover I've bitten my tongue hard enough to taste blood.

"I want you to understand," he crouches beside where I'm sprawled on the ground, "that your previous experiences with captivity—with negotiations, with hope of rescue—those rules no longer apply."

He reaches out and almost gently adjusts my collar, which has shifted during the convulsions.

"This is not a kidnapping. This is not a hostage situation. This is ownership. You belong to me now, until I decide otherwise. Your compliance is not requested—it's programmed."

Around me, the others struggle to sit, still shaking from the aftershocks. Rebel's face is gray, and I think she might have passed out completely. Mia has vomited, the acidic smell mixing with the tropical heat.

"The beauty of these devices," Malfor says, standing again, "is that I don't need to break you individually. I can condition you as a group. When one of you disobeys, all of you suffer. When one of you tries to escape, all of you pay the price."

He smiles down at us, and it's the expression of a man who's thought this through completely.

"You'll learn to police each other. To value group compliance over individual resistance. To see your sisterhood as a liability rather than a strength." He pockets the remote. "It's remarkably effective."

The implications hit me through the lingering neural static. Not only are we individually controlled, but we're responsible for each other's pain. Every act of resistance will be paid for by everyone. Every escape attempt will bring agony to women I've come to care about.

It's psychological torture disguised as technology.

"Your quarters are being prepared," Malfor says, turning away from us. "Rest well. Tomorrow, we begin your education and integration."

He walks away without looking back, leaving us collapsed on the burning stone of his courtyard, wearing his collars, breathing his air, completely at his mercy.

For the first time since this nightmare began, I understand that rescue might not be coming fast enough to matter.

The collars pulse once—a gentle rhythm against our throats, like a heartbeat. Or a countdown.

SIX

The Hunt Begins

HANK

THE COMMAND CENTER AT GUARDIAN HQ HAS A PARTICULAR energy during crisis operations. It's not chaos—chaos is undisciplined. This is controlled urgency.

Laser-focused intent.

Every asset is in position. Every operator has a purpose.

I've seen this configuration a hundred times, but never from this side of the equation. Never as the one with everything to lose.

Workstations form a horseshoe around the central holographic display. Mitzy's techs occupy the right wing, each hunched over monitors tracking maritime traffic, drone signatures, and satellite feeds. Intelligence analysts are sorting incoming data, monitoring chatter, and parsing patterns from noise.

Sam stands at the command station; his face carved from granite as he reviews satellite imagery. Forest paces nearby, expression unchanged since Jenna's apartment. If someone lacks tactical training, they might miss the subtle indicators of his rage

—the precisely measured steps, the controlled breathing, the absolute economy of movement.

I recognize it because I'm implementing the same protocols.

Compartmentalization.

Controlled emotional resources.

Tactical focus.

The alternative is unacceptable.

Every Guardian team is represented. Alpha. Bravo. Charlie. Delta. We represent some of the world's most lethal operators, all assembled in one room.

The collective combat experience in this space could topple governments; *has* toppled governments.

And at this moment, every bit of it is focused on one objective.

"Surveillance review confirms what we suspected," Forest begins without preamble. "This was meticulously planned and executed. Not opportunistic. Calculated."

The holographic display cycles through security camera stills: Harrison's arrival, the team's deployment formation, and the extraction sequence.

"Harrison's been Robert Collins's head of security for twenty years," Sam continues.

"Yet, somehow, he executed a perfect breach of our facility," I state, the words clipped, precise. "Which means either he's been gathering intelligence on us for Malfor, or Malfor has another source."

Sam nods once, the only acknowledgment necessary. "Sentinel's infiltration exceeded predicted capabilities. We're implementing full Sigma protocols."

Translation: trust no one.

"We've got drone fragments," Mitzy announces from her station. She looks exhausted, with her purple hair limp and eyes red rimmed from hours of analysis. "Recovered from the rooftop extraction point. Someone sabotaged the cameras up there, but we found trace components."

The display shifts to technical schematics, including propulsion systems, guidance hardware, and flight control mechanisms.

"These aren't anything on record," she continues. "Custom builds. Military-grade components with proprietary modifications. Whoever built these had access to top-tier technology and the engineering expertise to adapt it."

She magnifies a grainy image of the underside of one of the drones. "This power distribution system is revolutionary. It shouldn't be possible to achieve this payload-to-battery ratio." Her fingers tap across the keyboard. "I've never seen anything like it."

"Focus on the women," Forest redirects. "Where are they now?"

"Their initial trajectory indicates they headed west over the Pacific," Mitzy responds, bringing up a map with projected flight paths. "The drones departed at 21:48, and their last confirmed visual was at 21:53. After that, they disappeared from all monitoring systems."

I don't bother asking how she knows. I stopped trying to decode Mitzy's sources years ago—whether it's satellite piggybacks, underwater sonar taps, or something she cooked up in that neon-lit lab of hers. She sees what no one else does.

"Vanished?" Ethan asks, leaning forward.

"Completely." Mitzy's frustration is evident. "No thermal, no radar, no satellite tracking. It's like they went dark or—or somehow masked their signature."

"That's not possible," Walt counters. "Not even our stealth tech can do that."

"I know what I'm seeing," Mitzy insists. "Or rather, what I'm not seeing. They disappeared approximately three miles offshore.

We've been monitoring all vessel traffic within a 100-mile radius since then. Nothing suspicious."

I process this information meticulously. "Three miles is within range of a submarine pickup. Or a vessel running without transponders."

"A sub would require specialized docking equipment for drone retrieval," Gabe says beside me.

"Their drones are specialized." It punches out of me. Hard. Hot. "Why the hell wouldn't they have specialized subs too?" My voice cuts sharper than I mean it to, fury riding shotgun with helplessness. "Jesus, Gabe. Fucking *think*."

The room stills for a beat.

Gabe doesn't react—doesn't blink, doesn't flinch. Just shifts his weight, taps that familiar uneven rhythm against his thigh.

One-two-pause. Three.

It's his tell. Always has been. Movement when I go still. Fire when I freeze.

"I am *thinking*," he says quietly. Not calm—measured. Careful. For me, not him. "You're not."

I exhale through my nose. A harsh sound. My pulse is a war drum in my ears.

He leans in just slightly, lowering his voice.

"She's *mine* too."

That stops me cold.

I flinch.

Not from the words. From the truth of them.

Doesn't fix it. Doesn't make it better. But it anchors me—just enough.

"Shit." I drag a hand down my face, skin burning with tension. "I know."

Silence stretches.

Then Gabe blows out a breath, rubs a hand over the back of his neck. "Yeah. We're both a little broken right now."

A beat.

"I didn't mean to snap." I shift, jaw grinding. "I just—"

"I know." He cuts me off before I can finish. Not sharp. Not forgiving either. Just there—solid as always. "You're not the only one losing your mind."

He knows I'm strung tight. Knows I'm this close to cracking through the surface. And he doesn't take it personally—never does. Not when it comes to Ally.

He lets the silence hang between us, the kind that doesn't need filling. We've been here before. Different battlefield. Same war.

And I breathe—once, hard—grateful he knows when not to push, and how to steady the fire without putting it out.

I nod once. Slow. The weight of everything pressing against my spine.

Then I look him dead in the eye.

"We're getting her back."

"Yeah." His jaw ticks. "We sure as shit are." He's as calm as ever. No pushback. No challenge. Just giving me space to burn.

And just like that, we're aligned again. One mission. One woman. One war.

And we're bringing all of it.

We're both silent after that. Not because there's nothing to say. Because everything we need to know is already between us.

"A submarine would explain the disappearance," Ethan speaks up, his voice filling the silence.

"We've got SOSUS arrays monitoring the entire West Coast," Sam reminds us. "No submarine signatures detected."

"What about the facility breach?" I ask, shifting focus to the more immediate concern. "How did they penetrate Guardian HQ to begin with?"

This has been bothering me since the moment we found Jenna's apartment. Guardian HQ is a fortress, equipped with biometric security, motion sensors, armed patrols, and surveillance coverage. The fact that an extraction team walked in, took six women, and walked out is unprecedented.

Mitzy frowns, her hands stilling over her keyboard. "That's the other problem. We've found no breach in the perimeter security system. No alarms. No unauthorized access points. Nothing in the logs."

"That's impossible," Blake says, echoing all our thoughts.

"I know," Mitzy replies, clearly frustrated. "I've been running diagnostics all night. The system shows normal operation throughout the entire event window."

"Could they have hacked it?" Walt asks. "Inserted a loop in the security feed?"

"First thing I checked," Mitzy shakes her head. "Our systems are isolated. External access would leave traces. There's nothing."

"They got in somehow," I state flatly.

"There's something else," Mitzy adds, bringing up a new display. "We've been experiencing random electronic malfunctions across the compound for weeks. System glitches, power fluctuations, equipment failures. Initially, I thought they were isolated incidents."

Dr. Skye Summers enters the command center, nodding briefly at Forest before joining the briefing circle. Her medical scrubs are rumpled, hair pulled back in a messy bun—she's come straight from treating Max.

"How's Max?" I ask.

"Stable," she replies with the same economy of words. "Sedated. He'll recover."

I nod once. Information received. Assessment complete.

"At first, I thought the glitches might be connected to Ally's USB drive," Mitzy continues. "The one she brought back from

Kazakhstan. We suspected it might have contained a virus that activated when she connected it to our network."

"But you cleared it," Gabe notes, eyes narrowing.

"Multiple times," Mitzy confirms. "And the malfunctions were occurring before she ever plugged it in. Plus, they've affected isolated systems with no network connection."

"Like what?" Forest presses.

"Cell phones with rapid battery drain," Mitzy says. "Including yours and Gabe's." She nods toward us. "The system in the motor pool that tracks vehicle usage. Three different satellite uplinks that keep dropping signal."

Walt steps forward, arms crossed over his chest. "Don't forget the equipment at Guardian Grind. The espresso machine's been glitching for weeks. Register freezes constantly. Malia was ready to throw the coffee grinder through a window yesterday. Mike, the mechanic, has been back five times, and nothing stays fixed."

"I mean," Walt rubs the back of his neck, "he's a good guy. Always responds quickly, but the fixes never last. Malia was convinced he was doing it on purpose to keep coming back for free coffee."

"Has anyone vetted him recently?" I ask.

Forest catches my implication immediately. "Full personnel sweep," he orders. "Everyone with access to Guardian HQ in the last six months gets reassessed. Mike goes to the top of the list."

Mitzy's already typing. "Michael Drayson. Contractor. Hired eight months ago for general maintenance and repairs. Ex-military. Marine Corps. Honorable discharge." Her fingers pause. "Clean record, but limited background on his time before Guardian HRS."

"Has there been any particular pattern to these malfunctions?" Forest asks, voice tight. "Any correlation with locations, timings, personnel?"

Mitzy shakes her head. "Nothing I could identify. Just random equipment failures, power drains. We replaced some cell phones for tech team members when they kept dying. Rewired parts of the electrical system in the east wing. Replaced the satellite uplink twice."

"Mike is being brought in for questioning," Sam announces, reviewing incoming messages on his tablet. "We're implementing lockdown protocols. All personnel are to be accounted for. No one enters or leaves without Level 1 clearance."

The command center doors slide open, and Carter strides in. His face is drawn, jaw set with the same controlled anger I recognize in myself. His badge—Guardian Protector, not operative—hangs from his belt.

"They took Jenna," he says without preamble. The words are measured, but the force behind them is unmistakable. "Hurt Max."

"We know," Sam acknowledges, though his posture stiffens slightly. He understands what's coming.

"I'm going after her," Carter continues, moving to stand with our group. "I'm joining Charlie team."

Sam shakes his head. "You're a Protector, not a Guardian. You're not combat certified for this level of operation."

Carter doesn't flinch. "I've been training with Blake and Rigel for months. I can handle myself."

"This isn't a debate," Sam replies, his tone final. "This is a Category 1 operation. Full tactical team deployment."

"He's been running courses with us," Ethan interjects, surprising me with the support. "Combat scenarios, hostage recovery, tactical formation. He's solid."

CJ steps forward, his massive frame drawing all eyes. As operational commander of all Guardian teams, his word carries weight. "I've reviewed his progress. He's not at an operative level, but he's close. Better than some we've deployed."

Sam looks to Forest, clearly displeased with the interruption to protocol.

"Don't care what you say. They took Jenna." Carter says each word precisely. Controlled. "I'm going, just try to stop me."

I assess him clinically, noting his stance, muscle tension, and eye movement. He maintains strict control, channeling his emotions to focus rather than letting them compromise his judgment. I recognize and respect this trait.

"We'll need every asset," I state, supporting his position. "Carter brings years of experience as a detective. He *thinks* differently than we do. He's an asset, not a liability."

Rigel nods in agreement. "He's put in the work. Firearms qualification, combat fitness test, tactical simulations. He's ready."

Forest watches this exchange without expression, then looks directly at Carter. "You follow orders without question. You maintain operational discipline. You don't compromise the mission."

"Understood," Carter replies, not a flicker of emotion betraying the intensity I know he feels.

"Approved." Forest nods once. "Carter Jackson is temporarily assigned to Charlie team for the duration of this operation."

The chain of command adjusts and recalibrates. A new tactical element is integrated.

"This operation was meticulously planned," I observe, returning focus to the mission. "The timing was precise. They struck exactly when all Charlie team operatives were occupied with the security briefing following the attack on Alpha team."

"Which means they had inside information," Forest confirms.

"Or they've been monitoring us," Gabe adds. "Those electronic malfunctions could be more than random glitches."

Surveillance. Infiltration. Compromise.

"Guardian HQ has been under observation," I state,

converting suspicion to tactical fact. "For how long is the question."

"And to what extent," Forest adds grimly.

My eyes meet Gabe's across the command center. A silent communication passes between us—assessment, calculation, shared understanding.

This isn't about recovering the women.

This is about Malfor.

The man who tried to control global energy through fusion technology.

The man who took Ally once before.

The man who now has her again.

I catalog the anger and store it precisely where it will serve the mission. Cold focus is what will bring her back.

What will bring them all back.

"Mitzy," I say, my voice steady, controlled. "We need everything on those drones. Flight capability. Range. Technical signature. If we find how they're built, we find who built them."

"And if we find who built them," Ethan finishes, "we find our women."

"To start," CJ says, "we begin with Collins."

SEVEN

Separation & Forced Compliance

ALLY

Boots scrape against concrete as guards march us down a corridor. Water trickles down walls slick with condensation, filling the air with the stench of mold and something industrial—chemical cleaners maybe, or the sharp bite of disinfectant.

My legs spasm, muscles still rewiring themselves after the collar's attack. Each step grinds bone against nerve endings, yet my eyes refuse to stop scanning, cataloging, and measuring distances between doors and cameras.

A mechanical hum vibrates through the floor and into my feet, rattling my molars. Generators. Powerful ones. The low-frequency drone pulses in my chest cavity, a second heartbeat beneath my ribs. Copper and salt coat my tongue with each breath—the tang of blood from my bitten cheek and tongue, mixed with sea air forced through ventilation systems.

We round a corner into a prison block designed by someone who understands psychological torture. Six cells—individual compartments with thick metal doors and strategically barred windows between them. The architecture screams its purpose:

we'll hear each other scream, watch each other break, witness each other's suffering.

"Inside." A guard rams the butt of his rifle between my shoulder blades.

My body slams against the far wall, shoulder taking the impact. The door seals with the magnetic thunk of high-security locks. My collar chirps—a perverse, cheerful sound—and the tiny light flashes green as it connects to facility systems.

Metal surrounds me. Bunk welded to the wall; its thin mattress stained with substances I refuse to analyze. Toilet and sink combo bolted to the floor, exposed to anyone walking past. No sheets, no blankets, no personal items. Nothing to pry loose, weaponize, or use for escape.

Through the barred window into the adjacent cell, Jenna curls into herself on her metal bunk, her forehead pressed against her knees, her fingers white-knuckled around her shins. The woman who led our self-defense classes, who never broke stance, has collapsed into a tight ball of silence.

Malia's cell echoes with the metronome of her pacing—five steps, pivot, five steps back. The purple-black bruises on her forearms stand stark against her skin as she rubs them absently, wincing at her own touch.

Across from me, Rebel leans against the concrete, cradling her shattered arm. Sweat beads on her gray-tinged skin. Bone fragments press visibly against flesh, distorting the contours of her forearm. Yet her eyes—clear, focused, predatory—track every movement in the cellblock.

Mia sits rigid on her bunk, her face turned toward the wall, but her spine is straight as rebar. Her fingers drum a precise pattern against her thigh—not nervous energy but calculations, timing, planning. When she briefly glances my way, her eyes burn with barely contained fury, a biochemist's mind no doubt cataloging exactly what compounds would dissolve our captors most painfully.

At the row's end, isolated by design, Stitch stands at her bars. Our eyes lock through the narrow space between cells. Her jaw tightens, nostrils flare. The message passes between us wordlessly—survive, resist, remember. These bastards don't know what we're capable of.

Boot heels announce new arrivals before they appear—measured, confident steps, not the hurried shuffle of guards. Different cadence. Different purpose.

Malfor appears at the cellblock entrance flanked by two men in pristine lab coats. Their presence strikes deeper than any armed guard could. These aren't hired muscle but educated men—PhDs, colleagues, peers who've chosen this path with open eyes. ID badges hang from breast pockets, laminated proof of their complicity.

"Time to get to work." Malfor rubs his hands together, cologne wafting through the bars—sandalwood and amber, jarringly refined against the reek of fear and blood. "We have schedules to keep."

A guard unlocks Stitch's cell. She rises without prompting, spine straight as steel, face emptied of everything but cold calculation.

"We'll start with her." Malfor flicks two fingers toward Stitch, casual as selecting produce. "I need someone to analyze our network security protocols, find the vulnerabilities. Shore up our defenses."

"Go fuck yourself." Stitch's words drop like stones, each syllable precise and deliberate.

Malfor's smile doesn't falter as his hand slides into his pocket. "I was hoping for an early demonstration."

Pain explodes through my nervous system before I can draw breath. Every muscle seizes simultaneously, my back arching so violently that something pops in my spine. White-hot electricity courses through blood vessels, setting nerve endings ablaze.

Around me, the others convulse in identical agony—Rebel's scream cuts off as her throat locks, Malia slams against her cell bars, Jenna's teeth clack audibly as they snap together.

The assault lasts three seconds. Five. Ten. An eternity.

When it stops, I'm face down on the concrete, tasting blood and bile. My vision fragments into kaleidoscope patterns that refuse to resolve.

"Collective punishment." Malfor's voice floats above the ringing in my ears. "One refuses; all suffer. Simple behavioral conditioning."

Stitch drags herself upright, palms scraped raw from the concrete, expression murderous. "When I get free—"

"You won't." Malfor cuts her off. "You'll analyze my security systems because the alternative is watching your friends suffer until their hearts give out. And you're many things, Stitch, but you've never been someone who sacrifices others for principles."

The words land like grenades. Stitch's face contorts, not from physical pain but from the impossible choice laid before her.

Malfor pivots toward my cell, index finger tapping his chin in theatrical contemplation. "And you. You're going to work with Dr. Elkin and Dr. Rafeeq. Help them build what only you can."

Blood pounds in my ears, drowning everything but his voice. "Me? Build what?"

"The quantum entanglement network that will control my nanobots once they've infiltrated the world's financial systems." His smile spreads like an oil slick, teeth too white, too perfect. "I need a robust control mechanism that can't be jammed or intercepted. Your research is the key."

"Nanobots?"

"Yes." There's something slimy about his smile. As if he's savoring a secret only he knows.

I'm not up for playing his games. Instead, I focus on what makes sense.

"That's …" My throat constricts around the words. "That's global terrorism. Financial collapse. Millions would die in the aftermath."

Malfor's hand slides toward his pocket, fingers hovering over the outline of the remote.

"Wait!" My palm shoots out, fingers splayed. Everyone's ragged breathing fills the silence. "I'll try. But the mathematics are incomplete. The quantum coherence breaks down at scale—it's why I was still researching it. What you're asking might not be possible with current technology."

"Oh, I believe you'll find a way." His hand remains near his pocket, a constant threat. "Your motivation is quite literally staring you in the face."

"Rebel needs medical attention." I gesture toward her cell, where she's slumped against the wall. "Set her arm, give her antibiotics. Please. She'll die from infection if—"

"Perform first, rewards after." Malfor's voice turns sickeningly sweet, the tone one might use with a trained animal. "That's how this works. You give me results, and your friend gets medical care. You delay, she suffers. Simple cause and effect."

"She can't wait that long. The bone—"

"Is an excellent motivator." He cuts me off, eyes glittering with something beyond cruelty—a clinical fascination with our pain. "Work quickly, work well, and perhaps she'll keep that arm. Fail me, and infection will be the least of her concerns."

Rage burns white hot behind my eyes, so intense my vision blurs at the edges. This man, in his expensive, yet rumpled, clothes, with his educated voice, reducing us to experiments, to leverage. The scientist in me wants to explain the progression of sepsis, the inevitability of tissue death, but the words die in my throat. He knows. He just doesn't care.

"Time is wasting, Miss Collins." His smile doesn't reach his eyes. "Every minute you spend arguing is another minute closer to septic shock. For a physicist, your grasp of biological time-frames seems—lacking."

Metal groans as my cell door unlocks. The sound reverberates through bone and tissue, settling into my marrow. One thought crystallizes through the fog of fear—Rebel's arm, the bone frag-ments pressing against skin, the infection that's inevitable without treatment.

"Her arm needs to be set." My words scrape against raw vocal cords as I point toward Rebel's cell. "I'll do it. I'll build your network. Whatever you want. But please, her arm needs medical attention now."

My voice cracks, pride dissolving in the face of Rebel's agony. "You can see the bone. She'll die from sepsis before I can finish your work. Please. I'm begging you."

"I believe I was clear." Malfor's voice drops to a dangerous softness. "Work first. Rewards after. No negotiations."

He thumbs the remote without warning. Five bodies hit the ground simultaneously. The sound of Rebel's broken arm striking concrete cuts through the symphony of agony—wet snap followed by guttural howl that doesn't sound human.

"Stop!" The word tears from my throat, stripping tissue raw.

Malfor releases the button, tilting his head like a bird exam-ining a particularly interesting insect. The screaming stops, replaced by ragged breathing and soft whimpers.

"You want to help your friend?" Malfor steps close enough that his breath warms my face, mint and coffee masking some-thing rotten underneath. "Then work. Cooperate. The sooner you give me what I need, the sooner everyone gets what *they* need."

"I told you not to argue with me." His voice remains conver-sational, as though discussing weather rather than torture.

"These are the consequences of questioning my instructions. Do you understand the rules now, Miss Collins? Or do I need to provide another demonstration?"

He hovers his thumb over the remote again, eyebrows raised in polite inquiry.

My legs wobble as I step into the corridor, muscles liquefied by fear and lingering pain. "No, you don't need to. I'll comply."

"Good girl." The words land like a boot on my chest, his tone dripping with patronizing satisfaction. "We finally understand each other. Dr. Elkin and Dr. Rafeeq don't have time to waste. Neither do you."

Guards materialize on either side of me, close enough that their body heat radiates against my skin, their weapons cold against my ribs. At the corridor's far end, Stitch walks away between her own escorts, head high despite everything.

Our eyes connect across the distance—hers narrowed, calculating, certain. One blink. Deliberate. The message burns between us: remember your training, remember who you are.

The hallway stretches before me in endless white, security doors punctuating the path at measured intervals. My brain struggles to map our route—left turn, right turn, another left—but sedatives still cloud my thoughts, fragmented memories slipping away like smoke. The guards maintain absolute silence, their breathing the only proof they're human.

We halt before a reinforced door marked with a keypad. One scientist—older, gray-haired, with wire-rimmed glasses—punches in a six-digit code, his fingers casting shadows under the harsh fluorescents. The door whispers open on pneumatic hinges.

Cold air slaps my face as we enter the lab. The temperature drop raises goosebumps along my arms, deliberate atmospheric control to keep equipment stable. Antiseptic and electronics fill my nostrils—hot silicon, solder, the acrid scent of new circuit boards. Three terminals line the far wall, screens pulsing with code I recognize instantly—my algorithms, my formulas, my life's work twisted into weapons.

A steel table dominates the center, littered with components that tighten my throat—motherboards, wiring harnesses, drone chassis components, power cells. Pieces of a puzzle designed to kill.

The scientists move to workstations without acknowledging my presence, backs turned as they tap at keyboards and adjust equipment. Then the older one turns—Dr. Elkin, based on his ID badge, revealing a face that might belong to a kind professor in another reality. Gray temples, laugh lines around his eyes, hands that have spent decades manipulating delicate equipment.

"We were told you might be difficult." He removes his glasses, polishing them with a microfiber cloth pulled from his pocket.

As he tilts his head, the high collar of his lab coat shifts, revealing a metal band identical to mine circling his throat. His eyes meet mine, a flash of shared understanding passing between us.

"Don't be." His voice drops lower, almost a whisper. "It won't help anyone, least of all your friends. Or mine."

The realization hits me like a cold wave of clarity—these scientists aren't willing collaborators. They're prisoners too, collared and controlled just like us. Different cell, same cage.

My collar pulses once against my throat, a phantom finger tracing my carotid artery. The guards take position by the door, weapons loose in practiced hands, expressions bored behind tactical glasses.

The chair's metal surface chills my skin through thin fabric as I lower myself before the third terminal. Familiar code pulses on the screen—quantum entanglement protocols I spent years developing, algorithms that should have revolutionized communication systems. But they've added subroutines, twisted my elegant equations into something grotesque, something designed to target and destroy.

My research, my beautiful theorems meant to connect people across impossible distances, perverted into death.

The lab door seals with hydraulic finality. No exit. No options. No hope of rescue arriving in time.

My fingers hover over the keyboard. Ice fills my veins, not panic but something colder, more calculated. Something that lets me analyze scenarios without emotion. I won't give Malfor his weapon, but I'll give him the illusion of compliance while I find a way to sabotage everything he's built.

The keys click beneath my fingertips, cold plastic against flesh. And I begin.

EIGHT

The Betrayer

GABE

RAGE HAS A TEMPERATURE.

Most people think it's only hot, explosive, wild, and uncontrolled. But that's amateur hour. The pros know rage comes in flavors. Hot, cold, and everything between.

Right now, mine is nuclear—the kind that irradiates from the inside out. The kind that burns so hot it circles back to ice. The kind that lets you think clearly while plotting murder.

I stand against the wall of Guardian HQ's command center, watching Mitzy prep the video feed. Her fingers fly across the keyboard as she mutters commands to her tech team. The room is charged with a particular kind of tension—the dangerous quiet before something irreversible happens.

Telling a father his daughter is missing is one thing.

Telling Robert Collins that his head of security betrayed him and took his only child? That's igniting a thermonuclear device.

And I'd know. I've set off enough of them.

"Connection establishing," Mitzy announces, her voice tight. "Secure uplink in three, two—"

The central display flickers, then stabilizes. Robert Collins materializes on screen, his silver hair immaculate, his posture rigid even at this hour. He's in his home office—that austere space of polished mahogany and floor-to-ceiling windows overlooking the city. A half-empty tumbler of whiskey sits by his right hand.

His eyes instantly scan the room, cataloging faces. When he reaches mine, the first flicker of awareness ignites—that slight narrowing of the eyes, the infinitesimal tightening around his mouth. He doesn't know yet, but he feels it.

The wrongness.

"This is unexpected." Collins's voice is measured and controlled.

Around me, the team goes still. Blake shifts his weight, a subtle tell of tension. Walt's breathing changes rhythm, barely perceptible. Rigel crosses his arms, muscles bunching under his shirt. Carter's face is stone, jaw locked so tight I'm surprised it doesn't crack.

Hank stands beside me, a glacier to my volcano. His stillness is absolute—the kind that makes predators invisible before they strike.

Forest steps forward, facing the screen directly. No preamble. No softening blow.

"Harrison has betrayed you," he says, each word precise as a blade strike. "He's taken Ally."

The words land like artillery shells. One. Two.

Boom!

I watch it hit—the electromagnetic pulse before the blast. Collins doesn't move, doesn't blink, doesn't breathe. His face empties of all expression, a whiteout, his mind unable to process the words.

One second stretches to three.

Then—

"That's not possible." Each syllable is carefully controlled.

Denial, not out of stupidity, but self-preservation. "Harrison has been with us for twenty years. He wouldn't—"

"He did," Forest cuts in, unmoved. "We have him on camera leading a tactical team into Guardian HQ. They took Ally and five other women. It was a premeditated, coordinated attack."

Collins's face transforms—age etching itself into every line as the reality hits. Ten years older in ten seconds. His hand moves toward his phone.

"I'll call him. There must be—"

"He won't answer." Forest's voice remains measured. "His communication devices went dark immediately after the extraction. We've been monitoring all channels."

Collins tries anyway, fingers jabbing at his desk console. We watch him dial once, twice. The muscle in his jaw twitches with each unanswered ring.

I catalog every micro-expression—the flare of his nostrils, the whitening of his knuckles, the rapid blink pattern signaling cognitive overload. This isn't just a billionaire losing an asset. This is a father realizing his daughter is gone, taken by someone he trusted.

"Mr. Collins," Hank says, his voice like steel. "We need everything you have on Harrison. Any changes in behavior. Any unexplained absences. Financial issues. Pressure points. Anything unusual in the past six months."

Collins doesn't respond immediately. His gaze goes distant, processing. Then, like watching a transformation in real time, something shifts.

The shock recedes.

The confusion hardens.

The grief calcifies into something dangerous.

I've seen this before—on battlefields, in hostage situations. The moment when emotion transforms into lethal purpose.

Robert Collins, grieving father, disappears.

In his place sits the man who built a tech empire from nothing. The strategic genius who crushed competitors and reshaped global markets. The ruthless tactician who doesn't just play the game—he rewrites the rules.

"Whatever you need," he says, voice dropped an octave, resonating with absolute certainty. "Whatever it costs. Bring her back."

His eyes lock with mine for a beat too long—recognition passing between predators of different species but similar appetites.

"We will," I respond, the promise a blood oath.

Forest nods to Mitzy, who brings up a secondary display. "We need full access to your security systems. All footage of Harrison for the past three months. Communications logs. Building access records. Everything."

Collins doesn't hesitate. "Authorization codes incoming. You'll have unrestricted access to all systems."

Mitzy's tablet pings with the transfer. She nods once, already diving into the new data stream.

"Tell us about Harrison," Ethan presses, stepping forward. "Anything that could explain this."

Collins runs a hand through his silver hair—the first truly human gesture since the news hit. "Harrison has been our head of security for twenty years. Before that, he was with the State Department's diplomatic security service. Before that, the military. Impeccable record. Rigorous vetting. I trusted him with my daughter's life. With my life."

The betrayal cuts deeper when it comes from someone positioned to protect. I know this firsthand. So does everyone in this room.

"Family?" Hank asks, voice clinically detached.

"Divorced over a decade ago. Two adult children—son and daughter. Both estranged, from what I understand. He never spoke much about his personal life."

"Financial status?" I ask, mind already mapping potential vulnerabilities. Men break for two reasons—money or loved ones.

"Comfortable. Not extravagant. We pay well, and he's been smart with investments." Collins frowns, thoughts visibly accelerating. "But there have been—changes. Subtle things."

Rigel leans forward slightly. "What kind of changes?"

"He's been more distant. Preoccupied." Collins's eyes narrow in thought. "Missed a security briefing last month—first time ever. Claimed it was a dental emergency. And he's been unusually interested in Ally's research. Asked detailed questions about her quantum work after Kazakhstan."

That clicks something into place for me—a detonator finding its charge. Harrison asking about Ally's research. About the work Malfor wanted.

"Accessing records," Mitzy interrupts, eyes fixed on her tablet. "I'm seeing multiple unauthorized entries into the Collins family secure server over the past month. File access timestamps during off-hours."

"What files?" Forest asks.

"Ally's research notes. Her academic records. And—" Mitzy's fingers pause over the screen, "—personal medical files from after the Kazakhstan incident."

I exchange a glance with Hank. There it is. The connection we needed.

"He was looking for something specific," I say, the pieces aligning in my head with the precision of a well-designed explosive. "Malfor wanted Ally for her quantum research in Kazakhstan. Now Harrison is accessing those same files."

"It's not about ransom," Hank concludes, his voice cold enough to freeze nitrogen. "It's about whatever Ally knows. Whatever she can do."

"Security footage," Mitzy announces, pulling up video on the main screen. "Collins residence, past month. Multiple instances of Harrison making calls from secluded areas. Outside normal security channels."

The footage shows Harrison in various locations around the Collins's estate—garden pathways, empty corridors, the perimeter fence line. Always alone. Always checking his surroundings before engaging his phone.

"Look at the body language," I note, pointing to his stance in the most recent clip. "Weight shifted forward. Shoulders tense. He's stressed, but trying to project confidence. That's not a man making normal calls."

"Can we recover the communications?" Forest asks.

Mitzy shakes her head. "Not from this. He was using a personal device, not security-issued equipment. Smart. Kept it completely separate from monitored channels."

"Mr. Collins," Hank asks, eyes never leaving the footage, "did Harrison have any connection to fusion research? Energy technologies? Quantum physics? Anything that might link him to Malfor's interests?"

Collins's brow furrows. "Not that I'm aware of. His background was strictly security and protection. He's detail-oriented, methodical, but not scientific."

I study the man on screen—Harrison's careful movements, his vigilance, his precision. There's something practiced in his caution. The kind of behavior that comes from extended planning, not sudden opportunity.

"This wasn't an impulsive betrayal," I say, more thinking aloud than addressing the room. "He's been setting this up for months. Maybe longer."

"But why?" Collins demands, frustration finally breaking through his controlled exterior. "Why would he do this? After everything—after years of loyalty—why turn now?"

"It's either money or coercion," I reply, eyes still tracking

Harrison's movements in the footage. "Men like Harrison don't flip without reason. If it's not financial, then he's being controlled."

"Could be family," Ethan suggests. "Even estranged children can be leveraged."

The memory of Sophia hits me—her desperation when she confessed how Malfor used her son Luke to force her betrayal. How she sabotaged Guardian systems, leaked information, compromised security—all to keep her child alive.

Rebel did something similar. Disappeared after being rescued, only to be found working on the wrong side of a human trafficking ring. All in a desperate attempt to find her sister's child, Zephyr.

It happens.

"We need everything on Harrison's family." I turn to Mitzy. "Every detail. Current locations. Communications. Financial transfers. If someone's got hooks in them, we'll find it."

"I'm on it," she responds, fingers already flying. "Running deep background now."

Collins watches this exchange, his expression hardening with each revelation. "I want to be clear," he says, voice dropping to that dangerous register that made him a business legend. "I don't care what it takes. I don't care about collateral damage. I want my daughter back. And I want Harrison to pay."

"Mr. Collins," Forest replies, matching his tone, "I assure you —Harrison will face consequences, but our priority is recovering the women. All of them."

Collins nods once, sharp and decisive. "My resources are at your disposal. Aircraft. Security teams. Satellite access. Name it, it's yours."

"We'll need your complete security logs," Hank says. "Everything Harrison touched. Every location he accessed. Every system he interfaced with. The pattern will tell us where he's vulnerable."

"And where he took Ally," I add.

As Collins issues commands to his staff off-screen, I let my mind work the problem from other angles. Harrison knows Guardian HQ's security protocols. He knows Collins's resources. He knows Ally's routines, preferences, and vulnerabilities.

Which means he's planned for our response. For this exact moment.

I close my eyes briefly, letting the technical details cascade through my consciousness. Drone specifications. Flight paths. Oceanic currents. Vessel traffic. Satellite blind spots.

Harrison is good. But I'm better.

He might understand security systems, but I understand destruction. The precise application of force. The exact pressure needed to break things—or people.

When I open my eyes, I catch Hank watching me. That glacier-cold assessment that says he's thinking exactly what I am.

Harrison made one critical mistake.

He took what's ours.

And there is nowhere on this earth—or under its oceans—that will protect him from what's coming.

NINE

Cold Fury

HANK

"WHAT WE'RE SEEING HERE IS UNPRECEDENTED," FOREST SAYS, standing at the head of the conference table. Dark circles rim his eyes—he hasn't slept since the abduction. None of us have.

The command center thrums with restrained fury. Charlie team occupies the left flank of the room—Ethan, Rigel, Walt, Blake, Carter, Gabe, and I. Seven men with one shared purpose. Max and Brady, team leaders from Alpha and Bravo teams, stand along the back wall. Their expressions range from grim solidarity to barely concealed tension.

Forty-two hours since the women were taken. Forty-two hours of nothing but dead ends and false starts.

I catch Ethan's eye across the room. As Charlie team leader, he maintains his composure, but I see what others miss—the microscopic tremor in his right hand, the way his jaw pulses every few seconds. Rebel's absence cuts into him like a blade.

Blake stands motionless, face carved from stone, but his usual easy demeanor has vanished. Walt's restlessness manifests in controlled micro-movements—his fingers tapping silent rhythms against his thigh, his eyes constantly scanning the displays. Rigel's stillness is more pronounced than usual, a predator conserving energy before the hunt. And Carter—the newest, official addition to our ranks—radiates cold fury.

His place is well-earned. I've watched him during training. He processes differently than we do, but his dedication to finding Jenna matches our own.

Gabe paces along the outer edge of the gathering, unable to remain still. I recognize the restraint in his movements—the explosive energy he's banking for when it's needed. It mirrors the cold burn in my chest, though our expressions differ.

"We need to consider all possibilities," Forest continues. "Guardian HQ has never been breached. Not in its entire operational history. Yet someone walked in, took six women, and walked out—without triggering a single alarm."

"It's been breached once before." Blake's voice cuts through the room like broken glass.

The silence that follows is immediate. Heavy. Every man in the room knows exactly what he's referring to.

Who he means.

Blake's jaw works, muscles ticking beneath the skin. His hands are steady, but his breathing changes—shallow, controlled. The cost of saying it aloud.

"Malfor used Luke against Sophia," Forest says quietly, his voice carrying the weight of command decisions that haunt leaders. "She did what any mother would."

Blake's throat works, but he doesn't speak. Doesn't need to. Forest just said what Blake couldn't—the defense of the woman he loves coming from the man who had to make the call to trust her again.

The room stays silent. We all remember. The betrayal that wasn't really betrayal. The way Sophia had to look us in the eye, work alongside us, earn our trust—all while systematically dismantling our security from the inside. How she cried when confessing. How Blake held her while she broke apart from the guilt.

"Different circumstances," Ethan says finally, but his voice is gentler now. Understanding. Rebel went through something similar—the impossible choice between loyalty and survival.

Blake's hands curl into fists, then deliberately relax. The silence stretches, heavy with shared memory and understanding.

"He had inside help. Had to." Gabe stops his pacing to lock eyes with Sam. "We already know Harrison betrayed Collins. Who's to say he's the only one?"

"What's Malfor's endgame here?" Brady from Bravo asks. "Taking Charlie team's women is tactical. Deliberate."

"It's a trap," Ethan states flatly. "He's using them as bait."

"Of course, it's a trap," Gabe says, the words sharp enough to cut. "But we're still going in."

No one argues. Not even the team leaders whose women weren't taken. They understand the unwritten code—any one of us would do the same for any one of them.

"The electronic malfunctions I've been tracking," Mitzy looks up from her station. "They've accelerated since the abduction. Three more satellite uplinks went down this morning. Six communications systems in the east wing are experiencing packet loss. Something systematic is happening."

"Sabotage, obviously." CJ leans against the far wall. "Physical tampering with equipment."

"We've checked," Mitzy counters. "There's no evidence of manual interference. No unauthorized access to secure areas where the equipment is housed."

"What about software?" Walt's voice is rougher than usual. Malia's absence weighs on him, visible in the tightness around his eyes. "Could someone have introduced a virus into our systems?"

Mitzy shakes her head. "That was my first thought. I've run

every diagnostic, every security protocol. Nothing. Whatever's causing this doesn't follow conventional attack vectors."

"We're missing something." The room quiets at my words. "We need to reconsider our approach."

Doc Summers steps forward. She's been examining the survivors of the attack—Sophia, Violet, and the children. Her medical scrubs are rumpled, her usually perfect appearance showing signs of the same strain we're all under.

"I may have a perspective on this." Her voice carries that precise clinical tone that commands attention. "Have you considered it might be a virus?"

Mitzy snorts softly. "Of course. First thing I ruled out. Ally's USB drive is clean. So is her laptop. No malware signatures, no unauthorized data packets. I ran every scan I have, even created a sandbox environment to test replication. Nothing."

"I don't mean a computer virus." Skye folds her arms across her chest. "In medicine, when we track outbreaks, we always start with one question. Who got sick first? We call it 'Patient Zero.' Sometimes, symptoms don't make sense at first and don't fit expected patterns. But there's always a source."

Mitzy frowns. "You think this is a biological agent?"

"No," Skye says slowly, "I'm saying maybe you're looking at the wrong kind of infection. Viruses don't always spread through code or networks. What if something else is propagating through the system? Not malware—but something new? A kind of exposure."

Mitzy stills. Fingers hovering over the keyboard. "You want me to find the—*equipment* zero?"

"Trace it back," Skye nods. "Figure out the very first system that glitched. What failed first? What changed around that time?"

Silence settles for a beat. Tense. Heavy with implication.

Then Mitzy mutters, "That's actually—not a bad idea."

Forest gestures. "Do it. Start building the timeline. Every incident. Every piece of tech. I want the entire history cross-referenced against personnel movement, new arrivals, and asset transfers."

Gabe glances at me, then at Skye. "You think this started with Ally?"

"I don't know how it started. Or, if it began with a person. The thing is, we have no idea. Something happened, and now we're missing six women." Skye's expression is unreadable. "I think it started somewhere. We won't know until we find the thread."

I process this, seeing the tactical application immediately. "You're suggesting we treat the electronic malfunctions like a disease outbreak."

"Exactly." She nods, acknowledging my understanding. "If we track backward through the system failures, find which one happened first, then second, we might identify the source. The 'patient zero' of this electronic epidemic."

Gabe shifts, his focus intense. Our gazes meet briefly across the room—silent communication honed through years of operations together, years of sharing women, sharing space, sharing life.

Now, sharing Ally.

The thought of her in Malfor's hands burns cold in my chest. The same fire runs in Gabe's eyes.

"So instead of looking at what's failing," he says, voice rougher than usual, "we look at the pattern of failure. The spread."

"Precisely," Doc Summers continues. "In disease outbreaks, we map infections—who infected whom, where the transmissions occurred, and the timeframe between cases. The pattern tells us about the pathogen itself—its incubation period, transmission method, vulnerabilities."

"Can the same approach work with technology?" Forest asks.

"It's worth trying," Mitzy interjects, already typing. "I've been focused on the failures themselves, looking for malicious code or hardware tampering. But if we map the chronology, the pattern of spread ..."

"We might find the source," I conclude, the implications already forming in my mind.

"And possibly the method of infection," Doc Summers adds. "Which could give us a way to neutralize it."

"Do it," Sam orders. "Mitzy, reconfigure your approach. I want a complete timeline of every electronic failure for as far back as you started noticing an on-going issue. Locations, affected systems, and personnel interactions. Everything."

Mitzy nods, already redirecting her team. "I'll access the logs for all electronic equipment malfunctions. Maintenance records. Usage patterns."

Doc Summers steps closer to the table. "There's something else to consider. If this behaves like a virus or pathogen, we need to consider transmission vectors. How is it spreading from system to system?"

"Physical contact?" Walt suggests. "Someone manually tampering with each device?"

"Too time-consuming," Gabe counters. "And too visible. Security cameras would have caught that."

"Network connections?" Blake offers. His voice is flat, controlled, but I catch the tension underneath. Sophia might be safe, but the thought of her nearly being taken again has him on edge.

"Some of the affected systems aren't networked," Mitzy shakes her head. "The coffee grinder at Guardian Grind, for instance. Completely stand-alone device. Same for their register."

"Wireless transmission?" Rigel suggests. "Could be broadcasting on frequencies our security doesn't monitor."

"Possible," Mitzy concedes, "but our radio frequency sweeps are comprehensive. We'd have detected unusual signals."

"What about something more—exotic?" Carter speaks for the first time, his detective's mind working differently than our tactical training. "Something biological, maybe. Or a hybrid."

The room goes quiet as everyone considers this possibility.

"Like what, exactly?" Sam asks, skepticism heavy in his voice.

Carter shrugs. "I don't know. But in my experience, when conventional explanations fail, it's time to look for unconventional ones." Sam may have had reservations about Carter, but he thinks like a detective, and that's what we need right now.

"What about proximity?" I ask. "Could it jump from one device to another when they're close enough?"

"Like airborne transmission in a biological pathogen," Doc Summers says slowly. "That would explain the pattern we're seeing—clusters of failures in the same locations, spreading outward."

"Start with the timeline," Sam decides. "Find patient zero. Then we'll determine how it's spreading."

The meeting breaks. Teams form. I remain still, processing the new tactical approach and recalibrating.

Six hours later, we've made no progress.

The command center has transformed into a war room dedicated to tracking electronic failures. Wall displays show timelines, device locations, and personnel movements. Red markers indicate affected systems spread across the virtual map of Guardian HQ like a disease.

"This doesn't make sense," Mitzy says, frustration evident in her voice. "I've tracked back seventy-three separate equipment failures over the past three months. No consistent pattern in system types, no logical progression. Just random malfunctions."

"Nothing's random." I study the display. "We're missing something."

Gabe paces behind me, energy rolling off him in waves. We haven't spoken much in the past six hours, both focused on the mission, but the shared purpose binds us. Finding Ally. Our woman. The one we swore to protect.

We failed her once. We won't fail her again.

"What about Mike?" Gabe asks, stopping his pacing. "The maintenance guy who kept 'fixing' the espresso machine at Guardian Grind?"

"We've interviewed him twice," Sam reports. "Nothing suspicious. His background checks out, his movements around the facility match his work orders, and his technical knowledge is limited to basic repairs."

"What about environmental factors?" Doc Summers suggests. "Changes in temperature, humidity, power fluctuations?"

"All within normal parameters," Mitzy responds. "And they wouldn't explain how isolated systems with separate power sources are affected."

I study the timeline, looking for patterns others might miss. The failures started appearing approximately three months ago. Small issues at first—devices losing power, communications dropping momentarily. Then escalating in frequency and severity.

"What happened three months ago?" I ask. "Major events, personnel changes, new equipment installations?"

The room falls silent as everyone searches their memory.

"The Kazakhstan extraction," Ethan says finally. "That was three months ago."

TEN

False Hope

ALLY

FOURTEEN HOURS.

That's how long I've been staring at screens, building simulations, fighting against my own mind. My fingers twitch over the keys, muscles locking tight from hours of stillness. The tendons in my shoulders tug like overstretched cables, aching with every breath. Blinking does nothing—grit scratches across my eyes like ground glass. Overhead, the lights strobe just enough to twist the inside of my skull, each flicker a nail hammered behind my eyes. I press my palms to my temples, as if outward pressure can keep my head from splitting open.

The work itself is the real torture. Every line of code I write brings Malfor's system closer to functionality. Every problem I solve moves the quantum entanglement network toward viability.

I deliberately introduce subtle flaws—mathematical inconsistencies that will cause cascading failures—but can't risk making them too obvious. Malfor's other scientists might not understand quantum physics at my level, but they're still brilliant.

And just as trapped.

Guards change shifts.

Dr. Rafeeq brings me lukewarm tea that tastes faintly of metal. Dr. Elkin nods at my progress, his collar gleaming under the harsh lights. No one speaks beyond necessary technical exchanges. The unspoken hangs between us—we're all building something that could destroy millions of lives, and none of us have a choice.

When they finally march me back to the cellblock, my body moves on autopilot. The rhythm of boots against concrete, the distant crash of waves against the island's shore. A curious hollowness has replaced fear, as though my emotions have retreated somewhere beyond the collar's reach.

The first thing I notice when they unlock my cell door is Rebel's arm.

It's been properly set. Professional splint, actual medical gauze, and even the swelling is reduced. Her color has improved from death-gray to merely exhausted. She catches my eye across the cellblock and raises her good hand in a tiny gesture of acknowledgment.

The door locks behind me with that same magnetic thunk. My knees give out, dumping me onto the thin mattress. The cellblock remains silent for several minutes as we all listen for departing footsteps, for any sign the guards remain within earshot.

"You look like shit." Rebel's voice drifts across the space between us, rough with pain but alert.

"Better than you." The words scrape my throat raw.

"Debatable." Her laughter turns into a wince. "At least I got the good drugs."

Before I can respond, boot heels tap their deliberate rhythm down the corridor. Not guards—they shuffle and stomp. This measured cadence belongs to only one person.

Malfor appears before my cell, hands clasped behind his back, satisfaction radiating from him like heat.

"Productive day, Miss Collins?" His smile never reaches his eyes.

My silence only broadens his smile.

"I see you've noticed your friend's medical care." He gestures toward Rebel. "Quality work results in professional attention for your friend. Even appropriate pain management." His voice shifts into that same condescending tone. "See how this works? You perform well, they benefit. Simple positive reinforcement."

"What do you want?" The question slips out before I can stop it.

"To show you something. A little—*motivation* for tomorrow's work."

He produces a tablet from his jacket pocket, taps the screen, and holds it up so we can all see. The image resolves into a familiar space—The Guardian Grind café at Guardian HRS headquarters. The footage is real time, high-definition. I recognize Mitzy hunched over her laptop in the corner booth, her signature pixie cut and psychedelic hair. Two Guardian operatives I don't know well, Brady and Booker from Bravo team, stand at the counter ordering coffee.

"How …" The word dies in my throat.

"How am I watching your friends in real time?" Malfor's smile widens. "You brought me inside, of course. You, Malia, and her brother. Kazakhstan was not a *total* loss. The Guardians rescued you, as planned, and you gave me an incredible opportunity."

What?

He wants me to ask. He's waiting to tell me something, but I'm not going to play his game. A chill does run down my spine, just as he intended.

As planned?

Malia makes a choked sound from her cell.

"Kazakhstan was just the beginning." He swipes to another feed—this one showing Hank and Gabe in what looks like a planning room, surrounded by tactical gear and maps. "When they rescued you from the reactor, we made sure you left with more than just your research on your USB. Nanobots, Miss Collins. Microscopic machines that have been replicating and spreading throughout Guardian HRS's systems since the moment you walked through their doors."

The ground tilts beneath me. Those headaches after Kazakhstan. The way my laptop kept glitching. The way electronic devices sometimes malfunctioned around me. It wasn't radiation exposure or PTSD. It was this. I was the carrier. The Trojan horse.

"The espresso machine." Jenna's voice comes out strangled. "That's why it kept shorting out. Poor Mike spent days trying to fix it."

"Hank's and Gabe's phones." I grip the cell bars. "Their batteries kept draining for no reason."

"My tablet would restart randomly during meetings." Mia's clinical detachment slips, voice rising. "We thought it was buggy software."

"Very observant." Malfor swipes again, showing another room at Guardian HRS—the tactical planning center. "Every system, every computer, every piece of electronics. All are compromised. All are feeding me information." He leans closer to the bars. "They're planning your rescue right now. Their team compositions. Their backup plans. Their contingencies for their contingencies."

He holds up the tablet so we can see and hear CJ outlining extraction points. The audio is crystal clear.

"Fascinating to watch them scramble." Malfor's voice drops to a confidential whisper. "They have no idea I'm already three steps ahead. That I know their plans before they finish making them."

"You're lying," Stitch speaks from her cell, voice flat. "Guardian HRS systems have quantum-level security protocols. No nanobot could bypass them."

"No ordinary nanobot, certainly." Malfor turns to her, eyebrows raised. "But these aren't ordinary. They're based on Miss Collins's quantum entanglement research. Worked like a charm for fusion stabilization. It also allows instantaneous communication across any distance, completely undetectable by conventional security."

My breath freezes in my lungs. My research. My work. Turned against the very people trying to save us.

"That's why you need me." The realization cuts like glass. "The nanobots are deployed, but you need a more robust control system. Something that can't be disrupted."

"Exactly." He tucks the tablet away. "Your friends at Guardian HRS will never find them, because they don't know what to look for. By the time they realize they've been compromised, it will be far too late."

He steps back, surveying our cells like a collector admiring his specimens. "Rest well. Tomorrow brings much more work. For all of you."

His footsteps fade down the corridor, leaving us in silence broken only by ragged breathing.

"I did this." My voice sounds distant, detached. "I brought them inside."

"We both did." Malia slumps against her cell wall. "Malikai too."

"This isn't on you." Jenna's voice hardens. "Malfor planned this. He used you."

"Doesn't matter whose fault it is." Rebel shifts, wincing as her splinted arm moves. "What matters is that Guardian HRS is walking into a trap, and we can't warn them."

The reality settles over us like a shroud. We've compromised the very people we were counting on to save us.

"What do we do?" There has to be a way to warn them, but I can't figure out how.

Silence claims the cellblock. Each of us retreats into our own thoughts, the weight of what we've learned crushing any remaining optimism. Hours pass. The overhead lights dim slightly—night cycle in our windowless prison.

"You know what this means," Stitch says.

"No, what?" Mia asks.

"If he's watching them," I say, knowing exactly what Stitch is thinking. "He's watching us. Everything we do, or say, he knows. There's no way to get a message out. No way that he won't discover."

A ripple of awareness passes through the cellblock.

"Every system has vulnerabilities," Stitch speaks from the darkness, her voice floating between cells. "Even ones built on quantum entanglement."

For the first time in hours, something stirs in my chest. Not hope—we're still trapped, still collared, still forced to build weapons of mass destruction.

But a tiny flicker of possibility lights within me. But how to capitalize on it?

"If they're using my research ..." The thought coalesces slowly. "Then maybe I understand their weaknesses better than Malfor does."

Night deepens around us. Rebel's breathing evens out as pain medication pulls her under. Malia whispers equations to herself, a self-soothing ritual I recognize from our days working together. Jenna and Mia maintain a silent watch, taking turns sleeping in shifts.

Through it all, my mind races through quantum possibilities, through entanglement protocols and signal degradation patterns. If Malfor is using my work to control the nanobots, then perhaps —just perhaps—I can find a way to use that same work against him. Maybe I can get a message out?

Not rescue. Not escape. But resistance.

It's all we have left.

ELEVEN

Patient Zero

HANK

The Kazakhstan extraction. Three months ago.

"When was the first documented system failure?" I ask.

Mitzy pulls up the data. "Guardian Grind register. The espresso machine. Exactly seventy-two hours after the extraction team returned."

I move toward Mitzy's workstation, where her team is already assembling the timeline Doc Summers suggested. They've created a virtual map of Guardian HQ, with each affected system marked in red, timestamps floating beside each marker.

"Show me." I position myself where I can see the entire display.

"We've documented 147 separate electronic failures over the past eleven weeks," Mitzy explains, bringing the visualization to life.

The markers appear one by one, chronologically, spreading across the map like a time-lapse of infection. "Starting here."

The first red dot appears over Guardian Grind. The coffee shop where Ally works. Where Malia works.

Where they spent most of their time after returning from Kazakhstan.

"The espresso machine register," Mitzy confirms. "First reported malfunction, exactly 72 hours after the extraction team returned."

The second dot appears nearby. "Malia's cell phone. Battery completely drained despite being fully charged. 12 hours later."

A third dot. "Ally's laptop. Power regulation issue."

Doc Summers frowns, studying the display. "Wait. Where was Ally's laptop when it failed?"

"Nowhere near Guardian Grind," Mitzy confirms, checking the logs.

"That's significant," Doc Summers says, her medical training kicking in. "If this were a traditional pathogen, we'd be looking at two separate outbreaks. Two distinct patient zeros. The espresso machine at Guardian Grind, and Ally's laptop in a completely different location."

The pattern expands outward, like ripples in water, each new failure connecting to previous ones through proximity or usage patterns. But now I can see what Doc Summers sees—two epicenters of infection, spreading simultaneously.

The electronic contagion moves through Guardian HQ like a slow-motion explosion. "From person to person, device to device."

"The timing is too precise to be coincidental," Mitzy agrees. "And look at the concentration points."

She highlights specific areas on the map—Guardian Grind, the residential quarters where Malia lives, the research lab where Malikai worked, and our condo.

"Everywhere they went." The picture crystallizes in my mind. "Everything they touched. What else failed soon after?"

"Our phones," Gabe interjects, stepping forward. "Remember? Right after Ally plugged her USB drive into her laptop. Both our phones started draining faster than normal."

I nod once, the memory precise.

Everything Ally, Malia, and Malikai touched after returning from Kazakhstan subsequently malfunctioned.

Doc Summers frowns, her expression shifting as she accesses a memory. "There's something else. The medical scanners."

"What medical scanners?" Forest asks, turning toward her.

"The ones we used during the initial assessment of the Kazakhstan survivors," she explains, her words gaining momentum. "They weren't catastrophic failures, just—glitches. Calibration errors. Signal dropouts. I thought it was just equipment fatigue from the field deployment."

"When was this?" I ask.

"Immediately after extraction," she replies. "On-site, before transport back to HQ. Standard medical protocol for all rescued hostages."

"That would make the medical scanners patient zero," Mitzy says, already updating her timeline. "Even before they arrived at Guardian HQ."

"They were packed back up with the rest of our gear and haven't been anywhere else. The likelihood of them transmitting whatever this is to other systems is virtually nil. However, Guardian Grind and Ally's computer and the connection with Malikai all point to the fact that each one of them was an epicenter of spread."

"What about the other rescuees from Kazakhstan?" Walt asks.

Doc Summers shakes her head. "None of them came to Guardian HQ. They went to The Facility, where they were processed, treated, and offered standard rescue services. Ally, Malia, and Malikai were the only ones who came here."

"Which means whatever is causing this came back with them

from Kazakhstan." I look at Gabe. Ally. Our Ally. Used as a vector for Malfor's infiltration.

"Mitzy," Sam says, "gather all potentially affected devices. Full forensic analysis. Isolate and destroy."

"I don't think isolation protocols are necessary," Mitzy says, already moving. "If these devices are carrying something, it's already spread throughout our systems. It's better to examine them in their current state. Not to mention, we shouldn't destroy anything until we know what we're dealing with."

"Get it done." Sam accepts Mitzy's expertise.

I'm like Sam. I want to burn everything to the ground, but what Mitzy says makes sense. The first step in destroying an enemy is understanding them, and there's a lot we don't understand right now.

Hours pass.

Mitzy's lab is a fortress of advanced technology. She gathers equipment and sets up diagnostic systems. Ally's laptop sits on the central workstation, surrounded by our phones, the register component from Guardian Grind, and circuit boards from various failed systems throughout the facility.

"If there's something embedded in these devices," Mitzy explains as she initializes the diagnostic sequence, "it has to be microscopic. Our standard security scans would have caught anything larger."

I watch as she methodically scans the laptop's components. Power regulation system. Battery connection points. Circuit boards. Nothing appears unusual at standard magnification.

"Nothing visible at baseline," Mitzy mutters, frustration evident in her voice. "This doesn't make sense. Something is affecting these systems, but I can't find any physical or digital evidence."

"What's the maximum resolution on that scanner?" Gabe asks, his eyes fixed on the display.

"Standard electronic microscopy tops out at around 10,000x magnification," Mitzy responds, "but we rarely need to go beyond 1,000x for component analysis."

"Push it higher," I instruct, a hunch growing despite the lack of visible evidence.

She gives me a questioning look but complies, adjusting the equipment. "2,000x … 5,000x … still nothing but standard electronic components."

"Keep going," Gabe insists, leaning forward, hands braced on the workstation.

"Interesting." She increases magnification, zeroing in on what appears to be corrosion along one of the connection points.

"What's that?" I ask.

The image sharpens. Increases magnification again. And again.

"8,000x …" Mitzy continues, the resolution increasing. "Wait, there's something …"

"That's not corrosion," I say, my voice controlled, measured.

"You're right." Mitzy's voice carries the weight of discovery.

At 10,000x magnification, the "corrosion" resolves into distinct structures. Mechanical. Organized. Purposeful. Along the power coupling, clustered like metallic barnacles, there are hundreds of microscopic machines.

"My God," Mitzy breathes, fingers freezing over the controls, "those are nanobots. Advanced ones, no less." Mitzy pulls up comparative images. "Nothing like this exists in any unclassified research I've ever seen. They're targeting power regulation systems, communications interfaces, anything that processes data or manages energy flow."

"They're concentrating around the communications, security, and tactical systems."

She immediately switches to our phones, examining the

battery connections. The same microscopic machines appear at the same magnification.

"They're in everything." Her voice is tight with disbelief. "Every device the Kazakhstan survivors touched. And from there, they spread to other systems through proximity or direct contact. It's an infestation."

"Can you determine their function?" I ask.

"I'll need to analyze their architecture first," Mitzy responds, capturing detailed scans of the nanobots. "But based on their positioning near power and data connections, they appear designed to siphon energy and intercept information."

"Surveillance?" Gabe states, the word sharp with rage. "Do you mean Malfor's been watching us through our equipment?"

"Surveillance and interference, more likely than not." Mitzy studies the magnified structures.

The door to the lab slides open, and Doc Summers enters. Her expression is grim.

"I've been reviewing the medical data from the Kazakhstan extraction. The scanning equipment began malfunctioning exactly 47 minutes after first contact with the survivors. Malfor must have introduced these nanobots into their systems during captivity. Most likely through topical application—medical procedures, contaminated surfaces, even something as simple as a handshake with an infected handler."

"On them?" A bad feeling comes over me. "If they were on their skin …" I don't want to think my next thought. Fortunately, I don't have to.

"I need skin samples from everyone," Doc Summers says. "We can start with those closest to them." Doc Summers turns her warm brown gaze on me and Gabe. "I need to take skin swabs from you both. Call Walt in, as well. The three of you had the most contact with them. If you're infected, then we start testing everyone."

"I don't like the sound of that." I turn to Gabe and see the same thought swirling in his head. He dials Walt, calls him in, then notifies Ethan.

"Give me a moment to get swab kits. I'll be back soon." With that, Doc Summers disappears.

Walt and Ethan arrive a few minutes later, and that's when the questions begin. Questions for which no one has any answers. When Doc Summers returns, she makes quick work of collecting skin samples from our hands, forearms, and faces.

One of Mitzy's technicians takes the swabs and preps them for scanning via electron microscopy. Doc Summers and Mitzy settle down in front of the controls and examine the samples.

"I found something." Doc Summers transfers data to the main screen. Microscopic images appear, and among the dead skin cells and normal bacteria, tiny metallic structures cling to the surface like technological parasites.

"Nanotech," she explains. "They're on your skin. Explains the spread from device to device. I've never seen anything like this outside of experimental research."

"That's how they got past our security." The pieces fall into place. "No alarms because the security system itself was compromised."

But infiltration technology can be reverse-engineered.

"Mitzy." My voice is flat, controlled. "Can you isolate an intact specimen? They have to communicate somehow. Can we trace them back to their source?"

TWELVE

Contamination Protocol

HANK

MITZY EXTRACTS ANOTHER NANOBOT SPECIMEN FROM ALLY'S laptop. Each second burns through my control like acid eating through steel. Ally could be anywhere by now—another continent, another hemisphere, another grave.

The variables expand exponentially with distance and time.

I force the thought aside. Cold focus serves the mission. Emotion doesn't.

"Got it," Mitzy announces, her voice tight with concentration. The extracted nanobot—barely visible even under maximum magnification—sits isolated in a specialized containment field. "Intact specimen secured. Beginning architectural analysis."

The Guardian HRS lab has transformed into a sterile war zone over the past three days. Every surface gleams under harsh fluorescent lighting. Every breath tastes of antiseptic and desperation. Doc Summers moves between workstations like a surgeon during triage, coordinating skin sample analysis with electronic forensics.

"What do we know?" I ask, my voice flat. Control through precision.

Doc Summers approaches, tablet in hand, loaded with contamination data. "Charlie team is heavily contaminated. Everyone who touched the Kazakhstan survivors. The coffee shop. Everything they used."

She pulls up a contamination map on her tablet. "Guardian Grind frequent customers show elevated concentrations. The techies working on their equipment also test positive. The other Guardian teams show minimal contamination—occasional contact through shared facilities, but nothing like what we're seeing with direct exposure groups."

Every system is compromised.

Every communication is monitored.

We've been fighting blind while he watched our every move.

Gabe paces behind me, raw energy barely contained. I feel his frustration radiating like heat from a blast furnace. We're complementary forces—his fire, my ice—but right now both of us are burning.

"Individual units are primitive, but when they network together, they create collective intelligence, like a beehive. Hundreds of them working together can process information, adapt, and coordinate complex operations."

"Collective intelligence." The tactical implications are daunting.

"Malfor didn't just tag the Kazakhstan survivors—he turned them into unwitting carriers of a distributed intelligence network. Living deployment vectors."

"That explains how he knew *when* to take our women," Gabe adds, his voice rough with controlled rage. "He's been monitoring our communications, our movements, our vulnerabilities for months."

Forest enters without announcement. Coffee and fatigue cling to his weathered frame. "Charlie team. Conference room. Now."

We follow him through corridors that feel different now—compromised, violated. Every camera could be feeding Malfor intelligence. Every communication system is potentially broadcasting our plans to the enemy.

The secure conference room houses our senior command structure: Forest, Skye, Sam, CJ, Mitzy, and the team leaders from Alpha through Delta. The atmosphere carries the weight of a funeral.

"Situation assessment," Forest begins without preamble. "Skye, what do you have?"

Doc Summers activates the wall display, showing a three-dimensional map of Guardian HRS with red contamination markers spreading like a virus through the facility.

"Total facility contamination confirmed. Nanobots are present in 89% of all electronic systems and 67% of all personnel. The devices have been active for approximately three months."

"Operational impact?" CJ asks, his massive frame tense.

"Complete operational compromise." My voice carries the weight of tactical analysis. "Malfor has real-time intelligence on all our activities. Communications, planning, deployment schedules, and personnel movements. He knows our capabilities, our limitations, and our responses to every scenario."

"Including our response to the kidnapping," Gabe adds. "He knew exactly how we'd react, where we'd deploy, what resources we'd commit."

Forest's expression doesn't change, but I catch the slight tightening around his eyes. "What are our options?"

Mitzy steps forward. "I'm trying to reverse-engineer their communication protocols. If these nanobots are using quantum entanglement for data transmission, they have to be paired with receiver colonies somewhere. Find those, and we find Malfor's command center."

"Timeline?" I ask.

"Unknown. The quantum encryption is unlike anything I've seen. Could be hours, could be weeks." Mitzy's doing her best, but it's not enough, not for Gabe and me. We need Ally like we need air to breathe.

"We don't have weeks." Each passing hour reduces our chances of recovering the women alive. Malfor isn't keeping them for ransom or intelligence. They're bait. Which means he'll dispose of them the moment we activate his trap.

"There's another option," Doc Summers interjects. "If we can't break their communication, we can disrupt it."

"How?"

"Electromagnetic pulse. Targeted EMP deployment could disable the nanobots without permanently damaging our critical systems."

"That creates its own problems," Sam points out. "EMP deployment would announce our knowledge of the contamination. Malfor would know we've discovered his surveillance network."

"He already knows," Gabe counters, anger bleeding through his control. "The moment we started this investigation, every nanobot colony in the facility reported our activity. We're fighting a war where the enemy knows our every move."

"In the meantime," Forest says, "we assume all communications are compromised. All planning sessions should be moved to Faraday cage environments. All operational details need to be compartmentalized to essential personnel only."

"That severely limits our coordination capabilities," CJ observes.

"Better than operating with zero security," I reply.

Forest nods once. "Implement it. Charlie team, you have operational priority. Whatever resources you need."

As the meeting disperses, I catch Gabe before he can leave. There's something burning in his eyes—impatience mixed with accusation like this is somehow my fault.

"What?" I ask.

"Nothing." But his tone says everything. Sharp. Clipped. The way he gets when he's building toward an explosion.

"Say what you're thinking."

"I'm thinking we're wasting time while she's out there." Gabe gestures vaguely toward the door. "More meetings. More protocols. More fucking analysis while Malfor does God knows what to them."

"Analysis keeps us alive. Keeps them alive." Gabe's spiraling. It's hard to watch, and each time I try to talk to him, his agitation only increases.

"Does it?" The question carries an edge that makes my jaw tighten. "Because from where I'm standing, we're sitting here analyzing nanobots while she's out there getting tortured."

"That's not—"

"Isn't it? We followed procedure. Secured the area. Ran diagnostics. Did everything by the book." His voice rises, drawing looks from the dispersing command staff. "And while we were being methodical, Malfor was already ten steps ahead."

Heat builds in my chest, matching his energy despite my training. "You think rushing in blind would have prevented this?"

"I think if we moved faster, acted on instinct instead of waiting for perfect intelligence—"

"You're thinking like a demolitions expert," I cut Gabe off. "Blow things up first, worry about collateral damage later."

"And you're thinking like a fucking robot. Calculate everything to death while real people suffer the consequences. We need to extract the women now." He snarls and slams his hand on the table. The sound echoes like a gunshot. "Before he moves them."

"Moves them?" I shake my head with incredulity. "We don't even know where they are, or were, or anything. What intel do you want us to act on?" My voice stays level, which only makes me angrier. "We don't know location, defenses, or extraction routes."

"We know he's watching us plan. Every second we delay gives him more tactical advantage."

"Every second we rush gives him exactly what he wants—us walking into a trap." It's like we're operating on different wavelengths.

Glitching.

That's never happened before.

The room watches as the tension between us escalates. Carter shifts in his seat, the fabric creaking beneath him. Blake's eyes ping-pong between us like he's tracking a live grenade. This isn't a tactical disagreement.

It's personal.

"Maybe if you cared more about getting her back than your precious protocols—" Gabe's voice cracks like a whip, sharp and reckless.

My spine locks. "What the fuck did you just say to me?"

"You heard me." Gabe closes the distance in two strides, his chest nearly brushing mine. "While you're calculating acceptable losses, Ally is being tortured."

"We don't know that." Fury spikes, hot and immediate.

"We don't not know that." He jabs a finger toward the ops table.

Why is it so damn hard to get him to listen?

"It makes no sense for Malfor to torture them." I grit the

words, each one clenched between my teeth.

Gabe snorts, incredulous. "Why the hell not? He's using them for bait."

"Exactly," I snap. "Which is why torture doesn't make sense. You damage bait, you weaken leverage."

His jaw flexes. Mine does too. The air between us buzzes with unspoken threats and years of brotherhood fraying at the seams.

"That's enough." Ethan's voice cuts through like a blade—cold, commanding. "Both of you. Outside. Cool off."

Silence snaps into place like a vise.

No one moves.

The whole team feels it now—the fracture line. Wide. Splintering. And it's got both our names on it.

"I'm not going anywhere with him," I snap, but my eyes never leave Gabe's face.

"Then separate," Ethan says coldly. "But the two of you need to get your shit together. Because right now, you're more dangerous to this mission than Malfor is."

Around us, our teammates pretend not to notice the fracture line running through Gabe and me.

But they all see it.

The way Gabe's hands clench into fists. The way my breathing has shifted to combat-ready. The space between us feels electric with unresolved violence.

"We'll continue this later." I keep my voice level despite the fire building in my chest.

"Will we? Because every hour we wait is another hour *my woman* spends in his hands." Gabe spins on his heels and walks away, leaving me standing in the conference room with the taste of blood in my mouth from grinding my teeth.

Two hours later, we're back in the secure conference room, but the tension from earlier hasn't dissipated.

If anything, it's gotten worse.

My woman.

Did he really say that?

To me?

Ethan spreads reconnaissance photos across the table. "Based on Mitzy's preliminary analysis, we're looking at three potential locations where the quantum signature originates."

Gabe leans against the far wall instead of taking his usual seat beside me. The distance is deliberate. Pointed.

"We go in three teams." Ethan traces routes on the tactical map. "Coordinated assault, multiple entry points. Alpha takes primary breach, Charlie handles extraction, Bravo provides overwatch and containment."

"That's exactly what he'll expect," Gabe counters, pushing off from the wall. "Standard Guardian HRS tactics. He's been watching us for three months—he knows our playbook better than we do."

I lean forward, supporting Ethan's assessment. "Which is why we stick to proven methodologies. Discipline under pressure—"

"Discipline?" Gabe laughs, but there's no humor in it. "We should hit hard and fast. Overwhelming force before he can adapt."

"With what intelligence? We're flying blind."

"Better than paralysis by analysis."

Walt shifts uncomfortably in his chair. Blake and Carter exchange looks. Rigel's jaw tightens as he watches our partnership disintegrate in real time. The whole team feels the fracture line running through their leadership.

Ethan tries to regain control. "Maybe we should take a step back—"

"We stick to proven tactics," I state, backing my team leader. "Coordinated assault gives us the best chance of success with minimal casualties."

"We're days behind and still clueless about where she is."

Gabe's pacing now, fists clenched at his sides, jaw flexing with every ragged breath. "We're discussing tactics like we know where we're headed. One of three *potential* locations?"

"Gabe." Ethan's voice is calm. Contained. "You're making it worse——"

"I don't care!" Gabe spins back, voice sharp. "She's out there alone. Scared. And I'm stuck here watching hours bleed away."

The room stills.

No one dares interrupt him.

He drags a hand through his hair, eyes red-rimmed and wild. "I should be with her," he mutters. "She needs me. God, she ..."

A beat of silence.

Then, softly. Broken.

"I promised I'd protect her."

Not us. I.

"I should've never let her out of my sight," he goes on, voice cracking now. "I should've been there. I should've ..."

My heart stops.

Gabe doesn't even hear himself. Doesn't notice the shift. But every word twists like a knife between my ribs. Because in his mind, right now——it's just him and her.

No we.

No us.

No space for what we built between the three of us.

Just him. Her. And the guilt eating him alive.

My hands curl into fists, and just like that, I feel it——the splinter, deep and raw. The slow bleed of something breaking between us.

Blake shifts like he feels the fracture too.

Rigel glances at me, eyebrows furrowing.

The conference room goes dead silent except for the hum of electronics and the whisper of ventilation systems. Blake's coffee mug hovers halfway to his mouth. Carter's pen stops moving across his notepad. Walt's medical bag sits forgotten on the table between us.

Gabe stares at me for a long moment, something like satisfaction flickering in his eyes. Like he wanted this confrontation. Needed it. He walks out, leaving Ethan to salvage what's left of mission planning.

THIRTEEN

Training Exercise Gone Wrong

GABE

Charlie team gears up for what should be a routine training exercise. I know what it is—something to keep us busy while the techies try to figure out where the fuck Malfor's keeping our women.

The magazine clicks into place with the same sound it's made a thousand times before. Familiar. Reliable. Except today, even that small mechanical certainty feels wrong.

Everything feels wrong when the most important person in your world is missing.

The practice drill is a standard building clearance exercise. A simulated hostage rescue. The kind of drill we've run a hundred times and can execute in our sleep.

But my hands shake slightly as I check my rifle's action, and I have to force myself to focus on the mechanics. Muscle memory takes over when conscious thought fails.

The kill house sits at the far end of Guardian HQ's training grounds—a modular structure designed to simulate urban combat scenarios. Today, it's configured as a three-story office building with multiple entry points, blind corners, and designated "hostage" locations marked by sensors.

Simple scenario: terrorists have taken civilian hostages on the second floor. Charlie team's job is to neutralize threats and extract the friendlies without casualties. Basic Guardian HQ doctrine—coordinated entry, systematic clearance, overwhelming tactical superiority.

We should dominate this.

"Final equipment check," Ethan announces, his voice carrying the crisp authority of mission command.

Around us, the team performs their pre-deployment ritual—magazines seated, comms tested, gear secured. Walt adjusts his medical kit. Blake checks his breaching charges. Carter inspects his rifle optics with the methodical precision of a man who's never missed a shot that mattered.

The familiar choreography should be comforting.

Usually is.

But today, every movement feels like we're all going through motions while something fundamental has shifted beneath us.

I watch Hank at the tactical display, studying building schematics with that focused intensity I've seen a thousand times. His jaw works silently—the tell that means he's processing multiple variables, building contingency plans for contingencies. When he catches me watching, his expression hardens into something cold and professional.

We haven't spoken directly since yesterday's briefing room blowup. Haven't looked at each other except when necessity demands it. The space between us thrums with unresolved tension, words that cut too deep to heal with simple apologies.

"Primary breach point, south entrance," Ethan announces, studying the tactical display. "Gabe and Walt, you're first through. Hank follows with Blake and Carter. Rigel provides overwatch from the north stairwell."

Standard formation.

Proven tactics.

Precisely the kind of methodical approach that's kept us alive through missions that should have killed us.

It's also precisely the kind of careful, calculated precision that's been eating at me for three days.

Hank nods his approval of the plan. "We'll take our time with this one. Methodical approach, systematic clearance. No unnecessary risks."

Take our time.

The phrase sticks in my throat like glass. Three days ago, "taking our time" meant Ally was safe in her lab, probably wrestling with some quantum equation. Now it means going through training motions while she's …

I force the thought away, but my jaw clenches involuntarily.

"Questions?" Ethan asks, scanning the team.

The word hangs in the air.

Questions?

I've got plenty of questions. Like, why are we running practice drills while our women are in hell? Like, why does every conversation include phrases about "proper intelligence" instead of action?

"All good," I say, but the words come out clipped.

Walt glances over, that careful expression that means he's reading the temperature in the room. Blake's watching me too, probably noticing the way my hands keep flexing into fists.

"Breach in three," Ethan's voice crackles through comms as we approach the kill house. "Wait for my signal."

I stack behind Walt at the entry point, muscles coiled with three days of accumulated frustration. Through my earpiece, Rigel confirms overwatch position. Blake reports breaching charges armed, and Carter settles into his position with the team.

Everything is by the book. Everything is calculated. Everything is designed to minimize risk through overwhelming coordination.

Everything feels like wasted time while Ally suffers.

"Two," Ethan continues the countdown.

My finger taps against my rifle's trigger guard. The movement is small, unconscious, but Walt notices. He shoots me a look over his shoulder—a question and a warning combined.

But I'm thinking about quantum signatures and all the hours we've spent talking instead of moving.

"One."

Instead of waiting for the coordinated assault, I hit the door early. Alone. Without backup.

Frustration overrides years of tactical training. The entry explodes inward as I breach the threshold, rifle up, scanning for targets. The simulated environment unfolds before me—furniture arranged to create firing lanes, mannequins positioned as hostile targets, and sensors that will register hits and determine mission success or failure.

I should wait for backup. Should establish positions and advance systematically.

Instead, I push deeper into the structure, hunting targets with single-minded intensity.

"What the fuck are you doing?" Hank's roar fills the comm channel, raw fury bleeding through his usual control.

But it's Ethan's voice that cuts through the chaos: "Gabe, fall back and regroup. That's an order."

The first simulated hostile appears around a corner—a pop-up target designed to test reaction time and accuracy. I engage immediately, double-tap to center mass, moving forward before the target even registers the hit.

"Gabe, fall back NOW," Ethan commands, team leader authority demanding compliance.

But I'm already committed. Already moving toward the stairwell, where intelligence suggests the hostages are being held. Already proving that sometimes action beats analysis.

It feels good to actually do something.

The second hostile catches me in a crossfire I should have anticipated. Would have anticipated if I'd waited for backup, if I'd followed protocol, if I'd trusted the team to do their jobs while I did mine.

The training laser tags me center mass.

I'm dead.

Simulation over.

Mission failure.

"Target down," the automated system announces with mechanical indifference. "Exercise terminated."

Static fills the comm channel. Not the comfortable silence of a team that's just executed flawlessly, but the poisonous quiet that comes after someone has fucked up catastrophically.

The debrief room feels smaller than usual when we file in fifteen minutes later. CJ stands at the head of the conference table like a judge about to pronounce a sentence. He shows no emotion, but the way his fingers drum against the tabletop telegraphs controlled fury.

We take our seats—a team that just failed a basic exercise we should have dominated. The shame radiates off everyone like heat from a fever.

"Explain to me," CJ begins, his voice carrying the weight of command authority and bitter disappointment, "how my best team just failed a drill that Academy recruits complete successfully."

Silence stretches across the room. Walt stares at his hands. Blake's jaw works silently. Carter's cop instincts tell him to stay quiet and let someone else step on the landmine.

Ethan shifts in his chair, team leader responsibility weighing on his shoulders. "There was a breakdown in—"

"My fault." The words come out before Ethan can finish. "I jumped the gun."

"Explain." CJ's flat stare locks onto mine.

The honest answer?

I'm sick of analyzing everything to death while our women suffer. Sick of Hank's careful variables and contingency plans when what we need is action. Sick of "methodical approaches" and "systematic clearance," when every second we waste planning could be Ally's last breath.

The honest answer is that I snapped because I can't stand one more second of tactical patience while the woman I love is in hell.

"No excuse," I say instead.

But everyone knows the real story. That I'm coming apart at the seams and taking it out on the person closest to me. That I've been picking fights with Hank for three days because doing something—even something destructive—feels better than doing nothing.

That when you're drowning in helplessness, the easiest target is the man who's always been your anchor.

Hank's hands clench into fists. Ethan's heavy gaze darts between us, reading the fracture lines that started the moment our women disappeared. The way Walt and Blake exchange looks like they've been watching a slow-motion car crash, waiting for the inevitable impact.

"Charlie team is suspended from active deployment pending remedial training," CJ announces, his words hitting like physical blows. "You'll spend the next week running basic exercises until you remember how to function as a unit."

Suspended.

The word tastes like ash. While Ally suffers in Malfor's hands, we'll be playing training games because I couldn't control myself for five fucking minutes.

"CJ," Ethan begins, "if we could just—"

"The decision is final." CJ's tone brooks no argument. "When you can complete a basic hostage rescue without going cowboy, we'll discuss operational deployment."

He moves toward the door, then pauses. "Gabe, stay behind. The rest of you are dismissed."

FOURTEEN

Compromised

GABE

THE TEAM FILES OUT IN SILENCE, LEAVING ME ALONE WITH CJ's judgment. They gather outside—Ethan's shoulders rigid with command stress, Walt shaking his head, Blake's fists clenched.

And Hank. Standing apart from the others, staring back at the building with an expression that makes my chest tighten.

"Seventy-six hours," CJ says quietly, settling back into his chair. "Seventy-six hours since the women were taken, and you just sabotaged your team's readiness to get them back."

The words hit like armor-piercing rounds. "I—"

"You're compromised." The assessment cuts through my attempt at explanation. "Emotionally, tactically, operationally. The Gabe I know would never abandon his team in a firefight."

"The Gabe you know never had to watch the woman he loves disappear."

"Neither has the rest of your team." CJ's voice stays level, which makes it worse. "You think you're the only one suffering? The only one desperate to bring them home?"

The question hits because I do think that. Have been thinking that. Wrapped so deep in my rage that I've forgotten everyone else is bleeding too.

"What I think," CJ continues, "is that you're so busy being angry at Hank for not moving fast enough that you've forgotten how to be angry at the right target."

"Hank's not the problem—"

"Hank's the only reason this team functions. He's your anchor. His planning keeps you alive. His discipline compensates for your impulses." CJ leans forward. "And now you're destroying it. Tearing apart the most effective partnership in Guardian HQ because you can't handle the fact that getting Ally Collins back requires patience instead of explosives."

The truth burns like acid. Because everything I've accomplished, every mission I've survived—it's all been built on the foundation of Hank's steady presence.

"Learn some fucking patience." CJ stands, moving toward the door. "Because right now, you're more dangerous to your team than Malfor is."

He pauses at the threshold. "One week. One week to remember who you are and why your team trusts you with their lives. Fuck this up, and I'll transfer you to a desk where your emotional compromises can't get good people killed."

My teammates wait in the hallway. Not dispersed. Not gone. Standing there like they've been holding a vigil for my sanity.

The silence stretches between us, heavy with three days of accumulated tension and the fresh wound of our suspension.

"Meeting room," Ethan says quietly. "Now."

We file back into the conference room we just vacated. The air still carries the weight of CJ's disappointment, but something else has shifted. Something darker.

Blake settles into his chair, jaw tight. "Getting emotional won't fix this, Gabe."

The words hit like a slap.

"Emotional?" Like I'm some fucking rookie who can't keep his shit together. I'm in his face before I realize I've moved, chest bumping against his. "Six women are gone, Blake. Our women. And you want me to stay calm like some fucking robot?"

My hands ball into fists, knuckles cracking. Every muscle coiled for violence. "Easy for you to say, isn't it? Sophia's safe. Luke's safe. You don't have skin in this game."

The words are out before I can stop them, before I can think about what I'm saying.

"What the hell did you just say to me?" Blake's chair hits the floor as he surges to his feet.

The room goes electric. Everyone else freezes.

"Whoa, hold up, Gabe—" Ethan starts, hands raised.

"Not cool, man," Rigel says sharply. "That's way out of line."

Carter steps forward. "Gabe, you need to apologize right now."

It's all a buzz of static.

"Not taking it back. You heard me." But even as the words come out, I know I've crossed a line. "Your family's tucked away nice and safe while—"

"How dare you?" Blake's voice drops to something dangerous, deadly quiet. His hands slam into my chest, shoving me back a step. "How fucking dare you talk to me like I don't bleed with you." Another shove, harder this time, making me stumble. "Like I don't breathe with you. Like, I don't fight with you. Like, I wouldn't die for you."

But I surge forward again, shoving him back just as hard. "Yeah? Then where the fuck were you when they needed you? Where were you when Harrison walked through our front door?"

"Those women are like sisters to me, you piece of shit. Ally's my little sister. Jenna's my little sister. Rebel, Mia, Malia, Stitch— every single one of them. And if you think for one goddamn second that I don't feel every moment they're gone like a knife in my chest, then you don't know me at all."

The raw pain in his voice hits like a physical blow, but rage has its hooks in me now, driving me forward past reason, past brotherhood.

"Then why aren't you doing something about it?"

"Whoa, you're totally out of line." Carter springs to his feet, defending his twin. "Take that back."

I round on Carter, heat blazing through my chest like napalm. "You're just a freaking stand-in. You're not even really part of this team." I'm in his face now, jabbing my finger into his chest with each word. "You got fast-tracked because your girl-friend got taken. That doesn't make you one of us."

Carter's jaw tightens, cop instincts warring with the urge to hit back. "That woman out there is my world, and I'll be damned if I let you or anyone else tell me I don't belong in the fight to get her back."

"And what's your brilliant plan, Carter?" The words come out like venom. "More cop psychology? You think you can talk Malfor into giving them back?"

"And what would you have us do?" Blake's control starts to fray. "Storm off half-cocked without a plan?"

"Better than sitting on our asses making plans that get trans-mitted to the enemy in real time."

"Look, we're all frustrated—" Rigel spreads his hands, trying to find middle ground.

"Frustrated?" The word comes out like a roar. I take a step toward him, fists still clenched. "Frustrated is when your coffee order gets fucked up. This is systematic failure on every level."

"That's enough." Ethan stands, movement sharp.

"Is it? Because from where I'm standing, it looks like we're all real good at talking and real shit at actually doing anything."

That's when Hank speaks.

Cool. Measured. Clinical as always.

"We need actionable intelligence before we can mount an effective operation."

The sound of his voice—that same controlled precision he uses when the world is burning—detonates what's left of my restraint.

"Actionable intelligence?" I spin toward him, heat blazing through my chest. "We need ACTION. Period. While you're sitting there analyzing variables, Ally could be dead. They all could be dead."

"We follow protocol." Hank delivers each word with military precision.

"Fuck protocol." The words explode between us like shrapnel. "Six women kidnapped because we didn't see the infiltration coming."

Hank's jaw tightens—the only sign my words hit their target. "Operating without intelligence gets people killed."

"Operating without urgency gets people killed." I step closer, invading his space. "But you wouldn't understand that, would you? Everything's just another equation to solve."

"And everything's just another target to blow up for you." His voice drops, carrying an edge I recognize. Dangerous territory. "That's not how we get them back."

"At least I want to get them back." The words explode out of me, spittle flying. "At least I'm not sitting here calculating acceptable losses while Ally is being tortured."

Hank's eyes go flat, deadly calm. "You think I don't want Ally back? You think I'm not dying inside thinking about her in that bastard's hands?"

"I think you're too fucking controlled to feel anything." I'm chest-to-chest now, close enough to see the muscle ticking in his jaw. "I think you've compartmentalized getting her back into a tactical problem."

"You're too fucked up to think straight." His voice stays level, which makes it worse. "Emotion compromises judgment. Always has with you."

"Emotion?" I laugh, but there's no humor in it, just raw violence looking for a target. "You want to see emotion? You want to see what happens when I stop thinking and start feeling?"

The room feels smaller suddenly. Everyone else fades into background noise. None of it matters.

Just me and Hank.

Staring at each other across a chasm that's been building for days.

"Outside." Hank's voice cuts through the static in my skull. "Now."

"Fuck off." The words come out like a snarl. "I'm not going anywhere with you."

His hand clamps down on my arm like a steel trap, fingers digging into muscle hard enough to bruise.

"You want to fight about this? Then we fight. But not here. Not when you're like this." His voice drops to that command tone that's gotten us through a hundred operations. "Get the fuck outside, Gabe."

"Let go of me." I try to jerk away, but his grip tightens.

"Move." He doesn't raise his voice, doesn't need to. The authority in it cuts through my rage like a blade. Even pissed off and spiraling, part of me recognizes the hierarchy in our relationship.

I plant my feet, try to resist, but Hank's got leverage and momentum. He drags me toward the door, my boots sliding against the polished floor.

"You're tearing apart the team when we need to be united." His grip never loosens as he hauls me down the corridor. "You want to lose your shit? Fine. But you do it with me, not them."

The team watches in stunned silence as Hank marches me out of the conference room like I'm some kind of unruly animal. My face burns, but the fury burning in my chest is stronger.

It's been seventy-six hours, fifty-seven minutes.

Charlie team is suspended.

Ally is still missing.

And the partnership that defined my life is lying in pieces because I couldn't control my rage for five fucking minutes. All because I forgot that when you're drowning, you don't drag down the people trying to save you. Least of all, your anchor.

FIFTEEN

The Fight

GABE

The Guardian HRS gymnasium occupies an entire football field. It's an industrial space with exposed steel beams overhead, fluorescent lights casting harsh shadows across rubber flooring. Spray mats cover the center area—a familiar arena where we've worked through countless conflicts over the years.

But this feels different. Charged. Dangerous.

Ethan follows us in. He knows what this is. What it could become. His presence serves as both witness and insurance—someone to call a halt if we cross lines we can't uncross.

"This is about the exercise," Hank says as we enter the gym. "About you going rogue."

"This is about you being too fucking careful while our women are out there getting tortured."

"And this is about you thinking with your dick instead of your brain."

That's when I know we're going to fight. Really fight. Not spar, not train. Fight like enemies instead of brothers. Hank wants to get personal?

Well, I can give him that.

"Strip down," Hank says, already pulling off his tactical shirt.

I shed my gear, muscles coiled with three days of accumulated rage. The familiar ritual should calm me. Usually does. But today the anger burns hotter, more personal.

We step onto the mats.

Hank moves first—a testing takedown attempt that I counter easily. Standard grappling. Light contact. Feeling each other out.

But my energy's too high, my movements too aggressive. What should be controlled technique comes out sharp and violent. When I go for an arm drag, I use more force than necessary.

Hank responds by using precise counters that make me look sloppy.

Which pisses me off more.

"Talk to me." Hank slips out of my attempted triangle choke. Slippery fucker.

"Nothing to talk about." I explode up from the mat, reset our positions. "We should be hunting that bastard instead of rolling around on fucking mats. She's out there." The words come out strangled as I break his grip. "Probably hurt. Scared. And we're twiddling our thumbs on training exercises."

"Rushing in blind gets everyone killed."

The calm certainty in his voice breaks something loose in my chest. All that rage I've been containing, all that helpless fury at watching Ally disappear into Malfor's hands—it needs somewhere to go.

I throw a real punch.

Not sparring contact. Not training intensity. A real hit meant to hurt.

Hank slips it by millimeters, counters by taking me down hard enough to drive the air from my lungs. His knee settles across my chest, pinning me down.

"You done?" he asks.

Instead of answering, I buck hard, use my hips to throw him off balance, then scramble to my feet. This isn't sparring anymore.

This is fighting.

"You don't get it," I growl, circling him like a predator. "You never get it. Everything is just a tactical problem to solve. But she's not a fucking variable, Hank. She's—"

"What?" His voice carries an edge now, control fraying. "What is she, Gabe?"

"Mine." The word tears out of me raw and primal.

"What the fuck?" Hank's voice explodes, all that controlled precision shattered. "Yours? She's yours?" His hands slam into my chest, driving me backward. "I've heard a lot of *me's* and *mine's* out of you lately. You're a fucking bastard, she's *OURS*. I'm dying on the inside just like you, and you going off the deep end isn't helping anyone. It sure as shit isn't helping Ally."

He lands a series of punches—hard, precise hits to my ribs, my shoulder, each hit punctuating his words. I block what I can, but his rage finds its target.

"That better be the last fucking time you claim her as your own, fucktard. She belongs to both of us."

"Shit, is that what this is about? A pronoun?"

"When you start claiming her as *yours* instead of *ours*, you bet that's what this is about." His voice breaks on the last word—raw, guttural, not just anger but pain. I barely register the shift before his fist slams into my jaw. White-hot pain explodes behind my eyes as my head jerks to the side with a crack.

"She belongs to both of us," he snarls, following it up with a punch to my ribs that knocks the air from my lungs. "Not just you. Not just me. *Us*. She doesn't belong to you."

"Shit, it was just a—"

His fist crashes into my face again, fiercer this time. No holding back. No warning. My vision blurs, and blood fills my mouth. I stumble, trying to stay upright, but he's already moving.

He drives his knee into my gut. My body folds, instincts screaming, but there's no time to recover. His elbow slams down across my back like a battering ram, dropping me hard to the mats.

I hit with a grunt, stunned. The room spins.

"You selfish piece of shit," Hank spits, voice cracking like thunder. "You think you're the only one who loves her? You think you're the only one who's fucking destroyed?"

Another kick to my ribs as I try to get up. Real violence. Calculated brutality from a man who's spent years learning exactly how to hurt people.

"I held her when she had nightmares about Kazakhstan. I watched her smile when she felt safe again. I felt her trust when she submitted to me." Each word comes with another strike—fists, knees, elbows. "She's mine too, you fucking psychopath."

I roll away, blood in my mouth, but Hank follows. Relentless. His boot catches me in the shoulder, spinning me across the mat.

"Every second she's gone, I die a little more. Every breath feels like I'm drowning, but I don't get to fall apart because someone has to think clearly enough to get her back."

He drops down, pins me with his knee across my throat. Pressure building. Stars dancing at the edges of my vision.

"And you ..." His voice drops to something deadly, unrecognizable. "You want to throw it all away because you can't handle sharing her with me. Is that what this is? You think she's fucking yours?"

"She may call you Sir, but she kneels for me. Suffers for me." I drive my elbow into his ribs, hard. "She cries for me."

Hank freezes for a split second—just enough.

I twist, break the chokehold, and slam my forearm into his throat as we flip. We're both bleeding, panting, torn between killing each other and collapsing under the weight of what we've lost.

I refuse to tap out. Use dirty techniques to break free. Elbow strikes that would be illegal in competition. The controlled violence we usually share becomes something uglier. More personal.

"This isn't about Ally," Hank says, breathing harder now. "This is about you needing someone to blame."

"Fuck you."

We crash together again, grappling to hurt. Sweat makes our grips slippery. Breathing comes in sharp bursts. My shoulder screams where it impacts the mat wrong.

"You want to know what this is about?" I hook his leg and take him down harder than necessary. "This is about you sitting there like a fucking robot while the woman we love suffers."

"And you losing your shit helps, how exactly?" The clinical tone in his voice—even now, even with me trying to hurt him—destroys the last of my control.

I land a solid hit that actually rocks him. Hard enough to split his lip.

Blood on his mouth. Surprise in his eyes.

For a heartbeat, we both freeze.

Then Hank's counter comes harder than it needs to. A warning. His elbow connects with my ribs hard enough to make me see stars.

We're both breathing hard now. Sweat-slicked. Real anger bleeding through. We're about to cross a line we can't uncross.

"Stop." Ethan's voice cuts through our labored breathing. "Both of you. Just fucking stop."

We separate slowly, warily. Like animals backing away from a fight that almost turned lethal.

Hank wipes blood from his lip. I press a palm to my ribs, feeling for damage.

We stare at each other across a chasm that feels like miles.

"We're falling apart." The admission tastes like eating lead, but it's fitting. I've been an ass, and not just to Hank. I owe several apologies. "When we need each other most, we're fucking falling apart."

"Yeah." Hank's voice carries cold fury. "Because you can't lock down your emotions long enough to think straight. Because you'd rather tear apart the team."

The silence stretches.

That's when it hits me. The solution burns through the rage and frustration like white phosphorus.

"We need somewhere these fucking things can't hear us."

Hank's eyes sharpen, tactical wheels already turning.

"We're *infested.*" Hank takes a step back and wipes blood from his mouth. "Or did you snooze during that part of the briefing?"

"Don't be an ass. I didn't snooze." I press my palms against my eyes, trying to think through the rage and pain. "But we need somewhere they can't hear us. Somewhere without electronics, without … Fuck!"

My brain spins through options. Guardian HRS is compromised. Every building, every room, every piece of equipment is crawling with those microscopic spies. Even if we go off-compound, how do we know we're clean? How do we know they haven't spread to our vehicles, our gear?

"Forest mentioned a Faraday cage." Hank wipes blood from his split lip.

"Maybe, but who knows if these quantum things follow normal electromagnetic rules?" I pace across the mats, boots squeaking against rubber. Think, dammit. Somewhere without tech. Somewhere isolated. Somewhere, the nanobots couldn't have spread.

"Water," I say suddenly. "Saltwater disrupts electronics. If we go somewhere remote enough …" An idea starts forming, pieces clicking together like an explosive device assembly.

"The beach." The solution crystallizes as I speak. Below Insanity. Doc Summers' and Forest's place. No tech down there. Nothing but sand and saltwater and the sound of waves."

For the first time in three days, something like hope flickers in Hank's expression.

"We'll need to get everyone clean first." Hank slips back into operational mode as if we didn't just try to kill each other. "EMP exposure to fry any nanobots. Then move to a secure location for actual planning."

"Now you're talking."

But Hank's eyes stay cold. Blood trickles from his split lip, and when he wipes it away, his gaze never leaves mine. He's compartmentalizing what happened between us, filing it away for later reckoning.

I know that look. I've seen it when he's about to eliminate a target.

"Hank—"

"We're not done with this conversation." His voice cuts through my attempt at reconciliation. "Don't think for a second this is over. What we need to focus on right now is how to get them back. Until then, I'm not dealing with your shit."

He stands slowly, favoring his ribs where I landed a solid hit. When he looks at me, there's something broken in his eyes. Something that might never heal.

"You think I'm going to forget what you said?" His voice stays deadly quiet, but I hear the fury underneath. "You claimed her like I was nothing. I won't forget. Not today. Not tomorrow. Not ever."

The words hit harder than any punch he threw because I know Hank. When he says never, he means it.

"Look. I fucked up, and that's not what I meant. I would

never cut you out of what *we* have with Ally. I was lost and confused and enraged and fucked in the head. She's *ours*. Always will be." I run a hand through my hair to hide its shaking.

Did I fuck it all up? I hope not.

But I can't take back the words I said. Somehow, I'll have to make it up to Hank. To him. To Blake. To Carter. Hell, to the whole damn team. It's time I stop my personal pity party and get to work.

The fracture between us doesn't evaporate—it widens. Every breath, every heartbeat drives the wedge deeper. He won't forget what I said about Ally being mine. Won't forgive the claim I tried to make.

"I'm not going to apologize for loving her, but I know I fucked up. I'll lock it down."

"You better." He points vaguely in the direction of Charlie team's bullpen. "And you've got apologies to make. The shit you said to Blake? To Carter?" Hank shakes his head. "Fix it. As for us, Ally *needs* both of us. You can't give her what she needs. You're not *enough* for that."

SIXTEEN

Ghosts and Echoes

HANK

I GUIDE MY SUV DOWN THE COASTAL HIGHWAY TOWARD HOME. Gabe sits in the passenger seat, jaw clenched, staring out at the Pacific like it holds answers. The silence between us carries weight—dense, suffocating, broken only by the low rumble of the engine and the distant crash of waves against the cliffs.

Ethan looked between us in the gymnasium, blood on our faces and murder in our eyes, and made the call. "Go home. Both of you. Wait for instructions."

Not a suggestion. An order from someone who's seen too many partnerships fracture under pressure.

I downshift as we approach the turnoff to our cliffside road. The motion sends a sharp pain through my ribs where Gabe landed solid hits. Good. The physical discomfort helps me focus and keeps my rage under control.

"You're favoring your left side," Gabe observes, his first words in twenty minutes.

"You hit like a sledgehammer when you're pissed off."

"Yeah, well. You fight dirty when you're angry."

The admission hangs between us. Neither apology nor accusation. Just a statement.

Our home comes into view—glass and steel perched on the cliff's edge, designed for privacy and defensibility. Usually, the sight of it settles something in my chest.

Home. Sanctuary.

The place where Ally learned to trust us completely.

Today, it feels like a mausoleum.

I park, engine ticking as it cools. Neither of us moves to get out.

"She's everywhere in there," Gabe says quietly.

"I know."

"Her coffee mug is in the sink. That book she was reading on the nightstand. Her fucking perfume still on the pillows."

"I know."

He turns to look at me, and for the first time since the fight, his expression carries something other than rage. Pain. Raw and unfiltered.

"How do you do it? How do you—compartmentalize?"

The question hits like a heat-seeking missile because the truth is, I can't. Not completely. Every room in this house reminds me of her. Every trace of her is a knife between the ribs.

"I don't," I say finally. "I just don't let it show."

If only it were that simple.

Her scent hits me immediately—vanilla and something uniquely Ally—lingers in the air despite three days of absence. The morning light streaming through the floor-to-ceiling windows illuminates everything she touched, everywhere she's been.

Her coffee mug sits with lipstick still on the rim. A hair tie lies forgotten on the granite surface of the counter, along with one of her pens—the expensive kind her father buys by the dozen.

Gabe stops in the doorway, hands clenching at his sides.

"This is fucked," he mutters.

I move past him like he didn't speak. Like he's not even there. My shoulder bumps his as I push past into the kitchen, close enough to be deliberate, distant enough to make my point. He wants to voice his pain? He can do it to someone who gives a shit.

Muscle memory carries me through familiar routines. Check the security logs. Scan for any signs of intrusion. Catalog potential threats.

Nothing.

The house is exactly as we left it before we discovered the girls had been taken. We haven't been home since—seventy-six hours of sleeping in Guardian HRS break rooms and surviving on vending machine coffee while we planned and replanned, yet got nowhere.

The tactical part of my brain files away the details. The emotional part—the part I usually keep locked down—notices everything else.

Ally's sweater draped over the back of her favorite chair—the one by the window where she likes to curl up with her research. The indent in the couch cushions where she spent hours working on quantum equations, I'll never understand.

"I need …" Gabe starts, then stops. Shakes his head. "I can't be in here right now."

He disappears down the hallway toward his suite, leaving me alone with the ghosts.

I find myself standing in the doorway of my bedroom.

Aimless.

Our bedroom.

The place where all three of us sleep when we're together. California king bed, dark sheets, reinforced frame to handle our combined weight and activities. It sits unmade from when we left in a hurry, Ally's pillow still holding the impression of her head.

A book lies open face down where she was reading before

sleep: some quantum physics text that makes my head hurt just looking at the equations. Her clothes are scattered around—not messy, Ally's actually quite tidy. A silk camisole drapes over the chair. Her jeans are folded on the dresser.

I pick up the camisole, fabric soft between my fingers. It smells like her. Like vanilla and that soap she uses.

A memory slams into me without warning.

Ally standing at the dresser in nothing but this camisole, brushing her hair while Gabe made coffee in the kitchen. She caught me watching and smiled—that slow, knowing smile that meant she was planning something.

"You're staring," she said.

"You're worth staring at."

She turned, silk sliding against her skin, and walked over to where I sat on the edge of the bed. "We have that meeting with Mitzy today. The one about my research."

"We do."

"After that, I want to try something new." Her fingers traced the collar of my shirt, touch feather-light but loaded with intent. "Something I've been thinking about."

"What kind of something?"

Her smile turned wicked. "The kind that requires both of you. And these." She held up silk restraints, the expensive kind from the collection in Gabe's suite.

The memory fractures, leaving me holding ruined silk. I'm staring at the torn fabric in my hands when footsteps echo from the hallway.

Gabe appears in the doorway, but he looks different. Calmer. His hair is damp—he's showered—and he's wearing clean clothes that don't hide the bruises I put on his ribs.

"Feel better?" he asks, eyes going to the destroyed camisole.

"No."

"Good. Because if destroying her things made you feel better, I'd have to beat the shit out of you again."

Despite everything, my mouth almost twitches toward a smile.

Almost.

"Found this on my pillow," he says, holding up a hair elastic. "She must have left it there the last time she ..." He doesn't finish. Doesn't need to.

Gabe's suite serves a specific purpose in our dynamic. It's where he takes Ally when she needs what only he can give her—the intensity, the edge, the kind of surrender that requires specialized equipment and absolute trust.

"She was nervous that first time," he continues, voice dropping. "When you brought her to my room. Remember?"

I remember.

"I trust you," she said, standing in the doorway of Gabe's suite, taking in the St. Andrew's cross, the suspension points, the carefully organized collection of implements. "Both of you. But this is ..."

"Scary," Gabe finished, understanding immediately. "It's supposed to be a little scary. That's what makes it intense."

"But you'll stop if I ask you to?"

"The second you say your safe word."

She nodded, then looked at me. "You'll be there?"

"Every second," I promised. "Watching. Making sure you're safe."

And I was there. Watching as Gabe guided her through her first real scene. Watching as she discovered parts of herself she had never explored. Watching as she learned to trust us with her darkest fantasies.

"She came so hard that night she couldn't speak for five minutes," Gabe says softly. "Just lay there shaking while I held her."

"I remember."

"She told me later that was the moment she knew. Not just that she loved us, but that she belonged with us. That we completed something in her that she didn't know was missing."

The words hit hard. Ally isn't just our submissive, our lover, or our partner. She's the piece that makes us whole. The bridge between Gabe's fire and my ice. The center around which everything else revolves.

"I fucked up," Gabe says suddenly. "What I said about her being mine."

"Yes. You did." I set down the ruined camisole, meeting his eyes.

"She chose us both. Not me, not you, but both of us. And I shouldn't have claimed her as mine alone ..." He stops, jaw working. "I betrayed our friendship. I betrayed her choice."

"Damn straight, you did."

"I just ..." His voice cracks. "When I think about what that bastard might be doing to her, when I imagine her scared and alone, I want to tear the world apart."

It's not a complete apology. The hurt between us is still too fresh, the words we used as weapons still too sharp. But it's an acknowledgment. Recognition that our personal damage matters less than getting Ally back safely.

"We've been partners for years," I finally say. "Sharing everything. Women, missions, life-and-death situations. We don't let one crisis destroy that."

"Even after I acted like a possessive asshole?"

"Even then."

We stand there for a moment, two damaged men in a room full of memories, trying to figure out how to be whole again when everything between us has shifted.

The silence stretches, filled with the distant sound of waves and unspoken understanding. We're both thinking about her. About the way she looks between us in this bed, safe and satisfied and home. About the trust she's placed in us and how catastrophically we've failed to protect it.

My phone buzzes, cutting through the quiet. Ethan's name is on the screen.

"Ethan."

"Time for a road trip," his voice is carefully neutral. "Remember that place Doc Summers mentioned? The one with the good acoustics?"

Insanity. The beach below Angel Fire's group home. Where sound carries differently, where conversations can't be overheard.

"How long?"

"Now would be good."

The line goes dead.

I look at Gabe. "Ethan needs us. Now."

Understanding flickers in his eyes. Whatever Ethan has planned, whatever solution he's found to our communications problem, it's time.

We move through the house, gathering what we need for an extended absence.

As we head for the door, I take one last look around. At Ally's coffee mug and reading glasses. At the sweater that still smells like her perfume. At all the small traces of the life we've built together.

"We'll bring her home," Gabe says, following my gaze.

"Yes," I agree. "*We* will."

Because the alternative—a future without her laughter in this kitchen, without her body warm between us in that bed, without her presence filling every corner of this house—is unthinkable.

SEVENTEEN

Punishment Protocol

ALLY

DREAMS OF HOME SHATTER AS THE OVERHEAD LIGHTS SNAP ON without warning. My muscles contract automatically, my body remembering pain before my brain fully wakes. The collar feels heavier today. The metal edge digs into the raw skin of my throat.

It's been two days since Malfor's revelation about the nanobots. Despite my best efforts, I'm no closer to figuring out how to use that knowledge to our benefit. There has to be a way to send a message. Warn Guardian HRS about the nanobots.

Three hours of sleep. Maybe four. Not enough to clear the fog of yesterday's work from my brain, not enough to steady my hands or ease the throbbing behind my eyes.

Across the cellblock, Stitch is already awake, standing at her bars. Our gazes meet through the narrow spaces between cells. Something shifts in her expression—a subtle tightening around the mouth, a glint in her eyes that wasn't there yesterday.

My stomach twists. She's taken a risk, and from the almost imperceptible nod she gives me, it was calculated.

Deliberate. Dangerous.

"Stay sharp." Jenna's voice carries from her cell, deliberately casual despite the undercurrent of exhaustion.

Boot steps echo down the corridor before anyone can respond. Not the usual shuffling gait of morning guards but the precise rhythm of Malfor's personal security team.

The cell doors unlock simultaneously, the now-familiar magnetic thunk preceding the guard's barked commands.

"Out. Line up."

They grab Stitch first, roughly, shoving her against the wall. Her expression remains neutral, but her eyes track everything— guard positions, weapons, the slight disruption in their usual routine.

My guard digs his fingers into my arm hard enough to leave bruises, marching me forward to stand beside Stitch. The back of my neck prickles with warning. Something's wrong. The tension in the air tastes metallic, sharp enough to cut.

"What did you do?" The words barely carry between us, lips barely moving.

Stitch's eyes flick toward mine, then away. "Took a chance."

No time for more as we're marched down the now-familiar route toward the labs. Left turn, right turn, left again. With each step, the guard's grip tightens on my arm. With each turn, more security personnel appear in the corridors, faces tense beneath tactical visors.

Dr. Elkin waits outside the lab door, shoulders hunched beneath his lab coat, fingers working nervously at his collar. His eyes meet mine with something that might be pity or might be fear.

"Inside." He steps aside, revealing the lab beyond.

The usual space has transformed overnight. Additional monitoring equipment crowds the workbenches. Two armed guards stand at each terminal. Three men in suits I've never seen before pore over printouts and screens. And at the center of it all,

Malfor stands with his back to the door, perfectly still, hands clasped behind him.

"Miss Collins." He doesn't turn, voice pitched low and controlled in a way that sends ice water through my veins. "Your colleague has been quite busy."

He pivots, smiles tightly with those cold eyes. "Did you know about her little project? Were you part of it?"

"I don't—"

"Don't insult us with denials." He gestures toward a monitor where lines of code scroll past, sections highlighted in angry red. "Three hundred and seventeen lines of rogue code. A beacon, buried in our security protocols. Designed to broadcast our location on a very specific receiver frequency."

My heart stops, then restarts at twice its normal speed. Stitch tried to signal Guardian HRS. A desperate gamble using the very systems Malfor forced her to secure.

One of the suited men approaches Malfor, speaking in low tones. Malfor's expression doesn't change, but something hardens in his eyes. He turns to the nearest guard.

"Take them all to the courtyard. Now."

The guard's grip shifts from painful to bruising. Dr. Elkin steps forward, hand half-raised.

"The project timeline—"

"Will be adjusted." Malfor doesn't look at him. "Some lessons require demonstration, Doctor. You of all people should understand that."

They drag me back through the corridors, past Stitch. Our eyes lock for one fractured second, and I read the message there: *Worth the risk.*

When they throw us back into our cells, it's only for minutes. Just long enough for the guards to collect the others. Rebel's face has gone pale, her arm clutched protectively against her chest. Malia trembles. Mia keeps her face blank. Jenna catches my eye across the cellblock, a question in her expression. I shake my head slightly.

Not now. No way to explain safely.

The cell doors slam open once more.

"Out. Courtyard. Now."

Sunlight hits with a blinding force after days in fluorescent hell. The courtyard blazes white as the tropical sun is reflected off the concrete and metal surfaces, instantly causing sweat to bead on my skin. Gulls wheel overhead, screeching freedom we can't reach.

They've arranged a semicircle of guards around a central post—metal, about seven feet tall, with restraints mounted at the top. Beside it stands a small table with objects I don't want to identify.

Malfor waits beside the post in his rumpled suit. Sweat beads on his forehead but doesn't diminish the cold calculation in his expression.

The guards force us into a line facing the post. Stitch, they drag to stand before Malfor. She stands straight, chin raised.

"I want to be clear about what's happening here." Malfor's voice carries across the courtyard, pitched to reach all of us. "This isn't punishment. It's education."

He paces before us, each step measured, hands clasped behind his back.

"One of you believed you could outsmart me. Could use my systems against me. Could signal your friends." His gaze sweeps across us. "Let me explain why that was a profound miscalculation."

He nods to the guards, who grab Stitch, forcing her against the post. Metal cuffs snap around her wrists, ankles, and waist. A final restraint locks around her throat, forcing her head up, immobilizing her completely. Her eyes remain defiant despite her vulnerable position.

"The signal was intercepted before it went anywhere." Malfor moves to the table, running his fingers along the objects laid out there. "Your friends at Guardian HRS remain oblivious, still planning their doomed rescue mission. But this attempt suggests a failure in my conditioning program."

His fingers select something from the table—a thin metal rod about two feet long. He tests its weight in his hand.

"The first lesson: disobedience has collective consequences."

His thumb finds the remote in his pocket, and all our collars activate simultaneously. The pain is worse than before, not just stronger but somehow deeper, reaching parts of my nervous system that shouldn't be accessible.

My spine arches, muscles contracting so violently I feel tendons tear. My vision whites out, then returns in fractured pieces. Around me, five bodies contort in identical agony.

When it stops, I'm on my knees, blood filling my mouth where I've bitten through my tongue. Jenna lies motionless beside me. Malia vomits weakly. Rebel makes a sound no human throat should ever produce. Mia groans, clutching her belly.

"That was thirty seconds at level four." Malfor sounds like he's discussing the weather. "There are three more levels available. I don't recommend experiencing them."

He turns back to Stitch, still immobilized against the post, her body trembling from the aftereffects of the shock.

"The second lesson: personal consequences for the instigator."

Malfor turns back to the table, lifting two implements for us all to see. In his left hand, a bullwhip coiled like a sleeping snake, its leather tip worn from use. In his right hand, a thin metal rod, the kind prison guards might carry—heavy enough to break bone, light enough for precise control.

He steps toward me, both weapons extended. "Choose."

The word doesn't register at first. My brain refuses to process what he's asking.

"Choose which one I use on her." His voice softens to a terrible gentleness. "Or I use both."

Stitch's eyes lock with mine over Malfor's shoulder. Even restrained, even bleeding, dignity radiates from her like heat. Her slight head shake tells me not to play his game.

But refusing means both weapons. Means twice the damage to her already battered body.

"The rod." The words scrape my throat raw. The metal will hurt, will bruise, might crack ribs—but the whip will tear flesh and leave scars that never heal.

"Excellent choice." Malfor hands the whip to a waiting guard, weighing the rod in his palm. "You see? Cooperation is so much simpler."

The metal rod cuts through the air with a whistle, connecting with Stitch's ribs. The sound of impact—metal on flesh, bone—echoes across the courtyard. Stitch doesn't scream. Not for the first strike. Not for the second that lands across her thighs.

The third blow breaks her silence. Her scream tears through me worse than any shock from the collar, flaying something essential from my soul. And behind that scream, the knowledge that I chose this for her. That my hands might as well be wielding the rod.

"Stop!" The word rips from my throat as I lunge forward, only to be caught by guards on either side. "She was following orders. My orders."

Malfor pauses mid-swing, turning toward me with eyebrows raised. The silence stretches between us, broken only by Stitch's ragged breathing.

"Your orders?" His voice drops lower, intimate almost. "How interesting."

He hands the rod to a waiting guard, then walks toward me. His shoes stop inches from where I kneel on the concrete.

"And what orders were those, Miss Collins?"

My mind races, constructing a lie that might divert his rage from Stitch to me. "I asked her to create a backdoor. A way to communicate with the quantum systems remotely."

"Remarkable." He crouches before me, bringing his face level with mine. His cologne—that same expensive sandalwood— mingles with the metallic scent of Stitch's blood. "And did you also instruct her to encode it to Guardian HRS frequencies?"

My hesitation costs me. His hand shoots out, gripping my jaw with bruising force, fingers digging into the hinge of my mandible until my vision sparks with pain.

"You protect each other. How touching." His thumb traces my lower lip, the gesture obscene in its gentleness. "But it's ulti- mately futile."

He releases me with a shove that sends me sprawling onto the hot concrete.

"The third lesson for all of you to learn is that interference will not be tolerated, nor will lies." His voice carries an almost academic interest. "Any attempt to lie and reduce another's punishment results in doubled consequences for the intended beneficiary."

He nods to the guard, who hands him the bullwhip he set aside. Malfor uncoils it, letting the leather drag across concrete.

"You chose the rod to spare her the whip." He tests the whip with a flick that cracks the air like gunfire. "Now she receives both."

"No—" The protest dies in my throat as the first lash cuts across Stitch's back, tearing through her shirt, leaving a crimson line in its wake.

Stitch's body jerks against the restraints, muscles tensing as she fights to remain silent. The second lash crosses the first, forming an X of blood that soaks through the torn fabric. Her restraint breaks on the third—a guttural sound that doesn't sound human escaping through clenched teeth.

Jenna lunges forward only to be caught by guards. She's forced back to her knees. Malfor doesn't acknowledge the attempt; he is too focused on his demonstration. Three more lashes, each precisely placed to maximize pain without risking unconsciousness.

When he finally stops, Stitch hangs in her restraints, blood streaming down her back, her breathing shallow and ragged.

"The fourth lesson is responsibility."

Guards haul me upright, dragging me toward the post where Stitch hangs in her restraints. Up close, the damage is worse— blood soaks through her shirt where the metal broke skin, bruises already darkening across visible flesh.

"Look at her." Malfor stands at my shoulder, voice soft in my ear. "She bleeds because you lied to me."

He grabs my hand, forcing something into my palm. A cloth. White. Clean.

"She suffers because you resist what's inevitable." His fingers close around mine, making me grip the cloth. "Clean it."

I try to pull away. "No."

His hand finds my collar, thumb pressing against the control node at its base. Pain sparks behind my eyes, a warning of what's to come.

"Clean it, or I will continue the demonstration on each of your friends. One by one. Starting with the one with the broken arm."

My gaze finds Rebel, still on her knees, face gray with agony, arm clutched protectively against her chest. Then Malia, tears streaming silently down her face. Jenna, struggling to stand despite the tremors wracking her body. Mia, blood trickling from her nose where she hit the ground during the shock.

The cloth feels like lead in my hand. Stitch's eyes meet mine above the restraint around her throat. She blinks once, deliberately. *Do what you have to do.*

Bile rises in my throat as I step forward, wiping blood from the metal post. The white cloth turns red, stark evidence of my submission. Of my complicity.

"Very good." Malfor's approval lands like acid on my skin. "Now you understand."

He moves back to the center of the courtyard, addressing us again. "The final lesson is that obedience brings rewards. Resistance brings pain. This is the simplest equation. Even brilliant minds like yours should be able to solve it."

He turns to the guards. "Return them to their cells. Double security on the work details."

They throw us into our cells with more force than necessary. Stitch, they carry, her body limp between two guards, blood trailing on the concrete floor. They dump her on her bunk, her head lolling at an angle that sends fresh panic through me until I see the slight rise and fall of her chest.

For hours, we maintain silence, too afraid to risk triggering another demonstration by even whispering. The guards patrol more frequently, stopping to peer into each cell, hands resting on their collar remotes in silent warning.

Night falls outside our windowless prison, marked only by the dimming of overhead lights. The guards change shifts, voices murmuring in a language I don't recognize—not Spanish this time, something harsher, with more consonants.

When their footsteps fade to the far end of the corridor, I crawl to the bars separating my cell from Mia's.

"Can you see her?" My voice barely carries the few feet between us.

Mia shifts on her bunk, angling toward Stitch's cell. "Still breathing. Bruising looks bad. Possible fractured ribs."

Stitch stirs on her bunk, a small sound of pain escaping before she stills again. My throat tightens around words I can't voice. Apologies won't help her. Guilt won't heal her wounds. Despair won't break our collars.

I watch the faint outline of her breathing through the night, counting each inhale and exhale like prayer beads. Each breath is a victory. Each minute she survives is a testament to her strength. To what we might all still have inside us, buried beneath compliance and fear.

This isn't over.

Not by a long shot. I will do whatever it takes to bring Malfor to his knees.

EIGHTEEN

Insanity

GABE

The Pacific crashes against the rocks below—relentless, violent, perfect for how I feel right now. My hands grip the steering wheel harder than necessary as we wind up the coastal highway toward Insanity. Each curve reveals more of the sprawling estate perched on the cliff like some kind of fortress.

Seagulls wheel overhead, their cries cutting through the engine noise. Sharp. Demanding. Like the rage burning in my chest that won't quit, no matter how many deep breaths I take.

Hank sits in the passenger seat, silent as stone. The space between us thrums with everything we didn't say after that clusterfuck in the gym. His split lip is healing, but I know the words we traded are going to take a hell of a lot longer to mend.

Maybe never.

And it's my fault.

The ocean breeze carries the scent of salt and seaweed through the open windows, mixing with the aroma of eucalyptus from the trees lining the road. It should be calming. Should remind me of the mornings Ally would drag us out to the deck to watch the sunrise over the water, her hair whipping around her face as she pointed out dolphins in the distance.

Instead, it makes my chest feel like someone's taken a blowtorch to it.

"Turn here." Hank's voice is flat, professional. As if we're heading to any other tactical briefing instead of the place where we're going to figure out how to get our woman back.

The outer gate to Insanity stands twenty feet high, wrought iron twisted into patterns that look like musical notes if you squint. The intercom crackles before I can reach for it.

"About time." Forest's voice carries through the speaker, rough with exhaustion. "Drive straight up to the main house. Everyone's waiting."

The gate swings open with a mechanical hum, and I gun the engine up the winding drive. The mansion sprawls across the clifftop like it grew there—all glass and stone and impossible angles that probably cost more than most small countries' GDP. Multiple levels cascade down the cliff face, connected by bridges and terraces that make the whole place look like something from a dream.

Or a rock star's wet fantasy, which is probably more accurate.

I park behind a cluster of tactical vehicles. The whole gang's here for whatever Ethan has planned.

Gravel crunches under our boots as we walk toward the main house. The full scope of Insanity spreads out before us as we round the corner. The clifftop estate stretches for what has to be acres, with multiple buildings connected by covered walkways and gardens. To our left, the separate house where Forest, Paul, and Sarah live sits like a smaller echo of the main mansion, complete with its own terraced gardens and ocean views.

But it's the scene at the gondola station that catches my attention.

Charlie team is clustered around the boarding platform—

Ethan, Rigel, Walt, Blake, Carter, and the rest of the crew. Mac from Alpha team stands with his arms crossed, his expression grim. Brady from Bravo leans against the gondola's control housing, while Jenny from Delta paces in small circles like a caged predator. Forest stands near the back of the group, a mountain of packed muscle that makes everyone else look small by comparison. Paul hovers nearby, his dark eyes scanning everything with automatic vigilance.

Doc Summers is there too, her attention focused on the center of all the activity.

And in the middle of it all, Mitzy crouches beside the gondola mechanism with a toolkit spread around her like she's performing surgery. Her psychedelic hair, currently sporting streaks of electric blue and hot pink in a sharp pixie cut, catches the afternoon sunlight as she works, her snarky attitude evident even in the way she handles her tools.

Forest spots us approaching first. "Heard you two had a moment." His dry tone makes it clear he knows exactly what kind of moment we had. "Are you done tearing each other apart?"

The question hits differently coming from him. Forest knows what it's like to have the person you love torn away. He, Paul, and Sarah have been through their own version of hell, and the way his eyes search my face tells me he's looking for the same fractures that almost broke him apart.

"We're functional." Hank's response is controlled and precise. The kind of answer that says everything and nothing.

Paul steps closer, his gaze moving between us. "Functional's a good start, but you two look like you've been beating the shit out of each other."

Forest's eyes narrow as he takes in Hank's healing split lip and the careful way I'm holding my ribs. "Please tell me you didn't take it that far."

I shrug, not meeting his eyes. Hank's silence beside me answers more than words would. We didn't work through shit— just beat the hell out of each other and agreed to coexist in tense silence for the sake of the mission.

"What did Mitzy find?" I deflect, needing to move past the uncomfortable territory.

"That's what we're all trying to figure out." Paul jerks his head toward where Mitzy continues working. "She's been crawling all over that thing for the past hour, muttering about quantum interference patterns and electromagnetic signatures."

"She won't tell us what she found," Forest adds, "just keeps saying she needs to 'verify the baseline parameters' before she explains anything."

"Sounds like Mitzy." Hank's voice carries the first hint of warmth since we left Guardian HRS. Dealing with the tech division's resident genius has a way of putting everyone on the same page—specifically, the page labeled *what the fuck is she talking about now?*

"Finally." Blake straightens when he spots us approaching. "Thought you two might have killed each other before you made it here."

Rigel punches him in the arm. "Tactful as always."

Blake grins, but there's genuine concern behind it. "We all know about the gym."

I owe this man an apology—a big one—for the shit I said when I lost control. For questioning his loyalty to the team. For implying he didn't care about the women as much as the rest of us.

"About what I said." The words come out rough, but they're real. "About Sophia being safe. That was way out of line."

Blake's expression softens, understanding passing between us. "Don't worry about it. We're all stressed. It's fine."

Hank tenses beside me. Our fight is still fresh.

"You two good?" Ethan's question is straightforward. No bull-shit, no dancing around the subject.

Hank and I exchange a look. The hurt is still there, the anger still simmering under the surface, but underneath all of that are years of shared missions, shared women, and shared everything that matters.

"We're good," Hank confirms, his voice carrying the kind of certainty that ends discussions.

"Good enough to work together?" Walt asks, arms still crossed.

Hank and I exchange another look, both of us shrugging at the same time.

"Yeah, sure. We're fine. Let's go."

Ethan's expression is unreadable. As Charlie team leader, he's been holding everything together while Hank and I figure out our shit. The weight of that responsibility shows in the tension around his eyes.

"I'm ready to work." I roll my shoulders, feeling some of the coiled tension start to release. Being here, surrounded by the team, with a concrete mission ahead of us—this is what I need. Action instead of analysis. Movement instead of sitting around thinking about all the ways we failed to protect Ally and the others.

The ocean breeze picks up, carrying the scent of kelp and salt spray. Above us, seagulls continue their raucous conversations, diving toward the rocks below where the surf crashes in endless rhythm. The sound should be soothing, but it just reminds me of the morning Ally stood on our deck, wrapped in one of my shirts, watching the waves roll in.

Mitzy suddenly straightens, her tools clattering as she shoves them back into the kit. When she turns to face us, her expression is unreadable behind safety glasses that have definitely seen better days.

"Well?" Ethan's patience has its limits, and we've apparently reached them.

Mitzy pulls off the glasses, revealing eyes that are bright with discovery and something else—something that makes my skin crawl with anticipation.

"You boys ready for a field trip?" She gestures toward the gondola with a grin that's equal parts excitement and menace. "Because we're going down to the beach."

"What did you find?" Brady steps forward, his team leader instincts demanding answers.

Mitzy's grin widens, and she loads her tools back into their case. "Questions later. Right now, you all need to pair up and get in the gondola. Two by two, like a very tactical Noah's ark."

"Mitzy—" I start, but she cuts me off with a wave.

"Nope. No questions, no explanations." She straightens, hands on her hips, looking like a teacher dealing with particularly slow students. "Just get in, boys. Time's wasting."

The gondola sits suspended over the cliff edge, rails disappearing into the mist below. Small, built for a maximum of four people, but with guys our size, two is the practical limit.

"Alright, you heard her." Ethan steps toward the boarding platform. "Rigel, you're with me. We'll go first."

They climb into the gondola, the small car swaying slightly under their combined weight. Mitzy operates the controls, and the car slides smoothly down the track, disappearing into the fog that clings to the cliff face.

The rest of us spread out along the platform, settling in for what's obviously going to be a long wait. The thing's got to go all the way down, unload, then climb back up before the next pair can go.

"So what's the betting pool on what Mitzy found?" I move toward Hank. We always pair up for shit like this, but Hank steps to the side, putting distance between us as he examines the gondola mechanism. Not looking at me.

He walks away to stand near Forest and Doc Summers.

What the fuck? I thought we were good.

The gondola reappears through the mist, empty now, as it climbs slowly back toward the platform. Ten minutes, maybe twelve. This is going to take forever.

Blake and Forest step toward the gondola as it reaches the top, climbing in without ceremony. The car descends again into the fog.

"Anyone else think this gondola's moving slower than usual?" I ask the group when the conversation lulls.

"Seems normal to me," Walt says, watching the cables.

"Could just feel slow because we're waiting," Paul adds.

The gondola returns. Doc Summers and CJ climb in next.

Now there's fewer of us—Hank, Walt, Carter, Mac, Brady, Jenny, Paul, and me. Eight people waiting. Mac and Brady go down next. Then Jenny and Paul.

Four of us are left waiting up top. The space feels bigger now, the silence more pointed.

"Think the waves are getting rougher?" I ask.

"Hard to tell from up here." Walt glances at the ocean.

Hank examines his fingernails like they're the most fascinating thing in the world.

The gondola returns.

"Walt, you're with me," Hank announces as the car reaches the top.

Walt glances between us, confusion flickering across his features. "Uh, sure thing."

They climb into the gondola. Hank still hasn't looked at me directly.

As they descend, I'm left alone with Carter on the platform.

The ocean breeze picks up, carrying salt spray and the distant cries of seagulls. It should be peaceful. It should be calming.

Instead, it just gives me time to think about how my best friend, my brother, just spent the last hour actively avoiding me. The gondola returns for its last load. Carter and I climb in without ceremony and spend the entire trip in silence.

I stare down at the beach growing larger below us. The ocean roars below us, and the gondola tracks cut down the cliff face like a scar. At the bottom, a small platform sits just above the tide pools where the Pacific pounds the rocks into submission.

Whatever Mitzy found down there better be worth this bullshit.

NINETEEN

Faraday Cage

GABE

THE GONDOLA LURCHES AS WE HIT THE STEEPER SECTION OF track, wheels grinding against the rails with a metallic shriek that cuts through the ocean air. Carter grips the safety rail beside me, but I let the momentum rock me forward, watching the cliff face slide past in layers of weathered stone and stubborn vegetation clinging to impossible angles.

The Pacific stretches endlessly ahead of us, afternoon sunlight turning the surface into hammered silver. Waves roll in steady sets, crashing against the rocky shoreline with enough force to send spray fifty feet up the cliff face. Beautiful, violent, relentless.

Like everything else in my life right now.

Below, the beach resolves into focus—small stones instead of sand, mixed with tide pools, scattered driftwood, and the small platform where this ride ends.

My ribs ache where Hank landed solid hits in the gym. The split on his lip is healing, but the fracture between us feels like it's widening.

We bump to a stop, and Carter pushes the door open. The

ocean breeze hits immediately, carrying the sharp scent of kelp and brine. Seagulls wheel overhead, their cries mixing with the constant rumble of waves against stone.

I step off the platform onto uneven ground, boots crunching on a mixture of sand and rock. The beach stretches maybe two hundred yards before the cliff face curves away, creating a natural amphitheater protected from the worst of the wind.

And there, right in the center of it all, sits the most elaborate unlit bonfire I've ever seen.

Massive logs form a perfect circle, each one easily four feet across, weathered smooth by years of salt air. Inside the circle, stacks of driftwood and split lumber form a pyramid that stands eight feet tall.

Ready to light. Waiting for a match.

Everyone else lounges around the setup like they're at some kind of tactical beach party. Blake sits on a piece of driftwood that's been worn into a natural bench, idly tossing pebbles toward the tide pools. Rigel examines something in the rocks, probably cataloging marine life out of habit. Walt and Ethan stand near the water's edge, boots just out of reach of the advancing foam.

Hank leans against one of the massive logs, arms crossed, staring out at the horizon. Still not looking at me.

"What the hell is this?" I mutter to Carter as we approach the group.

He shrugs. "Looks like someone planned a barbecue."

The whole scene has a weird communal vibe to it, like we're here for some kind of team-building retreat instead of a tactical operation. Which makes no fucking sense, because moving to the beach doesn't solve our nanobot problem. If those things are still active, they're reporting our location, our conversations, our plans back to Malfor just as efficiently as they would anywhere else.

My suggestion about finding a secure location was supposed to be about isolation, not—whatever this is.

"Alright, gather 'round." Mitzy's voice cuts through the sound of waves and wind. She stands near the bonfire, toolkit in one hand, that characteristic grin spreading across her face. "Everyone, take a seat. Time for show and tell."

The team moves slowly, settling onto logs and driftwood with the kind of reluctance that comes from too many briefings in uncomfortable locations. I find a spot on a sun-bleached log, deliberately not looking to see where Hank positions himself.

"So what's going on?" Brady asks, voicing what we're all thinking. "Why are we down here playing summer camp?"

"Yeah," I add, my voice sharper than intended. "Last I checked, moving to a different location doesn't magically solve our surveillance problem."

Mitzy's grin widens. "Oh, but it does. See, that's the beautiful thing about this whole setup." She gestures toward the gondola platform. "Do any of you know what a Faraday cage is?"

A few nods around the circle. Most of the guys have at least basic knowledge of electromagnetic principles.

"For those who don't," Mitzy continues, stepping into the center of our makeshift circle like she's lecturing a physics class, "a Faraday cage is an enclosure made of conductive material that blocks electromagnetic fields. Named after Michael Faraday, who figured out in the 1830s that electricity flows around the outside of a conductor, not through it."

She pulls a small device from her toolkit, something that looks like a handheld radio crossed with a smartphone. "The principle is simple. Build a metal cage, and electromagnetic radiation— radio waves, microwaves, even electromagnetic pulses—can't penetrate to the inside. The electrical current flows around the cage, leaving the interior completely shielded."

Blake shifts on his driftwood bench. "Okay, but what does that have to do with—"

"Everything." Mitzy's eyes find mine across the circle. "Gabe, when Ethan called and told me about your suggestion—finding a place where we could talk where the nanobots wouldn't listen—it just lit up my mind."

The pieces start clicking together in my head, but I let her explain.

"See, you may not have realized it, but that gondola is its own little Faraday cage. When you stepped in and took the ride down, we turned on the electromagnetic shielding. Inside that shielded environment, we emitted a small, controlled EMP burst."

She holds up the device in her hand. "That EMP should have eliminated any nanobots on your person or embedded in your gear. Fried their circuits. Turned them into microscopic pieces of dust."

The implications surged through me like a tidal wave. "You EMP'd us? Without warning?"

"Small burst. Targeted. Completely safe for biological tissue and shielded electronics." Mitzy waves off my concern. "But lethal to nanoscale surveillance devices."

Doc Summers steps forward, medical kit in hand. "Which is why we need to do some confirmation testing."

She and Mitzy move around the circle, Doc Summers taking skin swabs from everyone while Mitzy runs a scanner over our gear. The process is methodical and clinical. Swab, scan, move to the next person.

When they finish, Mitzy claps her hands together. "Okay, you guys are cut loose. This is going to take a couple of hours to process."

"Cut loose?" Walt looks around the group. "What do you mean, cut loose?"

Carter starts to stand, probably heading back toward the gondola. "We can head back up while you—"

"Nope." Mitzy shakes her head. "Everyone has to stay down here."

"What the fuck?" The words explode out of me. "What do you mean, stay down here?"

"We need to confirm that the nanobots were deactivated," Doc Summers explains, already setting up what looks like a portable lab station on a flat section of rock. "If any of you go back up to the compound before we know for certain, you could re-contaminate yourselves."

Forest appears from somewhere near the tide pools, carrying a case of medical equipment. "Think of it as quarantine. Better safe than sorry."

"How long?" Ethan asks, his team leader instincts kicking in.

"Couple hours, minimum." Mitzy connects cables between various pieces of equipment. "Maybe longer, depending on what the analysis shows."

She straightens, dusting grit off her hands, and grins at all of us. "You guys are on your own. Check out the tide pools. Skip some rocks. We'll call you when we're ready."

The dismissal is clear. We're stuck here until further notice.

I look around the circle at the rest of the team. Blake's already wandering toward the water. Rigel's examining something in the rocks again. Walt and Carter are discussing the merits of different driftwood configurations.

Normal conversation. Casual banter. The kind of shit guys talk about when they're not focused on missions or operations or life-and-death situations.

Hank remains where he is, leaning against his log, staring at the horizon like it holds answers to questions I can't even guess at.

The afternoon sun hangs lower now, maybe two hours from

dusk. The tide pools reflect the sky in perfect miniature, and somewhere in the distance, a seal barks from the rocks.

We're stuck here. All of us. With nothing to do but wait.

And talk.

And the one person I need to talk to is giving me the fucking cold shoulder.

I push off my log and walk over to where Hank's still leaning against his, arms crossed, studying the horizon like it's a tactical map.

TWENTY

Tide Pools

HANK

THE CONVERSATION REPLAYS IN MY HEAD LIKE A TACTICAL briefing gone wrong. Gabe's words from the gym, sharp as broken glass: *She's mine.* Not ours. Mine. Like the years between us meant nothing.

Like Ally's choice meant nothing.

I've heard him say a lot of stupid shit over the years. Reckless plans. Dangerous theories. The kind of explosive thinking that makes him brilliant in the field and impossible to predict.

But he's never tried to split up what we had.

Never tried to claim exclusive ownership of the woman we both love.

The surf crashes against the rocks twenty feet away, salt spray catching the afternoon light. Seagulls wheel overhead, their cries mixing with the constant rumble of waves.

It should be peaceful.

It should help me process this mess between us.

Instead, it gives me time to think, and I don't like the direction of my thoughts.

An hour passes. Maybe two. The sun drops closer to the horizon, turning the ocean surface into molten gold. The team spreads out across the beach—Blake and Rigel comparing rock formations, Walt carving something on a piece of driftwood, Carter examining a tide pool with the focused attention of a detective studying a crime scene.

Everyone's getting restless. Hungry. The kind of low-level agitation that comes from forced downtime when your mind wants to be anywhere else.

I separate from the group, walking toward the far end of the beach where the cliff curves inward, creating a series of deep tide pools cut off from the main shoreline. The water here is crystal clear, undisturbed by the larger waves that pound the outer rocks.

My boots splash through ankle-deep water as I move from pool to pool. Sea anemones cling to the rocks like green and purple flowers, their tentacles swaying in the gentle current. Hermit crabs scuttle between patches of seaweed, carrying their borrowed homes on their backs. Small fish dart between underwater crevices, silver flashes against the dark stone.

Perfect miniature ecosystems, each one complete and balanced. Each one exists in isolation while connected to something larger.

Ally, Gabe, and I—three separate people who became something more when we came together. A system that worked because each part understood its role, its boundaries, and its purpose.

Until Malfor tore it apart.

Until fear made Gabe claim ownership of something that belonged to all of us. Until I let pride and anger drive a wedge between us when we need each other the most.

I crouch beside one of the larger pools, watching a sea star slowly make its way across the bottom. Methodical. Patient. Focused on the simple task of moving from one point to another despite the obstacles in its path.

The water reflects my face back at me. I'm tired, but underneath the exhaustion, there's something else. The need for Gabe and me to be solid.

For the foundation to hold.

Without that, I'm not sure I can get through *this*.

I don't want to end things with Gabe, but there's still friction between us. A fight and some words don't erase that. He apologized, admitted he overstepped, but there's lingering uncertainty in my mind about whether we can trust each other with the thing that matters most.

Whether I can trust him with her.

A wave larger than the rest crashes against the outer rocks, sending spray shooting thirty feet into the air. The mist drifts over the tide pools, carrying the scent of the deep ocean and ancient salt, reminding me that some forces are greater than one individual.

Some things require working together to survive.

Footsteps crunch through the rocky shore behind me. Every muscle in my back tightens. I don't need to look to know who it is. Gabe's got a particular kind of presence—wired too tight, shoulders buzzing with tension, jaw clenched like he's trying not to scream.

He's been circling me all damn day like a dog that knows it pissed off the alpha and doesn't know how to fix it.

"Got a minute?"

"Not really." The words scrape across my nerves, brittle and forced, and I don't bother turning around.

I look around the beach—at Blake skipping stones, at Rigel cataloging tide pool specimens, at the rest of the team scattered across the rocks.

"Well, what the fuck are you gonna do for the next couple of hours? Just sit there and keep ignoring me?"

His voice has an air of something. It's strained and desperate.

Like he knows he fucked this up and doesn't know how to reel it in.

"I'm not ignoring you." My voice remains flat, controlled. "I'm processing."

"Processing, what? We worked things out at the gym and then at home."

My laugh comes out sharp, bitter. "You think a couple of punches fix this?"

"What I said was wrong. I didn't mean it." The words feel clumsy, inadequate. "I just … I need us to be good."

"There's nothing good about this."

I need space, need oxygen, need distance before I forget how many years we've stood side-by-side in blood and fire.

But Gabe grabs me.

Hand wrapped around my forearm, tight enough to make my skin pulse with heat. It stops me cold.

"You don't understand." The desperation creeps into his voice despite my efforts to control it. "I need us to be solid. You're the only anchor I have right now. I'm going to slip up. Say stupid shit and do even stupider shit. If things aren't right between us, I don't know if I can get through this."

I uncross my arms and turn to give him a long look. Something shifts in his expression.

"Don't worry about it. We're good."

"We're not good." His words come out hard. "If we were good, this wouldn't feel like shit."

"If you need to kick my ass again, just do it already. We've got plenty of time, and I'll take the hits. I earned them." The words spill out fast, ragged, like they've been clawing at the back of his throat and he's finally letting them loose. "Whatever you need to do, just—fucking do it. I want to *fix* this."

"What I need," I grit out, voice low and shaking with

restraint, "is for you to give me some space and leave me the fuck alone."

I need him to take it back. Not with words. With something deeper. Something that says he understands the line he crossed.

He's already bracing, like he knows what's coming. Shoulders squared, mouth drawn in that stubborn line that used to mean loyalty and brotherhood. Now it just looks like a wall I want to tear down with my fists.

"You sure about that?" he asks.

"Yeah. I'm sure." But I'm not. Too much anger and hurt stir in my blood. I take a shot because I fucking *need* to take it.

My fist slams into the side of his jaw before I know I'm moving.

A clean hit.

All my fury coiled into that single, punishing strike. His head whips sideways, his body dropping like I cut his strings. He hits the rocky shore hard, a grunt punching out of him as he rolls.

He doesn't get up.

For a second, he lies there, blinking at the sky like he's trying to make sense of gravity. Then he groans, pushes up on one elbow, and spits the blood trailing from his mouth. He swipes at it with the back of his hand, eyes finding mine with a look that might've been disbelief if it weren't for the edge of something else.

Pain. Shame.

"What the fuck, Hank?"

"You told me to take a swing," I growl, stalking forward. "I did. You gonna bitch about it now?"

"I didn't think you'd actually—" He doesn't finish the sentence. Doesn't have time.

My boot connects with his ribs, hard and fast. He folds around the impact with a sharp curse, arms curling in as he drops to his side, teeth bared in pain.

"Shit! Fuck, man—what the hell?" He coughs, dragging in a breath through clenched teeth, voice tight and raw. "That's not cool—kicking a man when he's down."

I stand over him, breathing hard, fists still clenched, chest heaving like I've just come out of combat.

"That?" I snarl, voice low and vibrating with rage. "That's nothing. That's a whisper of pain compared to what you did. What you said."

He's still gasping, still doubled over, but his gaze finds mine again, and this time there's no disbelief—just regret.

Honest, heavy regret.

But I'm not ready to hear it. Not now. Not with her missing. Not with all of them gone and everything unraveling at the seams.

"You don't get to tear us apart when she needs us the most." My voice shakes, not from weakness, but from the weight of everything crumbling between us.

"I know," he mutters, wincing as he sits up straighter. "I fucking know."

"Then why the hell did you say it?"

He doesn't answer. Just sits there in the grit and rock, blood smeared along his mouth, and for the first time in eight years, I don't recognize him. And that scares the shit out of me more than any mission ever has.

Because if I can't trust him now—when everything's on the line—then what the fuck do we have left?

And if this falls apart … We all do.

Gabe wipes at his mouth again, smearing blood along his jaw. He still doesn't stand. Doesn't argue. Just looks up at me like he's trying to find the right words in the middle of the wreckage he created with a single goddamn sentence.

Then, finally, quietly, he says, "She's not mine. Never was. She's ours. She chose both of us, and I know that. I knew it was wrong when I said it—I just … I was scared. Fucking terrified. Of losing her. And now …"

"What about now?"

"Now, I'm losing you and that fucking kills me, all because I should've kept my mouth shut." His voice cracks on the last word, and it lands like a punch in my chest.

But I don't let it show. I can't.

Not now. Not with Ally missing. Not with the others gone and time slipping through our fingers like sand we can't hold onto.

I drag in a breath, slow and shaky, chest still tight from the swing I threw and the ones I didn't.

"We're not doing this." My voice comes out low, rough. "You broke something, and I don't have time to figure out if it can be fixed."

He nods once, like he knew that was coming. Like he knows he deserves it.

"Ally needs us whole." My gaze stays on him, brutal and unflinching. "I'll do whatever the hell it takes, and I know you'll bleed for her just like I will. This thing between us needs to take a back seat. It's a distraction that's dangerous."

"I know." Gabe presses a hand to his ribs and nods again, slower this time. He understands, and maybe that's all I need right now.

I step back, chest heaving, pulse still pounding like a drum in my head. The crunch of boots behind us snags my attention, heavy and purposeful.

I glance down at Gabe—still on the ground, blood running from his mouth, and feel the weight of everything we almost lost. Everything we still might lose. Eight years of side-by-side, live-or-die trust. Of knowing without speaking. Of never once having to question where we stood. Until now.

I hold out a hand, my breath burning in my lungs. Gabe takes it, and I pull him to his feet. We turn and find Ethan watching us. He's still a few feet back, arms crossed, jaw tight. He doesn't speak right away. Just drags his gaze from Gabe to me and back again.

"We got a problem here?" Ethan's voice cuts through the salt and wind, sharp as ever. "You said you were good. I can't have this—"

"We're fucking right as rain." The words are steady, but they're not enough.

"I need more than that." Ethan doesn't blink. "Tensions are high enough without this shit between the two of you. The whole team is rattled. We're all dealing with the same shit. Our women are missing, and two of my best guys are throwing punches in the dirt. Don't tell me the two of you are *"right as rain."* Don't fucking insult me. I'm going to ask once, and you better answer me clean —do we have a problem that's going to fuck with the success of this mission?"

"We're good." Gabe doesn't look at me when he speaks.

"We're good," I echo Gabe's words.

Ethan watches us a second longer, like he doesn't quite believe it. Then he shakes his head, snorts under his breath, and mutters, "This is why you don't share women."

It hits harder than it should, even if it's meant half as a joke. Gabe doesn't react, but the words land between us like another grenade, just in a different place.

Ethan doesn't get it. None of them do.

They don't understand that I don't know how to hold a woman without Gabe by my side. Or that he feels the same. We need each other. Always have.

Whatever this thing is between us, it's not about sex. It's never been about that. It's deeper than friendship. Deeper than the blood of brothers. It's not clean and it's impossible to describe, but it's everything. It's the way we move in sync. The way we balance each other. It's how I can feel his pulse from across a room and know exactly what he's about to do before he does it.

I need him in ways I've never been able to put into words, and as much as he broke something in me the second he said *she's mine,* he needs me just as much as I need him. Maybe even more so.

But none of that matters right now.

What matters is Ally and the rest of our women.

All that matters is bringing them home.

So I push my anger down. I shove it so deep I don't have to feel it until this is over. Until they're safe. Until I can bleed in peace.

"We're solid," I say again. This time with more weight behind it. I feel the shift in me. The determination to do whatever it takes to bring Ally home. I'm done fighting with Gabe. I need my friend standing beside me. The rest?

We'll figure out the rest later.

Ethan gives us one last look, then jerks his chin toward the rest of the team, already gathering by the waterline. "Good. Saddle up. Manic Mitzy is ready for us."

As he walks off, Gabe limps beside me, quiet and slow.

We don't speak. Not yet.

This mission just became the only thing holding us together. I'll be damned if I let either of us fall apart before Ally's back in our arms.

Because none of this means a damn thing if we don't get her back.

"We're calling a truce." My voice is low but firm. No edge, no venom. Just finality. "We're calling it because we don't get to fall apart right now. Not when she's out there. Not when she needs *both* of us."

He turns toward me, and I catch the side of his face—

bruised, smeared with blood, jaw clenched around whatever emotion he's still swallowing.

"I'm with you," he says quietly. No hesitation. No ego. "We get her back. Together. You and me. Like it's meant to be, and I'm going to make it up to you."

I nod once. It's not absolution. Not even close. But it's something. I glance out toward the surf, where the tide creeps in like time, slow and merciless.

For a second, we stand there—two men held together by loyalty and the ghost of the woman we'd burn the world down to protect.

It's not forgiveness, but we're no longer at war. Gabe and I stand together. As we always have.

TWENTY-ONE

Clean Slate

HANK

We follow Ethan across the rocky beach toward the massive bonfire setup. Smooth stones shift under our boots, the kind worn round by decades of Northern California surf. Tide pools dot the shoreline like scattered mirrors, reflecting the late-afternoon sky in perfect miniature.

Gabe walks beside me, not behind, not ahead.

With me.

Charlie team spreads around the unlit bonfire like they've been waiting for orders. Blake's eyes immediately catalog Gabe's swollen left eye.

I grab a seat on one of the weathered logs. Gabe settles beside me. It's the way things should be, the two of us gravitating toward each other.

But that moment from just minutes ago still burns in my mind. When I took a swing at Gabe and he just—took it. Didn't counter. Didn't try to block. Just absorbed the hit like he deserved it.

That's not the Gabe I've known for years. The Gabe who

fights like a cornered animal when pushed. The Gabe who never backs down from anything.

The guilt is eating him alive and making him dangerous in ways that have nothing to do with explosives or tactical expertise.

Mitzy steps forward with Skye, both wearing expressions I haven't seen since this nightmare began. Something that looks dangerously close to hope.

"Alright, everyone's here," Forest announces, his face showing the strain of three sleepless days. "Mitzy, Skye. What's the verdict?"

Mitzy's grin spreads across her face—the first genuine smile any of us have seen since this nightmare began. Her psychedelic hair catches the afternoon light as she raises a tablet displaying microscopic analysis results.

"Gentlemen, I have excellent news."

The circle goes dead silent. Good news became a foreign concept the moment Harrison betrayed us.

"The improvised EMP pulse we administered during your gondola rides was completely effective." She turns the tablet so we can see the data. "Zero active nanobots detected on any personnel. Zero contamination in the electronics you brought down. Zero quantum signatures in any biological samples."

Skye steps beside her, medical scanner in hand. "We've tested everyone twice. Skin samples, blood work, full spectrum analysis." Her warm brown eyes move around the circle, meeting each of our gazes. "You're clean. All of you."

The words detonate through the group like incoming artillery fire. Ethan lets out a long breath he's been holding for days. Blake actually laughs—short and sharp, but real. Walt's shoulders drop as the tension he's been carrying since Malia disappeared finally releases.

"About fucking time," Ethan mutters, scrubbing his hands through his hair.

"No more performing for that bastard," Blake adds, something approaching relief creeping into his voice.

But even as the good news settles over us, reality reasserts itself. Being clean doesn't bring the women home.

Ethan voices what we're all thinking. "This is temporary, though. The moment we go back up to the compound …"

"Recontamination," I finish, the implications crystal clear. "We'll be compromised again within hours."

Mitzy nods grimly. "Which is why, from this point forward, all critical meetings happen here. This beach is our clean zone. Our sanctuary. The only place we know with absolute certainty that we can speak freely."

Forest moves to the center of the circle, command presence asserting itself. "That's not just a recommendation. That's operational protocol. Real meetings happen here, on this beach, where we know things are clean. Up there, we're performing for Malfor, and you need to think of it like that. We're starting a campaign of misinformation specifically for him. Down here is where we do the real planning. Where we know it's safe."

"What about coordination with the other teams?" Rigel asks, always thinking about the larger tactical picture.

"Limited," Forest admits. "We'll maintain normal operational façades when we're back up there. Standard briefings, routine communications. But anything that matters—anything that could compromise our ability to find them—gets discussed here."

Sam rises from his position on a smooth boulder, drawing our attention—Forest's slight nod transfers operational command.

"Listen up," Sam begins, his voice carrying the weight of battlefield leadership I've heard in a dozen combat zones. "Being clean means we can finally plan without enemy surveillance, but we still have a fundamental problem."

He pauses, letting the gravity of our situation settle over the group.

"The trackers in Stitch and Jenna aren't broadcasting. They're not responding to pings. Until we get a location, there's nothing for the Guardian teams to do except wait for actionable intelligence."

The admission burns through my chest, but it's accurate. Without target coordinates, all our tactical expertise becomes meaningless.

Walt's voice carries the weight of Malia's absence. "So what do we do? Just sit here and wait?"

"No," CJ interjects, his massive frame commanding attention as he steps forward. "We work the problem from every angle. And we're not working alone anymore."

"Collins?" Ethan asks.

Sam nods. "Ally's father is deploying serious resources. Corporate assets, private contractors, research facilities. This just became a different kind of war."

I process the implications. Robert Collins has the kind of financial backing that can move mountains when properly motivated. And losing his daughter twice to the same enemy? That's the kind of motivation that reshapes entire landscapes.

"What kind of war?" Carter asks, his tactical mind already working through possibilities.

"Two-fronted," Mitzy answers, excitement building in her tone. "One part of this war will be conducted exactly as Malfor expects—where we have to assume he can see and hear everything we do. Our *misinformation campaign*. Traditional Guardian operations, visible deployments, obvious tactical responses."

Blake leans forward on his driftwood seat. "And the other part?"

"Complete black operations," Sam continues. "A close team of Mitzy's best AI experts working with Collins's nanotech specialists. Their mission is twofold—find a way to locate the women, and eliminate the nanobots entirely."

"Or better yet," Mitzy adds, her grin turning predatory, "use the nanobots to launch our own Trojan horse directly into Malfor's infrastructure."

I like it. Dual operational tracks—one visible, one invisible. Force Malfor to fight on multiple fronts while never knowing the true scope of our capabilities.

"Timeline?" I ask because operational parameters always matter.

Mitzy's excitement dims slightly. "Unknown. The quantum entanglement technology is beyond anything I've reverse-engineered before." She shrugs. "But with Collins's specialists and resources backing us up, maybe we get lucky."

"And in the meantime?" Walt's question carries desperation he's trying to hide.

"In the meantime, we maintain operational discipline," CJ responds. "Visible operations continue as normal. Training drills. Guardian teams deploying on actual missions—all except Charlie team. We respond to calls, run missions, and maintain the image that we're operating under normal conditions."

"While the real work happens here," Forest adds, approval clear in his weathered features. "Every piece of critical intelligence gets processed in this clean zone."

I absorb the new operational paradigm, adjusting my mental frameworks to accommodate the shift. It's sound tactical doctrine—compartmentalized intelligence, multiple operational tracks, strategic deception.

But the fundamental variable remains unchanged. Ally is still missing. They're all still missing.

Rigel asks the question that's been burning in all our minds. "Collins's resources? What exactly are we talking about?"

Sam's expression grows thoughtful. "Tech billionaire resources. The kind of money that can buy access to information networks, hire the best specialists, and deploy corporate assets in ways that complement our tactical capabilities."

"Manpower?" Brady asks.

"Intelligence gathering," CJ clarifies. "Collins has connections in the tech world that we don't. Corporate espionage capabilities, financial tracking, and digital forensics. Different tools for a different kind of war."

It makes sense. The most crucial advantage Collins brings isn't just money or connections—it's the ability to establish a completely *clean* facility. Somewhere separate from all nanobots, where his specialists can work without Malfor's surveillance. We don't have that luxury at Guardian HRS. Every time we go back up that cliff, we're compromised again, and if we do something about the nanobots, that tips our hand, letting him know we're aware of the infestation.

"So we wait," Gabe states, resignation bleeding through controlled fury. It's the first time he's spoken since we sat down, and his voice carries an edge I don't like.

"We wait *strategically*," Sam corrects. "Every hour we're clean is an hour we can use for preparation. For planning. When coordinates come in, we need to be ready to move fast and hit harder than Malfor expects."

The circle settles into a different kind of quiet. Not the desperate silence of the past three days, but something approaching patience. The kind that comes when operators finally have a plan, even if that plan requires waiting for the right moment to execute.

The strategy feels solid. More solid than anything we've had since this nightmare began. But it still requires the one thing none of us wants to accept.

Patience.

"We're setting up a temporary field office here," Mitzy explains. "A way to search for evidence of where they are."

"How?"

"Not sure, to be honest." Mitzy shrugs. "But he took Stitch and Ally. Between the two of them, I have to think they're going to do whatever it takes to send a message. Some way to tell us where they are." She doesn't say the obvious thing because none of us wants to hear it.

If Guardian HRS were going to find them, we would have already. We've exploited every advantage, yet we've nothing to show for it. Finding our women rests with them now.

The sun hangs lower now, painting the waves in shades of gold and crimson. Tide pools reflect the changing sky like scattered mirrors across the rocky shore. Somewhere out there, beyond the horizon, Ally and the others wait for rescue.

None of it is possible unless *they* find a way to reach us.

No comms. No trackers. No clean tech. Nothing but the minds of two people caught in Malfor's cage.

We're blind.

Deaf.

Waiting in the dark while the people we love are being used as pawns in a game we're already losing.

No signals. No trackers. No way in.

If Ally and Stitch don't find a way to send us a message—something clever enough to slip past Malfor's surveillance and brutal enough to cut through the noise—

Then this beach becomes our graveyard.

Not just for hope.

For them.

TWENTY-TWO

Uneasy Allies

GABE

Two days back from the beach and nanobots have reestablished their microscopic surveillance network. Every breath is monitored. Every conversation is transmitted. Every tactical discussion feeds directly back to Malfor.

The knowledge sits in my gut like swallowed glass.

Hank falls into step beside me as we approach the Charlie team ready room.

We don't talk about the beach. Don't acknowledge the moment when guilt made me absorb his punch instead of defending myself. Right now, everything centers on Ally. Personal grievances get filed under "deal with later" until she's home.

But we're back and united, if a little bruised and battered. Hank and I will make it through this. I no longer doubt it.

The ready room buzzes with the kind of restless energy that comes from operators with nothing to operate on. Blake sits at the table pretending to read equipment manifests, but I catch him reading the same line three times. Walt stares at his coffee like it holds answers to questions he's afraid to ask. The mug trembles slightly in his grip—barely noticeable unless you know what to look for. Rigel cleans gear that's already pristine, the repetitive motion keeping his hands busy while his mind races. Carter maintains his usual vigilant silence, but tension radiates off him in waves, and his fingers drum Morse code patterns against his thigh, probably spelling out violent threats against our enemies.

Hank drops into a chair, fingers drumming against the table. "So we're just gonna sit here with our thumbs up our asses while they're out there?"

"What else do you want to do?" Ethan glances at him. "Storm random buildings until we find them?"

"Better than this bullshit." Blake doesn't look up from his manifest, but his voice carries the kind of edge that comes from too much caffeine and too little sleep. "Sitting around talking about equipment rotations while our women are God knows where is *exhausting*."

"You could always clean your rifle again," Rigel suggests without looking up from his gear. "Pretty sure I saw a speck of dust on the barrel."

"Fuck off," Blake mutters, but there's no real heat in it.

Walt shifts in his seat, the movement sharp and agitated. "It's been days …" He stops himself, jaw working like he's chewing glass.

"I know, man." Carter's voice is quiet, steady. "We all know."

The silence that follows carries weight. Each of us is lost in our version of hell, our imaginations going wild with what might be happening to the women we love.

However, we can't discuss it. Not here. Not with nanobots recording every word for Malfor's entertainment.

"Anyone catch the game last night?" Ethan asks, the question so obviously forced that it would be laughable under different circumstances.

"What game?" Rigel plays along, understanding the need for normal conversation.

"I dunno. Lakers? Thought maybe the distraction would help." Ethan's admission carries more honesty than the casual question suggested.

"Did they even play last night?" Blake asks.

"No idea." Ethan tips his head back and stares at the ceiling.

Walt snorts. "Nothing's gonna help until they're home."

The honesty cuts through our attempts to pretend this is just another day. Because Walt's right.

Food tastes like cardboard.

Sleep comes in fractured nightmares.

Even breathing feels wrong when the most important people in our lives are missing.

The conversation hangs in the air, loaded with implications we can't voice. Plans we can't discuss. Promises we can't make out loud. But the understanding passes between us anyway—when this is over, Malfor won't just pay for what he's done.

He'll suffer for it.

We're each taking a piece of him.

A knock on the door interrupts the growing tension. CJ enters, carrying a carefully neutral expression that indicates he has intel he can't share in this contaminated space.

"Gentlemen." His eyes sweep the room, making contact with each of us. "I need everyone at Insanity this evening. Consider it a team-building exercise following your catastrophic failure the other day on the hostage drill."

The phrasing is careful. Deliberate. Anyone listening would hear about plans for team-bonding activities. Those of us who know better understand precisely what he's saying.

Evening fog rolls in from the Pacific as Charlie team makes the familiar trek to Insanity. The gondola waits at the cliff edge like a portal between contaminated and clean worlds. One by one, we step into the metal cage, submit to Mitzy's EMP deconta-mination, and descend toward the only place on earth where honest conversation becomes possible.

The beach bonfire blazes against gathering darkness when we arrive. Massive logs arranged in perfect formation, flames reaching toward stars emerging between breaks in coastal fog. Sam and CJ stand near the edge of the fire, their faces painted by the dancing firelight. Mitzy crouches beside her equipment array, psychedelic hair catching fire-glow as she monitors decontamina-tion readings.

And there, sitting on weathered driftwood with silver hair immaculate despite the beach environment, is Robert Collins.

Ally's father. Tech billionaire. The man whose resources could reshape this war. The man whose daughter sleeps in our bed and calls us both the loves of her life. Two men who navigate an uneasy truce.

His pale-blue eyes track our approach with the kind of sharp focus that built corporate empires. When they land on me, then shift to Hank, I catch something that might be resignation flick-ering across his features.

This is the reality he's had to accept. His daughter chose both of us. Not one or the other—both. And whatever his personal feelings about that arrangement, he's smart enough to know, that right now, we're his best hope of getting her back alive.

"Mr. Collins, thanks for coming down here." Sam takes point on what promises to be delicate diplomatic terrain.

Collins rises from his driftwood perch with easy confidence that speaks to expensive trainers and disciplined self-care. His handshake carries boardroom authority—firm, controlled, weighted with hostile takeovers and corporate negotiations.

"Forest gave me the basics, but I'm guessing there's shit you couldn't say over normal channels." His voice commands even in this informal setting.

"More than shit. We're completely fucked." CJ's response carries grim finality.

Collins's eyes sharpen. "How fucked?"

"These nanobots aren't just listening devices. They're full infiltration tech. AI colonies designed for long-term intelligence gathering and network penetration." Mitzy steps forward, tablet in hand, technical enthusiasm barely contained despite the gravity of our situation.

She activates the display, showing microscopic images that make my skin crawl with how thoroughly we've been violated.

"Every conversation for the past three months. Every planning session. Every private moment. That bastard has recordings of everything." Her voice carries scientific fascination warring with human revulsion.

Collins processes this with the kind of clinical detachment that made him successful in cutthroat industries.

"Harrison." The name carries more weight than a death sentence.

"Your head of security didn't bring in the nanobots. The Kazakhstan survivors carried them in. Ally, Malia, Malikai—they were infected during captivity. The nanobots spread from there." Sam's confirmation cuts through Collins's assumptions.

"Twenty years. Twenty fucking years I trusted that man with my daughter's life." Collins speaks more to himself than to us. The betrayal cuts deeper when it comes from someone who is supposed to protect.

I recognize the particular rage building behind his expression—cold fury that comes when trust gets weaponized against you.

"We need your help setting up operations outside Malfor's surveillance network. A clean facility where tech specialists can work without contamination." Mitzy steps forward, her technical expertise taking point on the explanation.

Collins's gaze shifts between Hank and me, assessment sharp as surgical steel. "And in return?"

"We get your daughter back." I let an edge creep into my voice. The implied challenge hangs in salt air between us—*do you doubt we can do it?*

Something passes across Collins's features. Not doubt exactly. More like distaste wrapped in paternal protectiveness. He's watching two men who share his daughter's bed, who've seen her in ways that make fathers uncomfortable, who represent everything about her adult life that exists outside his control.

"The facility's not a problem. I've got corporate research sites that can be completely isolated and secured within hours. But we need to be clear about what we're discussing here." His response comes after careful consideration. "Whoever goes in can't come out. They go in, get EMP'd to destroy any nanobots, then they stay locked inside working on a solution. Complete isolation until this is over."

Collins's jaw tightens. He's accustomed to controlling situations through financial leverage and corporate influence. Guardian protocols don't accommodate billionaire micromanagement. He shifts that attention to me and Hank.

"You love her." His voice carries grudging acknowledgment.

"More than our own lives." Hank's confirmation rings with absolute certainty.

"Enough to die for her," I add steel to the promise.

Collins nods slowly. "Then we're on the same page."

"So what can you give us?" Sam steps back into the conversation before tension can reignite.

Collins's demeanor shifts back to corporate efficiency. "I've got a research campus in Palo Alto that can be completely cut off from all external networks. Clean rooms designed for quantum computing."

"Faraday cage setup?" Mitzy's eyes light up with technical enthusiasm.

"Military grade. Built for classified government contracts. Completely invisible to outside surveillance." Collins's confirmation carries satisfaction.

"What about personnel?" CJ presses for specifics.

"Twelve specialists. Quantum physicists, AI researchers, and nanotech engineers. Best minds in their fields." Collins pauses, then adds with paternal steel, "People who know failure's not an option."

The resources he's offering represent capabilities that dwarf government budgets. Corporate research and development unconstrained by bureaucratic limitations or oversight committees.

"How fast can you deploy?" Sam continues the tactical assessment.

Collins checks his watch. "Team assembly within six hours. Full operational capability within eighteen."

"Money talks." Blake whistles low.

"Money screams. And right now, I'm prepared to be real fucking loud," Collins corrects with grim satisfaction.

The strategy crystallizes around us. Dual operational tracks. The visible Guardian activities that Malfor expects, and invisible technical warfare he can't monitor.

"How do we communicate between sites?" Rigel asks, always thinking about operational details.

"Courier runs. Physical transfer of intel between clean sites. No electronic communication that could get intercepted." CJ's response is short and direct. "We rotate Guardians at weekly intervals. They carry any necessary communication."

"Who's running the tech side?" Sam asks the critical question.

"I am." Mitzy's voice carries absolute authority. "But I can't be the one who goes in. I need to stay here, coordinate between the clean site and our beach operations, manage the flow of intelligence."

"Then who goes in for the techies?" CJ presses.

Mitzy looks around the circle. "Jeb. He's got the technical background to work with Collins's specialists, and he knows my systems better than anyone."

"And security?" Collins asks.

"I like your idea of two Guardians." Sam's tone makes it clear this isn't negotiable. "Hank and Gabe on the first rotation."

Collins nods, but I catch something in his expression. "How do we explain their absence from Guardian operations?"

"Training exercise," Forest suggests. "Extended deployment simulation. Happens all the time."

"That works for a few days," Ethan points out. "What about longer term?"

"We cross that bridge when we get to it," Sam responds.

But there's another issue burning in my mind. "How do we know your people are clean?" I ask Collins directly. "Harrison worked for you for twenty years. How do we know there aren't others?"

Collins's expression hardens. "Because I'm personally vetting every specialist who goes in. People I've worked with for years, people whose backgrounds I know inside and out."

"That's what you thought about Harrison," Hank points out, his voice carrying cold logic.

The challenge hangs in the salt air. Collins stares at us both, then nods slowly. "You're right, which is why every one of my people gets the same EMP treatment you do. Full decontamination before they enter the facility, and once they're in, they stay in until this is over."

"Anyone who enters that facility commits to seeing this through to the end," Mitzy adds.

"What if your specialists don't like our methods?" I test his commitment.

"Then they can find new jobs. I didn't build my company by putting up with bullshit." Collins's smile carries predatory satisfaction.

Walt shifts on his driftwood seat, the question he's been holding back finally emerging. "How long before we know something? Before we get intel we can actually use?"

"Unknown. This quantum entanglement tech is going to take time to crack." Mitzy's admission carries scientific honesty.

"We don't have weeks." Carter's statement rings with flat certainty.

"Then we make sure it takes days." Collins's expression hardens, and his voice carries the certainty that whatever resources are required, whatever specialists need to be acquired, whatever obstacles need to be eliminated, he'll make it happen.

Because his daughter is missing and somewhere out there, beyond the horizon, Ally waits for rescue.

"Collins, get your facility up and running," Sam says. "Mitzy, pick your team and get ready for immediate deployment. Everyone else keeps up the normal routine until further notice."

Collins rises from his seat, movements carrying boardroom authority even in this informal setting. "I'll do whatever it takes to bring my daughter home. Whatever resources you need. Whatever rules need breaking. Whatever enemies need eliminating." His pale blue eyes lock with mine, then shift to Hank. "But when this is over, we're gonna have a talk about my daughter's future."

"Looking forward to it. Should be a hell of a conversation." I let my own steel show.

"Real interesting." Hank nods beside me.

I catch his eye and something passes between us—a shared moment of amusement at Collins's assumption that he'll have any say in how this conversation goes. For a split second, Hank's mouth quirks up at the corner, and I feel my own grin starting to form. It's the first time we've been on the same wavelength since our fight, that automatic synchronization we've always had when facing down someone who thinks they can intimidate us.

The moment feels good. Right. Like the partnership that's kept us both alive through hell and back is on the mend.

"Yeah, I think it will be." Collins studies us both for another moment, then shakes his head. As he heads toward the gondola platform, I catch Hank's eye across the dying firelight.

Ally's father doesn't approve of us, but he needs us.

And right now, that's enough.

The war just gained a new front.

Time to see if money and desperation can accomplish what tactical expertise hasn't. I'm not a techie, but it finally feels as if we're doing something rather than spinning our wheels.

TWENTY-THREE

The Choice

ALLY

Morning arrives like a slap. Crusted blood cracks at the corners of my mouth when I attempt to swallow. Muscles scream from yesterday's electricity—no, not yesterday. Longer. Time bleeds here. Stretches. Contracts. Becomes irrelevant until pain marks its passing.

There's no window, no clock. Just the steady cycle of meals I haven't touched and the weight of fatigue anchoring my bones. My body remembers more than one sleepless night. More than one round of screams echoing from Stitch's cell. The silence now feels—recent. Like the kind that follows a storm no one dares name.

Across the corridor, she hasn't moved since they dragged her back. Not even to drink. The dried rust on her collar tells me no one's cleaned her up since.

Boots thud—six pairs, not four. Heavier. Intentional. A plastic container swings from one gloved hand—gauze, antiseptic, bandages. Not mercy.

Maintenance.

"Stand." The lead guard unlocks Stitch's cell first.

Stitch remains motionless, a broken thing. Long seconds pass before she moves, each shift telegraphing invisible damage—broken ribs, torn muscles, lacerations hidden beneath blood-stiffened clothing. Her face remains unmarked—calculated cruelty.

Malfor wants her brain to be functional, her fingers to be operational, and her expertise to be accessible.

The rest is expendable.

A medic enters her cell, cloth scraping wounds, antiseptic hissing against open flesh, gauze wrapping lacerations. Stitch endures the torture without sound, eyes fixed somewhere beyond the walls. Treatment finished, they haul her upright by her arms.

The key turns in my lock next.

"Move."

No medical attention for me. My damage, a split lip, bruised jaw, and muscles spasming from electric punishment, doesn't impair my usefulness.

Jenna's knuckles whiten around her cell bars as they drag me past. "Stay sharp," she mouths, eyes burning with warning.

Corridors stretch endlessly today, the distance to the lab multiplying with each step. Guards press closer than they did yesterday, fingers hovering near the remote triggers, eyes tracking every muscle twitch for signs of resistance. New cameras swivel at each intersection, black lenses following our path like predators tracking prey.

The lab's transformation strikes like another punishment. Four additional guards flank the room, their rifles pointed inward rather than downward. Three monitoring stations bristle with screens displaying our workspace from every angle. Even the air hurts to breathe—colder, sterile, saturated with implied violence.

Dr. Elkin hunches smaller at his terminal, shoulders curved inward as though trying to disappear into his equipment. Dr. Rafeeq's hands quiver against keyboards, the tremors traveling up his arms. Their collars dig deeper today, skin beneath raw and weeping.

A guard positions Stitch at the furthest workstation, one standing close enough behind her that his tactical vest brushes her shoulders. Her fingers move mechanically across the keys, inputting security protocols, one slow tap at a time.

My terminal glows with yesterday's progress—quantum entanglement algorithms approaching viability. The interface shows remarkable progress since yesterday—someone worked through the night, tearing down the barriers I constructed, dismantling the problems I planted to slow progress.

Dr. Elkin appears beside me, voice barely audible. "Specialists arrived after yesterday. Added resources." His eyes dart toward a camera. "Don't repeat yesterday's error."

I won't, although I wish Stitch told me what she was trying to do. Using code, Malfor was destined to discover her subterfuge, but she's given me an idea. Perhaps I can leverage the quantum entanglement and turn the communications from one-way to two-way.

I could get a message out.

Succeed where Stitch failed.

Dr. Elkin's warning costs him. A guard steps forward, his thumb pressing a remote. Dr. Elkin's body jerks, a puppet with yanked strings, as his collar activates briefly—not as punishment, but as a reminder. He stumbles backward, fingers scrabbling at his throat, eyes watering.

It should serve as a warning. What Malfor did to Stitch and how his guards enforce discipline should stop me, but the others would want me to try, especially after what he did to Stitch.

It's a risk, but it's worth it. All I have to do is figure out how to send a message and tag it with geo-location.

Time dissolves into code. Quantum formulas spill from my fingers—entanglement protocols, communication systems engineered to be unjammable, untraceable, unstoppable once deployed. Work that once filled me with wonder—particles communicating across impossible distances, defying conventional physics—now twists into obscenity as Malfor weaponizes my research.

Lunch arrives—tasteless protein bars and lukewarm water delivered silently. No breaks permitted. Bathroom visits are conducted under direct observation, dignity stripped alongside freedom.

By mid-afternoon, the system reaches a critical stage of integration. The quantum processor requires calibration with the communication arrays—a delicate procedure demanding precise timing and frequency adjustments. Dr. Rafeeq announces the phase, drawing attention from supervisory staff.

A suited technician approaches my terminal. "Proceed with quantum calibration sequence."

The perfect moment unfolds. Guard rotation begins at the door. It's a momentary distraction as personnel exchange positions. Dr. Elkin moves to assist Dr. Rafeeq with hardware connections, pulling monitor eyes toward the server rack. The surveillance camera above my station sweeps toward the main array, creating a ten-second blind spot.

Ten seconds. My fingers fly as I introduce a mathematical cancer into the calibration algorithm. Not crude sabotage—nothing as detectable as Stitch's beacon attempt. Just a fractional shift in the quantum frequency resonance. A change so small, it slips past every failsafe. Small enough to be overlooked. Devastating enough to rot the core from the inside out.

But that's not all I bury.

While the system digests the poisoned algorithm, I embed something else. A subtle phase modulation, hidden within the entanglement handshake. One that doesn't just receive, but transmits.

A ghost-pulse.

A whisper buried in the static, a signal bleeding outward, carried on the same frequency Malfor thinks he controls.

It won't light up any screens. I'll never know if it worked.

But Mitzy will. If anyone can hear a scream inside silence, it's her.

I mask the alteration beneath a layer of performance tweaks, burying my intent beneath simulated efficiency. My pulse thunders. My hands are steady.

Green lights flash. Calibration complete. The system stabilizes.

They'll think they've won.

Let them.

Thirty seconds pass normally. The system runs diagnostics, checking connections and verifying integrity. Then—a ripple. Tiny at first, barely registering in quantum field stability. Then another, larger.

Amber warning lights pulse across the central console.

"Field instability detected," the automated system announces. "Quantum coherence at 92 percent and declining."

Silence crashes through the lab. Dr. Rafeeq's hands fly across connections. Dr. Elkin frantically scans diagnostic data. Suited technicians swarm the central server, keyboards clicking in desperate rhythm.

"Explain." The lead guard advances, hand shifting to a weapon.

"Entanglement degradation." Dr. Rafeeq's voice fractures at the edges. "The quantum field's coherence is failing."

"Fix it."

"Working." Dr. Elkin pulls system logs and scans data streams. "Could be hardware interference, environmental factors, or—"

His words die. Eyes lock onto his screen, then shift to me—a flash of horrified understanding before his expression empties.

"Found it." His voice flattens. "Calibration algorithm modification. Quantum frequency resonance altered by 0.0037 hertz."

"Accidental?" The technician leans forward.

"Impossible." Dr. Elkin's resignation saturates each syllable. "That specific value creates harmonic distortion in the entanglement field. Deliberate."

The door hisses open. Malfor enters, hands clasped behind his back, his face carved from ice—that terrible calm that precedes his worst cruelties.

"System failure reported." His voice carries no anger, no surprise. Only expectation.

Dr. Elkin steps forward. "Quantum calibration error, sir. We're working to—"

"The nature and source are already known." Malfor cuts him off. "Miss Collins appears determined to test boundaries despite yesterday's education."

His gaze pins me like an insect to a corkboard.

"I didn't—" The words die on my tongue. Malfor doesn't care. "No! The calibration completed normally. Perhaps the hardware—"

"Enough." His hand rises, silencing me. "The modification carries your signature—that particular harmonic distortion pattern appears in your published research. It's elegant, but stupid."

"It's in my research because it's part of the science. I didn't do anything."

I did *something*, but I didn't do that.

The error isn't the ghost-pulse. That was buried too deep, masked within harmless phase modulation, encoded to mimic background quantum noise. What's unraveling the system isn't my message—it's the foundation Malfor built it on.

A flaw he introduced by forcing entanglement across incompatible nodes. An error seeded not in sabotage, but in arrogance. He used my published equations without understanding the boundary conditions. My framework included failsafes—counterbalancing variables meant for lab conditions, not brute-force deployment under threat of violence.

He overclocked the calibration protocol. Boosted resonance to force faster integration. Layered his hardware across protocols never designed to overlap. The distortion wasn't my doing—but it carries my name because the math originated from me.

That's what Elkin saw. Not a betrayal. A misfire. A consequence of pushing a fragile theory into unstable territory.

The ghost-pulse—my real defiance—remains hidden. Quiet. Untraceable.

But this? This is visible. Malfor thinks it's rebellion because he's too blind to see the damage is his own reflection.

He's going to punish me for breaking what he already broke.

Guards seize my arms, yanking me upright. Malfor extracts the collar remote from his pocket, thumb hovering over the activation button.

"Your resistance grows tiresome."

Agony explodes through my nervous system as the collar activates. It's worse than previous punishments, lasting far longer. My body convulses against restraining hands, my vision fracturing then reassembling in broken pieces. When it finally stops, my muscles liquefy. My legs buckle.

"Courtyard." Malfor tucks away the remote. "Bring the others."

"No. Please. Just me—only me. I swear I didn't do this. It's a fundamental flaw—"

"Silence!" He leans closer, his voice intimate. "You persist in believing your actions exist in isolation. That your choices affect only you."

Guards drag me through corridors. Behind us, more guards extract Stitch from her terminal. Dread crushes my lungs, each breath shallower than the last.

Sunlight stabs my eyes as they haul me into the courtyard—the same space where Stitch bled. The metal post stands dead center, dark stains marking where her suffering painted the concrete. Today, a steel table gleams beside it, something cloth-covered resting on its surface.

Guards force the others from their cells—Jenna walking upright, Rebel cradling her splinted arm, Malia stumbling forward, Mia's face that barely masks terror.

They arrange us before Malfor, who stands between the post and table, hands behind his back, his expression unnaturally serene.

"Your previous lesson proved insufficient." His voice carries across the courtyard. "Perhaps my teaching methods require greater clarity."

The guards force me forward until we stand face-to-face. Malfor strikes like a snake, fingers digging into my jaw, wrenching my face upward.

"Quantum calibration sabotage. Subtle approach, I grant you. Progressive damage, difficult to trace." His thumb traces my lower lip, the touch raising bile. "Cleverer than your friend's crude beacon."

"You don't understand." Tears fall freely now. My gaze flicks toward Stitch, whose face remains expressionless despite her injuries. "I didn't do anything. I'll accept whatever the punishment is, but it's not what you think."

"No." Malfor shoves me backward. "You fundamentally misunderstand the lesson. This isn't about punishing you. When children misbehave, sometimes the most effective discipline comes from watching their siblings suffer the consequences of their actions. It creates powerful associative memory. Direct links between action and consequence."

"No. Please," I beg, but it's useless when dealing with a madman.

"Choose." He turns, eyes reptilian. "One friend will receive the consequence of your sabotage."

"I can't." The words scrape through raw tissue. "I won't. I didn't do anything. You have to believe me. It's a flaw introduced by forcing entanglement across incompatible nodes. It was bound to happen."

"Silence! I'm tired of your lies." His smile never touches his eyes. "Choose one of your friends to accept the punishment."

"I won't. Take me. Please."

"Utterly pointless." He steps closer. "You've demonstrated a willingness to suffer for your principles. Admirable but useless to me."

His hand sweeps toward the others. "Choose now. Or all collars activate at level six until someone's heart fails."

Rebel's arm remains broken, healing improperly. Additional trauma might permanently disable her. Stitch barely stands after yesterday's beating, her body already past the breaking point. Mia's smaller frame suggests less physical resilience against severe injury. Malia trembles constantly now, her composure fraying under stress.

"Pick me." Mia's chin snaps up.

"I'll take the punishment." Malia trembles, but she stands tall.

They don't know what they're doing. None of us do. All we know is Malfor is a psychopath. Whatever he has planned, it's going to be monstrous.

"You have to choose me." Jenna stands the tallest. "I'm the least injured thus far. Most likely to recover from—whatever."

The logic twists my stomach, acid burning upward. There is no acceptable choice. Only gradations of monstrosity.

Exactly what Malfor intends. He wants to turn me into a monster.

"Ten seconds, Miss Collins." Malfor's voice slices through panic. "Or everyone pays."

"Jenna." Her name tears free, barely audible.

"Louder." Malfor's smile widens. "Ensure everyone hears your decision."

"Jenna." My voice shatters on her name.

TWENTY-FOUR

First Breakthrough

HANK

THE NUMBERS TRACK THEMSELVES AS I CRACK OPEN A BEER ON our condo balcony. A day has passed since the beach meeting with Collins, and the Pacific stretches endlessly before us, painted gold by late-afternoon sun. Somewhere out there, Ally waits for rescue. But for the first time since Harrison's betrayal, we have a plan that might work.

Gabe settles into the chair beside me, his beer already half empty. The tension that's been riding his shoulders since our fight has eased, replaced by something resembling the focused calm I recognize from mission prep.

"Training exercise starts tomorrow." I keep my voice level, conversational. The kind of statement that would sound routine to anyone listening through nanobots. "Could be a week, maybe longer."

"About time." Gabe takes another pull from his bottle. "Been going stir-crazy sitting around here."

The casual banter masks the truth we can't speak aloud. Tomorrow, we disappear into Collins's facility to begin the real work. The work that might finally bring our women home.

A seagull lands on the balcony railing, head tilting as it studies us with one black eye. Gabe tosses a piece of the sandwich he's been picking at and the gull snaps it up.

"Remember that deployment in Syria?" I grin, and for a moment it's like the old days. "When you spent three hours calculating blast patterns for a door that turned out to be unlocked?"

"It wasn't unlocked when I started the calculations," Gabe counters. "You just got impatient and kicked it open."

"Worked, didn't it?"

"Pure luck."

"Skill," I correct, then pause. "Besides, someone had to balance out your overthinking."

The easy rhythm of our banter feels good. Right. Like pieces of ourselves clicking back into place after days of distance. We've been partners too long to let personal shit destroy what works between us.

"This new assignment," I continue for our invisible audience, "sounds like it'll test everything we've learned."

"Good. I'm ready to put our training to use." Gabe's response carries an edge that anyone listening would interpret as professional eagerness.

But I hear the real message underneath. We're both ready to do whatever it takes to find Ally.

The next day, we travel down to Palo Alto. The facility appears unremarkable from the surface—just another corporate campus—but Collins leads us through security checkpoints that reveal what he has built underneath.

"Standard decontamination protocols," Collins explains as we approach an airlock system. "Corporate policy for all classified projects requiring clean room procedures."

He gestures to what appears to be a high-tech car wash. "Same process Guardian HRS uses, I'm sure."

The process takes twenty minutes. We strip down, submit to electromagnetic pulses that make my teeth ache, then dress in clean clothes. When we emerge, Jeb, who came ahead of us, runs a scanner over each of us.

"Clean," he confirms. "No electronic signatures detected."

Only then does the massive vault door swing open, revealing what Collins has built for us.

"Complete electromagnetic isolation," Collins explains as we enter. "No signal gets in or out unless we want it to."

The facility stretches out like something from a science fiction movie. Clean rooms, advanced equipment, specialists in lab coats.

"Dr. Rachel Kim, quantum physicist. Dr. James Rodriguez, AI researcher. Dr. Michael Okafor, nanotech engineer." Collins makes introductions. "They understand what's at stake."

Dr. Kim steps forward, offering a firm handshake. "We've been briefed on the tactical situation. I want you to know—we understand what's at stake here."

The extraction process unfolds over the next hour. Dr. Kim operates electromagnetic field generators while Dr. Rodriguez monitors quantum signatures. Gabe and I watch from outside the sealed chamber, ready to abort if anything goes wrong.

"Isolation field active," Dr. Kim announces. "Quantum entanglement signatures decreasing."

Minutes stretch like hours. Each movement tested and verified.

"Extraction complete," Dr. Okafor finally announces. "Specimen isolated and secured."

Relief floods the room. Collins exhales slowly. Jeb grins like he's witnessed magic.

"Phase one complete," Dr. Kim says. "Now the real work begins."

"Individual units have limited processing power," Dr.

Rodriguez explains, manipulating holographic displays that show the nanobot's internal structure. "But they're an adaptive learning system and share information through quantum entanglement, creating a distributed intelligence network. At scale, the hive mind has processing capabilities that rival supercomputers."

"How distributed?" Gabe asks the question I'm thinking.

"Global, potentially," Dr. Okafor responds grimly. "Every nanobot in the network has access to information gathered by every other nanobot. Complete intelligence sharing in real time."

The implications stagger me. Malfor hasn't just been watching Guardian HRS—he's been building a worldwide surveillance network using nanobots deployed through various operations.

"But we don't need a full hive to reverse-engineer them," Dr. Kim adds, excitement building in her voice. "The quantum entanglement connection should work both ways. If we can decode the communication protocols from even isolated specimens ..."

"We can track the network back to its source," I finish, understanding flooding through me.

"Exactly. Every nanobot maintains constant communication with its origin station. Find that station and we'll locate Malfor's operational centers."

Collins leans forward, billionaire intensity focused like a laser. "How long?"

"Unknown. The quantum encryption is unlike anything we've seen, but ..." Dr. Kim hesitates.

"But?" I press.

"We're analyzing the communication protocols from the isolated specimens. If we can decode how they work, how they authenticate with the network, we might be able to replicate them."

"Replicate them?" Gabe asks.

"Build our own nanobots," Dr. Rodriguez explains. "Trojan horses that look identical to Malfor's but carry our payload instead of his."

"What kind of payload?" Collins leans forward, billionaire intensity focused.

"Disruption code. Network viruses. Maybe complete a system shutdown, like a dead man's switch." Dr. Okafor lists the possibilities. "We don't know what's possible yet. The quantum entanglement technology is beyond anything we've seen. But I see why he took Miss Collins."

"Why?"

"Her research is specifically about quantum entanglement applications. He needs her expertise to maintain and expand his network," Dr. Rodriguez adds.

"Which means wherever he's running his quantum operations from, that's where we'll find her," Gabe concludes.

"Exactly. But we get one shot at inserting our Trojan horse. The moment Malfor detects foreign nanobots in his network, he'll shut everything down and relocate."

"Clock starts ticking the moment we deploy," I state, understanding the reality.

"Maybe less if his security systems are more sophisticated than we think," Dr. Kim warns.

"We do it," Collins states with finality. "Whatever it takes."

I study the faces around the room—scientists driven by curiosity, a father desperate to save his daughter, and specialists willing to risk everything for a chance at justice.

But experience has taught me that hope can be the most dangerous emotion in tactical operations. Hope makes you take risks. Hope makes you see opportunities where only traps exist.

TWENTY-FIVE

The Price of Resistance

ALLY

Jenna's eyes lock with mine across the courtyard. Her expression holds no accusation. No horror. Only calm acceptance and the slightest nod.

"*It's okay.*" She mouths the words, telling me she understands.

Maybe one day, she'll forgive me.

Guards move instantly, seizing her arms, dragging her toward the metal table. She doesn't resist, doesn't struggle. She maintains her dignity even as she's forced to her knees.

Malfor approaches the table, lifting the cloth to reveal what waits beneath. The brutal simplicity of the tool empties my stomach—bolt cutters, industrial grade, handles wrapped in black rubber, blades gleaming under the tropical sun.

"Secure her hands on the surface." Malfor's command mobilizes the guards.

They force Jenna's arms forward, palms flat against the steel. Zip ties lock her wrists to rings embedded in the table edge. She kneels upright, face composed.

"Dominant hand?" Malfor asks conversationally.

Jenna's silence hardens her jaw, her teeth clenched against response.

"Irrelevant." He lifts the cutters, testing their weight. "We'll improvise."

He positions the cutters' jaws around the base of Jenna's right pinky finger. The metal gleams against her flesh.

"Miss Collins." Malfor looks up. "Understand why this happens. Your sabotage delays my project. Costs time, resources, and progress. So I take something equally valuable from your friend."

Malia sobs openly now. Rebel strains against restraining hands, cursing through clenched teeth. Mia's scientific detachment shatters, horror contorting her features.

"Stop." The word rips through my vocal cords. "Please. I'll fix everything. I'll work without rest. Anything you demand."

"I know you will." Malfor's voice softens. "That's precisely this exercise's purpose."

The bolt cutters close.

The sound—metal cutting through bone and tendon—will haunt every future silence in my life. When Jenna screams, her voice is primal and raw, wounded, shredding the air between us.

Blood sprays across steel, across Malfor's immaculate suit. He doesn't flinch, doesn't pause. He repositions the cutters around her ring finger.

"Please!" I lunge forward only to be caught and restrained.

The cutters close again. Another finger falls. Another scream splits the sky.

Jenna looks at me through her agony, and somehow, impossibly, she forgives me.

"Cauterize the wounds." Malfor returns the bloody cutters to the table. "We don't want her bleeding out before the lesson concludes."

A guard advances with a device glowing orange at its tip.

Burning flesh joins the coppery tang of blood as they press it against the nubs where Jenna's fingers once were. Her screams intensify, and then she falls silent as she collapses.

"Return them to their cells." Malfor turns away, already dismissing us. "Miss Collins resumes work tomorrow. The calibration will be corrected." He pauses beside me, voice dropping to an intimate register. "Remember this feeling. Remember what defiance costs."

Guards escort us back to our cells. Jenna is carried between two guards who dump her onto her bunk. Her injured hand hangs over the edge of the bed, blood dripping onto the concrete floor.

Hours pass in silence. The only sounds are Jenna's shallow breathing and occasional sobs from Malia's cell. It's Mia who breaks the silence.

"We need to check her hand." Her voice forces clinical calm. "The cauterization should protect against infection, but it looks like she's still bleeding."

"How? The guards won't release us." Rebel shifts on her bunk.

"Pass any clean fabric to me." Mia's voice steadies with purpose. "I'll make bandages and feed them through the bars."

We all respond, fabric tearing, small bundles passing cell to cell until reaching Mia, who fashions makeshift bandages.

"Jenna." Her voice is insistent. "Jenna, wake up."

A low groan from Jenna's cell is the only thing we hear.

"Your hand needs cleaning and wrapping." Mia folds the strips of fabric. "You have to get up."

Jenna groans, then stirs. She moves off the small cot and crawls over to Mia.

Mia works through the bars, her voice guiding Jenna through the process of cleaning her wounds with water and wrapping the stumps in fabric strips.

I remain frozen on my bunk, guilt crushing my chest and stealing my breath. Each of Jenna's pained inhales, each rustle of bandages drives my guilt deeper.

"This is my fault." The words hang in the darkness between our cells. "I'm so sorry."

"This is Malfor's choice. Not yours." Jenna's response comes immediately, stronger than seems possible. "Don't apologize for what he's done."

"I shouldn't have—"

"Stop." The command in her voice silences me instantly. "He forced an impossible choice on you. There was no right answer."

"I chose you. I let him—"

"You chose the person most likely to survive." Her matter-of-factness stuns me. "I would have done the same thing."

"How can you not hate me right now?" The absolution burns worse than any accusation.

"Because hate is what he wants." She shifts position, wincing. "He wants us divided. Broken. Turning on each other."

"He's succeeding." Malia's voice sounds small in the darkness. "In breaking us, that is. Not in turning on each other."

"You're right. We won't let him pull us apart." Jenna's response carries surprising strength. "We decide that, not him."

Silence falls again, heavier but somehow different. Not the silence of isolation, but of shared pain and shared resistance.

Later, when the guard patrol passes and the others have fallen into exhausted sleep, Jenna's whisper finds me through the bars.

"Ally." Her voice barely carries the short distance between our cells. "This isn't your fault."

"Two fingers." The words catch in my throat. "You lost two fingers because of me."

"Your sabotage might have bought Guardian HQ more time." Her pragmatism shocks me. "Might have delayed whatever he's planning. It was worth the cost. You and Stitch did what any one of us would've done. We all would've taken a chance to disrupt his plans. None of this is your fault."

"I still feel terrible."

"And I'll still give you the biggest, strongest hug when we get out of here. Malfor wants to hurt us. He wants to drive a wedge between us. We don't let him. No matter what he does ..."

She means well. Jenna means to absolve me of my actions, but it will take time to forgive myself.

Sleep refuses to come. I lie awake watching the faint outline of Jenna's breathing through the bars, the irregular rise and fall revealing the pain she endures despite her brave words.

Malfor's strategy becomes clearer with each passing hour. He's not just breaking our bodies—he's breaking our bonds. Making resistance synonymous with another person's suffering. Creating a prison where the walls exist in our minds more than in concrete and steel.

The worst realization comes in the darkest hour before dawn: he's winning.

Not through the collars.

Not through beatings.

Not through psychological torture.

He's winning by making me afraid to fight back. By making the cost of resistance too high to bear.

I stare at the ceiling, imagining Guardian HQ planning their rescue, unaware of the nanobots monitoring their every move. I imagine Hank and Gabe working together, preparing for an extraction that will fail before it begins.

I imagine the quantum network Malfor unleashed spreading through financial systems, government infrastructure, and defense networks—all controlled by a man who cuts off fingers to make a point.

Whatever resistance remains, it can't be obvious. It must be subtle and invisible even to those closest to us.

Tomorrow I'll return to the lab. I'll fix the calibration. I'll work diligently on Malfor's quantum network. I'll be the model prisoner, the broken asset, the compliant tool.

And somewhere beneath that performance, I'll keep searching for the one thing Malfor doesn't expect me to find.

A way to bring it all down.

TWENTY-SIX

The Signal

GABE

I LEAN BACK IN THE FACILITY'S BREAKROOM CHAIR, WATCHING Hank methodically clean his sidearm for the third time today. A week locked in this underground bunker has taught me things about Hank I never noticed before—like how he arranges his gear in perfect right angles when he's processing complex information, or the way he hums barely audible classical music when he's content.

Today it's something that sounds like Mozart, which means he's optimistic about our progress.

The air recycling system maintains perfect temperature and humidity, but it can't replicate the salt tang of ocean wind or the sound of waves against rock. Seven days without natural light have left both of us pale as lab rats, but the work we've accomplished makes the confinement worthwhile.

"Blake and Walt should be here in an hour." Hank slides the weapon back into its holster, smooth and automatic. His actions carry the easy confidence that comes from a week of our friendship healing itself through working together again.

"About time. I'm ready to see sunlight again." I stretch,

feeling vertebrae pop after too many hours hunched over monitoring equipment. "Think they'll handle being locked up better than we did?"

"Blake will go stir-crazy by day three. Walt will probably reorganize the entire lab by day two." Hank's mouth quirks up at the corner—the closest thing to a grin I've seen from him since Ally disappeared. "At least they'll have results to keep them busy."

The past week has been a masterclass in controlled scientific breakthroughs. Dr. Kim and her team worked eighteen-hour days reverse-engineering nanobot architecture while Hank and I maintained security protocols. But more than that, we found our rhythm again.

Not the careful distance we maintained after our fight. The real friendship. The kind where I start a tactical assessment and he finishes it without missing a beat. Where he calculates blast patterns, and I instinctively know which direction to position charges.

It feels good. Right. Like pieces of myself are clicking back into place. He's a part of me as much as I'm a part of him.

"Hank, Gabe, you're gonna want to see this." Jeb's voice carries through the intercom system, crackling with excitement.

We follow the scientists to the main lab, where holographic displays show data streams that look like technological hieroglyphics to my demolitions-trained eyes. But the body language around the room tells me everything—Dr. Kim practically vibrates with excitement; Dr. Rodriguez keeps double-checking the readings, even stone-faced Dr. Okafor carries a hint of a smile.

"Our Trojan horse is fully integrated with the network," Dr. Kim announces. "Authentication successful. The hive mind has accepted it as legitimate."

"And it's receiving communication bursts," Dr. Rodriguez

adds. "Scheduled data transfers from the quantum control network."

Hank steps closer to the displays. "What kind of data?"

"Operational coordinates. Command instructions. Network maintenance protocols." Dr. Okafor pulls up geographical data that makes my pulse spike. "Including what appears to be the primary communication node location."

Holy shit!

The coordinates float in space like a promise of salvation. Longitude and latitude numbers that could lead us directly to Malfor's operational center. To Ally.

"Where?" The question scrapes out of my throat like broken glass.

"Remote island in the South Pacific. Eight hundred nautical miles southwest of Hawaii." Dr. Kim overlays satellite imagery showing a volcanic landmass jutting from endless blue water. "Isolated. Defensible. Perfect for covert operations."

"Infrastructure?" Hank asks, always thinking ahead.

"Significant. Multiple structures, communication arrays, deep-water harbor capable of handling substantial vessels." Dr. Rodriguez zooms in on obvious military construction. "It's a permanent installation."

"How confident are we in this intelligence?" Hank asks.

"The quantum signatures match perfectly," Dr. Kim responds. "Our Trojan horse is receiving direct instructions from this location. No intermediary nodes. This is the source."

I scan the room, noticing the scientists exchanging glances. Jeb's barely suppressing a smile, and Dr. Kim keeps looking at something on her tablet that she hasn't shown us yet.

"What?" I ask. "What aren't you telling us?"

Dr. Kim and Jeb exchange another look. Dr. Rodriguez suddenly becomes very interested in his coffee mug.

"We were going to wait until the full briefing," Jeb says, his voice attempting seriousness but failing to hide his excitement.

"Tell us now," Hank demands, his instincts clearly picking up the same vibe I'm getting.

Dr. Kim takes a deep breath. "There's more. Not only have we tracked the primary communication node, but ..." She pauses, looking at Jeb.

"But we also received a signal," Jeb finishes, unable to contain himself any longer. "A direct transmission from the facility."

My heart stops. "What kind of signal?"

"It's encrypted," Dr. Okafor explains, "but using a very specific pattern. One that matches protocols developed right here in this lab."

"Specifically," Dr. Kim says, her eyes locking with mine, "it uses the quantum encryption algorithm Ally designed last year."

The air leaves my lungs. "You're saying—"

"We believe it's Ally," Jeb confirms, his face breaking into a full grin now. "Or possibly Stitch. But given the encryption pattern, our money's on Ally."

"Show me," I demand, stepping forward.

Dr. Kim taps her tablet, and a string of code appears on the main display. To most people, it would be meaningless, but I recognize pieces of it from watching Ally work countless nights.

"The signal contains geographic coordinates that match exactly with the facility location we already identified," Dr. Rodriguez explains. "Plus, there's this embedded in the data stream."

He highlights a sequence that, when isolated, repeats in a pattern familiar to anyone with military training.

"SOS," Hank says quietly.

"Not just SOS," Dr. Kim adds. "There's more data embedded in the transmission. We're still decrypting it, but preliminary analysis suggests it contains information about the facility's security systems."

"She's giving us a way in," I breathe.

Hank and I exchange looks across the lab space. For the first time since Harrison's betrayal, we have actionable intelligence. A target we can hit. A place where Ally isn't just waiting for rescue —she's actively helping us get to her.

"We need to brief the team," Hank says, his brain switching to mission mode.

The transition from artificial underground lighting to natural Pacific sunset hits hard. After the drive from Palo Alto and the gondola ride down the cliff—complete with Mitzy's micro-EMP treatment to fry any nanobots that might have attached themselves since leaving the clean facility—Hank and I emerge onto the beach, squinting against golden light that paints the waves in colors no holographic display could replicate.

Salt air fills my lungs, carrying scents of kelp and distant storms that make the facility's recycled atmosphere taste like plastic by comparison.

Charlie team waits around the familiar bonfire setup, faces painted bronze and shadowed by dancing flames. Sam and CJ stand near the water's edge, their presence commanding even in this informal setting. Mitzy crouches beside her equipment, psychedelic hair catching firelight.

Collins paces near the bonfire's outer edge, expensive shoes crunching against smooth stones with restless energy that screams billionaire impatience.

"Report." Sam's single word cuts through the sound of waves against rock.

"We have coordinates." I drop the intelligence like a live grenade into the circle. "Our Trojan horse integrated with Malfor's network. We know where he is."

The reaction is immediate.

"Where?" Collins demands, stopping his pacing mid-step.

"South Pacific. Remote island installation approximately eight hundred nautical miles southwest of Hawaii." Hank provides coordinates with his usual precision. "Significant infrastructure. Deep-water harbor. Communication arrays. Everything consistent with a major operational center."

"How confident are we?" CJ cuts straight to the heart of it.

"Quantum signatures confirm direct communication with this location," I respond. "No intermediary nodes. No relay stations. This is the source of the network controlling the nanobots."

Hank and I exchange a quick glance. We'd agreed to hold back the most important piece of intelligence until we could verify it further, but the weight of it burns in my chest like a live coal.

Collins stops pacing completely, his focus converging on mission possibilities. "How fast can you deploy?"

"We need to plan this properly first," Hank's voice stays level, controlled. "Verify the intel. Figure out what we need. Make sure we do this right."

My jaw tightens. I want to move now, screw procedure.

"Standard mission planning protocols," Sam decides, his voice settling the debate. "Seventy-two hours minimum for intelligence assessment and operational preparation."

"Seventy-two hours?" Collins's voice rises. "We're talking about my daughter's life."

At least, I'm not the only one who wants to move yesterday. Good to have Collins on my side, even if Hank isn't.

"We're talking about all their lives," CJ responds with granite certainty. "Getting them killed because we rushed into a trap doesn't serve anyone."

Each man knows that proper operations require time, patience, methodical preparation.

"Forty-eight hours," Collins negotiates like he's closing a corporate deal. "Surely that's enough time to plan a rescue mission."

Collins stares at me across the firelight, his intensity meeting my demolitions expertise in a contest of wills that could determine mission success or failure.

"If the intelligence is solid," CJ states, "we can move faster."

I can't hold it back any longer. "There's something else." All eyes turn to me. "We received a signal from the facility. Encrypted with Ally's personal algorithm."

The revelation lands like a thunderclap.

"What?" Collins steps forward, eyes wide. "You're saying my daughter made contact?"

"We believe so," Hank confirms, shooting me a look that's half exasperation, half understanding. "The signal contains an SOS plus what appears to be security information about the facility."

"She's alive," Collins whispers. "And she's fighting."

"This changes everything," Sam says, his tactical mind already recalculating. "If we have someone on the inside—"

"—someone who knows the facility and can provide real-time intelligence—" CJ continues.

"We can cut prep time significantly," Hank finishes, nodding. "Forty-eight hours might work."

The waves crash against rocks in eternal rhythm, indifferent to human struggles playing out on this narrow strip of clean beach.

Somewhere out there, beyond the horizon, Ally isn't just waiting for rescue—she's reaching out to us. Along with Jenna, Rebel, Mia, Malia, and Stitch. Six women whose only crime was loving men who attract danger like magnets attract metal.

The fire crackles and sparks, sending embers spiraling into the night like prayers made of light and heat.

For the first time since this nightmare began, those prayers might actually be answered.

TWENTY-SEVEN

Countdown

HANK

The beach has transformed into something between a command center and a military camp. What started as our sanctuary—the only place we could speak freely—has become our base of operations.

Walt and Hank were pulled from their rotation at Collins's facility, joining the rest of us as we regroup and strategize, the firelight flickering over faces too exhausted to pretend anymore.

Waterproof equipment cases dot the rocky shore. Portable communication arrays stretch between higher rocks above the tide line, their cables snaking across stone worn smooth by decades of Pacific surf. The salty air carries the metallic scent of electronics and the sharper tang of gun oil.

I kneel beside a makeshift table we've constructed using driftwood and flat stones, studying satellite imagery downloaded to secure tablets an hour ago.

The photographs show Malfor's island in high resolution—every building, every guard tower, every potential approach vector mapped in detail.

"We've got a perfect tide window," Gabe drops beside me, small rocks shifting under his knees as he spreads maritime navigation data across our makeshift planning surface. "Low tide hits at 0347. Gives us about ninety minutes for a beach landing."

The intelligence is better than anything we have a right to hope for. Guard rotation schedules. Communication array specifications. Even architectural blueprints of the main facility complex. Each piece of data builds a picture of an operation that's not just possible—it's achievable.

"What's the perimeter defense situation?" Defensive capabilities always determine approach vectors.

"Pretty light," Sam approaches our makeshift planning area, his boots crunching against shells and seaweed. "Automated systems focused on deep-water approaches. Minimal ground coverage on the north beach."

Ethan moves to the center of our planning area, taking charge like he always does. "Alright, let's break this down piece by piece. We've got good intel, but I want every angle covered."

"Approach vectors?" Rigel asks, already thinking like the methodical operator he is.

"Three viable options," I respond, pointing to different sections of the satellite imagery. "North beach during low tide, east cliff face for technical climbers, or direct assault on the main harbor."

"North is our best bet," Walt states, finally looking up from his weapon maintenance. His voice still carries that roughness, but there's steel underneath it now. Purpose. "Minimal coverage, natural concealment from the rocks."

"Agreed," Blake adds, moving closer to study the photos. "East cliff gives a height advantage, but it's a bottleneck if we need to extract fast."

"Harbor's suicide," Carter observes quietly, speaking for the first time in an hour. When Carter talks, everyone listens. "Too exposed. Too many kill zones."

The tactical situation becomes clear. Malfor built his facility to repel large-scale military assault, not small-team infiltration. The kind of oversight that creates opportunities for operators who understand how to exploit defensive blind spots.

"So Charlie team goes in as one unit," Ethan continues, taking charge like he always does. "Six-man insertion, sweep, and clear as a team."

"We need a support structure," Sam interjects, looking to his operations chief.

"Alpha team provides covering fire from elevated positions," CJ responds, taking over the broader deployment planning. "Bravo handles communications and coordination. Delta takes overwatch."

"What about extraction?" Rigel asks, always thinking about the way out.

"We extract together," Blake responds, tracing paths on the satellite photos. "Primary route via beach. Secondary, through the east cliffs if the beach gets compromised. Helicopter pickup if everything goes to hell."

"Which it might," Carter adds with characteristic understatement.

Walt looks up from his weapon. "What's the building layout look like? Where are they most likely holding the women?"

I point to a central structure on the satellite imagery. "Main facility, probably underground levels. That's where I'd put high-value assets."

"Agreed," Ethan nods. "Charlie team goes in together, sweeps and clears as one unit, locates targets, extracts as a team before they can mount serious resistance."

"Time on target?" Blake asks.

"Fifteen minutes, max," Gabe responds, his demolitions mind already calculating. "Any longer and we lose the element of surprise."

"Fifteen minutes to find six women in a facility that size?" Walt's skepticism shows.

"That's why we move fast and stay together," Ethan explains. "No splitting up once we're inside. We clear room by room, systematic and quick."

"Actually, we won't be going in blind," Mitzy speaks up from her analysis station, excitement building in her voice. "I can deploy my bumblebee drones ahead of you. They'll rapidly map the interior of the facility and locate the women in real time."

"How fast?" Blake asks.

"Three minutes to map a standard facility layout," Mitzy responds. "The drones are silent, nearly invisible, and can transmit location data directly to your tactical displays. You'll know exactly where they're holding the women before you breach the building."

Walt's expression shifts from skepticism to hope. "That changes everything."

"Cuts our search time from fifteen minutes to maybe five," Gabe adds, his tactical mind already recalculating. "Get in, get them, get out before anyone knows we're there."

The plan takes shape with the efficiency that comes from men who've worked together long enough to anticipate each other's thoughts. Every man has a role. Every role serves the mission. Every mission objective serves one purpose—bringing our women home.

"What about air support?" Walt asks, his voice carrying a roughness that's been there since Malia disappeared.

"Collins has helicopters positioned offshore," CJ responds, consulting waterproof tactical notebooks that contain every operational detail we've planned. He shifts his massive frame on the piece of driftwood he's claimed as a seat, the wood creaking under his weight. "Medical extraction and fire support if we need it."

"What about rules of engagement?" Blake's question carries weight. We all know this isn't a standard hostage rescue where we worry about collateral damage or legal consequences. He looks up from the weapon he's been field-stripping, blue eyes hard as winter ice.

"Whatever it takes," Forest states with granite certainty. His weathered face shows no emotion, but I catch the way his eyes sweep the beach, taking in every man under his command. "Primary objective is recovering our people alive. Everything else is secondary."

"Not everything," Sam interjects, his voice carrying the weight of broader tactical concerns. "We need to neutralize Malfor and eliminate the nanobot threat. Those nanobots could spread worldwide if we don't shut down his operation completely."

The reminder settles over the group like cold water. Rescuing the women is personal, but stopping a global surveillance network from falling into the wrong hands affects the entire world.

"Secondary objective then," Forest acknowledges. "Destroy the facility and eliminate Malfor's operational capabilities."

"With Alpha, Bravo, and Delta already assigned support roles, we're stretched thin for a dual-objective mission," CJ observes, consulting his tactical notes.

Sam and Forest exchange looks, recognizing the need for additional resources beyond Guardian HRS capabilities.

"Time to call in favors," Sam states, pulling out a secure communication device. "Cerberus Protection Specialists. We've worked with them before."

"Ghost?" Forest asks.

"If anyone can handle the secondary objective while we focus on extraction, it's Mason Blackwood's team."

The mention of Ghost brings nods of approval from Charlie team. Cerberus is a smaller operation, but Mason draws exclusively from special operations—highly trained operatives who are familiar with how Guardian HRS operates and can be trusted with high-stakes missions.

"Good call," CJ says with a nod. "Blackwood's team is surgical. No collateral, no mess, no traces."

His tone carries the respect of a professional who recognizes equal skill. In our world, that kind of acknowledgment doesn't come easy.

"Cerberus?" Collins questions, his billionaire instincts kicking in. "Are they reliable? This isn't just any extraction—this is my daughter we're talking about."

"They're the best," CJ assures him. "And Ghost has saved our asses more than once."

Collins's shoulders relax slightly. "Then spare no expense. Whatever they need, they get."

"Glad to have Cerberus help on this," Rigel says quietly, but there's satisfaction in his voice. "No more playing by rules that don't apply to bastards like Malfor."

"Damn right," Walt adds, his hands finally still on his rifle. "Time to show him what happens when you take our women."

Carter nods once, which, from him, is equivalent to a rousing speech. Blake grins for the first time in days, the expression sharp and predatory. The authorization settles over Charlie team like armor—no restrictions, no limitations, no mercy for anyone who stands between us and the women we love.

"Equipment loadout?" Ethan asks, moving through the checklist with team leader efficiency.

We're getting down to operational details.

Finally.

Gabe likes to think I overthink and over plan, but I'm just as eager as him to get in there and shoot shit up. It feels good to be planning rather than sitting around with our thumbs shoved up our asses doing nothing.

"Standard assault kit plus demo charges," Gabe responds. "Breach and clear, fast and violent."

"Communications gear for everyone," Rigel adds. "Redundant frequencies in case they jam primary channels."

"Medical supplies?" Blake asks.

"Full trauma kit," I respond. "We don't know what condition they'll be in."

The words hang heavy between us. None of us want to think about what Malfor might have done to them, but tactical reality demands we prepare for worst-case scenarios.

"Equipment decontamination?" I voice the concern that's been nagging at me.

"Mitzy's working on a solution," Sam responds. "Portable EMP units that won't fry our electronics. Should have something ready before we deploy."

"Should?" Walt looks up sharply.

"Will," CJ corrects with granite certainty. "Mitzy doesn't miss deadlines when lives are on the line."

That's reassuring. Mitzy's track record speaks for itself. Everything about this mission is coming together exactly as we need it to.

"Training drills?" We can't run mission-specific drills down here on the beach, but we also can't let Malfor see what we're preparing for.

"Cover operation," Sam responds immediately. "We'll run standard hostage rescue scenarios at Guardian HQ. Multiple facility types, various approach vectors. Make it look like we're preparing for several possible targets."

"Misdirection," Blake nods approvingly. "Smart. Malfor sees

us training for a dozen different scenarios; he won't know which one is real."

"If any of them," Ethan adds. "For all he knows, it's all routine training exercises."

The deception makes tactical sense. Train for the skills we need while hiding the specific target. Let Malfor's surveillance network see our preparation without revealing our true intentions.

"What's the weather looking like?" Meteorological conditions can disrupt even the best-planned operations, and ocean weather changes rapidly.

"Clear skies. Light winds. Minimal wave action." Mitzy looks up from her portable analysis station, where she's been monitoring quantum signatures for signs of nanobot activity. "Perfect conditions for getting in there."

The weather window aligns with everything else. We've got good intelligence, a sound tactical approach, and optimal timing. For the first time since Harrison's betrayal, all the pieces are falling into place.

"How confident are we in this intel?" Ethan asks.

"Rock solid," I answer without hesitation. "This intel came directly from Collins's secure research facility. We're not getting this secondhand or from questionable sources—we're getting it straight from the inside of his operation."

"Everything looks solid," Sam responds, consulting data sheets that contain verification protocols.

"Facility seems well-suited for our approach," I observe. The defensive weaknesses are exactly what we need to exploit for a successful infiltration.

"Remote location works in our favor," CJ suggests. "Limited backup, restricted reinforcement capabilities."

"And overconfidence," Blake adds, reassembling his rifle with smooth efficiency. "Malfor thinks his island location makes him untouchable."

Both explanations make tactical sense. Remote island locations can create complacency in defensive planning. Overconfidence is a documented weakness in high-profile targets who believe geography provides sufficient protection.

Collins approaches our planning area carrying an expensive thermal container. Steam rises from the cup, carrying scents of premium coffee and barely controlled anticipation. His silver hair is perfectly styled despite the beach environment, but dark circles under his eyes betray sleepless nights of paternal worry.

"Is the timeline locked in?" The question comes out sharp, eager. His free hand taps against his thigh—nervous energy that he's trying to control.

"Insertion at 0300 hours tomorrow night," Sam responds. "Gives us eighteen hours for intelligence verification plus training time. Facility penetration thirty minutes after insertion. Extraction window opens at 0400."

Collins nods, anticipation radiating from him like heat from a fire. "So we're ready to go tomorrow night."

"After final verification," Sam states. "Standard operational procedure. Confirm intelligence through secondary sources, then we execute."

"How long for verification?" Collins asks.

"Twelve hours should be sufficient," I estimate. "Satellite thermal imaging, communication intercepts, standard confirmation protocols."

"Excellent," Collins responds, satisfaction clear in his voice. "Finally, we're moving forward."

Nobody else speaks, but the energy around our planning area has shifted completely. Charlie team has run operations like this before. We know our roles, understand our objectives, and accept the risks involved in rescuing people we'd die to protect. But more than that, we trust each other. Trust that every man will do his job, watch his brother's back, and bring everyone home.

This is what Charlie team looks like when we're united. Men who've bled together, fought together, and survived impossible odds together. Each of us brings different skills to the mission, but we're all committed to the same outcome.

Bringing our women home.

TWENTY-EIGHT

Emergency Response

GABE

Mitzy's alarm cuts through our mission planning like a fire alarm in a munitions depot. Everything stops. Every conversation dies. Every head snaps toward her analysis station where lights flash patterns I've never seen before.

"What kind of spike?" Sam barks, command authority cutting through sudden tension as he moves toward Mitzy's equipment.

"Massive quantum entanglement activity," Mitzy responds, fingers flying across her tablet interface. "The signature is coming directly from the target coordinates. Whatever's happening there, it's happening right now."

I'm on my feet, moving toward her station with the rest of Charlie team. The equipment displays show wave patterns that look like seismic readings during an earthquake, except these measure quantum communications instead of ground movement.

"Could be facility preparation," CJ suggests, his massive frame leaning over Mitzy's shoulder to study the readouts.

"Or prisoner movement," Forest adds grimly.

"Or execution prep," Walt states with brutal honesty, voicing what we're all thinking.

The words hit like incoming artillery. Ally could be dying right now while we sit here planning training exercises and forty-eight-hour verification protocols.

"How confident are we in this reading?" Hank asks, his analytical brain still processing data while mine screams for immediate action.

"Completely confident," Mitzy responds without hesitation. "This isn't equipment malfunction or atmospheric interference. Something major is happening at those coordinates. The quantum activity suggests either massive data transfer or ..." She pauses, checking her readings again. "Or they're preparing to move the entire operation."

"Relocate?" Blake asks.

"Yes," Mitzy confirms. "If Malfor knows we're coming, he might be evacuating the facility. Moving the hostages. Destroying evidence."

The tactical situation becomes crystal clear, like det cord laid out for maximum destruction. We have a window of opportunity that's closing fast. Maybe hours. Maybe minutes. Not the forty-eight hours we had planned for verification and preparation.

"We go tonight," I state before anyone else can voice what we're all thinking.

"Tonight?" Collins's voice carries desperate hope mixed with fear. "Can we be ready?"

"We have to be," I respond, my chest tightening with that familiar pre-explosion tension. "Because if we wait for perfect conditions, there might not be anyone left to rescue."

Sam and Forest exchange looks. They feel the shift from deliberate planning to emergency response. CJ consults his tactical notes, already calculating revised timelines. Ethan's team leader instincts engage, processing equipment requirements and coordination challenges.

"Cerberus won't make it in time," Sam observes, pulling out his secure communication device. "I'll contact Mason, see if they can provide backup support from a secondary location."

"We go without them if necessary," I respond, because waiting for perfect backup could cost us everything. "Charlie team can handle primary and secondary objectives if we have to."

Walt nods grimly. "Damn right we can."

Blake's already breaking down his weapon for transport. "Whatever's happening to them, we end it tonight."

"Equipment decontamination?" Rigel asks, always thinking about operational details.

"Mitzy's portable EMP units," CJ responds. "We'll have to trust they work as advertised."

The beach transforms into organized chaos as our carefully planned forty-eight-hour timeline compresses into six hours of rapid preparation. Equipment cases get sealed for transport back to Guardian HQ. Communication gear is disassembled and packed. The makeshift command center we built over days gets dismantled in minutes.

"Back to Guardian HQ for final prep," Forest announces. "Cover mission goes active immediately. We need to look like we're spinning up for routine training exercises."

The gondola ride back up the cliff carries a different energy than our descent hours ago. Instead of relief at reaching a clean space where we can talk freely, we're heading back into contaminated territory with emergency deployment pressing down on us like a live explosive.

But we don't have a choice.

The real preparation must occur where we have access to our complete equipment buildouts and transportation resources.

Guardian HQ buzzes with controlled activity when we arrive. Alpha team runs building-clearing drills in the east wing, their movements sharp and aggressive. Bravo team practices communication protocols in the west training facility, voices crackling through radio static. Delta team conducts equipment familiarization exercises with new gear, weapons clicking and sliding as they test mechanisms.

To anyone watching—including Malfor's surveillance network—it looks like routine training escalation across multiple teams.

But only Charlie team knows which training exercise is real.

"Full equipment decontamination in the armory," CJ directs as we enter the main building. What he doesn't say is that Mitzy's EMP units are already set up and tested.

We know.

The armory has been transformed into a sterile processing zone. Mitzy's portable electromagnetic pulse devices create clean corridors, allowing us to prep mission-specific gear without nanobot contamination. It's not as thorough as the beach environment, but it's functional for our immediate deployment needs.

"Assault kit plus demo charges," I confirm, selecting weapons and explosives from the decontaminated equipment racks. My hands move with familiarity—rifle, sidearm, breaching charges, det cord, timers. Everything I need to blow holes in whatever stands between us and Ally and the other women.

"Communications package," Rigel adds, testing radio frequencies and backup channels. His fingers dance across the equipment like a pianist warming up, each touch deliberate and practiced.

"Medical trauma kit," Walt states, loading supplies that none of us want to think about needing. Bandages, surgical tools, morphine. The kind of gear that means someone's coming home hurt.

"Insertion timeline?" Ethan asks, checking GPS coordinates and navigation equipment.

"Transport leaves in two hours," Sam responds, consulting updated operational schedules. "Gets us on target during optimal weather and tide conditions."

"Almost like it was planned," I mutter, loud enough for Hank to hear.

His eyes meet mine across the equipment table. "What do you mean?"

"The timing," I explain, trying to put my finger on what's bothering me. "Quantum spike happens exactly when we're ready to deploy. The weather window aligns perfectly. Tide conditions are optimal. The facility apparently is unprepared for an assault."

"We know we're walking into a trap," Hank responds, but I catch something in his voice that suggests he's thinking the same thing.

"I know, and the first step in avoiding a trap is knowing it's there." I rub the back of my neck. "It's just, I've got an uneasy feeling about this."

My words settle between us like an armed explosive device. Because the timing is convenient. Everything is aligning exactly when we need it to align.

The quantum spike is real, and if we don't move tonight, we might lose our only chance.

"Pre-deployment briefing in thirty minutes," Ethan announces. "Final coordination with air support and backup teams."

I shoulder my gear and follow the team toward the briefing room, but the nagging feeling won't go away. Something about this whole situation feels like a perfectly laid charge—all the components in place, timing synchronized, just waiting for someone to trigger the detonation.

The question is whether we're the ones setting off the explosion, or if we're walking directly into the blast radius.

"Transport status?" Sam asks as we gather in the secure briefing room.

"Four helicopters standing by," CJ responds. "Primary insertion with Charlie team. Secondary with air support and emergency extraction capability."

"Weather confirmed optimal," Rigel adds. "Clear skies, minimal wind, calm seas."

"Gear up," Sam orders. "Wheels up in thirty."

The team disperses, each member moving to collect specialized equipment for the mission ahead. I check my demolition kit one final time—custom charges, remote detonators, the specialized breaching tools we might need to access secured areas of Malfor's facility.

Ninety minutes later, we're boarding Collins's private G650, the kind of luxury transport that seems incongruous with our tactical gear and weapons. But the jet's range and speed make it ideal for reaching our Pacific staging area without military attention.

"Any word from Cerberus?" I ask Sam as we settle into the leather seats that seemingly cost more than my annual salary.

He checks his secure comm device. "Blackwood confirms they're mobilizing, but they're dealing with a logistic issue. Their transport had mechanical problems in Singapore. They're securing alternative transportation now."

"Timeline?" Hank asks, the concern evident in his voice.

"They'll be approximately four hours behind us," Sam responds. "Not ideal, but not mission-critical either. Our primary objective is extraction of our people. Cerberus was always going to handle the secondary objective."

The secondary objective—securing or destroying Malfor's

quantum network infrastructure—is important, but not as important as getting Ally and the others out alive.

"They'll make it," CJ asserts with quiet confidence. "Blackwood's never let us down before."

The flight across the Pacific passes in a blur of final preparations, tactical briefings, and equipment checks. When we finally touch down at a private airfield on one of the smaller Hawaiian Islands, the sun is just beginning to rise, painting the horizon in shades of gold and crimson.

Four Black Hawk helicopters wait on the tarmac, their rotors already spinning lazily in preparation for immediate departure. Collins arranged them through private channels—former military aircraft now owned by a shell corporation that can't be traced back to him or Guardian HRS.

"Comms check," Mitzy calls, distributing the quantum-shielded communication devices she's been modifying throughout the flight. "These should resist any attempt by Malfor's systems to intercept or jam our signals."

"Any update on Cerberus?" Hank asks as we move toward the waiting helicopters.

Sam checks his device again. "They've secured transport. ETA to our position is now three hours behind schedule. We'll be on-site before they arrive."

"Do we wait?" CJ asks the question we're all thinking.

Sam considers for a moment, then shakes his head. "Negative. We proceed as planned. The extraction window is too critical to delay. Cerberus will join us when they can."

"They'll catch up," I add, trying to convince myself as much as anyone else. "Blackwood's resourceful."

We load into the helicopters—each Guardian team taking their own bird. Hank and I board the third helicopter with the rest of Charlie team, while Alpha, Bravo, and Delta spread out among the remaining three. Sam and CJ, along with Mitzy and her techies, remain on the tarmac. Their role as command leadership keeps them at the staging area, where they'll coordinate the entire operation from a secure tactical center.

"Mission is a go," Sam's voice comes through our comms as the rotors spin up to full speed. "Maintain radio discipline. Next check-in at waypoint Zulu."

"Copy that," I respond, watching through the helicopter window as Sam and CJ grow smaller, heading back toward the command center.

CJ raises a hand in a final salute—part good luck, part silent order to bring everyone home.

As the formation of helicopters lifts off and banks toward the southwest, I catch a glimpse of the vast Pacific stretching out before us. Somewhere in that blue expanse lies Malfor's island facility.

Somewhere ahead, Ally is waiting. Somewhere behind, Cerberus is racing to catch up.

"You ready for this?" Hank asks.

"Always ready to blow shit up," I respond automatically. "Question is whether we're blowing up the right shit."

"Meaning?"

"Meaning this feels like we're walking into someone else's demolition sequence," I admit. "Like all the charges are already set, and we're just providing the trigger."

The helicopter vibrates around us, rotors chopping through night air thick with the promise of violence.

All of us process the same reality—we're flying toward an island where Malfor has had time to prepare for our arrival. The helicopter's engines drone through the night sky, carrying us toward our destination.

"Contact bearing two-seven-zero," the pilot's voice snaps through the headset, clipped and urgent. "Multiple aircraft. High speed. Closing fast on our position."

Out the window, dots of light slice the dark sky, flying fast and tight—military precision, not some drunk tourist joyride.

"How many?" Ethan's voice cuts through comms, low and hard.

"At least six aircraft. ETA to intercept, ninety seconds."

Beside me, Hank shifts, his face carved in red shadow, jaw clenched tight.

This isn't a surprise.

"Looks like our welcoming committee's early." My voice is flat, stripped down to steel. We're still three miles out over open water.

Not ideal.

No cover. No place to run. Just the hum of the rotors and a sky that's about to ignite.

The thrum in my gut turns sharper. We were always flying into a trap. The only question now is how many of us make it to shore, and how many go down in flames.

TWENTY-NINE

The Broadcast

ALLY

A METALLIC THUD SLAMS THROUGH MY SKULL—BOOT AGAINST steel. I jolt upright, heart in my throat, sleep shattering around me. The outer door crashes open, hinges shrieking like something wounded.

Four guards flood the space, weapons drawn, visors reflecting the wide-eyed panic I can't hide fast enough.

"Up. Now."

Their voices slice through the stale air, sharp and cold. No explanation. No delay.

Just the snap of urgency that means something's changed—and not for the better.

Rough hands seize my arms, drag me upright. My legs—asleep from hours curled on the metal bunk—refuse to support my weight. Boots scrape concrete as they haul me into the corridor.

Across the cellblock, more guards extract the others. Malia emerges curled inward, arms wrapped around her midsection, eyes swollen from tears. Mia follows, face blank, her fingers trembling against her thighs. Stitch moves stiffly, her body still carrying the wounds from the whip beneath blood-stiffened clothing.

Rebel emerges last, defiance etched in every line of her body despite her splinted arm. A guard shoves her forward, eliciting a hiss of pain but no submission.

Jenna stands shakily in the corridor, bandaged hand clutched against her chest. Gray circles shadow her eyes—a testament to hours spent battling infection and pain. Her cauterized stumps must throb with each heartbeat, yet her spine remains straight, chin high despite everything.

"Move." The lead guard gestures with his rifle barrel.

They herd us down unfamiliar corridors, not the route to the labs or work details. Overhead lights flicker, casting our shadows as fractured ghosts against concrete walls. The air changes—salt and heat replacing the sterile chill of interior spaces.

We emerge into the courtyard, but nothing here resembles yesterday's execution ground.

The transformation stops my breath. A massive screen is mounted on the compound wall. Speakers flank the display, professional-grade audio equipment gleaming despite the darkness. A drone hovers overhead, camera lens focused downward, recording everything.

The setup resembles a theater. Or an execution chamber.

Malfor stands before us, hands clasped behind his back, smile curving lips too thin for genuine warmth. His suit—charcoal gray today—absorbs light rather than reflects it. Guards flank him like extensions of his will.

"Good evening, ladies." His voice carries the smooth confidence of a man who owns everything he surveys. "A change of schedule. Something special I've arranged for your—education."

His voice crawls beneath my skin like burrowing insects. My silence only widens his smile.

"You're wondering about this setup." He gestures toward the

screen. "I thought you deserved to witness something firsthand. A demonstration of futility."

Ice spreads through my chest. Whatever comes next will break something vital inside us.

Malfor steps away, produces a remote from his pocket—not the collar control but something sleeker, designed for the equipment surrounding us. He presses a button.

The screen flares to life. Night-vision green bathes us in sickly light as aerial footage fills the display. The ocean stretches black and endless. The island edges are barely visible as jagged shadows against darker water. Stars speckle the upper portion of the frame, but something else moves among them, cutting through the darkness.

"What am I seeing?" Malia whispers, the first words any of us have spoken.

"Patience." Malfor adjusts something on the control panel beside the screen. "Context is everything."

The camera angle shifts, and an image resolves into mechanical shapes.

Helicopters. Four of them, flying in tight formation.

My heart lurches against my ribs. It can't be …

Targeting data overlays the screen, displaying altitude, speed, and distance. Numbers tick down as the aircraft approach. Another data stream shows perimeter defenses activating, tracking systems locking onto the incoming crafts.

"Interceptors deployed," announces a mechanical voice from the speakers. "Target acquisition in progress."

"What is this?" The question scrapes my throat raw. My hands fly to the collar around my neck, clawing at the metal edges. I can't breathe. Can't think past the roar of blood in my ears.

"Live feed." Malfor's smile stretches wider, and I catch the predatory gleam in his eyes as he watches my reaction. "Happening right now, just beyond the visual range of this compound. Your friends at Guardian HRS believe they've mounted a successful stealth approach." His chuckle lacks all humor. "My systems detected them twenty-seven minutes ago."

This has to be a trick. A manipulation. He's showing us old footage, archived material designed to break us. But the telemetry data streams in real time, coordinates updating second by second. The tactical displays show current weather conditions, wind patterns that match tonight's storm front approaching from the west.

Hope and terror war in my chest. Guardian HRS is here. They found us. They're coming.

But Malfor knows.

"Audio channel open," the mechanical voice announces.

Sound floods the courtyard—rotor wash, wind static, and beneath it—voices.

"Contact bearing two-seven-zero," a voice snaps through the headset, clipped and urgent. *"Multiple aircraft. High speed. Closing fast on our position."*

"How many?" Ethan's voice cuts through comms, low and hard.

"At least six aircraft. ETA to intercept, ninety seconds."

Malfor's smile turns predatory as he watches us break. He feeds on this—our pain, our helplessness, our love being weaponized against us.

"Your Charlie team," he says, voice silky with satisfaction, "is about to discover that heroism has its limitations."

We're standing. Exposed. Helpless. And he's watching us like it's the finest entertainment money can buy.

Because for him, it is.

"Interceptor One locked." The mechanical voice sounds almost pleased. *"Firing solution calculated."*

A streak of light cuts across the screen, so fast the eye barely registers movement. Something small, deadly efficient, launched from an unseen platform.

The lead helicopter has no time to react. No evasive maneuvers. No warning.

The explosion blooms white-hot against the eerie wash of night-vision green. The tail rotor shears away, spiraling into darkness. The helicopter lurches, spinning out of control, then slams into the ocean. The main cabin holds together as it hits, sending a geyser of seawater skyward. The wreckage sinks fast into black.

"Charlie team is down! Repeat. Charlie team is down!"

No one could've survived.

Screams tear through the courtyard—ours, raw and ragged, echoing the panic blaring from the speakers.

"Evasive maneuvers! Deploy countermeasures!"

The second helicopter jerks left, flares arcing out in a dazzling burst of light. The missile clips its tail, sending it listing—but it stabilizes, engines roaring as the pilot claws for altitude.

The third bird banks hard to the right, flares bursting like fireworks across the sky. It vanishes into the clouds and disappears into the night.

Then—silence. Nothing but an empty ocean where three aircraft had been. No survivors visible. No movement beyond burning debris flickering against the darkness.

My knees buckle. I hit the ground hard, gravel biting through thin fabric, but I barely feel it.

They're gone.

The words don't make sense. My brain rejects them, shoving back like a bad equation that refuses to balance. But the screen doesn't lie. The ocean swallows what's left—twisted metal, scorched foam, silence.

Hank.

Gabe.

Charlie team … Gone.

The pain doesn't come in a wave. It detonates. Shrapnel through bone. Through breath. Through my soul. I claw at the collar around my neck, needing air, needing them—needing it not to be true.

"Look at them," Malfor murmurs, voice like oil on water. "I said, look."

I can't not look. He's forced us all into a front-row seat to slaughter, made sure we watched—helpless, caged, collared like animals.

He planned this.

He wanted this.

He murdered them and made us watch.

"You bastard," I whisper, not caring if he hears. I want him to hear. I want him to burn.

Something inside me cracks open. Not just grief. Fury. White-hot. Acid-sharp. I don't care about consequences. I don't care if he kills me next.

He showed us this to break us.

But all he's done—is given me a reason to survive.

"You're a monster." Rebel's voice emerges strangled, half sob, half scream.

"I am what circumstance requires." Malfor steps into our line of sight, blocking the screen showing our last hope burning on black water. "But this lesson isn't about me. It's about you. About understanding your situation with perfect clarity."

He paces before us, measuring each step, hands still clasped behind his back. "I gave you hope. The promise of rescue. The knowledge that someone was coming for you." His smile never reaches his eyes. "Now I've taken that away. Hope is a luxury you can no longer afford."

"They'll send others." Jenna's voice remains steady despite everything. "Guardian HRS doesn't abandon its people."

"Perhaps." Malfor nods as though considering her point.

"But how many teams must die before they reconsider? How many bodies must wash ashore before the mission is deemed too costly?" He stops directly before her. "And how long can you survive waiting for them?"

The screen behind him shifts, replaying the destruction from different angles. Slow-motion footage of explosions tearing metal and flesh apart. Enhanced views of burning wreckage striking water. Close-ups of debris that might once have been human.

"Each of those men," Malfor continues, his voice taking on the cadence of a professor delivering a lecture, "died believing they were heroes." His smile becomes razor-sharp. "They were wrong."

The words are designed to inflict maximum psychological damage. He's not just reporting their deaths—he's defiling their memory.

"You'll need time to process this loss," Malfor speaks as though delivering a therapeutic intervention rather than psycho-logical torture. "Time to understand your new reality. Time to accept that resistance is not heroism—it's suicide."

He turns to the guards. "Return them to their cells. Double the watch. Suicide risk is elevated after events like these."

Rebel snaps.

It's not a scream—it's a sound, raw and inhuman, ripped from someplace wild inside her. She lunges so fast that the guards barely register movement. The collar jerks her back mid-charge, wrenching her to her knees with a crack of electricity that lights up her spine.

But, she doesn't stop.

Snarling, she surges up again, her arm catching Malfor's lapel. Fingernails shred fabric, leaving angry red lines across his chest before the guards slam into her from both sides, driving her into the ground.

Malfor steps back, brushing his suit like she's filth. Like none of it mattered.

But it did.

Because for one breathless second, she almost had him.

The beating comes fast, brutal—like they've rehearsed it. A boot slams into her ribs. Once. Twice. The third strike cracks something deep and real. She coughs, the sound wet, sharp. One guard drops to a knee, pinning her broken arm beneath him. Her scream splinters the air—high and raw, animalistic.

The third doesn't move. Just stands there like a monolith, hand on her collar's control, ready to press again if she so much as twitches.

Malfor brushes invisible dust from his lapel. Calm. Immaculate. Then he reaches into his coat pocket and pulls out something small—silver catching the light.

A blade.

"Impulsivity has consequences." He crouches beside her, voice smooth as silk pulled tight over broken glass. "Beauty is a privilege. Easily revoked."

Rebel snarls, lips bloodied, eyes blazing.

He slices her slowly, from temple to jaw. The blade moves with surgical care, skin parting clean, blood spilling in a crimson river down her neck. It's not meant to kill. It's meant to ruin.

To brand.

But she doesn't scream this time.

She just laughs.

Not loud. Not sane. Just the whisper of something broken and burning. Her eyes lock on his, gleaming with hate so pure it feels holy.

"Gonna need a sharper knife," she rasps, teeth red with her own blood. "If you want to cut out the fight."

Malfor pauses, only for a second, but it's there. A flicker of doubt.

And Rebel grins through the ruin of her face.

Unbroken.

Unbowed.

Unafraid.

"Take them back." Malfor rises, tucking the bloodied blade into his pocket. "Miss Collins stays."

The guards drag the others away—Malia still sobbing, raw sounds torn from her throat that echo down the corridors. Mia moves like a sleepwalker, white-faced with shock, her body going through the motions while her mind retreats. Stitch allows herself to be led mechanically, still dissociated, staring at nothing. Jenna walks with military bearing despite everything, already compartmentalizing the trauma. Rebel, they carry between them, blood dripping from her face to mark their path across the concrete, but her eyes still burn with defiant fire.

When we're alone, Malfor positions himself directly before me. His breath smells of mint and coffee, with a hint of something rotten underneath.

"No one is coming, little bird." His voice drops to an intimate whisper. "Not for you. Not ever."

His finger traces my jawline, the touch raising bile in my throat. "The sooner you accept your new reality, the easier your life becomes."

My voice emerges from some distant place, hollow and strange. "They'll never stop looking."

"They already have." He straightens, satisfaction evident in every line of his body. "By this time tomorrow, Guardian HRS will have officially listed the mission as a catastrophic failure. All hands lost. Search and rescue abandoned due to hostile conditions." His smile widens. "And you? You'll be listed as collateral damage. Presumed dead alongside your would-be rescuers."

The screen behind him continues its endless loop—helicopters approaching, exploding, falling. Approaching, exploding, falling. The death of hope on infinite repeat.

"I'll leave you with your thoughts." Malfor gestures to the guards. "One hour. Then return her to her cell."

He pauses at the courtyard entrance, silhouetted against interior light. "Tomorrow, you return to work. With renewed focus, I trust."

The screen plays on as he leaves. Helicopters die again and again before my eyes.

Grief has weight, has mass, has a gravitational pull that collapses lungs and crushes bone. It presses against my eyes until my vision darkens at the edges. It fills my throat until breathing becomes impossible.

They're gone.

Everyone who might have saved us.

Everyone who loved us.

Gone.

Yet we remain.

Collared. Imprisoned. Forgotten.

The hour passes in a haze of static and white noise. Guards return and drag me back through corridors that stretch forever. My feet move automatically. My body remembers how to walk even as my mind fractures around a loss too vast to process.

They throw me back into my cell. The door locks with that same magnetic thunk that once seemed like the worst sound in the world. Now it barely registers through the roaring in my ears.

Night deepens. Darkness wraps around the cellblock like a shroud. But we're not silent now. We're broken in different ways, each processing the loss according to our nature.

From Malia's cell comes the sound of quiet sobbing—not the raw keening from the courtyard, but steady tears that speak to profound grief. She loved Walt with everything she had, and now that love has nowhere to go except into the void where he used to exist.

Jenna's voice cuts through the darkness, barely above a whisper but carrying authority. "Stitch. Can you hear me?"

A long silence. Then, tentatively: "I'm here."

"Good. Stay with us. Don't go anywhere we can't follow."

Jenna's doing triage on our emotional casualties, making sure no one gets completely lost in their grief. Her pain is locked away, somewhere she can access later, when the immediate crisis passes.

"Mia?" Jenna calls softly.

"Present." The response comes shakily but promptly.

"Rebel?"

A bitter laugh echoes from her cell. "Still breathing. Still planning how to kill that bastard with my bare hands."

"Ally?"

I try to speak, but the words stick in my throat. Everything feels distant, unreal. The future Hank, Gabe, and I planned—lazy Sunday mornings, his coffee getting cold while we talked about everything and nothing, all of it gone in a streak of light across a night-vision screen.

"Ally." Jenna's voice carries gentle insistence. "I need you to answer."

"Here," I finally manage. "I'm here."

But I'm not. Not really. Part of me died with that helicopter, sank into the ocean with the men I loved. The part that believed in rescue. In happy endings. In love conquering all.

"We need to talk about what comes next," Jenna says quietly.

"What comes next?" Rebel's voice carries bitter amusement. "We're lab rats in a maze. The only thing that comes next is whatever experiment he wants to run."

"No." Jenna's response is firm. "We decide what comes next. Not him."

"How?" Malia's voice breaks on the word. "How do we decide anything when we're locked in cages?"

"Because we're still alive," Jenna replies with a conviction that cuts through the despair. "Because they died trying to save us, and giving up now makes their sacrifice meaningless."

Silence falls again, but it's different now. Not the silence of defeat, but of consideration. Of minds working through grief toward something resembling purpose.

"He'll expect us to be broken," I say finally, surprising myself with the steadiness of my voice. "Completely compliant."

"Then that's what we give him," Jenna agrees. "We show him broken women who've accepted their fate."

"While we plan," Mia adds, understanding creeping into her tone.

"While we survive," Stitch says quietly, her voice more present than it's been since the courtyard.

"While we prepare," Rebel finishes, dark promise in her words.

From my bunk, I stare at the ceiling and let grief settle into my bones alongside something colder. Malfor believes he's won. Believes he's broken us completely. He thinks we'll work obediently now, build his weapons, further his plans, and accept our captivity as inevitable.

Somewhere in the compound, Malfor sleeps easily, satisfied with his victory. Somewhere in the ocean, the bodies of our men drift with the currents. Somewhere in Guardian HRS headquarters, reports are being filed, missions aborted, and their losses tallied.

Here, in this concrete box, something dies inside me that will never live again, but something else takes its place.

Something cold. Something patient. Something that doesn't need hope, rescue, or salvation.

Hank and Gabe taught me many things during our time

together. How to defend myself. How to think tactically. How to survive when survival seems impossible.

And one lesson above all others: how to wait for the perfect moment to strike.

Tomorrow I'll return to the lab. I'll build his quantum network. I'll be the model of submission and defeat.

Beneath that mask, I'll become the weapon Hank and Gabe trained me to be.

Because monsters like Malfor never look closely at shattered things. They never notice the edge—until it slips beneath their skin.

Grief and fury braid together in my chest. I never got to say goodbye. But I swear on Hank and Gabe's memory—*I'll make sure you pay for every second of love you stole from us.*

The vow settles into my soul like armor. Tomorrow, I begin the long game.

Tonight, I mourn the future that died with Hank and Gabe, and forge a new one from grief and rage and the unbreakable bonds between women who refuse to be broken.

Even when everything else is taken from us, we still have each other.

And we still have the will to make Malfor pay.

THIRTY

Fathoms Deep

HANK

"Taking fire! Taking fire!" The co-pilot's frantic call crackles through the intercom a heartbeat before impact.

The first missile slams into our helicopter's tail. The concussion hits hard. A pressure wave compressing my lungs, the taste of burning metal and hot electronics flooding my mouth. The helicopter lurches violently sideways, throwing us against our restraints. Alarms shriek to life, their discordant wailing like wounded animals. Red emergency lights flood the cabin, turning familiar faces into blood-streaked masks.

The cabin fills with the acrid stench of burning hydraulic fluid and scorched wiring. My ears pop as cabin pressure shifts. Metal groans around us, the airframe protesting abuse beyond its design limits.

"Tail rudder hit!" The pilot shouts above the cacophony as a second impact rocks the fuselage. The helicopter pitches nose-down, then wobbles like a wounded bird.

G-forces press me into my seat as the aircraft shudders violently. Blake's tactical gear breaks loose across the cabin, scattering equipment that becomes deadly projectiles in the chaos. A med kit slams into Walt's temple, opening a gash that instantly wells with blood. Through the windows, I glimpse tracer fire streaking past—deadly lines of light cutting through darkness.

"Engine down. Hydraulics failing." The pilot wrestles with the controls, his voice strained but professional. "Losing altitude at twenty feet per second."

Six enemy aircraft circle us like predators, executing a coordinated attack pattern that leaves no escape vectors. This isn't random fire. This is a carefully orchestrated kill box.

"Options?" Ethan's voice cuts through the chaos, the single word carrying the weight of command.

"Water landing." The pilot fights the stick as warning indicators cascade across his console. The staccato beeping of failure alerts creates a hellish percussion against the alarms. "Only shot we've got." Sweat cuts tracks through the grime on his face. "Hit land at this speed and nobody walks away."

I assess our situation with the cold logic that's become second nature. Ocean temperature: 72 degrees. Distance from shore: 3.2 miles. Night visibility: minimal.

Not ideal. Better than becoming scattered wreckage across jagged terrain.

"Ninety seconds to water impact." The pilot maintains a death grip on the controls, voice level despite the tremor in his hands. We spiral down.

Impact imminent.

Beside me, Gabe reaches for his tactical vest, securing his dive gear. His face reveals nothing, but I recognize the tightness around his eyes—the look he gets when shifting into combat mode. We all carry standard equipment for coastal operations—compact rebreather good for sixty minutes, folding fins, thermal protection integrated into our undersuits.

"Ditch the bird." Gabe secures his sidearm in its waterproof holster, the sound of the snap loud even against the mechanical death throes surrounding us. "Not dying up here when Ally's still out there."

Our eyes lock across the shuddering cabin. Eight years of missions. Eight years of shared battles, shared beers, shared women. Two men who know each other better than brothers. No words needed.

Find Ally. Eliminate Malfor.

"Charlie team." Ethan's voice rises above the screaming alarms. "Brace for water evacuation. Buddy system. Secure your weapons, gear check now."

The team springs into action. Rigel and Blake double-check each other's equipment with the efficiency of men who've trained for this scenario countless times. Walt secures his medical kit, wiping blood from his eyes with one sleeve. Jeb checks his waterproof pack, ensuring his demolition supplies remain intact. Carter verifies his communication gear, establishing backup frequencies in case primary channels are compromised.

"Pilots." Ethan turns toward the cockpit. "Evacuation plan?"

"We'll ditch with you." The co-pilot half-turns in his seat. "No rebreathers up here. Standard vests only."

"Rigel, Blake—assist the pilots once we're in the water." Ethan's orders come without hesitation. "Share air if needed."

I verify my equipment. Rebreather secure. Folding fins attached to my calf straps. Waterproof tactical pack containing essential survival gear. Sidearm secured in its specialized holster.

"Thirty seconds!" The pilot's voice rises in pitch as our descent rate increases.

Through the windows, the ocean rushes toward us. Moonlight breaks across black water, turning the surface into a rippling mirror that reflects our approaching doom. The world outside blurs as we drop faster, the damaged helicopter surrendering to gravity one system at a time.

"Charlie team actual to all units." Ethan activates his comm unit. "We are going down. Repeat, Charlie team is going down."

"Acknowledged." The response crackles through static. "Engaging hostile aircraft to cover your descent."

"Negative." Ethan's eyes narrow, visibly calculating odds and opportunities. "Break off engagement. Let them think we're neutralized."

A heartbeat of silence on the line. "Understood, Charlie Actual. Disengaging. Good hunting."

"Brace! Brace! Brace!" The pilot's warning comes a second before impact.

We hit the water like slamming into concrete. The impact throws me forward against my restraints, pain exploding across my chest. The helicopter bounces once, twice, then settles with a sickening lurch. My teeth clack together from the force, copper taste of blood filling my mouth where I've bitten my tongue.

Metal tears as the rotors shear off on impact, the sound like some prehistoric beast being dismembered. The cabin fills with saltwater. Sweat and adrenaline mix with the metallic tang of blood and the chemical odor of burning electronics.

Water surges through shattered windows, a shocking assault that steals breath and clarity.

The cabin tilts sharply as water pours in—ankle-deep, then knee-deep in seconds. The aircraft groans around us, metal under stress, the death sound of a machine beginning its descent to the ocean floor.

"Move!" I hit my harness release, the buckle giving way with a satisfying click.

Water pours in. The helicopter shudders beneath us, listing further to port as the cabin floods.

"Out!" Ethan's voice rises above the chaos of rushing water and creaking metal. "Water egress! Sound off as you clear!"

"Rigel clear!" His voice comes first, professional even in crisis.

"Blake clear!" Second out, moving to secure the perimeter.

"Walt clear!" Our medic exits, medical kit secured to his tactical vest.

"Jeb clear!" Fourth man out.

"Carter clear!" Fifth voice confirming exit.

No word from Gabe. My pulse spikes.

"Status!" Ethan's command cuts through the rising water.

"Comms sealed. Rebreathers functional. Sidearms secured." I work my way toward Gabe's position, water now at chest level. "Gabe?"

"Webbing's jammed." Gabe's voice remains calm despite the water now reaching his sternum. His knife flashes in the dim light, sawing at the nylon restraints. "Release mechanism's bent."

"Go." Ethan jerks his chin toward the exit, already moving toward Gabe. "I've got him."

I hesitate, torn between helping my closest friend and following orders.

"Hank." Gabe meets my eyes, no panic in his expression despite the rising water. "Clear the bird. Do your job."

One quick assessment—Ethan has better leverage. The water continues to rise, now neck-deep. Thirty seconds at most before complete submersion.

The hardest step I've ever taken is the one that carries me away from Gabe, through the exit, into open water.

The Pacific closes over my head. Seventy-two degrees doesn't sound like it should be cold, but the shock of it steals my breath, muscles contracting involuntarily against the assault. My body wants to gasp, to fight, to panic. I suppress those instincts, channeling everything into controlled movements. Deploy rebreather. Establish position. Locate aircraft. Monitor team emergence.

I surface alongside Rigel, Blake, Walt, Jeb, and Carter. Moonlight catches on wet faces as we form a defensive perimeter around the sinking helicopter. The pilots appear next, coughing and sputtering as they emerge from the cockpit. Rigel and Blake immediately move to assist them, offering support.

Forty-three seconds pass before Ethan surfaces, dragging Gabe beside him. A jagged tear runs down Gabe's thigh, visible even in the dim light.

"Status." Ethan treads water, one arm supporting Gabe.

"Perimeter secure." Rigel scans the horizon, his voice barely audible above the water.

"Pilots stable." Blake helps the co-pilot adjust to a floating position.

"Rebreathers functional." Walt completes his equipment check.

"Comms working." Carter verifies our most vital link to the outside world.

"Ready to move." Jeb confirms his status.

"How bad?" I swim to Gabe's side, taking some of his weight from Ethan.

"Had worse." Gabe's jaw tightens against pain. "Metal fragment from the door frame. Clean cut."

Enemy aircraft wheel overhead, predatory birds seeking confirmation of their kill. Their spotlights cut through darkness, methodical search patterns sweeping the water's surface. The sound of rotors echoes across the open ocean, growing louder as they close in on our position.

"Ten minutes underwater." Ethan's order comes swift and clear. "Bearing zero-nine-zero toward shore. Rigel and Blake assist the pilots. Share rebreathers as needed. Surface only when clear of search pattern."

We float in silence, dark figures in darker water. Minimal movement. Every man's face half-submerged to reduce our thermal signatures.

"Alpha Actual." Static crackles from Ethan's waterproof comm. *"Visual on crash site. Confirmation of status requested."* Ethan's jaw

tightens. Ten seconds pass as he weighs options. *"All Guardian units. Charlie team is down. Repeat, Charlie team is down. All units fall back to secondary positions. Maintain operational security. Do not attempt recovery."*

The lie settles over us like a shroud. As far as Guardian HRS knows, we just died. As far as Malfor knows, his ambush succeeded.

We're ghosts now.

"Dive." Ethan's command sends us beneath the waves just as the search aircraft approaches our position.

THIRTY-ONE

The Trojan Betrayal

ALLY

THE EXPLOSION REPLAYS BEHIND MY EYELIDS EVERY TIME I BLINK. White-hot light consuming the helicopter.

Gone. They're gone. They're gone.

Guards drag me from my cell, but my legs won't support my weight. I stumble, catch myself against the concrete wall, and leave bloody fingerprints on gray stone. The collar chafes against raw skin, metal edges digging into wounds that never heal before new ones form, but physical pain barely registers through the emotional devastation hollowing me from within.

"Move." The lead guard's voice sounds like it's coming from underwater, distant and distorted.

I try to walk. My feet shuffle forward, but each step feels like betrayal. How can I keep breathing when they can't? How can my heart keep beating when theirs have stopped forever?

The corridor stretches endlessly ahead. Fluorescent lights flicker overhead, casting shadows that shift and dance like the burning wreckage I watched sink into the ocean. Every sound echoes—boot steps, breathing, the mechanical hum of ventilation systems—but underneath it all, I hear the flatline tone that will haunt me forever.

They died trying to save me.

The thought cuts deeper each time it surfaces. Our love, laughter, and shared dreams ended in a streak of light across night-vision screens. Hank and Gabe came for me, and Malfor murdered them for it.

The lab door hisses open, releasing a blast of frigid air that raises immediate goosebumps across my skin. The sudden temperature change triggers a violent shiver that has nothing to do with cold and everything to do with trauma my body can't process.

Dr. Julian Elkin stands at the primary workstation, shoulders hunched beneath his lab coat. He turns as we enter, and something flickers across his expression when he sees me—recognition of damage that goes beyond physical injuries.

"Jesus," he breathes, barely audible. "What did he do to you?"

The guards shove me toward him, and I stumble again, catching myself against the edge of a workstation. My hands shake so violently that I can barely grip the metal surface. Everything feels unreal, disconnected, like I'm watching someone else's life through thick glass.

"I'll take it from here." Elkin's voice carries careful neutrality, but his eyes never leave my face.

The guards position themselves at the door—far enough to create an illusion of privacy, close enough to intervene if necessary. Their collar remotes hang from belts, a constant threat without words.

Elkin approaches slowly, like I'm a wounded animal that might bolt. When he reaches for my restraints, I flinch violently, the movement involuntary and immediate.

"Easy." His voice is gentle. "I'm just removing the cuffs."

Blood rushes painfully back into my hands as the restraints fall away. I stare at the angry red circles around my wrists, evidence of captivity that seems insignificant compared to the gaping wound where my heart used to be.

"I watched them die." The words escape without permission, raw and broken. "He made me watch."

Elkin freezes, his face going pale. "Who?"

"Gabe. Hank. Charlie team." My voice sounds hollow to my own ears. "Helicopters. Missiles. Gone."

Something crosses his expression—guilt, perhaps, or recognition of Malfor's particular brand of cruelty. He doesn't offer comfort or platitudes. Instead, he gestures toward the terminal.

"He wants the quantum network operational by dawn," Elkin says quietly. "Communication scaffold. Entangled frequencies."

I stare at the screens without processing the information. Code fragments pulse like electronic heartbeats, but they might as well be hieroglyphics. My brain refuses to engage with anything that isn't grief.

"I can't." The admission costs everything. "I can't focus. Can't think. Every time I close my eyes, I see—"

"You have to." His interruption is gentle but firm. "Because if you don't, he'll kill the others too."

The threat penetrates the fog of trauma, sharp and immediate. Jenna. Malia. Rebel. Stitch. Mia. They're alive. Still breathing. Still depending on me to function when functioning feels impossible.

I force myself to the terminal, every movement deliberate and effortful. The chair feels wrong beneath me—too hard, too cold, anchoring me to this reality when part of me still orbits the moment those helicopters fell.

"Start with the base protocol structure," Elkin instructs, pulling up schematics on the main display. "The foundation has to be solid before we can build the communication layers."

My fingers hover over the keyboard, trembling. The first keystroke feels like sacrilege—working for the man who murdered the people I loved most. But the alternative is watching my sisters die, and I can't survive more loss.

The code begins to flow beneath my fingertips, muscle memory taking over when conscious thought fails. Numbers and symbols form patterns that my brain understands despite the trauma fracturing my concentration.

They died trying to save me. I'll make sure their deaths meant something.

The thought crystallizes with sudden, blazing clarity. Every line of code becomes an opportunity—not just to comply, but to ensure Malfor pays for what he's done. My quantum expertise turned against its master.

"What are you doing?" Elkin notices the pause in my typing, the way my hands have stilled mid-keystroke.

I look up, meeting his eyes directly for the first time. "Building what he asked for."

But that's not entirely true. Hidden within legitimate code structures, I begin nesting subroutines that don't belong. Recursive loops that appear functional but contain fatal flaws. Feedback triggers tied to external satellite arrays. The beginnings of a kill switch, buried so deep within the system's foundation that it looks like essential architecture.

Each line of sabotage is an act of love. For Gabe, who taught me to think tactically. For Hank, who showed me that patience and precision can topple empires. For the future we'll never have together.

My pulse hammers as I work, grief transforming into something colder and more focused. Sweat trickles down my spine despite the lab's arctic chill. The guards stare at my back, but they see only a broken woman following orders.

They don't see the weapon I'm becoming.

"Your hands are shaking." Elkin observes quietly, positioning himself to block the security camera's view of my screen.

"Grief." The word tastes like ashes. "It has physical symptoms."

But it's not just grief making my hands tremble. It's the adrenaline rush of rebellion, the terrifying thrill of building something that will destroy the man who destroyed everything I loved.

I type 'Gabe' instead of a variable name, catch myself, delete it, type the correct syntax. My subconscious keeps trying to memorialize them in code, to leave traces of their names in the digital architecture like flowers on a grave.

"He killed them to break me," I say softly, not looking away from the screen. "But all he did was give me a reason to be dangerous."

Elkin glances toward the guards, then back to me. Something shifts in his expression—recognition, perhaps, or respect for what I'm attempting.

"You'll get us both killed," he whispers.

"Maybe." I continue typing, sabotage flowing seamlessly into legitimate code structures. "But he killed them anyway. At least this way, their deaths serve a purpose."

Hours pass in a haze of keystrokes and carefully controlled breathing. Every few minutes, grief threatens to overwhelm me—a wave of loss so complete it steals my breath and blurs my vision. I force myself through these moments by focusing on the work, on the hidden poison I'm weaving into Malfor's digital empire.

The compile sequence finally completes. No alerts. No errors. The program appears perfect—a quantum communication network ready for deployment. The interface glows green with approval, unaware of the cancer nestled within its core.

Behind legitimate lines of code lies my legacy to Gabe and

Hank—a trigger that will blind Malfor's network when activated, scramble his commands, open backdoors for whoever might come next.

If anyone comes.

"It's done." My voice emerges steadier than I feel.

Elkin reviews the final output, his eyes tracking through code that looks flawless to external examination. Only someone with intimate knowledge of quantum entanglement protocols would notice the subtle anomalies, the elegant traps waiting to spring.

"You built a Trojan horse," he says quietly, something like admiration in his tone.

"I built a memorial." The correction feels important. "For the men who died trying to save us."

THIRTY-TWO

Three Miles

HANK

THE UNDERWATER WORLD ENVELOPS US IN EERIE SILENCE. Moonlight penetrates the first few feet, casting everything in ghostly blue-green light. I activate my rebreather, the familiar resistance as it scrubs carbon dioxide from my breath. Beside me, Gabe does the same, his movements slower but still precise despite his injury.

Fins deployed, we begin moving east toward shore. Rigel and Blake sandwich the pilots between them, sharing their rebreathers. Walt keeps close to Gabe, monitoring his condition. Carter and Jeb take point, establishing our heading.

Underwater movement brings its own challenges. The cold attacks more aggressively without the insulating layer of air between skin and water. Pressure builds in sinuses and eardrums. Vision narrows to shadowy shapes and vague directions.

We maintain formation, eight operators and two pilots moving through darkness with a singular purpose. The ocean above us lights up occasionally as search beams penetrate the surface, seeking wreckage or bodies.

They won't see us.

Ten minutes underwater feels like an eternity. Lungs begin to burn despite the rebreathers. Muscles protest the constant fight against water resistance. The cold seeps deeper, burrowing into bones.

Ethan signals our ascent. Slowly, cautiously, we rise to the surface, breaking the water with minimal disturbance. The pilots gasp for air, their limited underwater time taking its toll.

"Aircraft?" Ethan keeps his voice just above a whisper.

"Moving west." Rigel points toward distant lights. "Expanding search pattern away from us."

"They think we sank with the bird." Blake helps the co-pilot stay afloat.

"They think they killed us. Let's stay dead." Gabe breaks the silence, voice tight with pain. Blood continues to seep from his leg, but his eyes remain clear.

"They've done us a favor." I adjust my position to better support his position. "As of right now, we're off the grid. No one is tracking us. No one expects us."

"We've got about forty minutes before the cold becomes a serious problem." I check Gabe's leg again. "Bleeding's slowing. Needs attention when we hit land."

"What's the plan once we reach shore?" The pilot's question comes through chattering teeth.

Ethan doesn't hesitate. "We stick to the mission. Guardian HRS believes we're dead. So does Malfor."

"We find the women." Blake's voice carries quiet determination.

"We end this." Jeb's words fall like stones.

"Settle in. We swim for shore." Ethan looks at each of us in turn. "Conserve energy. Standard formation with wounded center. Questions?"

Silence answers him. We've trained for worse, survived worse. The parameters have changed, but the objective remains.

The aircraft lights disappear over the horizon, leaving us alone with the sea and the night.

"Move out." Ethan gives us our marching orders … Or rather, swim orders.

The ocean fights us with every stroke. Twenty minutes in, the cold seeps deeper. My fingers begin to lose sensation despite my thermal gloves. The first warning signs of hypothermia are setting in right on schedule.

"Keep moving." Ethan's voice carries across the water. "Halfway there."

Gabe's breathing grows labored as the combination of blood loss and cold takes its toll. I adjust my grip, taking more of his burden. He's hampered by the injured leg. Unable to swim effectively and keep up.

"I've got you." The words come naturally. Gabe and I are finally back in sync.

"Just like Bagram." Gabe's voice barely carries above the waves. "Remember?"

I do. Another extraction gone wrong. Another time I dragged his bleeding ass through hostile territory. "You were heavier then."

"Less swimming, more blood loss." His attempt at humor dissolves into a grimace.

The shore remains a distant shadow. My muscles burn with each stroke, the cold and exertion combining to drain strength. Still, I maintain my position, keeping Gabe afloat, matching my strokes to his weakening ones.

Thirty minutes in, the pilots begin to struggle, their lack of conditioning for this type of endurance evident. Rigel and Blake adjust their support, taking more of the civilians' burden. It's going to be a long ass swim.

"Status check." Ethan's voice is clipped. Strained.

"Moving." Rigel's reply comes between controlled breaths.

"Still here." Blake adjusts his position on the flank.

"Functional." Jeb maintains his position on point.

"Monitoring Gabe." Walt keeps medical watch.

"Comms intact." Carter confirms our connection to the outside world.

"Planning Malfor's retirement party." Gabe's voice weakens but still carries determination.

"Pilots stable." Blake reports on our civilian passengers.

"Two miles to go." I focus on the shoreline, now visible as a darker line against the night sky.

We push forward, each stroke a battle against the forces of physics and biology. The water temperature continues to leach our heat, sap our strength, and deteriorate our cognitive function.

"Current's shifting." Rigel's warning cuts through the sound of labored breathing. "Pushing us east."

"Compensate." Ethan adjusts his direction. "Forty-five degrees west."

We angle against the drift, burning precious energy to maintain course. My legs feel leaden, each kick heavier than the last. Drag from the packs slows us—extra weight, extra resistance. And that's before factoring in injuries.

Three miles through open ocean. Two-point-six nautical. In training conditions, that's an hour-eighteen. This? This is combat insertion. Wounded. Fully geared. Fighting currents and cold. Add another forty minutes. Maybe more.

At this pace, we're not just burning time—we're bleeding it.

And every minute lost is another minute too late. Two hours in, I hear it.

The rhythmic sound of waves breaking on the shore carries across the water. So close now, yet still so far. My legs kick, moving on willpower alone, muscles screaming for rest that can't come until we reach land.

"Watch for rocks." Ethan's warning brings renewed focus. "Coastline's jagged here."

The final stretch becomes a gauntlet. Waves grow stronger as we approach the shore, pushing us back, dragging us under—the land's last defense against invaders.

My hand strikes rock, then retreats with the wave. So close. Another stroke. Another. My knees scrape against stone, then lift with the retreating water.

"Forward." Ethan's command is barely audible above the surf. "Push through the break line."

One final wave crashes over us, tumbling bodies like rag dolls. I tighten my grip on Gabe, refusing to let the ocean claim him now. Not after everything we've survived.

And then—rock beneath my feet. Solid ground. The simple miracle of land after an eternity of water.

We drag ourselves past the water line, ten men collapse on wet rock, shivering violently as our bodies register the full extent of heat loss. No one speaks. No energy left for words.

One minute. Two. Just breathing. Just feeling solid ground beneath us.

"Status." Ethan finally breaks the silence, pushing himself to a sitting position.

"Alive." Rigel's single-word assessment is laughable.

"Checking Gabe's leg." I force myself to focus, examining the wound in the darkness.

"Perimeter secure." Blake scans the shoreline, professional even now.

"Need to get warm." Walt's medical training asserts itself. "Hypothermia setting in for all of us."

"Shelter first." Jeb forces himself to his feet, scanning the rocky shoreline. His eyes narrow, focusing on something in the darkness. "There."

I follow his gaze. A dark opening in the cliff face, barely

visible in the moonlight. Natural cave or coastal erosion, impossible to tell from this distance.

"How far?" Ethan struggles to his feet, swaying slightly.

"Hundred meters." Jeb points along the shoreline. "Looks accessible."

"Move." Ethan's command galvanizes us into action.

We help each other stand on shaking legs. Ten men who officially died in a helicopter crash, now ghosts on a hostile shore. Shivering, wounded, stripped of support and supplies.

I loop Gabe's arm over my shoulders, taking his weight. "One step at a time."

"Just like old times." His voice comes weak but determined.

"Shut up and walk." The familiar pattern of our interaction grounds me, gives me strength I didn't know I had left.

We make our way across the rocky shore, a ragged line of walking dead. Every step is an act of defiance against the ocean that tried to claim us, against the enemy who thinks they've won.

The cave mouth looms before us, a deeper darkness against the night. Jeb enters first, weapon drawn, clearing the space.

"Clear." His voice echoes slightly. "Goes back about thirty feet. Dry ground. Defensible position."

We stumble inside, helping each other over the uneven ground. The cave provides immediate shelter from the wind, and the temperature difference is noticeable even to cold-numbed skin.

We all reek of brine, blood, and exhaustion—except the two pilots laid out near the back, bundled in mylar, recovering from hypothermia.

Three miles in open ocean. In the dark. We nearly drowned out there, but it wasn't our day to die, but damn if it didn't try hard to be.

Rigel flops down next to Blake, huffing, dragging a hand through his drenched hair. "This is bullshit."

Walt moves to Gabe, helping him sit against the cave wall before examining his leg. "Need to clean and close this wound."

I help Walt clean Gabe's wound, holding the light stick while he works. The gash runs six inches down Gabe's outer thigh, deep enough to need stitches.

"Going to hurt." Walt prepares a needle from his medical kit, the thread already attached.

"Just do it." Gabe's jaw clenches in anticipation.

I place my hand on his shoulder, an unconscious gesture of support. "Remember Kandahar?"

"You mean when that farmer's kid tried to stitch me up with fishing line?" A ghost of a smile crosses his face, focusing on the memory instead of the present pain. "Said I'd live longer if I stopped screaming."

"You told him you'd live longer if he stopped sticking you with a rusty needle." I maintain eye contact as Walt begins stitching. "Then you gave him your last chocolate bar."

"Kid had steady hands." Gabe's fingers dig into my forearm as the needle pierces flesh again. "Unlike some medics I could name."

"Criticizing the guy with the needle?" Walt's voice carries dry humor despite the gravity of our situation. "Not a smart move."

The familiar banter helps all of us—gives Gabe something to focus on besides pain, gives Walt a rhythm for his work, gives me the illusion that something in our world remains normal.

Ten minutes later, Walt finishes the last stitch and applies a waterproof dressing. "That'll hold until we get somewhere with proper medical."

"Thanks." Gabe's face has gone pale, but his eyes remain clear.

"Rest now." Walt moves to check on the pilots, who look shell-shocked by their ordeal.

I help Gabe into a more comfortable position, arranging one

of the emergency blankets around both of us. Shared body heat is the most efficient way to combat hypothermia in field conditions.

"Like our first date." Gabe's attempt at humor comes through chattering teeth.

"You wish." I adjust the blanket to maximize coverage. "Our first date had a lot less blood and hypothermia."

"Debatable." His body shakes with cold, muscles involuntarily contracting as his core temperature struggles to stabilize.

"Gear assessment." Ethan slumps against the wall, voice ragged with exhaustion.

I check my waterproof pack, cataloging what survived. "Emergency blankets intact. Light sticks. Basic medical. Protein bars. Two magazines dry."

Similar reports come from the others. We've lost most of our equipment, but the essentials survived—enough to keep us alive, if not comfortable.

Ethan gestures to the team. "Everyone, pair up for warmth."

Standard cold-weather survival protocol. Shared body heat, emergency blankets, and minimal movement to conserve energy.

Across the cave, the others pair up—Ethan with one of the pilots, Walt with the other, Rigel with Blake, Jeb with Carter. Gabe and me.

Ten men reduced to shivering bodies huddled in a cave, fighting basic survival needs while planning their next move.

"Get some rest." Ethan's voice carries from the darkness. "Two-hour rotation for watch. Rigel first, then Blake, Walt, me."

"What's the plan?" Blake's question speaks for all of us.

"At first light, we assess our position, inventory gear, and treat injuries." Ethan's answer comes without hesitation.

The cave falls silent save for the sound of waves crashing against the rocks outside. Gabe shifts beside me, shivering from cold and blood loss.

I drift toward sleep, my body surrendering to exhaustion. Sometime later, Gabe's voice pulls me back.

"Hank." His words come softly, meant for me alone. "I hear something."

My eyes snap open; my senses are immediately alert, despite the bone-deep fatigue. I listen, filtering out the sound of waves, of breathing, of wind against rock.

Footsteps echo near the mouth of the cave—slow, deliberate. Every instinct fires hot. This place has no back door. No fallback. If someone found us, they mean to finish the job.

"Defensive positions." Ethan directs with hand signals, placing us to maximize cover and fields of fire.

"Just like old times." His attempt at humor does nothing to mask the gravity of our situation. I help Gabe into position behind a rock outcropping, ensuring he has a clear shot at the cave entrance while remaining protected.

"Shut up and aim straight." I position myself beside him, my SIG P226 feeling inadequate against an unknown number of hostiles.

Weapons rise in unison. Ethan lifts his rifle, Walt draws his sidearm, and Blake drops into a crouch beside me, jaw clenched.

We spent the night swimming three goddamn miles through freezing ocean in total blackness. No light. No comms. No rescue. And now someone's coming? Through this one entrance?

We stand or die here.

No one breathes.

THIRTY-THREE

Ghosts and Wolves

GABE

THE FOOTSTEPS GROW CLOSER. WHOEVER APPROACHES MAKES NO attempt at stealth. They know exactly where we are. The question is how—and who.

My pulse hammers against my ribs as I lock eyes with Hank. Firelight carves harsh shadows across his face, jaw tense, eyes calculating. We're cornered like wounded animals, cave wall at our backs, ocean beyond.

Rigel signals from the entrance—four figures approaching, heavily armed, moving toward our position.

I shift and hot pain lances through my leg. The bandage seeps dark again. If they're Malfor's men, we're cornered with minimal weapons and no escape. A perfect ending to their cleanup operation.

"If it's them, we make it count." Blake checks his sidearm, metal clicking against the damp cave walls.

I nod, tasting salt and copper. We won't go easily.

A silhouette steps into the light. Tall. Confident. Everything about him screams a different kind of predator.

"Easy, boys." His voice scrapes like gravel, tinged with amusement. "Unless one of you is feeling froggy."

"Identify." Ethan keeps the rifle trained on center mass.

"Ghost." The man steps forward, flanked by three others. Flickering light reveals battle-worn faces and dead eyes. He gestures to each shadow behind him. "Brass. Halo. Whisper."

Silence crashes down.

Cerberus. The unit that shouldn't exist. The ghosts that operate so deep in shadow, most of us thought they were just stories to scare recruits.

"Cerberus?" Blake straightens, disbelief raw on his face.

"How the hell are you here?" Ethan's voice stays glacial, but disbelief flickers in his eyes.

"Your little swan dive off that bird puts us exactly where we want to be." Ghost's voice cuts too smoothly, too calculated for what comes next. "Guardian HRS thinks you're dead, and so does Malfor."

The cave shrinks around us.

"What the fuck does that mean?" Blake's shoulders bunch up tight.

"It means you weren't informed, but your crash was part of the plan." Ghost delivers the bombshell without blinking.

"I don't know what the fuck you're smoking." Walt shakes his head violently. "Our chopper took a direct hit. I was there. I saw it."

"Yeah, that part wasn't in the plan." Ghost's eyes narrow slightly. "Made it look extra real though, didn't it?"

"Bullshit." Rigel surges to his feet. "We nearly fucking died out there."

"This?" I gesture to my blood-soaked leg. "This shit is real."

Ghost's shoulders rise and fall. "Sometimes shit happens. Mission complications. You weren't supposed to get injured."

Ethan takes a dangerous step forward. "Mission complications?"

"Injured?" Hank's voice drops to a whisper that's somehow more frightening than Rigel's shout. "You put us through hell without warning."

"You're saying that near-death ocean swim was intentional?" Hank's voice is low, menacing.

Ghost doesn't flinch. "The plan was always for Charlie team to go down. Chopper takes a hit. Team swims to safety. Cerberus provides shadow support."

"We were meant to crash?" The words slam into my chest. My throat closes. "To swim?"

"You knew?" Hank looks from Ghost to the pilots huddled under their mylar blankets.

One pilot drops his gaze. "Only the flight team was cleared. Full comms blackout. Couldn't risk Malfor intercepting anything."

Betrayal floods my mouth, bitter as bile. I remember endless strokes through black water, burning muscles, death circling behind us like a shark.

"Jesus." Blake rubs his hand down his face.

"Would've been nice to get the memo." Rigel's voice rises, heat blazing off him.

Ghost shrugs. "Three miles in the ocean, in the dark. Not your day to die. Guardian HRS knows that. Malfor doesn't. He doesn't know you're more resilient than he thinks."

Halo slams a battered black case onto the rocks. The lid hisses open, revealing rows upon rows of sleek, deadly bumblebee drones glowing under an ominous red light. Not a dozen—a hundred. Each is no bigger than my thumb but humming with lethal purpose.

"If you girls are done crying about your funeral and if your feelings aren't too butt-hurt no one sent you a sympathy card, maybe we can get back to saving your women?" Halo's eyes sweep over us, a smirk begging for someone to try him. "Or are we gonna sit here and braid each other's hair?"

The words sting like a slap.

Nobody speaks. Our eyes burn with enough fire to answer.

"Thought so." Halo flicks a switch. The drones blink to life—engines whining, wings flexing, sensors pulsing with predatory intent.

The swarm awakens.

I exhale hard. The sight of those drones—vengeful metal angels—sends fresh adrenaline flooding my system. My anger shifts, refocusing on Malfor and finding Ally.

"As you know, Collins pulled together a team of scientists for a Trojan horse project—some of you pulled guard duty, if I remember right." Ghost's voice drops low, charged with dark electricity.

"Yeah." Rigel grunts. "We didn't think it was done."

"It is. Those little stingers are full of it. Live, locked, and loaded." Ghost juts his chin toward the drones now vanishing into darkness. "They'll map the facility, locate your women, and infect Malfor's entire nanobot network at the source."

"This swarm isn't just recon—it's a kill switch?" The brilliance of it hits me in waves.

"You catch on quick." Ghost's smirk sharpens to a blade edge. "This Trojan horse doesn't just get us in. It burns his system to the ground from the inside out. We're not just saving your women. We're destroying everything that sick bastard built."

The swarm hum fades, but something inside me surges hotter—relentless, electric, impossible to extinguish. Vengeance taking flight.

Time to end this.

"The bees are weaponized?" Walt's eyes widen.

"They carry a nano payload." Halo taps the case. "Once the

hive releases, it finds the primary node Malfor's network uses to route updates. The Trojan horse piggybacks from there."

"Like a virus." Understanding clicks into place. "It'll look like a regular update to the system, but once it's in …"

"It corrupts everything." Whisper speaks for the first time. His voice sounds oddly gentle for a man bristling with enough firepower to level a village. "Malfor's nanobots will tear themselves apart."

"We didn't know it was finished." Hank's voice roughens. "Didn't know how it was going in."

"You do now." Ghost's eyes flick to mine.

The hum starts before we see movement—soft, electric. The swarm lifts and slips into the night through the cave mouth. I watch them disappear, knowing these tiny machines carry not just the hope of finding the women, but also of destroying Malfor's empire.

"Once they're inside, they'll start mapping." Brass checks a tablet screen. "They won't last long. Malfor's resident nanobots will identify and neutralize them quickly."

"But not before they deliver the payload." Ghost rubs his stubbled jaw.

"That's all well and good." Ethan gestures to our soaked, tattered gear. "But we lost everything in the crash. Our clothes are probably infested with nanobots already."

"Not likely." Ghost jerks his chin toward the pilots. "They EMP'd everything before going down."

The pilots nod in confirmation. Another round of crucial information they kept to themselves.

"That three-mile swim was good punishment for keeping that quiet." Carter laughs without humor. "Look at them—exhausted."

"Brought you boys some party favors." Ghost kicks a stack of waterproof bags I hadn't noticed before. "Clean gear. No nanobot infestation. Full tactical kits, helmets, headsets, ballistic vests, body armor, new boots, dry socks."

Brass tosses a box toward Blake. "MREs. Three thousand calories each. Swimming through three miles of ocean tends to burn through your reserves."

Blake tears into the packaging like a starving wolf. "Chili mac. Jackpot."

"Trade you for my beef stew." Walt already has his MRE open and eyes Blake's meal with naked envy.

"Not a chance." Blake clutches his MRE protectively. "I pulled this fair and square."

"Jalapeño cheese spread?" Rigel dangles the packet. "Prime trade material right here."

"Done." Walt snatches it instantly, surrendering his M&Ms without hesitation.

I rip into my own MRE. Doesn't matter what it is. Fuel is fuel, and my body screams for calories after the endless swimming and blood loss. The first bite hits my tongue—some kind of pasta—and suddenly I'm ravenous. We all are. The cave fills with the sounds of men devouring food.

"You animals ever hear of chewing?" Halo watches with disgusted fascination.

"Try swimming three miles with an injured leg." I don't look up from my meal. "Then judge my table manners."

Halo just snorts, but there's something almost like respect in his eyes.

We finish eating in minutes, crushing empty packets and stowing trash with the efficiency of men accustomed to leaving no trace. The calories hit my bloodstream like rocket fuel, clearing the fog that had settled in my brain. My body still aches, but the desperate emptiness is gone.

We take turns changing into dry gear. The relief of clean, dry clothing against the skin is almost as satisfying as the food. The bleeding in my leg has slowed to nearly nothing.

Brass sets another case by the wall. "Arms and munitions. Enough to outfit an army. Or eight determined men."

"Status?" Ghost glances at Whisper, who monitors the drone feed.

"First units reaching the compound perimeter now."

"Once the hive maps the compound—" Ethan watches the last drones vanish.

"—we find the girls." I finish his thought.

"And how are we supposed to get to them?" Hank's jaw tightens. "Waltz through the front gate?"

"Drainage tunnel. Sea-level. We scoped it out." Ghost laughs, the sound of stones grinding together.

"Another swim?" Rigel groans.

"Three miles at night should've been nothing for girls like you." Brass grins.

"Careful. I'm injured, not deaf." I glare at him.

The banter feels good and pushes back the anxiety gnawing at my mind. The fear that we might be too late. That Ally might already be—

No. Can't think that way.

The women are too valuable to Malfor. He'll keep them alive. They're bait in his elaborate game—chess pieces he's positioned carefully. This whole scenario reeks of a trap designed to lure in Guardian HRS and what's left of Charlie team. The women are his leverage, his insurance. He needs them breathing.

Which means we're walking straight into his trap. Unless— our untimely "demise" has already ruined his plans. The thought lands like ice in my gut. With Charlie team "dead," the women lose their value as bait. Maybe he's already decided to eliminate them, erase the evidence, clean up loose ends.

I glance at Hank across the shadowed cave. His eyes meet

mine, jaw muscle pulsing beneath his skin. No words needed. I can read it in the tight line of his mouth, and the slight forward tilt of his body, he's thinking the same thing.

Every second counts now.

"Okay, so we grab the girls. Then what? We're still behind enemy lines. What's our exfil?" Blake's voice scrapes rough.

"Yeah, how do we get them out? Through the front gate?" Walt's voice carries exhaustion and hope.

The question hangs over us all. Getting in is one thing. Getting out with civilians is another beast entirely.

"Exfil's already waiting." Ghost glances toward the cave mouth. "My team's got RIBs staged offshore. Once we've got the girls, we move to the drop point. Rappel down the cliffs, load up, and vanish into the dark. Clean. Fast. Silent."

A beat of silence.

"Copy that." Ethan nods once.

We have a way in and a way out—a real shot at pulling this off.

Ghost moves to the center of our makeshift shelter. "Once the hive feeds back info, we move out. You've got eight men. We've got four. That's twelve operators. We ghost in. We ghost out."

"Copy that." Ethan's voice hardens with resolve.

I shift, and pain spikes through my leg. But my pulse steadies. For the first time since hitting the water, something close to hope flares in my chest.

"They're inside." Whisper stares at his screen. "Starting to map. Getting layout data."

Malfor's about to learn what happens when you take something from men like us.

THIRTY-FOUR

Into the Drainage Tunnel

GABE

THE BUMBLEBEES LIMP BACK WITH FRAGMENTED INTEL. BROKEN. Destroyed. But not before delivering their deadly payload and mapping enough of the compound for our mission.

"Drainage tunnel entrance coordinates locked." Whisper's tablet bathes his scarred face in ghostly blue light, his eyes reflecting code sequences and death.

My SIG weighs a thousand pounds tonight. I slide my finger along the barrel, feeling every scratch, every kill etched into its metal. Around me, men transform into machines—methodical hands checking magazines, sealing waterproof packs, tightening tactical straps.

The cave holds its breath.

"Ninety minutes, max, before Malfor's system detects the corruption." Ghost cuts through our silence with a voice like gravel over bone. "Drone swarm released the Trojan package before neutralization."

"After that?" Ethan's eyes reflect firelight, twin flames of focused rage.

"After that, all hell breaks loose." Ghost's shoulders rise and fall, casual as discussing dinner plans. "Nanobots tearing each other apart. Security systems failing. Backup generators kicking in."

"Chaos." The word tastes metallic on my tongue, like blood and victory mixed. Perfect. We thrive in chaos when others drown in it. Hank grins beside me. Like him, I'm eager to get this show on the road.

Rigel crouches beside one of the pilots, who sits alert against the cave wall. "You good to man comms?"

"I'll be your eyes topside." The pilot checks the equipment. His hands steady.

The tablet, earpiece, and sidearm we leave him look pathetically inadequate against the crushing darkness of the cave.

"Three miles to target. Remember, we're ghosts. No trace." Ghost scans each face, memorizing our features like a commander tallying his troops before a suicide mission.

Hank stares through the cave opening where moonlight fractures across black water. "Just like old times."

Something electric crackles through the air. Understanding. Resolve. Hunger.

Yes. This time, we willingly embrace the crushing ocean. This time we choose to hunt. This time, we become the nightmares that stalk other men's darkness.

"Comms check." Whisper taps his ear, the tiny movement focusing everyone's attention.

Twelve voices breathe confirmation one by one. Whispers in the dark.

"Let's hunt." Ghost's nod sends us into motion.

The ocean swallows us whole. My injured leg screams rebellion. I shove the pain into a dark corner of my mind and lock the door. Pain belongs to tomorrow.

Black water. Black sky. Black purpose.

Waves smash against jagged rocks, spray raining down like ice shards. Every stroke resurrects yesterday's nightmare—endless miles, burning muscles, death circling beneath. But fear finds no purchase tonight. Tonight, I am the creature other men fear.

Ally's face appears in my mind each time I surface for air. Pale. Beautiful. Alive.

She has to be alive.

"Contact point ahead. Fifty meters." Ghost's voice slithers through my earpiece.

The cliff face towers above us, darker than the night sky it scrapes against. Waves hammer stone walls, spray whipping in the wind. I time my strokes with the surging water, letting it carry me forward, then fight its greedy pull as it retreats.

There is a deeper wound in the rock face. The tunnel mouth.

Ghost and Brass vanish into that darkness first. Whisper treads water beside me, tablet held above the churning surface. I follow Hank toward the opening, fighting currents that want to pulverize us against stone.

"Entrance secure." Ghost's voice crackles through the comms.

The tunnel swallows me, its mouth barely wider than my shoulders. Cold stone scrapes against my wetsuit as I haul myself inside. The stench hits like a rogue wave—rot and waste and chemical death. My stomach coils into knots.

"Grate ahead." Ghost's warning echoes back through darkness.

Walt edges forward, tools appearing in his hands like extensions of his fingers. His waterproof flashlight catches metal teeth —a rusted barrier blocking our advance. The snip of his cutters through corroded bars sounds deafening in the confined space.

"Real tight." Blake eyes the narrow opening as Walt pulls the grate free.

Rigel's teeth flash white in the darkness. "Too tight for you?"

"Watch me." Blake's eyes narrow to slits.

He forces his massive frame through the gap, shoulders scraping both sides of the passage. His grunt rebounds through the tunnel, amplified by concrete and water.

"Single file." Ghost's finger jabs forward.

The passage narrows further, angles upward. No more swimming—just crawling on elbows and knees over slick concrete that reeks of decades of filth. Water trickles past, carrying unidentifiable things that brush against my hands in the darkness. The stench intensifies—chemical waste, decomposing matter, and something metallic that coats my tongue and burns my sinuses.

My injured leg drags behind me, each movement detonating fresh explosions up my spine. My teeth clench against the pain.

Just keep moving.

The walls press closer. The ceiling lowers. Thousands of tons of earth and concrete crushing down from above. My breath comes faster, shallower. The darkness thickens, becoming almost solid. We're crawling straight into hell's throat.

"Motion sensor." Brass's urgent hiss halts our advance.

Every muscle locks. Brass extracts a small penlight from his pocket.

"Infrared bypass loop." His whisper barely carries back to us. "Oldest trick in the book."

My lungs burn. Sweat trickles down my back despite the cold. If that sensor triggers …

"Clear. Move slowly past this junction." Brass's voice releases us from our paralysis.

We inch forward, bodies pressed against slime-slick walls. The tunnel splits—one path continuing upward, another branching left.

"Maintenance access fifty meters ahead." Whisper consults his tablet. "Left."

The passage widens slightly. Our spines straighten from crawl to crouch, weapons ready. Water still trickles beneath our boots, but it's less now, barely covering the concrete.

"Hatch leads to a maintenance courtyard on the compound's south edge." Ghost pauses, voice dropping even lower. "Access point ahead."

"Security?" Ethan's question floats forward.

"Two cameras, wide-angle. Blind spot directly below the hatch."

My watch reads thirty-seven minutes since we entered the tunnel. The luminescent dial glows faintly green against the darkness.

Ghost stops at a metal ladder bolted into concrete. Above us, a circular hatch catches what little light penetrates this deep.

"Malfor's security focuses on the main gate and airfield." Ghost runs his fingers along the ladder's lowest rung. "Swarm intel shows minimal guard presence in this quadrant. This back corner houses machinery, water treatment, and power distribution."

"Perfect." Ethan's voice carries the first hint of satisfaction I've heard since we hit water.

Ghost turns his head toward Whisper. "Status on the Trojan horse?"

"Twenty percent integration." Whisper's eyes never leave his tablet. "Spreading through the system."

"Charlie team, head east once we're up." Ghost sweeps his gaze across our faces, eyes hard as flint in the dim light. "Your women are held in the subbasement of the main building, north quadrant. Cerberus will move west, secure the server hub, and ensure total system corruption."

"Rendezvous?" Ethan shifts his weight, already planning three steps ahead.

"North perimeter fence, zero-two-hundred. Extract through

the blind spot we identified. If anyone misses rendezvous, secondary extract at the cliff base, zero-three-hundred."

My fingers tighten around my weapon until my knuckles crack. We won't miss the rendezvous, not with our women.

"Questions?" Ghost scans our faces.

Silence answers. We all know what's at stake.

"I'll take point. Brass, cover. Everyone else, ten-second intervals." Ghost's hand reaches for the ladder.

The hatch opens with a whisper of metal. Ghost vanishes through the gap, then Brass follows. One by one, we ascend.

Cool night air rushes into my lungs as I emerge, the sudden absence of the tunnel's stench almost dizzying. A small concrete courtyard surrounds us, hemmed in by chain-link topped with glinting razor wire. Generator housings and massive water tanks create a maze of shadows. Distant lights from the main compound bleed against the low clouds, casting everything in a sickly yellow glow.

Somewhere beyond those lights, Ally breathes that same air.

We converge in the shadow of a towering water tank. Ghost kneels, unfolding a device that projects a ghostly blue blueprint onto the concrete.

"Security grid starting to glitch. Camera feeds are looping. Electronic locks are cycling randomly." Something almost like pleasure flickers across Ghost's face. "The Trojan horse is working."

"Maybe forty minutes before full system collapse." Whisper glances up from his tablet. "We've got a nice window."

"This is where we split." Ghost lifts his eyes to Ethan. "Charlie team, you know your objective."

"We do." Steel hardens Ethan's voice.

"Happy hunting." Ghost's hand extends between them. For a heartbeat, something almost human crosses his face.

"You too." Ethan clasps the offered hand.

Cerberus dissolves into shadows. Four wraiths swallowed by darkness, bound for a mission history will never record.

"Formation delta." Ethan turns toward us, voice barely disturbing the air. "I'll take point. Hank, you're two. Gabe, you're three. Walt and Blake cover our six. Rigel, Carter, and Jeb, watch our flanks."

My heart hammers against my ribs, adrenaline flooding my system, washing away the pain. Nothing exists but the mission. The objective. The hunt.

Ally.

"We move fast. We hit hard. We leave nothing behind but bodies." Ethan's eyes lock with each of ours, forging connections stronger than words.

"All of us." Hank's voice carries the weight of promise. "We *all* go home."

All of us. The men. The women. Ally. Everyone.

Ethan's sharp nod launches us into motion. "Move out."

We flow between shadows toward the main compound, eight separate killers merging into one lethal organism. Each silent footstep brings us closer.

Closer to our targets. Closer to our women.

The hunt begins.

THIRTY-FIVE

The Stranger's Gift

ALLY

HEAVY BOOTS ECHO FROM THE CORRIDOR, APPROACHING AT A clipped pace. My time runs out as the lab door hisses open, admitting four fresh guards with rifles slung across tactical vests.

"Back to your cell." The lead guard gestures with his weapon.

As they reapply restraints to my wrists, I look back at the terminal one last time. The quantum network sits there, innocent and deadly, waiting for deployment. Malfor will activate it, thinking he's gained ultimate power.

Instead, he'll have armed his own destruction.

"They're not coming," Elkin says as the guards prepare to lead me away. It's not a question.

"No. But what I built in their memory will outlive all of us."

The guards march me back through silent corridors, their grips unnecessarily tight against my arms. We're halfway to the cellblock when the floor beneath us shudders—a distant vibration that ripples through concrete like a stone dropped in still water.

The lights flicker once, twice, and then stabilize.

"Check that." The lead guard stops, head tilting as he listens to his earpiece. "Was that—"

Static breaks across their communication system, fragmenting whatever response comes through. The guards exchange glances, uneasiness bleeding through professional facades.

Another tremor rolls beneath our feet, stronger this time. Dust sifts from ceiling joints, powdering our shoulders with concrete snow. The guards' radios erupt with overlapping voices—too garbled to distinguish words, but the tone is unmistakable.

The first whispers of chaos.

They practically throw me into my cell, door slamming with that familiar magnetic thunk. The lead guard barks something into his radio, then gestures for the others to follow as they hurry back down the corridor, leaving only one man on watch.

Jenna lifts her head in the adjacent cell, eyes finding mine through the bars. No words pass between us, but understanding flows in that silent exchange—something's happening. Something outside Malfor's meticulous control.

"You're not winning," I whisper into the darkness, thinking of the quantum time bomb I've planted in his digital infrastructure. "Not tonight. Not ever."

The remaining guard paces before our cells, hand resting on his sidearm, eyes constantly checking his radio. The building trembles again, and somewhere in the distance, an alarm begins to wail.

Malfor's voice cuts through the cellblock speakers, calm despite the chaos unfolding around us.

"Containment breach in sector seven. All security personnel to assigned stations. This is not a drill."

The guard's radio crackles to life, spitting fragmented orders that send him running toward the exit, leaving our cellblock unguarded for the first time since our arrival.

"What's happening?" Rebel pulls herself upright, split face gleaming wetly in the dim light.

"I don't know." The admission costs nothing now. "But whatever it is, Malfor didn't plan for it."

"Another rescue attempt?" Malia uncurls from her protective huddle, something like awareness returning to her vacant expression.

"After what happened to Charlie team?" Mia's voice cracks with disbelief. "Who would try again?"

The memory of exploding helicopters cuts through me like a blade, but underneath the pain is something else—the cold satisfaction of knowing I've planted a weapon in Malfor's heart. Even if no rescue comes, even if we all die here, my sabotage will ensure he doesn't win.

I did it for you. Grief and fury braiding together in my chest. *I'll never see you again, but I made sure your deaths meant something.*

The alarms increase in pitch and frequency, echoing through the compound. The tremors intensify, and concrete dust now steadily drifts down from above. The lights flicker more persistently, plunging us into momentary darkness before reluctantly returning.

Hope is dangerous—more dangerous than despair, more painful than grief. But something is happening. Something unplanned. Something that has Malfor's perfectly controlled world fracturing at its edges.

And buried deep in his quantum network, my digital memorial to Gabe and Hank waits to activate, ready to turn his greatest weapon into his ultimate downfall.

The thought carries me through the chaos—not hope for rescue, but satisfaction that their sacrifice will not be in vain. Whatever comes next, Malfor will learn that some love burns too bright to be extinguished, even by death.

The cellblock door slides open with a soft hydraulic hiss. A figure appears in the threshold, silhouetted against emergency lighting, tactical gear gleaming dully in the red glow. Not one of

Malfor's regular guards—the profile is wrong, the stance unfamiliar.

"Containment located." The voice—female, accented, unknown—speaks into a communications device. "Six subjects confirmed alive. Proceeding with preparatory measures."

The stranger steps fully into the light, revealing a face mask and night-vision goggles that obscure all identifying features. Only one thing is certain—this is not Guardian HRS. Not their equipment. Not their extraction procedures.

"Who are you?" Jenna's question cuts through the uncertainty.

The stranger tilts her head, considering the question as she approaches the cells. "Consider me a—concerned third party." Her accent carries hints of Eastern Europe, precise consonants, and stretched vowels. "With interests that temporarily align with yours."

She produces a device from her tactical vest—a small, black rectangle with blinking lights that cast eerie shadows across the walls. When she presses it against the control panel beside Jenna's cell, the magnetic locks disengage with a soft click.

"Who sent you?" Stitch demands as the stranger moves to her cell next, repeating the process.

The locks on all six cells disengage in sequence, and the doors slide open. Freedom after endless captivity—the sensation overwhelms, vertigo threatening to buckle knees and steal breath.

But we all stand proud.

"The collars." My hand rises automatically to the metal band around my throat. "They're remote-controlled. Explosive."

"I'm aware." The stranger produces another device, this one more complex. "Hold still."

The collar around my neck clicks open, falling away like a dead thing. The sudden absence of weight brings tears to my eyes. The skin beneath is raw, tender—and when the air hits it, it stings. Freedom burns in its own way.

One by one, she removes all our collars, speaking only when necessary. When the last collar falls to the floor, she steps back, surveying us with clinical interest.

"You work for Guardian HRS?" Malia asks, hope threading through her voice as she rubs her newly bare neck.

"No." The stranger's response is clipped, final. "And my assistance ends here. I've disabled the corridor surveillance and security locks through the west wing. The rest is up to you."

"You're leaving us?" Rebel's face contorts with disbelief, the gash on her cheek pulling with the expression. "After getting us this far?"

"I have other objectives. More pressing matters." The stranger backs toward the door, never fully turning away from us. "Consider yourselves fortunate that our interests briefly aligned."

"Wait…" I step forward, desperate for answers. "Malfor's quantum network—"

"Will remain operational." Her hand rests on the door frame. "For now. That's a problem for another day."

Mia shakes her head in confusion. "I don't understand. Why help us at all if you're going to abandon us halfway?"

"I never said I was rescuing you." The stranger's voice softens fractionally. "I'm merely—evening the odds."

Before anyone can respond, she slips back through the door, pausing just long enough to add: "The west corridor leads to an equipment depot. Weapons, communications, and basic supplies. I suggest you hurry. This distraction won't last forever."

With that, she vanishes into the red-tinged darkness beyond, leaving six stunned women standing in open cells, collars lying useless on the floor around them.

"What the hell just happened?" Rebel breaks the silence, voicing what all of us are thinking.

"Questions later. Right now, we move." Jenna steps cautiously into the corridor, checking both directions before gesturing us forward.

"She could be leading us into a trap." Stitch's natural suspicion resurfaces with her freedom. "This could all be Malfor's sick game."

"Or it could be our only chance." I pick up one of the discarded collars and examine the deactivated circuitry. "Either way, standing here debating it wastes time."

The distant sounds of combat continue—gunfire, explosions, shouted orders carried through ventilation systems. Something significant is happening elsewhere in the compound, diverting attention and resources away from our cell block.

Malia helps Mia to her feet, steadying her as they move toward the corridor. "West wing. Equipment depot. That's what she said."

"Then west we go." Jenna takes point.

We move into the corridor as a group, six women finding strength in each other. The red emergency lighting transforms familiar paths into alien territory, shadows stretching and contracting with each flicker of failing systems.

The stranger's parting gift—freedom to choose our escape— feels simultaneously empowering and terrifying. No one is leading us. No one is guiding us. Just our wits and whatever mysterious distraction is occupying Malfor's forces.

Rebel pauses at the junction where the corridor splits east and west, looking back at the cellblock that held us captive for so long. "Who was that woman? And why would she help us?"

"Maybe she wasn't helping us at all." Stitch's voice carries the edge of someone piecing together a complex puzzle. "Maybe we're just convenient cover for whatever she's really after."

"Right now, I don't care." Jenna checks the western corridor before gesturing us forward.

Freedom tastes strange on my tongue—metallic and sharp, laced with adrenaline and fear. The absence of the collar feels wrong after so many days, my body not yet adjusted to its removal. My hand keeps rising to my throat, fingers finding only raw skin where metal used to be.

We've barely taken three steps when a sound freezes us in place—footsteps. Multiple sets. Moving fast. Coming our way.

"Back." Jenna's command is barely a whisper, urgent hand signals directing us to retreat.

We scramble back toward the cellblock, instinct driving us to the only territory we know. The footsteps grow louder—not the shuffling gait of regular guards but the precise, measured cadence of tactical teams. Professional. Dangerous.

Stitch pulls us into the cellblock, positioning herself beside the door frame, back pressed against the wall. The others follow her lead, flattening themselves against walls, ducking behind what little cover the room provides.

My heart slams against my ribs, sounding so loud I'm certain it will give us away. The footsteps approach, slowing as they near our position. A voice murmurs something unintelligible, followed by the distinctive sound of weapons being readied.

"Stack up." The voice is clearer now, male, commanding— definitely not Malfor's guards.

Malia's fingers dig into my arm, terror and confusion warring in her expression. Jenna signals for absolute stillness, her one good hand forming the universal sign for silence.

The door at the corridor's end hisses open. Then footsteps approach our final door.

"Three." The voice counts down, each number tightening the knot in my stomach. "Two. One."

THIRTY-SIX

Split the Pack

HANK

Ghost's team melts west into shadow. Our eight-man unit waits three heartbeats, then moves east through the maintenance yard. No words. No signals. Just years of training and the singular focus of men with nothing left to lose.

My pulse stays steady. Breathing even.

Ethan signals with his finger, tapping the air. I confirm, moving ahead through the narrow passage between industrial pumps and piping. Gabe stays on my right, compensating for his injured leg by moving in short, deliberate bursts.

Moonlight bleeds through cloud cover. Not ideal. Too much visibility.

The detention wing is located in the north quadrant, connected to the main lab complex by an enclosed walkway. Three stories down. According to Whisper's intel, our women are being held in a specially constructed containment cell.

My jaw locks at the thought.

"Two tangos, north corner." Ethan's voice whispers through the comms.

Guards in black tactical gear, carrying what look like modified P90s. Experimental shit. Wonderful.

I catch Carter's eye, tip my head slightly. He nods, understanding instantly. We move in perfect sync, hugging the shadows and closing the distance.

Ten yards. Five. Three.

The first guard never sees me. My forearm locks around his throat, cutting off blood flow to the brain. His partner turns just as Carter's blade finds the soft spot beneath his ear. Both men drop to the concrete without a sound.

Walt and Blake secure the bodies while Rigel keeps watch. Jeb grabs the weapon and examines it.

"Biometric lock," he murmurs. "Useless to us."

I nod. Expected as much. Malfor's tech doesn't play well with strangers.

We move deeper into the compound. The layout matches Whisper's schematics. A service door. A maintenance corridor. A security checkpoint.

"Camera," Gabe warns.

We freeze, pressing against walls. The camera swivels, mechanical eye scanning the empty hallway, then locks suddenly, jerking in place.

"The Trojan horse is working," Rigel breathes. "Glitching their systems."

"Thirty seconds," Ethan cautions.

We slip past in pairs. Gabe limps beside me, teeth clenched against pain. His bandage shows fresh blood. I don't mention it. He'd tell me to fuck off anyway.

Whisper's voice crackles through comms. "Charlie team, be advised. Cerberus has breached the server hub. Initiating system override."

"Copy," Ethan responds. "Status on subjects?"

"Detecting six female biosignatures. Sublevel B, east quadrant."

All alive. Relief floods my system, but I don't let it show.

Another corridor. Another silent takedown. My muscles move through the familiar dance of death, no hesitation, no regret. These men chose their side.

"Contact," Blake warns suddenly.

A guard rounds the corner ahead, spots Rigel before anyone can react. His hand flies to his sidearm.

Walt moves with startling speed for his size. Three steps and he's on the guard, massive hand clamping over mouth and nose. The guard's eyes bulge as Walt's other arm drives upward, the combat knife finding the soft underside of the jaw. Blood sprays across the wall in an arterial arc.

Too loud. Too messy.

We freeze, waiting for alarms. For shouts. For anything.

Nothing.

"Move the body," Ethan orders.

Blake and Walt drag the corpse into a maintenance closet. The blood trail remains, dark against white tile.

"Secure the junction," I tell Carter. "Jeb, watch our six."

We press deeper into the facility. The sterile corridors give way to a more clinical section. Labs. Testing facilities. The walls here gleam under harsh fluorescent light.

A familiar scent hits me. Floral. Delicate. My heart rate spikes.

"Hold," I whisper, moving toward a small table against the wall.

A woman's ID badge lies discarded beside a clipboard. The photo shows a face I don't recognize. Blood stains one corner of the plastic.

"Hank." Gabe's voice holds warning.

I pocket the badge, face grim. "Moving."

Ethan watches me, eyes unreadable behind tactical gear. He knows. We all know. The women aren't just alive—they're fighting back.

"Cerberus update," Whisper's voice returns. "Primary security grid compromised. Secondary systems engaged. Proceeding to the command center."

Through my earpiece, I catch muffled sounds of combat. Brass cursing. The wet impact of a knife finding flesh. Ghost's cold voice: "Clear."

Our path leads downward. Service stairs. Emergency lighting that flickers with the Trojan horse's spreading influence. The stairwell stinks of antiseptic and something else—a metallic, alien scent that makes my skin crawl.

Sublevels. Where men like Malfor hide their darkest work.

"Multiple heat signatures ahead," Jeb warns. "Lab coats, not tactical."

Scientists. Not fighters. Still dangerous in their own way.

"Bypass if possible," Ethan orders.

We edge along the corridor, finding an alternative route through what appears to be a storage area. Shelves of equipment. Boxes of supplies. Strange containers filled with shimmering liquid that seems to move with purpose.

"Don't touch anything," I warn.

"No shit," Blake mutters.

A sound above makes us freeze. Metal scraping against metal. The ceiling vents.

"Drone," Rigel breathes.

We press against the walls, weapons ready. A small spherical object drops from the vent, hovering at eye level. Not like any drone I've seen before. This thing pulses with inner light, its surface crawling with what looks like liquid metal.

"Shit," Walt whispers. "Nanobot construct."

The drone rotates slowly, sensors probing the darkness. My finger tightens on the trigger.

"Hold," Ethan commands. "It might trigger an alarm."

The drone drifts closer to Gabe's position. He doesn't breathe. Doesn't blink. The machine hovers inches from his face, then abruptly turns, rising back toward the ceiling vent.

"It's cataloging," Jeb whispers. "Mapping changes to the environment."

The drone disappears into the ventilation system.

"Move," Ethan orders. "Now."

We double-time through the storage area, reaching another corridor. The map says we're close. Two more junctions. A security door. Then the holding cells.

The overhead lights flicker, then die completely. Emergency lights kick on, bathing everything in a blood-red glow.

"Phase two initiated," Whisper updates. "Main power compromised. Backup systems failing."

Good. Chaos works in our favor.

"—reading unusual power fluctuations in your sector," Whisper continues, voice breaking through static. "Possible—"

The transmission cuts abruptly.

"Whisper?" Ethan tries. "Cerberus? Report."

Nothing but dead air.

"Comms are down," Carter confirms, checking his equipment.

"Keep moving," I say. "We stick to the plan."

"The plan was shit before we lost comms," Blake points out.

"The plan is all we've got," Gabe counters, voice tight with pain.

We continue forward, more cautious now. Blind. Cut off. The holding cells can't be far.

A voice suddenly booms through hidden speakers, echoing down sterile corridors. Smooth. Cultured. Amused.

"Gentlemen of Charlie team. How disappointing. I arranged such an elaborate funeral for you. And yet here you are, rudely refusing to stay dead."

Malfor.

"I must congratulate you on your resilience. Three miles is quite the swim, especially with injuries. And infiltrating my facility? Impressive. Truly."

I scan the ceiling, looking for cameras, speakers, any sign of surveillance.

"Your women have been quite resilient. Remarkable specimens. Though I'm afraid Ms. Collins has been particularly—difficult. Such spirit."

Gabe's eyes flash with rage. I place a hand on his arm.

"Steady."

"I'm afraid your little electronic infection is quite ingenious. It's causing all sorts of fascinating chaos in my systems. Unfortunately for you, I maintain analog backups."

Metal doors slam shut ahead and behind us. The sound of mechanical locks engaging echoes through the corridor.

"You have exactly two minutes before this section floods with a particularly unpleasant neurotoxin. I suggest you use that time to reflect on your life choices."

Ethan signals immediately. "Alternate route. Air ducts."

Walt rips a ventilation cover from the wall, metal shrieking as it gives way.

"Jeb, take point. Gabe, you're next," I order. No time for his pride. The injured go first.

"Fan access ahead," Jeb reports from inside the duct. "I can override it."

"Move," Ethan urges.

One by one, we pull ourselves into the narrow passage. I go last, scanning the corridor one final time before hauling myself up.

The duct is tight, barely wide enough for shoulders. We crawl in a single file, following Jeb's directions through the metal maze.

"Junction ahead," he calls back. "Sublevel B markings. East quadrant."

We're on track. Somehow.

Jeb pauses at a grate, peering through. "Clear below."

He works the cover loose, dropping silently into the room below. We follow one after another, each man knowing his role without being told.

A laboratory. Empty. Workstations are still active, screens glowing with data. On one monitor, cellular structures writhe and reform.

"Find the holding cell," Ethan orders. "Now."

We move through the lab to a secured door at the far end.

"Biometric and keypad." Blake examines the lock.

"Can you bypass?" I ask.

"Not without blowing it."

"Move." Gabe limps forward.

He pulls a small device from his tactical vest—part of Ghost's "party favors." He places it against the keypad. The screen flickers, numbers racing, until it settles on a six-digit code.

The lock disengages with a soft click.

"Cerberus are good friends to have." Gabe's mouth curves in a grim smile.

I take point, weapon ready. The door opens to a short corridor with another door at the end. This one is heavier.

"Stack up," Ethan orders.

We form into position, ready to breach. My heart pounds now, my adrenaline spiking.

So close.

"Three," Ethan counts down. "Two. One."

The final door opens.

Six women stare back at us. Their faces show exhaustion, fear, and defiance.

At the center of the room stands Ally, her hair falling loose around her shoulders, her body tensed like a cornered wolf. Her eyes widen as they land on Gabe, and then me.

"You're not real," she whispers. "You died."

The words hit me like a physical blow. Malfor's games run deeper than we thought. He didn't just take her—he made her believe we were dead. Showed her something to break her spirit.

Didn't work. The woman standing before us is battered but unbroken. Ally Collins to the core.

Gabe lowers his rifle, hands lifting slowly. His movements deliberate, careful, like approaching a wounded animal.

"Takes more than that to keep us away from you." His voice cracks with emotion he rarely lets show.

Ally's eyes dart between us, disbelief warring with desperate hope. "The helicopter," she breathes. "The explosion. Malfor— he showed us—"

"Later," I cut in, keeping my voice steady. Tactical mindset takes over. "Right now, we get you out."

Her fingers lift, trembling, reaching toward Gabe's face. She touches his jaw, traces the scar at the corner of his mouth. Testing if he's real or another of Malfor's illusions.

"You're real," she murmurs. Her voice breaks. Her throat catches on a sob that sounds ripped from somewhere deep and raw. "You're actually real."

Something shifts in my chest. A tightness I've carried since that night she and the others disappeared, finally begins to loosen.

"We'd crawl through fire to get to you," Gabe says, leaning in to press his forehead against hers. His hands cup her face with a gentleness I've rarely seen from him.

Then she's lifting on tiptoe, her lips finding his in a desperate kiss that speaks of weeks of fear and loss. Gabe's arms tighten around her, holding her like she might vanish if he loosens his grip even slightly.

When they break apart, Ally turns to me, her eyes glistening with tears. I move closer, my hand finding her back.

"We went to hell, sweetheart. We ripped the gates off to get here." My voice thickens with emotion I don't bother to hide. "Nothing—not death, not lies, not Malfor's sick games—could keep us from you."

She reaches for me then, her hand curling around the back of my neck. There's something in her eyes I can't name—something ancient and knowing, like she's seeing through me and into me all at once. Time slows as she pulls me down until our lips meet.

The kiss hits me like a bullet to the chest. Not desperate like the one she gave Gabe, but deep and devastating in its tenderness. A kiss that carries memories—rainstorms in safe houses, quiet mornings watching the sun climb over distant mountains, her laughter against my skin in the darkness. A lifetime of moments distilled into this single point of contact.

My fingers thread through her hair, memorizing its texture. I cradle her head as though it holds everything precious in this world, because for me, it does. I breathe her in—past the antiseptic smell of this hellhole, past the gunpowder and sweat of combat—finding that essence that is purely Ally. I commit it to memory with the desperation of a man who knows what it means to lose something irreplaceable.

Something passes between us in that kiss—unspoken but understood. A current of recognition so profound it aches. Like our souls are having a conversation our minds aren't privy to.

When we finally break apart, the world seems to have stopped spinning. Her eyes hold mine for one heartbeat, two, a universe of understanding passing between us.

She breaks then, pressing her face into my chest. Her body shakes with sobs she's probably been holding back for weeks. Survival mode giving way to release. I hold her so tightly my arms tremble with the effort, like I can somehow fold her into myself for safekeeping.

Gabe's arm wraps around her from the other side, his hand finding my shoulder in a grip that anchors us all. The three of us locked together in a circle that neither Malfor nor death itself could break. A trinity forged in blood and bullets, and this moment of impossible reunion.

I close my eyes, just for a second, and allow myself to feel everything—the weight of her against me, the warmth of her breath through my tactical gear, the subtle tremors of her body as she cries. I store these sensations away like a man packing provisions for a journey he knows he won't survive.

If this is to be our last moment of peace in this life, I'll take it. I'll carry it with me into whatever darkness comes next.

Around us, similar scenes unfold. Ethan pushes past me to reach Rebel, who stands tall despite the dark circles under her eyes. She doesn't cry—not Rebel's style—but when Ethan reaches her, her composure cracks just enough. She wears a splint on one arm. Her free hand grips his tactical vest like an anchor as he presses his forehead to hers, whispering words only she can hear.

Carter finds Jenna against the far wall. She's thinner than I remember, cheekbones sharp beneath her skin, but her eyes light up at the sight of him. Something's wrong with her right hand. Carter, normally so controlled, moves with uncharacteristic urgency, sweeping her into an embrace that lifts her off her feet.

Jeb stops when he sees Stitch and the careful way she holds herself. Then she's in his arms, sobbing, and that's when I see the blood covering her back.

Rigel and Mia's reunion is quieter. She steps forward, examining his face like she's cataloging every change since they last saw each other. When she finally speaks, I can't hear the words, but Rigel's shoulders drop as tension bleeds out of him.

Walt barrels past everyone to reach Malia, who meets him halfway. His massive frame dwarfs hers, but there's nothing but gentleness in the way his hands hover over her, checking for injuries before finally allowing himself to pull her close.

Blake stands awkwardly to the side, no woman of his own to find, but he's covering our backs while we have our moment. I catch his eye and nod my thanks. He returns the gesture, jaw tight with understanding.

"Can you walk?" I pull back slightly from Ally, tactical mindset reasserting itself.

Ally straightens, wiping tears with the back of her hand. Her chin lifts with that stubborn pride I've come to expect from her.

"I can run if I have to," she says.

That's my girl.

"Stay between us," I instruct, as Gabe checks her over for injuries.

"The others," she says, glancing at the women around us. "We stick together."

"All coming," I assure her. "Nobody gets left behind."

Gabe grips her hand, his eyes never leaving her face. "Not this time. Not ever again."

I signal to Ethan. "We're ready."

Time to get our women out of this hellhole. Time to make Malfor pay.

Mission accomplished. Now comes the hard part—getting everyone home alive.

THIRTY-SEVEN

The Cliff Extraction

GABE

For three heartbeats, nobody moves. Ally's words hang in the air between us.

You died.

"Not yet." My voice comes out rougher than intended. "Though not for lack of trying."

Her face transforms—disbelief to shock to something raw and primal. She crosses the room in three steps and slams into me with enough force to make my injured leg buckle. I don't care. Her body against mine, real and alive, is worth any pain.

"They showed us footage." Her voice muffles against my chest. "The chopper. The explosion. They told us no one could have survived."

"Malfor's good with special effects." I bury my face in her hair, breathe her in. Beneath the antiseptic hospital smell, she's still there. Still Ally.

Hank moves to us, his hand hovering for a moment before settling on Ally's shoulder. She turns, not letting go of me, and pulls him into our embrace. The three of us stand there, a tangle of arms and relief and shared breath.

"You're here," is all she manages, fingers digging into both of us like we might disappear if she loosens her grip.

For a heartbeat, the world narrows to just us three. This feels right. Normal. The way it's supposed to be. Not Ally and me. Not Ally and Hank. All of us together, the strange geometry of our relationship is somehow perfect in its complexity.

My eyes meet Hank's over her head. The tension from before—the fight, the harsh words, the distance—still lingers, but something else pushes through.

Understanding.

Shared purpose.

The knowledge that whatever bullshit lies between us, we both came for her. We both need her. And maybe, though neither of us would say it aloud, we both need each other too.

I want this for the rest of my life. Ally between us, safe. The three of us figuring it out together. I hope to God I haven't fucked things up with Hank beyond repair. We'll never go back to what we were, but maybe we can build something new from the ashes.

Something stronger.

Ally pulls back slightly, eyes moving between us. She sees something—the remnants of our conflict—and her brow furrows. But there's no time to untangle that mess now.

Around us, similar reunions unfold. Carter wraps Jenna in his arms, her face buried in his neck. Rigel cups Mia's face like she might shatter. Walt engulfs Malia in a bear hug that lifts her off the ground.

Ethan moves to the corner where Rebel sits. Blood cakes half her face from a deep laceration that runs from temple to jaw. Her right arm hangs at an unnatural angle—dislocated or broken, maybe both. Bruises mar the skin that shows beneath the torn medical scrubs, and her breathing comes in shallow, pained gasps.

She tries to stand as Ethan approaches, soldier's pride refusing to show weakness. Her legs buckle.

"Easy." He catches her before she hits the floor, his movements gentle despite the urgency in his eyes. His fingers brush hair from her face, revealing more bruising. Something dangerous flashes across his features—a cold fury I've rarely seen.

"What did they do to you?" The question emerges as barely more than a whisper, but the promise of violence behind it fills the room.

"Tried to break me." Her voice emerges stronger than her body, cracked but defiant. "Failed."

Ethan's jaw works silently. I know that look—he's cataloging every injury, storing it away, building a debt that will be paid in blood.

"Can you walk?" he finally asks.

She grits her teeth. "Not fast."

"I've got you." He lifts her, one arm supporting her shoulders, the other beneath her knees. She sinks against him, trust overriding pride.

His gaze sweeps the room, assessing each woman, each operator, calculating odds and options. When he speaks, his voice carries calm authority despite the storm I can see building behind his eyes.

"We have eighteen minutes to clear the compound before total lockdown. Every second counts. Stay tight, move fast, keep quiet. Questions come later—when we're safe."

Jeb finds Stitch against the far wall, quickly checking her injuries. She nods at his unspoken question—she can move on her own.

"Listen carefully," Ethan continues. "Stay close. Move when we move. Stop when we stop. We're getting you home, but I need you all focused. Clear?"

Six nods. These women aren't civilians anymore. Whatever Malfor did to them burned away hesitation.

"Jenna." Carter's voice tightens. "What happened to your hand?"

I notice it then—her right hand. Two fingers missing. The wounds look surgical, cleanly bandaged.

"Punishment." Her voice is flat, emotionless. "For fighting back."

Ally grips my arm, and her knuckles turn white. Her body trembles against mine.

A chill runs through the room.

"Ghost, this is Ethan." He adjusts Rebel in his arms. "Package secure. Six alive. Proceeding to extraction."

Static crackles, then Ghost's voice filters through. "Roger that. Cerberus has compromised security. Primary systems are offline. Backup systems are failing. You've got fifteen minutes before manual override kicks in."

"Copy. Charlie team moving."

Ethan turns toward the women, his eyes softening slightly despite the urgency. "Ladies, we move in Formation Bravo." He explains quickly for their benefit, though his team already knows the drill. "I'll take point with Rebel. Rigel with Mia. Carter with Jenna. Jeb with Stitch. Walt with Malia."

He pauses, glancing between me, Hank, and Ally.

"Ally stays with Gabe," Hank says, stepping forward. "Blake and I will take rear guard."

Ethan nods once, accepting the adjustment without comment. His team shifts into position without needing further instruction, years of training taking over.

Relief and guilt war inside me. Hank knows my leg is slowing me down. Taking rear guard means he's putting himself in the most vulnerable position—the last man out always faces the highest risk. But it also means Ally stays with me, where I can protect her.

The selfish part of me is grateful. The tactical part knows it makes sense—Hank on rear guard gives us the strongest possible defense at our most vulnerable point.

My leg throbs, but adrenaline dulls the pain. Nothing matters except getting Ally out. Getting everyone out.

Ally's eyes drop to my leg, noticing the dark stain spreading through the bandage. Her face hardens.

"You're hurt." Her fingers brush the edge of the bandage, coming away red.

"It's nothing."

"Bullshit." The word comes out sharp, focused.

She tears a strip from her scrub top, kneels, and wraps it tight around my thigh, reinforcing the existing bandage. Her movements are quick and efficient. When she finishes, she meets my eyes.

"You don't get to die on me twice."

Something in her voice sends warmth through my chest despite the circumstances. I touch her cheek briefly.

"Yes, ma'am."

We move through the detention block toward our exit route, the women taking in their surroundings with wary eyes. Ally stays close, her shoulder pressed against mine as we move. She positions herself on my injured side, her body subtly bracing mine whenever my weight shifts. It's not obvious enough that others would notice—she knows better than to wound my pride openly —but enough that I feel the support with each step.

Part of me loves her for it. Another part hates being the liability, the weak link, but her face shows only determination, not pity. She's been through hell, yet she's the one supporting me. The irony isn't lost on me.

We push through the detention block exit into a central corridor. Alarms blare throughout the facility, red emergency lights casting everything in blood-hued shadows. The Trojan horse is doing its work—security doors open and close at random, surveillance cameras swivel uselessly.

"Compound's in chaos," Ethan says, adjusting Rebel in his arms. "We go straight through. Mining access is two levels up, east wing."

"Contact back!" Blake calls, dropping to one knee.

Two guards round the corner, weapons raised. Hank and Blake fire simultaneously—controlled double-taps that drop both men before they can squeeze their triggers.

"Move!" Ethan orders.

We advance through the corridor at combat pace, the women keeping tight formation with their partners. Ally stays at my side, her movements fluid and focused. Whatever they did to her in captivity, they didn't break her.

More guards appear at a junction—three this time. Carter and Rigel engage while Walt provides covering fire. The firefight is brief, violent, and entirely in our favor.

"Stairs ahead," Jeb calls, eyes flicking over the schematic glowing on his tactical pad.

He moves with surprising ease, favoring the leg that nearly ended his Guardian career but never quite slowed him down. He's still got a slight hitch in his gait—a ghost of the old injury— but tonight, no one would dare call him the gimp. Not with the way he covers ground like every step is a promise of vengeance.

We hit the stairwell at full speed, climbing toward the upper levels. My leg burns with each step, but adrenaline keeps me moving. Ally notices my grimace, slides closer to support my weight without making it obvious.

A security team tries to ambush us on the landing—six men in tactical gear. They never stood a chance. We react as one, taking the fuckers out. Years of training make us death walking.

Six shots, six bodies.

"Emergency exit, next level," Ethan announces as we continue climbing.

An explosion rocks the building, vibrating through the concrete. The lights flicker.

"Cerberus at work," Hank says, a grim smile touching his lips.

We emerge onto a maintenance level. Signs of hasty evacuation everywhere—abandoned equipment, doors left open, papers scattered across floors. Malfor's staff is fleeing the sinking ship.

"Thirty meters ahead," Jeb confirms, checking his pad. "Service exit to the cliff face. Reinforced steel door."

We encounter no more resistance as we approach the exit. The door stands partially open, emergency protocols overriding the locks.

"That's our way out," Ethan points beyond the door. "Straight through to the cliff's edge."

"I must say, your persistence is admirable." Malfor's voice suddenly fills the air around us, crackling through hidden speakers along the cliff path. "Though ultimately futile."

Everyone freezes, weapons swinging toward corners and shadows. The metal grating beneath our feet sways slightly with the movement, two hundred feet of empty air between us and the jagged rocks below.

"Did you think I wouldn't have contingencies for my contingencies?" His cultured tone carries a hint of amusement. "I've known about this exit since I acquired the property. It's quite useful for—disposal purposes."

"Keep moving," Ethan orders quietly. "Ignore him."

"Your women have been such valued guests." Malfor's voice drips with mock courtesy. "Well, most of them. Ms. Collins proved particularly—unappreciative of my hospitality. Quite the fighter."

Ally's jaw tightens at his words. I squeeze her hand once, in quick reassurance.

"I suppose I should thank you for testing my security so thoroughly. The flaws you've exposed will be rectified. Though I'm afraid none of you will live to see the improvements."

A groan of rusted metal hits my ears half a second before the shriek. The rusted grating suddenly gives way beneath Carter's foot. He shoves Jenna forward with a startled shout. A desperate act of instinct and protection. She stumbles clear, landing hard on her knees just past the edge.

Carter's body follows the grating down.

For one frozen heartbeat, he's just—gone.

Then Rigel lunges. His arm snaps out, fingers locking around Carter's vest as the man's full weight jerks him toward the abyss. Walt is already there, diving low to grab Rigel's harness, anchoring him.

Hank and I whirl around just in time to see Rigel's muscles straining, boots grinding against crumbling steel as he hauls Carter back inch by inch.

"Don't let—don't you fucking let go ..."

Jenna scrambles on hands and knees, reaching. Walt throws himself forward, grabbing Carter's free wrist. Together, the two of them drag him back onto the platform, breath ragged and faces carved in panic.

Carter sprawls on the floor, heaving, blood running from a torn palm.

"That was too close," Walt mutters, brushing rust flakes off his arms.

Rigel stands, jaw clenched. "This whole place is a fucking death trap."

I look at Jenna—at the way her hands tremble, at the wild look in her eyes. She saw it. Carter didn't hesitate. He put her life above his own.

And we're not even out yet.

The wind screams past us again, whipping grit and salt across our faces as we press forward, the cliff's edge still yawning to our right like a hungry mouth waiting for its next meal. It's two hundred feet of sheer drop to the churning ocean below. Wind howls around us, carrying salt spray and the distant crash of waves against rock.

"Comms check," Ethan says, adjusting Rebel in his arms. "Ghost, confirm extraction."

"RIBs in position," Ghost's voice crackles through our earpieces. "Two hundred feet down. Lights will activate on your approach."

Ethan kicks open a heavy waterproof case stashed at the edge of the platform. "Rappel gear. Eight sets, six with passenger capacity."

"Let's move," he orders. "Walt, get the lines secured."

Walt quickly sets up the anchors and tests the rappel lines. His hands move without hesitation, checking and double-checking each connection. The women watch with tense faces.

"Pair up," Ethan directs. "I've got Rebel. Jeb with Stitch. Rigel with Mia. Carter with Jenna. Walt with Malia." He looks between me and Hank. "Gabe, you take Ally. Hank and Blake, you'll provide covering fire and come down last."

"My leg—" I start.

"Isn't a factor," Ethan cuts me off. "You're still our best climber."

No arguing with that. I help Ally into a harness, checking each strap.

"You've done this before?" She searches my face.

"A few times." I meet her eyes. "Trust me?"

A half-smile touches her lips. "Do I have a choice?"

"Always."

"First wave, go," Ethan orders.

Carter and Jenna step off first, followed by Rigel and Mia, then Jeb and Stitch. Each pair vanishes over the edge. Walt and Malia follow—she slips once, a small cry escaping before Walt adjusts their line, steadying her.

Ethan goes next with Rebel secured against his chest in a special harness. Their descent is slower and more careful due to her injuries.

My turn comes with Ally. I secure her harness to mine, double-checking the connections despite my shaking hands. Pain radiates from my injured leg as I take position at the edge, but I push it aside. Pain is just information. I refuse to be the weak link.

"Ready?" I ask Ally.

She meets my eyes, trust and determination mingling. "Let's go home."

We step backward into empty space, controlling our descent as we rappel down the cliff face. Wind buffets us, salt spray stinging my eyes. My injured leg screams with each push off the rock face, but I keep our descent steady.

Above us, Hank and Blake provide covering fire as drones appear on the horizon. Muzzle flashes illuminate the cliff top.

"Incoming!" Hank's voice crackles through comms. "Security drones, armed. Thirty seconds out."

A spotlight suddenly cuts through the darkness, sweeping across the cliff face. The beam catches us, momentarily blinding me as we continue our descent.

Above us, gunfire erupts. Muzzle flashes illuminate the cliff top as Hank and Blake engage the drones. Searchlights sweep the rock face, hunting for movement.

"Faster," I urge, increasing our rappel speed.

The ocean surges closer. I can make out the RIB now, Ethan and the first wave already aboard. Two hundred feet. One-fifty. One hundred.

A spotlight locks onto us.

"They've got us," Ally gasps.

I kick off hard from the rock, swinging us in a wide arc as bullets chip stone where we were a second before. We swing back, and I increase our drop rate to the edge of safety.

Fifty feet. Twenty-five.

The **RIB** appears directly below us, rocking violently in the surf. Carter and Jeb brace to receive us.

"Let go on my mark," I tell Ally. "Three, two, one—"

We drop the final fifteen feet, landing hard in the boat. Carter steadies Ally while Jeb helps me untangle from the rappel gear.

Above us, Hank and Blake descend last, providing covering fire even as they rappel. They're moving too fast—the lines smoking with friction—but with good reason. Spotlights track them, bullets pinging off rock all around.

Spotlights sweep the cliff face. Bullets ricochet off stone like angry wasps.

Then—*Crack.*

A round catches Hank. His body jerks, but he doesn't slow. Thirty feet. Twenty.

His body snaps midair, jerked off-line. He doesn't cry out. Doesn't even slow.

He releases early, dropping the final distance in free fall. He slams into the boat with bone-jarring force. Blake drops in hard right after him, rolling to his feet, scanning.

Hank doesn't move. Blood spreads in an obscene blossom across his tactical vest, already soaking through layers of Kevlar and cloth.

"GO!" Ghost yells from the cliff edge, his team providing covering fire. "PUNCH IT!"

The engines roar to life. The boat lurches forward, carving through the black waves as bullets stitch the sea around us.

I pull Ally to the deck and shield her with my body. Salt spray and gunfire mix in the air like metal and madness. Behind us, muzzle flashes continue to light up the cliff top. Cerberus, buying us time to escape.

"Hank," I call over the engine noise. "How bad?"

He doesn't respond, slumped against the side of the boat. Blood soaks his tactical vest—more than a scratch. Ally moves toward him, crawling, and presses a field dressing against the wound firmly. Her eyes meet mine over his unconscious form.

The vest's saturated. The blood won't stop.

He blinks slowly. Once.

Then his eyes roll back.

"Hank—" My voice cracks, panic shredding the edges.

"He'll make it," she says firmly. "We all will." Ally presses hard into the wound with a field dressing. "Pressure. Gabe, help me."

I crawl to them, heart hammering in my throat. "He's hit bad. He's losing too much."

I reach across, my hand finding Hank's limp one. Fear claws at my chest—raw, primal. Not just for a teammate or brother-in-arms. For Hank.

For what we are together. Something deeper than friendship, closer than brotherhood. A bond forged in blood and bullets and shared nights with Ally between us.

"He's not responding," I whisper.

"Don't say that," Ally snaps. "Don't even think that."

I grip his hand. It's already cold.

"Hank. Stay with me." My voice breaks, softer now. "Don't do this. Don't you fucking do this." I squeeze his hand, willing strength into him. "Don't you dare check out on us." His pulse flutters beneath my fingers—thready and fading.

The thought of losing him carves a hole inside me I didn't know could exist.

Ally looks up, eyes glistening. "He needs a trauma bay. He needs blood. And we're—what—miles out?"

Understanding passes between us. We might not make it in time.

She drops her gaze to Hank, but her hands are shaking.

Blake stares forward, jaw locked. Rigel's already on comms, voice tight with urgency, calling for med evac.

I look at the women we rescued—battered, traumatized, but alive. Alive and fighting. Just like us. But my focus keeps returning to Hank's pale face, to the blood soaking through the bandage Ally presses against his shoulder.

All I see is Hank. The man I would burn the world for.

His blood stains my hands, and all I can do is pray that whatever gods exist out here in this godforsaken dark are listening.

Because I can't lose him. Not now.

Not ever.

The boat speeds into the night, leaving Malfor's compound behind.

I grip Hank's hand tighter, a cold certainty settling in my chest as I watch his blood seep through the bandage, and pray.

THIRTY-EIGHT

Run Silent

ALLY

THE RIB SLAMS INTO ANOTHER WAVE. SALT SPRAY SLICES ACROSS my face, mixing with the sting of wind and blood. I don't flinch. I don't blink. I can't—because Hank's face is going slack, and if I lose sight of him now, I might never see him alive again.

Too much blood. Not enough time.

They came for us.

The truth doesn't just hit—it detonates, sharp and blinding, like shrapnel to the chest. My knees buckle. Breath locks in my throat. Every nerve fires at once, unable to process the impossible.

I saw their bodies explode. Saw the fireball swallow them whole. Watched the footage over and over, forced to memorize every frame while Malfor whispered what it meant—that they were gone. That I'd failed. That love could be obliterated with a single detonation.

But they're here. Bleeding. Breathing. And now, maybe dying.

I can't make sense of it. My brain stutters, glitching between grief and hope. Hallucination? Dream? Trap?

Gabe's eyes meet mine, and something inside me fractures.

I can't look. I can't not look.

My hands tremble. My vision blurs. The sound of the ocean, the girls crying, the motor's rumble—all of it fades beneath the roar of my own heartbeat.

"Keep pressure." I guide Malia's hands to the soaked field dressing on Hank's shoulder. The bullet went clean through, but that just means two holes bleeding out instead of one.

The night ocean churns black around us, our wake cutting a white path through the darkness. The wind tears at my hair, carrying away the smell of copper and gunpowder. The constant thunder of twin outboard engines nearly drowns out my thoughts.

Nearly, but not quite.

They came for us.

The realization keeps crashing over me in waves. These men who I mourned—who I saw blown to pieces in the crystal clear footage Malfor forced us to watch on repeat—they're alive. They came for us. And now Hank might die because of it.

Gabe crouches at the bow, a shadow carved in moonlight, rifle steady even as blood darkens his leg. He doesn't wince. Doesn't even acknowledge it. But I see the way his grip tightens every time the boat slams. His silence screams louder than the engines.

Blood seeps steadily from his leg, darkening his tactical pants. He ignores it, the same way he's ignored my attempts to check the wound.

I can't stop staring at him. Alive. Real. And it guts me— because the second I let myself feel that joy, I know I'm stealing it from Hank. There's not enough oxygen for both emotions. Not enough room in my chest for gratitude and grief.

"Status." Ethan's voice crackles through our comms from the second RIB.

"Still breathing." Carter pilots our boat, hands steady on the throttle. "RIB 1 holding together. Hank's stable—barely."

"Should've been me taking that rappel. Dammit." Blake's fingers curl into fists as he glances at Hank's too-still form.

"RIB 2 has some punctures." Walt's voice sounds strained. "Taking on water, but pumps are keeping up." He checks on Hank, placing his hand to his neck, then looks to me. "Pulse is slow, but holding. Just keep pressure."

My gaze drifts to the second boat, twenty yards off our port side. Rebel lies in the center. Jenna sits beside her, two fingers missing from her right hand, face hollow with exhaustion. Their RIB rides noticeably lower in the water.

"How far to extraction?" Blake stands at our RIB's rear gun mount, knuckles white on the grip.

"Twelve miles." Ethan's reply comes fast. "Trawler waiting at coordinates. ETA forty minutes. If we make it."

If we make it.

Three words.

Tiny. Hollow.

They rattle around inside me like shrapnel, echoing like a curse I'm too afraid to say out loud.

Because *if* feels fragile right now. Like a breath that won't hold. Like hope that can't survive the weight of blood.

Hank's blood.

He lies sprawled beside me, his face gray beneath the boat's flickering lights. The bandage I pressed to his shoulder is soaked through, the bleeding relentless. My hands are coated in it—slick, warm, sticky where it clings to my wrists like the memory of his body pressed against mine.

Only that memory doesn't match the man in front of me now.

I remember strength. Heat. The weight of him pinning me to

tangled sheets, his voice low and commanding, eyes full of fire and purpose.

Now he's limp. Pale. His lashes flutter, lips parted as if caught mid-plea or prayer.

He doesn't look like the man who once made me feel invincible.

He looks like a body. Like a loss I haven't had time to grieve.

I want to wrap myself in the miracle of Gabe's survival—but Hank is bleeding out at my feet. And I can't choose. I can't. So I don't. I split myself down the center and try to be enough for both.

I can't stop shaking.

He took the bullet mid-rappel—jerked hard in the harness but still fired three return shots, like he wasn't already dying. Then he let go early. Dropped the last thirty feet without hesitation. Crashed into the boat with a sound that will live in my nightmares.

He hasn't opened his eyes. Not once. Not even when I begged. That stillness terrifies me more than gunfire. More than death. Because Hank's not supposed to be still. He's supposed to tease me. Steady me. Catch me when I fall.

Gabe kneels opposite me, gripping Hank's limp hand so tightly his knuckles have gone bone-white. His jaw clenches once. Twice. A muscle ticks in his cheek.

But his eyes—

God, his eyes are wreckage.

I've seen Gabe angry. I've seen him cold. Focused. Dangerous.

But never broken.

Not like this.

He's bleeding too. His blood smells different from Hank's. Older. Drier. But it still clings to my fingers when I press his thigh. Still proof that I could lose him too.

"We're being tracked." Blake's voice slices through the night like a wire pulled too tight. Tension snaps across the boat. Every breath holds. Every heart waits to shatter. "Something in the water. Closing fast."

A current of dread curls low in my stomach.

"What kind of something?" Rigel asks, already moving toward the bow.

Blake glances at a handheld thermal scanner. "Not marine life. Not natural. Drone or torpedo. Maybe both."

Gabe doesn't flinch. Just shifts slightly, shielding Hank and me with his body.

I try to focus, but the world keeps narrowing to the wound beneath my hands. I press harder. Feel a sluggish pulse. Too weak. Too slow.

Please, no. Not him.

Another wave slams into the hull. Salt spray stings my raw neck where the collar used to be. The freedom burns more than the restraint ever did.

"Two contacts now," Blake growls. "They're flanking us."

I don't lift my head. Don't care. Let them come.

Just let me keep Hank.

"Stay with me," I whisper, dragging my sleeve across my face. "You said we were a team, remember? Three of us. All in. You don't get to leave."

He doesn't respond. Doesn't even twitch.

Gabe's breathing grows louder. Rough. Fraying. Like he's seconds from doing something reckless.

I meet his eyes. "We're not losing him."

His throat works, once, twice, three times before he finds the words.

"No. We're not."

He says it like a promise. Like a threat. Like a prayer.

Somewhere behind us, the boat's engines scream as the

throttle slams forward. Another explosion lights up the cliff face, turning the sea orange for half a breath. The team's still covering us. But I know—we all know—we're not out yet.

And Hank … Hank is barely hanging on.

His lashes flutter. Just once. I freeze, fingers splayed on his chest, afraid to believe it. His heart thuds once under my palm. Not strong. But there.

I lean down, press my forehead to his. Close my eyes. His skin is ice against mine.

I curl around him, shielding his body with mine as chaos churns just beyond us. His blood seeps into my clothes, warm and terrifying. I lower my lips to his ear, my breath shaky against his skin.

"I love you," I whisper, soft enough that only he can hear. "So you fight. You fight, Hank. For me. For Gabe. For us."

His eyelashes flutter against my cheek like the ghost of a promise. I clutch him tighter, refusing to let go of the warmth still in his body, the fight I swear I can still feel in his chest.

For a breath, there's only the hush of wind across the water. The thunder of my pulse. The ache behind my eyes. He stirs, and the world restarts.

A soft gasp escapes me at the faintest flutter of his fingers against mine. Not much. But real. Enough.

The scanner pings again.

"Contact right off the port side!" Blake shouts. "We've got sixty seconds before it's on us!"

The world narrows to chaos—yells, weapons drawn, team bracing for impact.

But I stay here.

In the blood.

In the silence.

In the space between breaths, where everything I love hangs in the balance.

If we make it.

No.

When.

Because I didn't survive hell to lose him now.

"We've got him, Ally. Trawler's rigged for trauma response. He'll make it." Carter curses, throttling up the engines.

Our RIB surges forward, slamming harder into the waves. Hank's body jolts with each impact. I brace myself against his side, trying to stabilize him.

"Multiple contacts," Walt confirms from the other boat. "Aquatic drones. And something on radar—aerial pursuit."

Rigel touches my shoulder, pointing to the night sky behind us. Tiny red lights blink in formation. Getting closer.

"Malfor's persistent." Jeb checks his weapon, expression grim.

Something changes in the air—a subtle electric charge raising the hairs on my arms. Mia's head snaps up in alarm. She feels it too.

"They're deploying nanobots!" I shout to Gabe. "Swarm pattern!"

The microscopic hunters will find us, tag us, and lead the drones straight to our position, no matter how fast we run.

Gabe's head turns sharply. "Blake—"

"On it." Blake digs in his gear, pulling out a cylindrical device with blinking lights. "EMP ready. Thirty-second countdown."

The aerial drones are close enough now to hear their high-pitched whine over the boat engines. Red targeting lasers sweep the water around us.

"Brace!" Carter throws our RIB into a hard turn.

Water explodes ten yards to starboard—a miss, but close enough to shower us with spray. Malia screams. Blake returns fire from the mounted gun, tracer rounds arcing into the night sky.

The second RIB veers sharply to the left as two aquatic drones breach the surface, their sleek forms gleaming wetly in the moonlight. Walt opens fire, driving one back underwater. The other launches something—a projectile that rips through their RIB's hull.

"Taking water!" Ethan's voice crackles through comms. "Hull breach!"

Blake activates the EMP device, tossing it high into the air between our boats. It detonates in a silent pulse of blue-white light. The pursuing drones falter, their lights flickering and dying as they plummet into the sea.

The electric feeling dissipates—threat neutralized.

Our momentary victory evaporates as Walt's voice cuts through: "We're going down! RIB 2 is sinking."

THIRTY-NINE

Safe Harbor

ALLY

CARTER IMMEDIATELY SWINGS OUR BOAT AROUND, BRINGING US alongside the damaged vessel. Water pours through multiple tears in their hull, the pumps clearly losing the battle.

"Transfer now." Ethan already moves Rebel toward our RIB.

What follows is a desperate scramble as we try to transfer six people from a sinking boat to ours—already crowded with eight. The RIBs knock together in the swells, making the transfers treacherous. Jeb nearly falls between the boats before Rigel catches his vest.

Jenna comes across next, then Mia. Ethan passes Rebel carefully to Carter and Blake, who lower her into our craft. Walt leaps across last as his boat settles deeper into the water.

A massive wave hits us broadside. The boats slam together violently. Blake, positioned at the edge helping Walt, pitches backward into the churning sea.

"Man overboard!" Carter shouts.

Before anyone reacts, Gabe dives.

For a heartbeat, time fractures. One second he's there—solid, alive, mine—and the next, he's gone again. A blur of movement swallowed by black water.

No.

My breath catches, lungs refusing to believe. Last time I saw him disappear, it was into flames. Into silence. Into death.

"Gabe!" I lunge toward the side. Rigel holds me back.

Eternal seconds pass. I scan the water, desperate for any sign. Please, not again. Not after getting them back.

Gabe breaks the surface first—violent, gasping, a dark shape erupting from the black water like something torn from the deep. He spins, scanning. Eyes locked. Focused. Terrifying in his precision.

Then—there. A ripple. A glint of gear.

He dives back under without hesitation.

Seconds stretch. My heart stops.

Then he hauls Blake up—fist gripped in the shoulder rig of his tactical vest, dragging him like dead weight. Blake sputters, coughing seawater, eyes barely conscious. His arm hangs limp, probably dislocated.

But Gabe doesn't slow.

He swims hard, one arm towing Blake, the other carving through water. No wasted motion. No hesitation. Just raw, unrelenting will.

I scramble to the edge of the boat, reaching for them, my voice raw from screaming. "Here! Gabe—here!"

His eyes lock on mine.

And suddenly I can breathe again.

Carter maneuvers our overloaded RIB around. Every hand reaches out as we haul the soaking men aboard. Gabe collapses on the deck, coughing up seawater, his injured leg bleeding freely now.

I clutch his shoulders, dragging him up onto the slick deck.

Water pours off him. Blood too. He coughs once, eyes finding mine through the chaos.

I press my forehead to his, fingers trembling as they dig into his shoulders. Relief crashes so hard it's nearly rage.

"You idiot," I whisper against his skin. "You could've drowned."

"Couldn't lose another one." His eyes meet mine, water streaming from his hair.

The sinking RIB disappears beneath the waves behind us, taking with it some of the men's weapons and gear. Our remaining boat sits dangerously low in the water with fourteen people aboard.

"We need to lighten." Ethan scans the overcrowded boat. "Anything non-essential goes overboard."

We dump spare gear, empty cases, anything we can live without. Carter coaxes a few more knots from the straining engines. We continue our desperate flight, everyone scanning the horizon for more pursuers.

Time blurs. I divide my attention between Hank's deathly still form and Gabe's barely conscious one. Both are losing blood. Both keep fighting. I won't lose either of them. Not now.

The eastern horizon begins to lighten. The first hint of dawn breaks over the ocean.

"Contact ahead." Ethan trains binoculars forward. "Hold positions."

I tense, expecting more drones. Instead, the ghostly silhouette of a ship emerges on the horizon. A fishing trawler, weathered and unremarkable.

"Authentication protocols active." Ethan checks through comms.

The trawler's lights blink in a specific pattern. Ethan responds with a flashlight, matching the sequence.

"We're clear." Relief edges into his clipped tone. "Approach port side."

As we draw alongside, figures move on deck—medics and security personnel. They throw down lines and secure our RIB.

We made it. Not intact. Not unchanged. But enough to fight another day. And that's everything.

"Wounded first," Ethan orders.

Hands reach down for Hank. I clutch his tactical vest, reluctant to let go.

"Ally." Gabe stands somehow beside me. "Let them take him. Best chance he has."

I release my grip. Watch as they lift Hank's limp form onto the trawler. Medical personnel immediately surround him.

Rebel goes next, then Jenna. Gabe tries to wave off assistance but collapses when he puts weight on his leg. Walt and Blake haul him up despite his protests.

One by one, we climb aboard. Exhaustion hits me as my feet touch the deck—bone-deep, mind-numbing fatigue that makes my knees buckle. Someone catches me before I hit the deck.

The RIB is stripped of anything useful, then scuttled. No evidence left behind.

I move to stand beside Gabe as a medic cuts away his pant leg, revealing the full extent of his wound. Infection is already setting in. His hand finds mine, squeezes.

"You found us." The words barely make it past the lump in my throat.

Gabe's gaze locks on mine. Fierce. Raw. "I'd walk through hell to find you. And I did."

His hand tightens around mine.

Dawn spills across the deck like a promise we're not sure we deserve.

But we're still here. Bleeding. Breathing.

And I swear to whatever's left of the stars—I'll never let them go again.

I look around at the survivors scattered across the deck. Soaked, bloodied, traumatized—but alive. The women I've come to see as sisters during our captivity. The men who came through hell to find us.

Not all whole. Not all intact. But alive.

Gabe's eyes close as the pain meds finally take effect. I keep hold of his hand, watching his chest rise and fall. A medic calls out from Hank's side—something about blood pressure dropping. More urgent activity.

I want to go to him, but the medics swarm him, fighting to save his life.

Dawn breaks fully across the water. Light catches the tears streaming down my face.

We made it out. But I know in my bones, we're not done. Not by a long shot.

FORTY

The Weight of Blood

COLD SPREADS THROUGH MY LIMBS LIKE ICE IN MY VEINS. EACH heartbeat pushes less blood, moves slower, carries me further from the surface where voices echo like distant thunder.

The trawler rocks beneath me, metal hull groaning against swells. Engine vibrations travel through the deck, up through the makeshift operating table, rattling my bones. Salt air mingles with the copper taste flooding my mouth—metallic and wrong.

Bright lights stab through my eyelids. Someone's pressing gauze to my shoulder—rough, urgent movements that send lightning through my chest. Scissors cut away my tactical vest, fabric parting with wet sounds that make my stomach clench.

"Blood pressure dropping to seventy over forty." The medic's voice cuts through static building in my ears. "Need another unit. Now."

Cold saline hits my veins. It's a temporary reprieve against the tide pulling me under. Hands work over my body—checking vitals, applying pressure, fighting a war they're losing inch by inch.

"Hank." Ally's voice breaks through the medical chaos like

sunlight through storm clouds. "You're not leaving us again." Her fingers thread through mine, warm against skin going cold. "Do you hear me? You don't get to leave us."

Our girl. The words won't form on my tongue. Too much blood, not enough air. My throat moves but produces only wet, rattling sounds.

Gabe's presence fills the space beside me—familiar even in this twilight between living and dying. His breathing is controlled but rapid. The smell of gunpowder and sweat still clinging to his clothes. His hand covers our joined fingers, grip tight enough to bruise.

Fighting something bigger than enemies or bullets or missions gone wrong.

Fighting time itself.

The monitor's beeping slows. Each tone stretches longer, spaces between them widening like cracks in ice before it shatters completely. Sixty beats per minute. Fifty. Forty-five.

My chest burns with more than bullet wounds. The weight of unfinished business crushes down—words unsaid, forgiveness unasked, the fight that drove a wedge between us when we needed each other most.

Need to tell them.

Memories surface through the fog of dying:

Gabe's face twisted with rage and pain. *"She's mine."*

My own voice, cold with fury. *"You selfish piece of shit. She belongs to both of us."*

The sound of fists on flesh. Blood on concrete. Jeb pulling us apart before we killed each other.

Three days of silence. Three days of treating each other like strangers instead of brothers.

And now I'm dying with those words between us—sharp-edged and cutting, poison that turned our partnership into warfare.

Can't leave it like this.

I force my eyes open. The effort costs everything, pulls me back from the edge where darkness waits. Blurred shapes swim above me—Ally's face streaked with tears, Gabe's jaw carved from stone.

Beautiful.

Both of them are beautiful, and mine.

"Hank." Ally leans closer, voice breaking on my name. "Stay with us."

Her hand cups my cheek, thumb tracing the line of my jaw. Skin soft as silk against the stubble I haven't shaved in days. Tears fall from her eyes onto my face, warm droplets that taste like salt and sorrow.

"We need you." The words crack in her throat. "I need you."

Blood bubbles on my lips when I try to speak. The medic shouts something about internal bleeding, arterial damage, and too much time elapsed. His voice fades to background noise.

None of it matters now.

Only them. Only this.

"He needs to conserve his strength." The medic's hands press fresh gauze to the exit wound in my back. "We're doing every-thing we can."

But we all know the truth. The wound channel tore through too much vital tissue. Nicked the subclavian artery, punctured lung tissue, probably severed nerves that will never heal. Even if I survive the blood loss, I'll never be the same.

Never be the operator they need. Never be the partner worthy of their love.

Better to go now, while I can still give them something meaningful.

Better to go with words that heal instead of words that destroy.

"Gabe." The word scrapes out like gravel over broken glass, each syllable a victory against failing lungs.

His eyes find mine, dark with grief and guilt and self-hatred, that I recognize all too well. The same look he wore after our fight, when words we couldn't take back hung between us like shrapnel embedded too deep to remove.

Blood pools in my mouth. I swallow it down, taste copper and iron, and the metallic tang of dying. Force words past the obstruction in my throat.

"She was never …" More blood. I cough, spattering red across the white gauze. "Just yours or just mine."

His face crumbles. Understanding hits him like incoming fire —recognition of forgiveness he doesn't think he deserves.

"Hank, don't." His voice breaks on my name. "Save your strength."

"No." The word costs me everything. "Listen."

My vision blurs, refocuses. The medical bay comes into sharp focus—steel walls painted hospital white, emergency lighting casting harsh shadows, the smell of antiseptic, blood, and fear. Ally's hair falls around her face like a curtain, long, silky waves I've run my fingers through countless times.

"She's yours now." My voice barely carries above the monitor's increasingly irregular complaint. "Take care of our girl."

Ally's sob cuts through me sharper than any bullet. Her forehead touches mine, tears falling warm against cold skin. I breathe in her scent—vanilla and fear.

"I love you both." Each word costs me everything left in my chest. Lungs struggling to inflate, heart skipping beats that it can't spare. "More than my own life. Build something beautiful from this."

Their hands squeeze mine—Ally's desperate and trembling, Gabe's steady despite the grief I can read in his grip. My vision narrows to their faces, memorizing every line and shadow. The freckle on Ally's left cheek. The scar through Gabe's eyebrow from a training accident years ago.

Details that matter. Details worth carrying into whatever comes next.

"Don't let this be the end of your story." Breath rattles in my chest, spaces between heartbeats growing vast as oceans. "Let it be the beginning …"

The words fade. Everything fades.

Except them. Always them.

The monitor's steady tone replaces my heartbeat, mechanical and final as a tolling bell.

FORTY-ONE

Where Grief Begins

ALLY

THE MONITOR LETS OUT A LONG, UNBROKEN TONE.

Not a beep. Not a warning. Just a single, piercing note that cuts through the chaos like a blade—cold, mechanical, final.

My breath hitches.

Hank's chest—where the medic's hands press rhythmically—stops moving.

Still. Too still.

Like the air has been sucked out of the room. Like time stutters.

No rise. No fall. No fight left in his body.

That sound—the flatline—it drills into my bones, fills my skull, drowns everything else. It's not just sound. It's a scream I can't make. A truth I can't hold.

I mourned him once. I can't do it again.

The thought shatters something inside me that I'd carefully rebuilt during our brief hours together on this boat. When I believed he was dead—when Malfor showed us that helicopter exploding—I'd already grieved him. Already said goodbye.

Already accepted a future without his steady presence, his quiet strength, his love that made me braver than I had any right to be.

And then he came back. Alive. Real. Bleeding but breathing, joking through pain, promising we'd figure out how to heal together.

We just got you back. We just…

The medic steps back, defeat written across his sweat-streaked face. Blood soaks through layers of gauze, stains the metal table beneath Hank's body. Dark pools that catch the harsh overhead lighting, reflecting it back like broken mirrors.

Too much blood. Too much time.

"Time of death, twenty-two forty-seven." His voice carries professional detachment that makes me want to scream.

"No." The word explodes from my chest, louder now, desperate. "Check again. Check again!"

But Hank's hand lies slack between mine. There's no pulse beneath my fingertips when I press them to his wrist, his throat, or the hollow of his chest where his heart beat moments before. His skin is already cooling, that vital warmth that made him Hank beginning to fade.

The silence where his heartbeat should be echoes louder than any explosion.

Gone.

"No," I whisper. The word breaks apart in my mouth. "No—no, please—this isn't fair. This isn't fucking fair!"

The rage hits me like a physical blow. He survived the helicopter crash. Survived hours in the ocean. Survived Malfor's compound and guards and bullets and everything designed to kill him. He made it to the boat. Made it to safety. Made it back to me.

And then he dies anyway.

Dies saving me. Again.

The cruelty of it steals my breath. I drop to my knees beside him, grabbing his hand, fingers slick with blood and seawater. Still warm. Still here. He has to be.

"We were supposed to have time," I sob, the words tearing from my throat like shrapnel. "You promised we'd have time to figure this out. You promised—"

But the line doesn't change. The medic doesn't move.

Only the silence pulses louder than the tone. Deafening. Paralyzing.

Gabe's voice cuts through it, ragged and unrecognizable. "Hank—don't you fucking dare—don't you dare leave us again!"

But the machine says otherwise.

The medical bay fractures into individual tableaux of grief, each person processing loss in their own devastating way.

Carter stands motionless by the far bulkhead, tears tracking down his cheeks. Silent, steady streams that he doesn't bother to wipe away. His hands hang loose at his sides, the eternal soldier suddenly looking every one of his years.

Walt moves forward on autopilot, medical training overriding personal devastation. His hands shake as he checks Hank's pulse points again—wrist, throat, chest—even though the monitor's flatline makes the gesture meaningless. "Come on," he whispers, pressing harder against Hank's throat. "Come on, brother. Don't do this."

Blake's fist connects with the bulkhead before anyone can stop him. The impact reverberates through the hull like a gunshot. "Fuck!" He hits it again, harder, blood spattering from split knuckles. "Fuck, fuck, FUCK!" Rigel and Carter move to restrain him before he destroys his hands completely.

Ethan's command mask slips for exactly three seconds—his face crumpling, breath catching on what might be a sob. Then he turns away, shoulders rigid, and walks to the far corner of the medical bay where he can pretend we can't see him falling apart.

"We just got you back," I breathe, leaning over Hank's still form. "We just … How is this happening? How can you be gone when you just came back to me?"

"Don't." Gabe's voice cracks as he moves to my side, his own hands hovering over Hank's body like he's afraid to touch and confirm the reality. "Don't do this. You can't—you can't go where he's gone. I can't lose both of you."

"He died saving me." The words taste like acid. "Again. He came back from the dead to save me, and I killed him anyway."

"He died doing what he chose to do." Gabe's response is fierce, desperate. "What he wanted to do. Don't you dare take that choice away from him."

But the guilt eats at me anyway. If I hadn't been captured. If I'd been stronger, smarter, more careful. If I hadn't needed rescuing in the first place.

Time fractures around the sound as the monitor screams its final note. Flat, unbroken. A blade through the air.

No one breathes.

Ethan stands frozen, arms wrapped around Rebel like she'll shatter if he lets go. Blood streaks from a brutal gash that slices from her temple to her mouth, dried and cracked. One arm splinted tight against her body. Her ribs grind when she breathes, each inhale a quiet sob buried against his chest.

She doesn't look at the screen. She doesn't have to. She feels it. We all do.

Jeb holds Stitch close. Her shirt clings to her back in dark, tacky patches—open lashes still oozing from where the whip tore her skin. She sways on her feet, pale and shaking from blood loss, from pain, from too much everything.

She was whipped. Caned.

Her legs tremble beneath her, but she stays standing because she refuses to collapse. Not yet. Not while Hank lies still on that table.

Carter braces Jenna against his side, his tears still falling silently. Her hand is wrapped in thick gauze, two fingers gone. A souvenir from Malfor's sick games. Her expression doesn't crack. Her lips are pressed into a line so tight it's colorless. But her eyes … God, her eyes. They're locked on Hank. Wide. Empty. Like something inside her broke and hasn't stopped falling.

Walt stands tall, one arm around Malia, his other hand still pressed to Hank's throat as if sheer will can restart circulation. Her arm's in a makeshift sling, and her skin's pale beneath bruises that haven't even started to fade. But she stays upright, chin lifted, eyes hard. Her body shakes, but her voice is steady as she whispers Hank's name like a prayer she's too afraid to believe in.

Blake cradles his bloodied knuckles against his chest, Rigel's restraining hand still on his shoulder. Shoulders squared despite the pain. Eyes red-rimmed but dry now, grief transformed into something harder, more controlled. Sophia wasn't taken. He was the only one of us who didn't feel that helplessness. But this? This is worse. Watching Hank die—there's no mission to complete. No enemy to shoot. Just silence, and that goddamn sound.

And then there's Rigel, holding Mia as gently as a man trained to kill can. She leans into him like she's been hollowed out. Her entire body bruised, battered, drained. Her cheek rests against his chest, lashes fluttering like she's on the edge of unconsciousness, but she won't let go. He murmurs something only she can hear, and whatever it is keeps her standing.

Barely.

They all loved him. Every person in this room owes their life to decisions Hank made, orders he gave, and sacrifices he chose. He wasn't just my lover and Gabe's partner. He was the heart. Their anchor. Their moral compass. The calm in the storm. The reason we're alive.

This isn't just loss.

It's a tearing.

A wound across every one of us, raw and open and screaming.

And now he's gone.

"Please," I whisper, but I don't know who I'm begging anymore. God? The universe? Hank himself?

The room stays silent, every soul inside it waiting for a miracle that won't come. I close my eyes, just for a second, but the monitor doesn't care. It blares the truth again—flat and final.

Why? The question burns through me. Why bring him back just to take him away again? Why give me hope just to destroy it more completely than before?

Gabe's shoulders jerk. One silent sob. His hand settles on Hank's chest like he can restart it with touch alone.

Then he roars in denial, his fist slamming into the bulkhead hard enough to crack fiberglass. The impact reverberates through the hull, metal groaning in protest. Blood spatters from his knuckles as he hits the wall again, then again.

This is the sound of the world breaking. None of us will ever be whole again.

"Don't." Blake catches his arm despite his own injured hands. "He wouldn't want you to destroy yourself."

"Don't fucking touch me!" Gabe whirls on him, eyes wild with grief and rage that has nowhere safe to land. "Don't you fucking dare!"

His chest heaves like he's drowning. Blood streams from split knuckles, drips onto the deck in steady drops that sound like rain on metal. The medics move around us, turning off equipment, preparing for transport, the business of death.

"I should have been faster," Walt says suddenly, his voice hollow. "On the rappel. I should have covered him better."

"Stop." Ethan's command voice cracks. "We don't do this. We don't tear ourselves apart with what-ifs."

"Then what do we do?" Blake demands, pain making his voice sharp. "How do we process this? How do we—"

"We honor him." Jenna's voice cuts through the chaos, steady despite everything. Military training holding her together when emotion threatens to shatter her completely. "We make sure his death means something."

One of the medics approaches with that dreaded white sheet—cotton that will erase Hank's face, hide the man we love behind sterile fabric.

"Wait." My voice cracks on the word. "Please. Just—wait."

I lean over him, memorizing details I should have paid more attention to while he lived. The scar on his chin from a childhood accident. The way his dark lashes look longer against pale skin. The callus on his trigger finger from years of service.

Features I've kissed, touched, and loved. Now still as a photograph.

"I'm sorry." The words tear from somewhere deep in my chest.

"Don't." Gabe's voice breaks completely. "Don't you dare. He chose to save you because you were worth everything to him. To both of us."

The medic's hand settles gently on my shoulder. "Ma'am, we need to—"

"I know." I don't look away from Hank's face. "I know what you need to do."

But I don't move. Can't move. Moving means accepting this is real. Moving means leaving him to whatever comes next—body bags and transport and all the administrative machinery of death.

"We need to call his parents," Ethan says quietly, his command voice steadier now that he has practical tasks to focus on. "His sister. They deserve to hear it from us, not through official channels."

"What do we tell them?" Carter asks, his tears finally stopping.

"The truth." Jenna's response is immediate. "That he died a hero. That he saved lives. That he was loved."

"That he was the best of us," Walt adds softly.

The sheet settles over Hank's face like snow. White cotton erasing the features I've memorized, loved, needed more than breath itself. My hand still holds his beneath the thin fabric, fingers intertwined with his cooling ones.

I sob, the sound cutting through me like a blade—not the controlled grief of before, but something wild and broken. The strength I've maintained through captivity, torture, and rescue finally cracks completely. My body shakes with the force of love and loss pouring out in waves.

Gabe stares at the covered body for a long moment, something terrible building behind his eyes. Then he turns and walks out of the medical bay without a word.

"Gabe—" I start to follow, but my legs won't support me. The breakdown I've been holding back hits full force.

"Let him go." Ethan's voice carries command authority even in grief. "He needs space right now."

"He needs—" I can't finish the sentence through my sobs.

"To process this in his own way." Ethan's eyes track to where Gabe's footsteps fade down the corridor. "We all do."

The women move as one, surrounding me in a circle of fierce, unspoken love. A sisterhood forged in captivity, in blood and bruises and whispered hope. They know what it means to love men who bleed for others.

Who would die to protect us.

Who have.

"Come here." Jenna's voice is soft but firm. She pulls me away from the table, away from the sheet-covered reminder of what we've lost.

"I can't leave him." Leaving feels like abandonment, like the final betrayal of everything we were together.

My legs feel disconnected from my body, muscles unwilling to obey simple commands. The medical bay has become the last place we were all together, the last space where love existed in its complete form.

"You're not leaving him." Malia takes my other arm, gentle but insistent. "But you can't stay here either."

"He'll always be with us," Rebel adds quietly, her damaged face showing fierce conviction. "Death doesn't end love. It just changes where it lives."

They guide me out of the medical bay, a procession of wounded women supporting each other through the worst night of their lives. Our voices fade as we move toward the galley, leaving the men to stand vigil over their fallen brother.

"Three days to home port," Ethan says quietly to the remaining team. "Captain's running dark, minimal communications. Gives us time to figure out our next steps."

"Memorial service?" Carter asks.

"Full military honors," Walt confirms. "Guardian HRS will want to—"

"No." Blake's interruption is sharp. "Not just Guardian HRS. This is bigger than that. Hank was—he was family to all of us."

"Private service first," Ethan decides. "For us. For the people who loved him. Then whatever official ceremonies Guardian HRS requires."

Three days on this boat with Hank's body in the ship's morgue. Three days to process what we've lost and decide what comes next.

Three days to figure out how to live in a world that feels fundamentally broken without him.

Three days that feel like a lifetime.

But also like no time at all to say goodbye to the future we'll never have.

I loved you, I think, grief settling into my bones like lead. *I loved you, and I'll keep loving you, and I'll figure out how to live with that love even when you're not here to receive it.*

The thought doesn't comfort. Nothing will comfort for a very long time.

But it's a place to start.

FORTY-TWO

The Space He Left

ALLY

THE GALLEY OF THE TRAWLER SMELLS LIKE COFFEE AND DIESEL fuel. Yellow light casts everything in warm tones that feel wrong for a night this dark. We claim the space, turning it into a sanctuary where grief can exist without judgment.

Jenna sits beside me on the worn bench seat, her bandaged hand resting on mine. The absence of her fingers hits me fresh—another piece of wholeness Malfor stole from us. Mia curls up in the corner, Rigel's jacket draped over her shoulders. He's somewhere above deck, keeping watch.

"He loved you both," Rebel whispers. Her voice rasps through swollen lips, one side of her face stitched and discolored. "Anyone with eyes could see it."

"Could see what?" My voice sounds hollow to my own ears.

I can't breathe. The air burns as it drags into my lungs. My chest stays hollow, no matter how tightly I wrap my arms around myself.

"How complete you made each other." Malia shifts beside me, wincing with the movement. One arm cradles her ribs, the other reaches out, brushing my back like she's afraid I might break apart. "The way you fit together like puzzle pieces. How you looked at each other like nothing else mattered. Like you found home in the same place."

My legs go. I drop, knees slamming against cold metal. Hands catch me—Stitch's, trembling from the lash marks that haven't stopped bleeding. Rebel sinks down beside me, pulling me in with her unbroken arm.

"And now? What do we do now?"

"Now you learn to fit together differently. You learn to live with the space he left behind," Stitch murmurs, crouching beside me, voice thick as the sea beyond the porthole. "But you're not empty. Not alone."

The women close in. A shield of love. Bruised, broken, bleeding—and still, they hold me.

The boat rocks gently, a rhythm that should be soothing but instead feels like a clock counting down to an uncertain future. Somewhere below, Hank's body lies in the ship's morgue. Somewhere above, Gabe bleeds on the deck rather than accept comfort.

"He'll come around," Jenna says softly, reading my mind. "Men like that—they process differently. They need to hit bottom before they can climb back up."

"What if he doesn't come back up?"

"Then you drag him." The certainty in Rebel's voice surprises me. "You grab him by the collar and drag him back to the surface, because that's what people who love each other do."

Mia uncurls from her corner and moves to sit across from me. "Rigel told me about the fight they had. Before the mission."

My stomach drops. "What fight?"

"Something about sharing you. About Gabe wanting more than Hank was willing to give." She reaches across the small table and covers my hands with hers. "Whatever he's carrying, it's eating him alive."

"He won't talk to me."

"He will. When he's ready to stop punishing himself." Stitch turns from the porthole, fixes me with eyes that have seen too much. "But you have to be ready to listen when he does."

The coffee in my cup has gone cold, a bitter film coating the surface. Outside, waves lap against the hull. Time moves forward whether we're ready or not.

"I should go find him."

"Give him another hour," Jenna advises. "Let him bleed a little more. Then go be the anchor he needs."

The next hours pass in silence, too heavy for words.

We take our grief in shifts. Plates of food go untouched. Rebel pours coffee, no one drinks. Malia dozes upright, pain etched between her brows. Jenna presses her forehead to Carter's shoulder, her eyes open but unfocused.

Rigel returns, wrapping Mia in his arms like he needs to feel her pulse just to believe she's real. Jeb finally coaxes Stitch into sitting, her eyes hollow, her back still seeping blood into borrowed fabric. Walt paces. Blake leans against the bulkhead, arms crossed, a silent sentinel.

No one mentions the empty seat at the table.

When I slip away, no one tries to stop me.

I find him on the forward deck, alone beneath a sky smeared with stars and smoke. His back rests against a rusting storage container, knees bent, elbows braced. The shadows cling to him, hiding the blood still drying on his knuckles, the rawness in his silence.

He doesn't move when I approach. Doesn't look at me. Just keeps staring out at the ocean, the way you do when you need it to swallow everything you're feeling.

I sink beside him, drawing my knees to my chest. The cold from the metal deck seeps through my borrowed clothes, through skin and bone, straight into the hollow he left inside me.

"I don't know how to hold this much pain by myself."

Still, Gabe says nothing.

"I know what you're doing," I say. "Bleeding it out, one inch at a time. Like if you punish yourself hard enough, it might somehow bring him back."

His head bows low. Shoulders quake once. Twice.

"It won't," I murmur. "But I'll sit here, with you, until you remember how to breathe."

Silence stretches again, except it's not empty now. It holds grief. Memories. The shape of a future neither of us knows how to face.

Finally, Gabe turns his face toward me. The ocean wind has dried salt on his cheeks that didn't come from sea spray.

"I should've died instead of him."

"No." I reach for his hand, wrap my fingers through the bloodied ones he won't care for himself. "You live. You live because Hank would've bled out a hundred times to make sure we both got out."

His eyes close.

"The only way through this is together."

His fingers tighten around mine. A broken thing reaching for another broken thing. And somehow, between us, it feels like the start of something whole.

"You missed dinner." I settle beside him, close enough to offer comfort, far enough to respect his need for space.

"Wasn't hungry."

"The women are worried about you."

"The women should worry about themselves." His voice carries no heat, just exhaustion that goes bone-deep. "They've been through enough."

Salt air cuts through the diesel fumes, carrying the scent of open water and distance. Stars reflect on the black surface, fractured by the boat's wake into a million glittering pieces.

"Talk to me."

"About what?"

"About why you're out here bleeding instead of letting someone help you."

He flexes his damaged hands, winces at the pain. "Pain feels appropriate right now."

"Hank wouldn't want you hurting yourself."

"Hank's dead." The words come out flat, matter-of-fact. "What he wants doesn't matter anymore."

"That's not true."

"Isn't it?" He turns to look at me for the first time since I sat down. "He's gone, Ally. Whatever he wanted for us, whatever plans he had—they died with him."

"His love for us didn't die."

"Love." He laughs, the sound bitter as salt water. "You want to know about love? You want to know what our great love story really was?"

My chest tightens. "Gabe—"

"It was me being a selfish bastard. It was me fighting him because I wanted you all to myself." The words tumble out like blood from a wound. "It was me telling him that you belonged to me, not us. That if he understood what you needed, he'd step aside."

The confession shakes me to my core. I sink back against the storage container, processing the weight of what he's revealed.

"You fought over me."

"We fought because I'm a possessive asshole who thought love meant ownership." He stares at his bloodied hands. "The last conversation we had, the last real words between us—I told him I wanted you as my slave. Complete submission, complete control. Just mine."

"What did he say?"

"That I was confusing possession with love. That I was too fucked up to tell the difference." His voice cracks. "And maybe he was right."

The boat rocks beneath us, carrying us through darkness toward an uncertain dawn. Below deck, his teammates sleep or try to sleep. Above us, stars wheel across the sky in patterns that have guided sailors for millennia.

"He forgave you."

"Did he? Because his last words sure sounded like he was trying to teach me something I was too stupid to learn while he was alive."

"His last words were about love. About taking care of each other." I shift closer, close enough that our shoulders touch. "He used his dying breath to forgive you and bless us. Both of us."

"I don't deserve forgiveness."

"Maybe not. But he gave it to you anyway." I take his damaged hands in mine, careful of the torn skin. "That's what love means. That's what family means."

He doesn't pull away this time; lets me hold his hands while tears he's been fighting finally fall.

"I don't know how to do this without him."

"Neither do I." The admission costs me everything. "But we're going to figure it out together."

"What if I'm just a possessive bastard? What if, without him to balance me out, I become everything he was afraid I already was?"

"Then I'll remind you who you are. The same way he would have." I squeeze his hands gently. "We'll teach each other how to love the way he wanted us to."

Above us, the stars shine down on two people learning how to carry impossible weight. Behind us, the wake of our passage stretches back toward a past we can never reclaim. Ahead, the horizon promises nothing but uncertainty.

But we're together. Broken and bleeding and barely holding on, but together.

The way Hank wanted.

The way we promised we would be.

FORTY-THREE

The Long Way Home

ALLY

I wake to the steady throb of engines and the smell of salt air mixed with diesel fuel. For one blissful moment, I forget. Then reality crashes down like a rogue wave—Hank is gone, and I'm curled against Gabe's chest in a narrow bunk aboard a trawler carrying us home incomplete.

Gabe's arm tightens around me when I stir. He's been awake for a while, I can tell by his breathing. Neither of us slept much. Every time I closed my eyes, I saw Hank's face going slack, heard that terrible flat tone of the monitor.

"Morning." His voice sounds like gravel over broken glass.

"Is it?" I don't move from his warmth. Outside the small porthole, gray dawn light filters through clouds. "Feels like the same endless night."

"Two more days." He presses his lips to the top of my head. "Then we figure out what comes next."

What comes next.

The phrase sits heavy between us, loaded with implications neither of us are ready to face.

What comes next is a house with three coffee mugs but only

two people to use them. What comes next is learning to be enough for each other when we've always been part of something larger.

A soft knock interrupts the silence. "Ally? Gabe?" Jenna's voice carries through the thin door. "Breakfast in the galley if you're up for it."

Food is the last thing I want, but the alternative is lying here, drowning in thoughts that lead nowhere good. I untangle myself from Gabe's arms, ignore the protest in my muscles, and reach for yesterday's clothes.

"We should go," I say when Gabe doesn't move. "The others need to see we're okay."

"Are we?"

The question hangs in the air like smoke. I don't have an answer, so I hold out my hand until he takes it.

The galley buzzes with quiet conversation when we enter. Charlie team sits around the scarred wooden table, picking at plates of eggs and toast. The women cluster together on the bench seats, coffee cups warming their hands. Everyone looks up when we appear, faces carefully neutral.

"There's coffee," Carter says, gesturing toward the pot. "Strong enough to wake the dead." His words fall into sudden silence. Carter's face goes white as he realizes what he's said. "Shit. I'm sorry ..."

"Hank would've appreciated that," Blake breaks the tension with a rough laugh. "Man lived on coffee and stubbornness."

"And those protein bars that tasted like cardboard," Walt adds. "Swore they were good for you even though they could probably stop a bullet."

A ghost of a smile touches Gabe's lips. "He made me eat one once. Tasted like punishment."

"*Collective suffering builds character,*" Rigel quotes in a passable imitation of Hank's command voice.

The stories start small—shared miseries and inside jokes. But they grow, becoming something larger. Someone mentions the time Hank got food poisoning in Thailand but still managed to complete the mission. Blake recounts an experience from last summer when Hank taught his nephew to fish, describing how patient he was with a hyperactive eight-year-old.

I find myself contributing too, telling them about that first morning at Gabe and Hank's condo when Hank was making breakfast. Gabe always said Hank's culinary skills were legendary among the team.

"He was so focused on getting the eggs just right," I say, smiling at the memory.

I don't mention how Hank looked at Gabe that morning, that subtle nod that communicated volumes between them. Don't tell them how Gabe lifted me onto the kitchen counter while Hank told Gabe to fuck me with that steady gaze that always made my pulse race. How afterward, with Gabe catching his breath, I slipped to my knees in front of Hank, following the silent command in his eyes. The way his hand tangled in my hair.

"Somehow he got completely distracted," I continue, meeting Gabe's eyes across the circle. His slight smile tells me he remembers exactly what I'm leaving out. "Smoke everywhere, alarms going off. And there was Hank, standing in the middle of his ruined kitchen, bacon burnt to a crisp, scrambled eggs somehow charred, looking absolutely bewildered about how it all went wrong."

It was one of our first times. Maybe the first. The three of us …

"He was so careful with everything else," I say, surprised by the steadiness in my voice. "Precise to the point of obsession. But put him in a kitchen …"

"He banned me from cooking after one tiny grease fire." Gabe joins in. "He called it self-preservation, but I did it on purpose. He was a virtuoso in the kitchen. That man could cook. Remember how he could turn MREs into something resembling actual food in the middle of a combat zone?"

The laughter that follows isn't bitter. It's warm, shot through with grief but not overwhelmed by it. For the first time since the medical bay, I can think about Hank without feeling like I'm drowning.

Day three brings rain. Gray sheets of water turn the ocean into hammered pewter. The weather matches the mood as we approach home waters. Tomorrow we dock. Tomorrow, this strange suspension between crisis and reality ends.

"He would've hated this weather," Rebel observes from her spot by the porthole. Her face has healed enough that the stitches are barely visible, but shadows linger in her eyes. "Always said rain during operations was God's way of making things unnecessarily complicated."

"He said that about everything," Ethan corrects. "Rain, snow, wind, excessive sunshine. According to Hank, optimal weather was seventy-two degrees, light cloud cover, and minimal humidity."

"Optimal conditions for optimal performance," several voices quote in unison.

The words hit like a gut punch—familiar, automatic, drilled into every one of them by the man they lost.

I laugh. I can't help it. It bursts out, sharp and aching, too close to a sob. Because even gone, Hank's voice still lives here. In their mouths. In their muscle memory. In the damn motto he barked before every mission like it was sacred scripture.

He made them better. All of them.

He made me better too.

The low thrum of approaching rotors cuts through the rain, growing louder until wind whips against the sides of the trawler.

We step out into the storm as the helicopter descends toward the deck, searchlights slicing through the mist.

The bird touches down hard, engine whining as the blades slow. The door slides open, and Forest steps out, rain flattening his usually polished hair and soaking the shoulders of his jacket.

Stitch appears behind me in the corridor, water dripping from her own coat.

"Forest wants everyone in the main cabin," she says. "Says we need to talk about tomorrow."

We gather in the larger space, cramped but together. Forest stands at the front, papers in his hands, the salt wind having wrinkled his shirt and darkened the fabric over his chest and sleeves.

"Port authority knows you're coming in with a KIA," Forest says without preamble. "Guardian HRS has sent a team to receive the body. They'll handle everything internally—no outside interference."

I look around the room at faces that have become family. These people who bled with us, who watched Hank die, who've spent three days learning how to carry his absence.

"Just us at the dock," Gabe says quietly. "No one else needs to be there."

"That will be arranged." Forest nods. "We'll keep it contained."

"Thank you." The words come out rougher than intended. "For everything."

"He was a good man," Forest says simply. "Deserves to be sent off right."

That evening, someone—I never figure out who—suggests we have a proper toast. Not the quick, desperate words we've been sharing, but something formal. Something worthy of the man we lost.

Walt produces a bottle of bourbon from somewhere. "Figured this qualifies."

We gather in a rough circle, plastic cups in hand. The bourbon burns going down, but the warmth that follows feels like courage taking root.

"To Hank." Ethan raises his cup first. "Who never let the team down, no matter what the mission threw at us."

"To Hank," Carter echoes. "Who never asked us to do anything he wouldn't do himself."

"To the man who could field-strip a rifle in thirty seconds but took an hour to pick a movie," Blake adds, earning soft laughter.

One by one, they share memories. Stories I've never heard, moments that happened in the field before I knew them. I learn that Hank once carried a wounded teammate three miles through enemy territory. That he never missed a shot when it mattered. That he sent money to the widow of a soldier killed on a joint operation, even though it wasn't his responsibility.

When it's my turn, the words stick in my throat. How do you summarize a man who became your foundation? How do you toast someone who taught you that love could be shared without being diminished?

"To Hank," I finally manage. "Who showed me what it meant to be cherished. Who made me believe I was worth fighting for."

"To the man who held us together." Gabe's voice cracks as he speaks. "Who forgave me when I didn't deserve it. Who died believing in us when I'd stopped believing in myself."

We drink in silence after that, letting the bourbon and the words settle. Outside, rain continues to fall, but inside this circle of grief and love, something like peace takes root.

"He'd want us to be happy," Jenna says softly. "All of us. He'd want us to build something good from this."

"He'd want us to take care of each other," Mia adds.

"He'd want us to remember that love doesn't die just because people do," Rebel finishes.

The truth lands hard—like breath knocked from my lungs, leaving me raw and exposed. Hank isn't really gone, not if we carry forward what he taught us. The way he loved—fiercely, completely, without reservation—that lives on in every choice we make.

Gabe's hand finds mine under the table, squeezes once. A promise. A commitment. A recognition that tomorrow we start the impossible task of learning to live without the best of us.

But tonight, we remember. Tonight, we honor what was and begin to imagine what could be.

FORTY-FOUR

Where Three Became Two

ALLY

MORNING COMES GRAY AND COLD, THE KIND OF WEATHER THAT seeps into your bones and stays there. I stand at the rail watching the familiar coastline emerge from mist, and my chest tightens with each mile that brings us closer to a life that doesn't include Hank.

"There." Gabe points toward the dock where a small group has gathered. Guardian personnel in dark suits. A black vehicle waiting to carry Hank away from us one final time.

The trawler's engines downshift as we approach the pier, their pitch dropping like a sigh. Dockhands move with quiet efficiency, lines thrown and caught, metal groaning against wood as the vessel eases into place. The mechanical routine of arrival unfolds, indifferent to the fact that my heart's tearing itself apart behind my ribs.

We gather near the stern—what's left of us.

The women flank me, bruised and broken and standing anyway. Malia, arm in a sling, eyes fierce with unshed tears. Rebel with her jaw swollen, stitches stark against mottled skin. Stitch leans on Jeb, who holds her like he'd take every lash for her if he could. Jenna's bandaged hand finds mine. Mia sways slightly beside Rigel, his arm wrapped tight around her waist.

And Gabe. At my side. Silent. Haunted. Not touching me, but I feel him anyway—his grief sharp and serrated, the storm he refuses to let loose.

Footsteps sound behind us—boots, six pairs. The men step forward together. Ethan. Jeb. Rigel. Carter. Blake. Walt. No words spoken. No discussion. They decided this quietly. Without asking. Without telling Gabe. So he could stay with me.

They move through the tight corridor to the small, cold room below deck.

And then they return.

Carrying Hank.

The coffin is simple. Clean lines. But it holds more than a body. It carries my heart.

I can't breathe.

The air thickens. The sound of their boots on the trawler's deck matches the pounding of my pulse.

Six across. Steps perfectly in sync.

This is brotherhood. This is love.

Gabe's arm comes around my shoulders, solid and grounding. His hand flexes once against my arm, a tremor he doesn't hide.

They reach the dock and descend the ramp, backs straight, eyes ahead. The coffin rests like it belongs to them—because it does. They don't hand him off. They carry him all the way to the waiting transport.

The rear doors open with a soft hiss.

He disappears inside.

The doors close with a gentle finality that punches the air from my lungs.

I sway. Gabe catches me.

"Where—" My voice snaps off, caught on a sob I can't swallow. I try again, quieter. "Where are you taking him?"

Gabe says something, but I hear none of it. The pain is too loud. The loss too much to bear.

The vehicle disappears, and no one moves. We stand there, suspended in the hush left behind.

"Ready?" Gabe asks beside me, voice rough with everything he isn't saying. None of us are. But we move anyway.

They bring a bus to carry us all home. Doors open and close in subdued clicks. No chatter. No ribbing. No comfort in routine.

Just silence.

The drive back to Guardian HQ is a blur of streetlights and reflection. Rain streaks the windows. Red taillights bleed across the glass. Rebel rests her head against Ethan's shoulder. Jeb runs his fingers gently along Stitch's spine, careful of the raw wounds beneath her shirt. Rigel doesn't take his eyes off Mia. Walt hasn't spoken since the trawler. Blake stares straight ahead like he's still carrying Hank's weight in his arms.

Gabe's thigh presses against mine. He doesn't speak. Doesn't look away from the dark outside. But his hand stays wrapped around mine like it's the only tether he has.

At HQ, no one lingers. There's no debrief. No gear unload. Just weary bodies peeling off into the night—each of us shattered in our own quiet orbit.

GABE LEADS ME TO HIS CAR, FINGERS BRUSHING THE SMALL OF MY back. He opens the door like he always did, like nothing's changed. But everything has.

The car door slams shut with metallic finality. Gabe's hands shake as he grips the steering wheel, knuckles still split and bloody from the bulkhead, from Malfor's face, from everything his fists could find to destroy in the aftermath of violence and loss.

I sit in the passenger seat, numb. My body feels disconnected, like I'm floating somewhere above myself, watching a woman who looks like me stare through rain-streaked glass at a world that doesn't make sense anymore.

The engine turns over. Gabe's breathing is too controlled; the kind of deliberate rhythm that means he's fighting something larger than grief.

The silence stretches between us, thick and suffocating. Not the comfortable quiet we used to share, but something raw and bleeding that neither of us know how to bandage.

"Is he really dead?" The words slip out before I can stop them, barely above a whisper.

Gabe's hands tighten on the wheel until his knuckles go white. "Yeah. He's really dead."

The confirmation hits like a physical blow. My chest constricts; my lungs forget how to expand properly. Some part of me has been waiting for this to be another nightmare, another trick, another psychological game Malfor was playing.

But it's real. The flatline was real. The sheet over his face was real. The cold skin beneath my fingers was real.

"I'm going to kill Malfor." Gabe's voice is flat, emotionless. "Torture him first. Make him suffer."

I turn to look at him—really look. His jaw is set in that dangerous way that usually means someone's about to get hurt, but his eyes … His eyes are empty. Hollow. Like he's used up every emotion he had and found nothing waiting underneath.

The rain starts again as we pull away from the curb, droplets spattering against the windshield like tears the sky can't hold back. The windshield wipers begin their rhythmic fight against the persistent moisture, back and forth, back and forth, a mechanical heartbeat in the silence.

We drive through familiar streets that now feel foreign. Everything looks the same, but nothing feels right. The world kept turning while our universe collapsed, and the disconnect is jarring.

"I keep waiting for him to call," I say softly. "To check in. To ask if we made it home okay."

Gabe's throat works like he's swallowing glass. "He always worried about the drive. Said it was more dangerous than our missions because people get complacent on familiar roads."

A sob catches in my throat. Such a Hank thing to say—practical concern wrapped in love, statistics disguised as affection.

Familiar landmarks scroll past. The coffee shop where Hank bought me my first latte, patiently explaining the difference between a flat white and a cappuccino while I pretended to care about milk foam. The park where the three of us walked on Sunday mornings, Hank pointing out birds while Gabe and I made fun of his amateur ornithology. The grocery store where he insisted on reading every ingredient label, not because he cared about preservatives, but because he liked the science behind food chemistry.

Memories layer over geography, turning the simple act of driving into an archaeological dig through our shared life.

"I never thought it would be him," Gabe says suddenly as we turn onto our street.

The words hang in the air, heavy with implications I'm not sure I want to explore.

"What do you mean?"

"I always figured if one of us didn't make it home, it would be me." His hands tighten on the steering wheel until the leather creaks. "I'm the one who takes risks. Who pushes boundaries. Who doesn't think things through." His voice drops to something barely audible. "Hank was supposed to be the steady one. The one who lived to be eighty and complained about his arthritis and taught our kids how to fish."

Our kids. The phrase cuts through me like a blade. Plans we made. Futures we imagined. Dreams that died with him on that metal table.

The house comes into view—weathered cedar shingles, wide deck overlooking the Pacific, windows that reflect the gray sky like empty eyes. Home. But how can it be home when the person who made it feel safe is gone?

"I don't know how to do this," I admit as Gabe kills the engine. The sudden quiet feels oppressive without the mechanical comfort of the wipers. "Walk through that door. See his coffee mug in the sink. Smell his cologne on the pillows."

"Neither do I." Gabe stares at the house like it might attack us. "We built this place for three people. Everything about it assumes he'll be there."

The kitchen with its oversized island designed for all of us to cook together, Hank chopping vegetables with surgical precision, while Gabe and I argued about seasoning. The living room with the sectional sofa arranged so we could all watch movies in a pile of limbs and contentment, Hank in the middle because he ran warm, and Gabe and I both got cold. The bedroom with the California king that seemed perfectly sized when we were all in it, but will feel cavernous with just two.

"Maybe we should sell it," I say, the words tasting like betrayal even as they leave my mouth. "Find somewhere new. Somewhere that doesn't have his ghost in every corner."

"Maybe." But Gabe doesn't sound convinced. "Or maybe we learn to live with the ghosts. Maybe we figure out how to honor what we had here while building something new."

Rain patters against the windshield, filling the silence while we both stare at a house that represents everything we've lost and everything we still have to lose.

"Do we keep the house?" I ask, voicing the practical concern that's been lurking beneath the grief. "Do we change everything? Move his clothes? Pack up his books?"

"I don't know." Gabe's honesty is brutal and necessary. "I don't know how to make those decisions yet."

"What about us?" The question scrapes my throat raw. "What happens to us without him to balance the equation?"

Gabe turns in his seat, reaches for my hands. His fingers are warm despite the cold that's settled into my bones, despite the violence those hands committed just hours ago.

"I'm scared," he admits, and the words cost him everything.

"Of what?"

"That I won't be enough. That without him to balance us, we'll fall apart." The confession tastes like poison in the air between us. "That you'll realize you don't actually want just me. That what we had only worked because he was there to make it work."

His words crack something open in me. A sob climbs my throat, raw and hot, but I choke it back, pressing his hands between mine as if I can force him to feel what I can't yet say.

"Our dynamic will be different," I say carefully, testing each word before I speak it. "The way we … The way we're intimate will change. The way we fight will change. The way we heal will change."

Gabe's jaw clenches. "What if we don't know how to be together without him there to show us the way? What if we try and it's all wrong?"

"Then we learn." The words come out stronger than I feel. "We stumble and fail and figure it out as we go. But we do it together."

"I fell in love with both of you," I continue, the admission feeling like stepping off a cliff. "That doesn't change because he's not here. He made me feel stronger, and you made me feel seen.

The two of you didn't split my heart—you expanded it. I can't breathe without you."

Tears blur my vision, salt and grief and truth mixing together until I can't tell where one ends and another begins.

"I'm scared too," I admit, voice breaking. "Scared of walking into that house without him. Of climbing into a bed that still smells like all three of us. Of reaching for you and feeling how different it all is."

Gabe closes his eyes, jaw clenched tight against words he doesn't know how to say.

"But I'd rather hurt with you than try to heal without you."

Silence stretches between us, thick with everything we've lost and everything we still might save.

"You are not a consolation prize," I say fiercely, needing him to understand. "You are not the piece that's left over after we lost the good part. You're the reason I want to keep breathing even though it feels impossible right now."

"But we're different without him. The dynamic changes. What if—"

"What if we become something different but equally beautiful?" I reach out and cup his face, thumbs tracing the familiar geography of cheekbones and stubble. "What if we honor Hank by refusing to let his death destroy what he helped create?"

Tears spill over, hot against the cold morning air. Gabe leans into my touch like a man dying of thirst.

"I love you," he says simply, and the words feel fragile as spun glass. "Not because you were Hank's too. Because you're you. Because even in the middle of the worst thing that's ever happened to us, you're still trying to take care of me."

His voice breaks on the last word, vulnerability cracking him open in ways violence never could.

"But I'm terrified we don't know how to love each other without him there to anchor us."

"Then we learn," I repeat, leaning forward until our foreheads touch. "We stumble and fail and figure it out as we go. But we do it together. The way Hank wanted. The way we promised."

Through the rain-streaked windshield, the house waits. Empty rooms full of memory and possibility. A life that needs to be rebuilt from whatever pieces we can salvage.

"Together," Gabe confirms, the word a vow, a prayer, and a promise all at once.

We sit in the car for another long moment, gathering courage for the simple act of going home. The rain continues its steady percussion against the roof, a rhythm that feels like time passing.

Finally, Gabe opens his door, and rain rushes in to remind us that the world keeps moving whether we want it to, or not.

The front door swings open on rooms that smell like him—coffee and soap and the faint trace of gun oil he never quite managed to wash off his hands completely.

I step across the threshold and freeze.

FORTY-FIVE

Living with Ghosts

ALLY

THE HOUSE SWALLOWS US WHOLE THE MOMENT WE CROSS THE threshold. Hank's presence saturates every surface.

His coffee mug still sits in the sink, half-full and growing a skin of mold because neither of us has the heart to clean it. His jacket hangs on the hook by the door, one sleeve twisted as if he just shrugged it off. The book he was reading still rests on the coffee table, bookmark exactly where he left it on page 247.

"Jesus." Gabe's voice cracks behind me.

Gabe stops in the entryway like he's hit an invisible wall. I watch his eyes track over familiar objects that have become arti-facts of a life that no longer exists. The house feels like a museum exhibit. Everything exactly as he left it, frozen in time while the world exploded around us.

"I'll make coffee," I say, because silence feels dangerous right now.

"I'm not—" He clears his throat. "I'm not really hungry. Or thirsty."

"Neither am I."

But I go to the kitchen anyway, needing something to do with my hands. The coffee maker sits next to Hank's favorite mug—black ceramic with "World's Okayest Operator" printed in faded white letters. A joke gift from last Christmas that he used every morning.

I reach for a different mug. Two different mugs. The mathematics of grief playing out in coffee cups and empty chairs.

Gabe wanders into the living room, then out again. Restless energy with nowhere to go. He picks up Hank's book and sets it down. Touches the remote, pulls his hand back like it burned him.

"Maybe I should stay in my room," he says suddenly. "For a while. Until—"

"Until, what?"

"Until it doesn't feel like we're betraying him just by being in the same space."

The coffee maker gurgles to life, filling the silence. Steam rises from the carafe, carrying the scent of the dark roast Hank preferred. Another ghost to add to the collection.

"He's not here, Gabe."

"Isn't he?" He gestures around the kitchen. "His fingerprints are on every surface. His voice echoes in every room. Hell, I can still smell his cologne on the couch cushions."

I can too. Sandalwood and cedar, faint but persistent. Like he just stepped out for a run and might come back any minute, sweaty and grinning.

"So what do we do? Burn everything? Pretend he never existed?"

"I don't know." Gabe slumps against the counter, exhaustion written in every line of his body. "I just know that every time I look at you, I see him too. And every time I think about—" He stops, shakes his head.

"About, what?"

"About touching you. About kissing you. About anything that

used to feel natural." His voice drops to barely audible. "It feels like cheating."

The words hit like a sucker-punch of reality. Because I feel it too—the wrongness that settles over us whenever we get too close. The way his hand pulls back when he reaches for me. The careful distance we maintain on the couch, on opposite sides of a space that used to hold three bodies in easy intimacy.

"We can't live like roommates," I say finally.

"Can't we?" He looks up, eyes red-rimmed with exhaustion and grief. "Maybe that's what we are now. Maybe the other thing—the us thing—only worked because he was the bridge between us."

The coffee finishes brewing with a final hiss. I pour two cups, add cream to mine, and leave his black the way he likes it. The way he's always liked it, since before Hank and me, since the early days when they were just partners learning to trust each other with their lives.

"You don't believe that."

"Don't I?" He takes the coffee but doesn't drink it, just holds it like a prop. "Think about it. When do we work best together? When he's there to translate between us. When do we fight? When it's just us trying to figure out what the hell we're doing."

"That's not—"

"The first time we had sex, all three of us, remember? You were terrified, but Hank made it okay. He made everything okay." Gabe's voice cracks. "What happens when there's no one to make it okay anymore?"

I set down my coffee mug with shaking hands because he's voicing the fear that's been growing in my chest since we walked through the front door. The fear that, without Hank's steady presence, Gabe and I will discover we're just two broken people who don't actually fit together.

"So we give up? We let his death destroy what he helped create?"

"Maybe what he helped create was always dependent on him being here to maintain it."

The words hang between us like smoke from an explosion. Heavy. Toxic. Impossible to take back once they're spoken.

I walk to the living room, sink onto the couch where we used to pile together for movie nights. The cushions still hold the impression of Hank's body, a shallow dent where he always sat. I curl into that space, breathing in the lingering scent of him.

"I miss him so much it feels like dying," I whisper.

Gabe follows but doesn't sit. Just stands in the doorway like he's afraid to contaminate the memory with his presence.

"I miss him too."

"But I miss us too. The way we fit together. The way you used to look at me like I was something precious." I meet his eyes across the room. "Now you look at me like I'm a problem you don't know how to solve."

"Because I don't." The admission costs him everything. "I don't know how to be with you without him here to show me how. I don't know how to touch you without feeling like I'm taking something that isn't mine. I don't know how to love you when half of what I loved about us is gone."

The truth of it settles over us like a ghostly shroud. We sit in Hank's house, surrounded by Hank's things, trying to figure out how to be Ally and Gabe instead of two-thirds of something larger.

"Maybe we're thinking about this wrong," I say finally.

"How?"

"Maybe we're not supposed to figure out how to be us without him. Maybe we're supposed to figure out how to be something new. Something that honors what we had while accepting what we've lost."

Gabe considers this, jaw working silently. Outside, the ocean crashes against the cliffs, eternal and indifferent to human grief.

"I'm scared," he admits.

"Of what?"

"Of touching you and realizing it doesn't feel the same. Of kissing you and tasting only loss instead of love. Of trying to make love to you and discovering that what I thought was desire was just proximity to him."

The fear in his voice breaks something open in my chest. I'm afraid of the same things. Afraid that without Hank's hands on my skin, Gabe's touch will feel foreign. Afraid that without Hank's voice murmuring encouragement, our intimacy will feel hollow.

"What if it is different?" Gabe takes a sip of his coffee.

"Then we figure out if different can still be good." I cross the room to where he's standing. "But we can't figure that out by avoiding each other."

"Ally—"

"No." I reach for his hands, feel the tremor in them that speaks to fear and want and confusion all tangled together. "We're going to spend the rest of our lives wondering if we could have made this work, or we're going to find out."

"What if—"

"What if we honor him by refusing to let his death steal our chance at happiness?" I step closer, close enough to feel the heat radiating off his body. "What if we owe it to him—and to ourselves—to try?"

Gabe's eyes search my face, looking for certainty I'm not sure I feel. But I know one thing for sure: this careful distance is killing us by degrees. Better to risk heartbreak than guarantee it through inaction.

"I don't know how to do this without him," he whispers.

"Neither do I. So we learn. Together."

I rise on my toes, press my lips to his in the softest possible kiss. A question more than a statement. A request for permission to try.

He freezes for a heartbeat. Then his hands come up to frame my face, thumb tracing the line of my cheek with the reverence I remember from before. Before grief. Before loss. Before everything got complicated.

I close my eyes and let his warmth seep into my bones, let his heartbeat remind me that life continues even when it feels impossible. Tomorrow we'll figure out how to live without Hank. Tomorrow we'll start the long process of healing.

Tonight, we hold each other and remember that love doesn't end with death—it just learns to exist in a different shape.

It's not the future we imagined. But it's the one we have.

"It feels wrong," he breathes against my mouth.

"I know."

"Like we're betraying him."

"I know."

"But I need you." The admission tears from his throat. "I need to know we still exist when it's just us."

"Then let's find out."

I take his hand, lead him toward the bedroom—Hank's room. Each step feels monumental, like we're climbing toward either salvation or destruction and won't know which until we reach the top.

The bedroom door stands open, revealing the California king that seemed perfectly sized for three and now yawns empty as a canyon. Gabe stops in the doorway, staring at that empty space.

"We don't have to do this in here," I say.

"Yes, we do." His voice carries newfound resolve. "If we're going to do this, we do it here. In our space. All of ours."

He's right. Running to another room won't change anything. The ghost of what we were will follow us wherever we go. Better to face it head-on, to claim this space for what we're becoming instead of what we've lost.

Afternoon light filters through the windows, casting everything in golden tones that should be romantic but feel melancholy instead. We stand beside the bed, suddenly awkward as teenagers, unsure how to begin something we've done a hundred times before.

"I don't remember how to do this," I admit.

"The mechanics are the same."

"That's not what I mean."

"I know." He reaches for the hem of my shirt, then stops. "Can I?"

The formality of the question breaks my heart a little. When did we become strangers asking permission for touches that used to be as natural as breathing?

I nod, and he lifts my shirt over my head. His eyes track over skin he's kissed and marked and worshipped, but now they hold uncertainty alongside desire.

"You're so beautiful," he says, as if he's just remembering.

"Touch me."

His hands settle on my waist, thumbs tracing the curve of my ribs. Familiar territory mapped by fingers that know every sensitive spot, every place that makes me gasp. But something's missing—the easy confidence that came from being part of a unit that knew exactly how to drive me to the edge of sanity.

I reach for his shirt, pull it over his head to reveal the body I've explored countless times. Scars I've kissed, muscles I've gripped, skin I've marked with my nails. Still beautiful. Still mine. But somehow foreign now that half our dynamic is gone.

We undress each other slowly, carefully, like we're handling something fragile that might shatter if we move too fast. When we're finally naked, standing beside the bed where we've made love hundreds of times, the silence feels heavier than before.

"This is weird," he says finally.

"Really weird."

We ease down onto the edge of the bed, but even that feels too loaded. Like we're trespassing in a memory.

Gabe lies back first. I follow, but instead of straddling him, I curl into his side, resting my cheek against his chest. His heartbeat stutters under my ear, not from arousal, but uncertainty.

Loss.

This isn't lust humming between us—it's the echo of something we're both afraid we've lost for good.

His fingers drift up my spine, trembling slightly. I press my mouth to the spot beneath his collarbone, where I once left teeth marks in a moment of passion.

Now my lips linger there, not from desire—but searching. Waiting for something to feel right.

It doesn't.

His breath catches—not in pleasure. In hesitation. His palm stills on my skin.

"I can't," he whispers, voice frayed at the edges. "I'm trying so damn hard to want this the way I used to, but—it feels like acting."

My eyes burn, tears pressing hot behind my lids. Relief and grief twisting together like vines.

"I'm glad you said it," I murmur against his chest. "Because I was pretending too."

He exhales a broken sound—half laugh, half sob—and covers his face with both hands. I sit up, pull the sheet over us, and we lie there in a silence that's finally honest.

Not pretending. Not forcing.

Just being.

"I wanted to feel close to you again," he says, voice muffled. "I thought if I touched you, it might bring him back."

I nod, throat too tight to speak.

We stare at the ceiling. The air between us feels less charged now, less full of failure and unmet expectations. Maybe just—understanding.

Grief doesn't follow a straight line. Sometimes, it loops back on itself. Sometimes, it lies in your bed, naked and aching and too scared to move forward.

I reach for his hand and lace my fingers through his.

"Let's just sleep."

His grip tightens.

And for the first time in days, we do.

FORTY-SIX

Finding My Way Back

GABE

THE BEDROOM FEELS DIFFERENT IN THE AFTERMATH. QUIETER. Like the ghosts that have been haunting us have finally decided to give us some space to breathe.

Ally sleeps curled against my chest, her breathing deep and even for the first time in days. No nightmares. No restless tossing. Just peace written across features that have carried too much pain lately.

I can't sleep. Too much adrenaline still coursing through my system, too many thoughts circling like vultures in my head. But for the first time since Hank died, they're not all dark thoughts.

We did it. We actually fucking did it. Made love without him and didn't fall apart. Didn't discover that everything between us was just proximity to his light. Found something that's ours—different from what we had before, maybe sadder, but definitely real.

Her hand rests over my heart, fingers splayed across skin she's marked with her nails. The sting feels good. Feels like proof that I'm still capable of feeling something other than grief.

"Can't sleep?" Her voice comes soft and drowsy, eyes still closed.

"Thinking."

"About?"

"About how that didn't feel like betrayal."

She shifts against me, tilting her head to meet my eyes. "What did it feel like?"

"Like coming home." I consider the question, searching for words that fit the tangle of emotions in my chest. "Like remembering who I am when I'm not drowning in guilt."

"Who are you when you're not drowning?"

"Yours." The word slips out before I can stop it, raw and honest. "I'm yours, Ally. I always have been."

Her eyes widen slightly. We haven't talked about that yet—the fight with Hank, the possessiveness that nearly destroyed us before grief finished the job.

"I know I fucked up before," I continue. "Thinking love meant ownership. Thinking I could stake a claim on you like you were territory to be conquered."

"Gabe—"

"Let me say this." I frame her face with my hands, need her to understand. "What we just did—that wasn't about possession. That was about choice. You choosing me. Me choosing you. Both of us choosing to build something new instead of letting grief bury us alive."

She kisses me then, slow and deep, and I taste hope on her tongue alongside desire. When she pulls back, her eyes hold something I haven't seen since before everything went to hell.

"Make love to me again," she whispers.

"Ally ..."

"Please. I need to know if we can do this more than once. I need to know if it gets easier."

I don't need to be asked twice. My body's already

responding to her proximity, to the way she looks at me like I'm something worth wanting instead of something broken that needs fixing.

This time there's less hesitation. Less careful navigation around empty spaces. I know how she feels beneath my hands now, how she responds when it's just us. The knowledge makes me bolder.

I roll her beneath me and pin her wrists above her head with one hand while the other explores territory that's always been mine to claim. She arches into my touch, breath hitching when I find the spot that makes her lose control.

"Better?" I murmur against her throat.

"Much better."

We move together with growing confidence, finding rhythms that belong to us alone. No ghost of a third presence. No phantom hands or imagined whispers. Just Ally and me, relearning how to set each other on fire.

When she comes apart beneath me, it's with my name on her lips and her nails digging crescents into my shoulders. When I follow her over the edge, it's with the knowledge that this—us—is going to survive whatever comes next.

I wake to pale morning light filtering through curtains and the soft sound of Ally's breathing beside me. The space where Hank should be doesn't feel like an open wound anymore. Just an empty pillow that reminds me of what we had without destroying what we have.

Ally stirs when I brush hair from her face, eyes fluttering open to reveal sleep-soft confusion that clears when she focuses on me.

"Morning," she says, voice husky with sleep.

"Morning."

We've made love twice in the last hour, and I'm already hard again. Already wanting her with an intensity that should probably concern me, but doesn't. This is who I am—the man who wants her constantly, who can't get enough even when she's wrapped around me.

Hank used to tease me about it. Called me insatiable. Said watching me try to control my need for her was like watching someone try to hold back the tide.

The memory doesn't hurt as much as it should. Instead of loss, I feel gratitude—for his understanding, for his willingness to share, for the way he never made me feel ashamed of how much I needed her.

"Again?" Ally asks, reading the intent in my eyes.

"If you're up for it."

"Always."

This time, I don't hold back. Don't treat her like she might break if I touch her too hard or move too fast. This time, I let myself be the dominant bastard she fell in love with, the one who knows exactly how to drive her out of her mind.

I flip her onto her stomach, hands gripping her hips as I position her exactly how I want her. She pushes back against me, demanding and eager, no longer the careful woman trying not to betray a dead man's memory.

"That's it," I growl when she meets me thrust for thrust. "Take what you need."

She does. She takes everything I give her and demands more, her body moving with the grace that always destroys my control. When I slide my hand between her legs, find the bundle of nerves that makes her scream, she shatters with an intensity that nearly takes me with her.

"Don't stop," she gasps. "Please don't stop."

I don't. Can't. I drive into her until thought becomes impossible, until there's nothing but sensation and connection and the primal satisfaction of claiming what's mine.

After, we lie tangled together, sweat cooling on skin marked by teeth and nails. Ally turns in my arms, studies my face with eyes that hold wonder alongside satisfaction.

"There you are," she says softly.

"What do you mean?"

"The man I fell in love with. The one who looks at me like he wants to devour me whole." Her fingers trace the line of my jaw. "I was starting to worry he was gone forever."

"Not gone. Just buried under a mountain of guilt and grief." I catch her hand and press a kiss to her palm. "Still working on digging him out, but I think he's going to make it."

"Good. Because I missed him."

"Missed who I am with you?"

"Missed who we are together." She shifts closer, eliminating the last inch of space between us. "This—what we just did—that felt like us. Like the real us, not some pale imitation."

She's right. The careful distance is gone, replaced by the easy intimacy that always existed between us. The way she fits against my body like she was designed for this exact purpose. The way I can read her needs in the arch of her spine, the catch of her breath.

"Shower?" I suggest. "Before we get too comfortable and spend the entire day in bed."

"Would that be so terrible?"

"Terrible? No. But I'm pretty sure we need to eat actual food at some point."

She laughs, the sound lighter than anything I've heard from her since the medical bay. "Fine. But I'm stealing your shampoo."

"You always steal my shampoo."

"Because it smells like you, and I like smelling like you."

The casual intimacy of the statement hits me harder than it should. These small things—shared shampoo, tangled legs, the way she steals my coffee in the morning—these are what make a life together. Not grand gestures or dramatic declarations. Just the accumulated weight of a thousand small choices to choose each other every day.

The shower is exactly what we need—hot water washing away the last traces of distance, steam creating a cocoon where only we exist. I wash her hair with the reverence she deserves, fingers massaging her scalp until she melts against me.

She returns the favor, hands mapping every inch of skin like she's memorizing me all over again. When she drops to her knees and takes me in her mouth, I have to brace myself against the shower wall to keep from falling.

"Fuck, Ally."

She hums around me, the vibration nearly destroying what little control I have left. When I fist my hand in her wet hair, she doesn't pull away. Just looks up at me with eyes that hold challenge alongside submission.

The combination unravels me completely. I come with her name on my lips and stars exploding behind my eyelids, knees threatening to buckle from the intensity.

She stands slowly, licks her lips with satisfaction that makes my spent cock twitch with renewed interest.

"Better?" she asks.

"You're going to kill me."

"What a way to go."

We finish the shower with hands that linger and touches that promise more later. When we finally emerge, pink-skinned and thoroughly satisfied, the world feels manageable for the first time in days.

I wrap her in the oversized towel she loves; the one that swallows her whole and makes her look impossibly beautiful. She does the same for me, movements gentle and reverent.

"I love you," I say, because the words feel important in this moment.

"I love you too."

"Even though I'm a bossy bastard?"

"Especially because of that." She rises on her toes to kiss me, soft and sweet. "I don't want you to be nice anymore, Gabe. I want you to be mine the way I'm yours. Completely. No reservations."

The words hit like absolution. Permission to be exactly who I am without apology or modification. Permission to love her with the intensity that always scared me before.

"Completely," I repeat, sealing the promise with another kiss.

We dress in comfortable clothes—jeans and T-shirts that feel like freedom after days of grief-soaked formal wear. Walk hand in hand toward the kitchen, already planning coffee and breakfast and the simple pleasure of a normal morning.

The plan evaporates the moment we reach the living room.

A woman sits on our couch like she owns the place, legs crossed, examining her nails with the kind of bored patience that speaks to absolute confidence.

Dark hair pulled back in a severe ponytail. Sharp features that would be beautiful if they weren't so calculating. Clothes that scream expensive and practical—a leather jacket, dark jeans, boots made for running or fighting.

She looks up when we appear, lips curving in a smile that doesn't reach her eyes.

"Well, well," she says, accent thick with Eastern Europe—Russian maybe, or Ukrainian. "Looks like the sex was every bit as good as it sounded. Very energetic. Very—thorough. Multiple times … She is a lucky woman."

Rage explodes through my system like white phosphorus. I'm moving, hand reaching for the weapon that isn't there, body shifting into attack mode automatically.

This woman—stranger, intruder, threat—has been listening

to us make love. Has been sitting in our house while we were vulnerable and naked and completely unaware of her presence.

"Gabe, stop." Ally's hand clamps around my arm, fingers digging into my muscles with surprising strength.

"Who the fuck are you?" I snarl, not taking my eyes off the intruder. "How did you get in here?"

"Locks are really more of a suggestion when you know what you're doing." The woman examines her nails again, completely unconcerned by the violence radiating off me. "And as for who I am ... Well, that's complicated."

"Uncomplicate it. Fast."

"Wait." Ally steps forward, head tilted like she's trying to place something. "Your voice ... Your accent ... I know you."

The woman's smile widens, becomes genuinely amused. "Do you now?"

"You." Ally's eyes widen with recognition. "You're the one who freed us from the cells. Who removed our collars."

"What?" I whip my head toward Ally, confusion cutting through rage. "What the hell are you talking about?"

"In Malfor's compound. The night of the rescue ..." Ally's voice carries growing certainty. "A woman came to us. She came. Disabled the surveillance, opened our cells, and removed the shock collars. She's the reason we were able to fight back when you found us."

"You never mentioned this in debrief," I say.

"We barely had any debriefs. Between Hank dying and ..." Ally's voice catches slightly. "There wasn't time to cover everything."

The woman—Ally's mysterious savior—rises from the couch with the kind of grace that speaks to extensive training. Military or intelligence, definitely dangerous.

"Touching reunion aside," she says, "I'm not here for reminiscing. I have information you need."

"What kind of information?" I ask.

"The kind that tells you exactly where to find the bastard who killed your lover."

The words hit like a physical blow. Malfor. She's talking about Malfor.

"Where?" Ally's voice comes out sharp as a blade.

"That depends. Are you interested in revenge, or are you planning to sit here playing house while he regroups and comes for you again?"

"We're interested," I say before Ally can respond. "Very fucking interested."

"Good." The woman reaches into her jacket—slowly, aware that I'm still coiled to strike—and produces a small device that looks like a modified phone. "Because I've been tracking him for three years, and I know where he's going to be."

She sets the device on the coffee table, screen displaying what looks like satellite imagery. A compound. Remote. Heavily fortified.

"Kazakhstan was just a pit stop," she continues. "His real base of operations is here. Off the coast of Montenegro. Private island, minimal security because he thinks no one knows about it."

"How do you know?" Ally asks.

"Because I've made it my life's work to know everything about Alexei Malfor." Something dark and dangerous flickers across the woman's features. "He killed someone I cared about. Someone who mattered. Now I'm going to return the favor."

She picks up the device, slides it back into her jacket.

"He'll be there for the next seventy-two hours. After that, he disappears again, and it could be months before another opportunity presents itself."

"Why tell us?" I study her face, looking for deception or a hidden agenda. "What's in it for you?"

"Nothing. Everything." She moves toward the front door with the same grace she's shown since we found her. "Let's just say that some debts can only be paid in blood and I need a weapon I can count on. That's you, if you hadn't figured it out yet."

"Wait." Ally hurries after her. "What's your name? How do we contact you?"

The woman pauses at the door, looks back with something that might be amusement or might be pity.

"You don't. You decide whether you want justice or not. If you do, you know where to find him."

"That's it? You just drop this bomb and walk away?"

"That's it." She opens the door, steps into morning sunlight that turns her dark hair to bronze. "Oh, and Gabriel?"

I tense, surprised she knows my name.

"Next time you want to fuck your woman senseless, might want to check for uninvited guests first. You're really quite loud." Her eyes glitter with amusement. "Though I have to say, I'm impressed by your restraint. That playroom of yours has some truly delicious toys, and yet you chose the bedroom. How—romantic."

My blood turns to ice. She's been in our playroom. The private space where Ally submits to me, where I keep the tools that drive her to the edge of sanity and back. The room that's more sacred to us than any church.

"You were in—"

"Everywhere." She cuts me off with casual indifference. "Lovely collection, by the way. That Saint Andrew's cross is a work of art. And the rope workstation? Very professional setup. Really, you should have made better use of it this morning."

The door closes behind her with a soft click, leaving us staring at empty space where life-changing information just waltzed in and out again.

"Did that really just happen?" Ally asks.

"Yeah." I run my hands through my hair, trying to process what we've just learned. "That really just happened."

Malfor. Alive. Hiding on some island compound, thinking he's safe from retribution.

The rage that's been simmering in my chest since Hank died crystallizes into something sharp and focused. Purpose. Direction. A target for all the helpless fury that's been eating me alive.

"We're going after him," I say.

"Gabe—"

"No discussion. We're going after the bastard who killed Hank."

She stares at me for a long moment, then nods slowly. "Yeah. We are."

Because some debts can only be paid in blood. And Malfor's debt is overdue.

FORTY-SEVEN

Assembly

GABE

THE SECURE PHONE RINGS TWICE BEFORE GHOST'S GRAVELLY voice cuts through the static.

"Figured I'd be hearing from you."

"Need to ask a favor." I pace the length of our deck, the ocean wind carrying salt and the promise of storm clouds gathering on the horizon. "Off the books. Personal."

"Malfor."

It's not a question. Ghost doesn't deal in questions when the answer's already carved in blood and grief.

"Got a location. Montenegro. Same area where he held Sophia and the kids." The coordinates taste like vengeance on my tongue. "Seventy-two-hour window before he disappears again."

Silence stretches across the encrypted connection. In the background, I catch muffled voices—Cerberus planning, always planning, turning violence into science.

"Guardian sanctioned?" Ghost's tone suggests he already knows the answer.

"Negative. This is personal."

"Best kind." The approval in his voice is unmistakable. "What do you need?"

"Transport. Support. Operators who know how to kill quietly and efficiently."

"Montenegro's not exactly a vacation destination. Rough terrain. Hostile government. Limited extraction options."

"We've been there before."

"Yeah, you have." Another pause, longer this time. "You realize this is suicide without proper intel and backup?"

"I realize Hank's dead because that bastard used our women as bait." The words come out sharper than intended, rage bleeding through professional composure. "Every day Malfor breathes is an insult to his memory."

"Fair point." Ghost's voice carries the weight of shared loss. "Usual rates apply. Plus combat pay for the personal touch."

"Done."

"Gear?"

"Everything. Long range. Close quarters. Demolitions. Whatever it takes to turn that compound into a crater."

"Brass is gonna cream himself. He's been itching for a real fight." Ghost's laugh holds no humor, just the dark satisfaction of men about to unleash hell. "Halo's got new toys he wants to field test. Whisper's been practicing his knife work."

"When can you be ready?"

"Already am. Question is, when do you want to move?"

The question hangs in salt air between us. Seventy-two hours. Three days to plan, execute, and extract before Malfor slips away again. Three days to balance the scales.

"Tomorrow night. 0200 hours."

"Cutting it close."

"Close is all we've got."

"Roger that. Rendezvous point?"

I give him the coordinates for a private airfield forty miles north of the city. Off the radar. Owned by someone who asks no questions as long as the money's clean.

"Martinez?" Ghost's voice stops me from ending the call.

"Yeah?"

"This won't bring him back."

The observation hits like a dagger through the heart. Because he's right—killing Malfor won't resurrect Hank. It won't restore what we've lost.

"No," I admit. "But it'll make sure he can't take anyone else."

"Good enough reason as any."

The line goes dead, leaving me alone with the ocean wind and the weight of decisions that can't be undone. Ally appears in the doorway behind me, her hair caught by the breeze, eyes holding questions she's not sure she wants answered.

"Ghost?" she asks.

"Ghost."

"Are you sure about this?"

The question forces me to examine my motivations—revenge versus justice, emotion versus logic, need versus wisdom. What I find isn't pretty, but it's honest.

"I'm sure Malfor needs to die. I'm sure we're the ones who should kill him. Everything else is just details."

She nods slowly, accepting what I've become in the aftermath of loss. Not the man who loved carefully and shared willingly, but something sharper. More focused. Distilled down to essential elements.

"What do you need me to do?"

The offer surprises me. After everything she's been through—kidnapping, torture, watching Hank die—she's still willing to walk into hell if it means standing beside me.

"Stay here. Stay safe. Let me handle this."

"Gabe—"

"No discussion." I turn to face her fully, see the argument

building in her eyes. "You've been through enough. You've lost enough. I won't risk you on a suicide mission."

"It's not your decision to make."

"Like hell it isn't." The words come out harsher than intended, but I don't take them back. "You're the only good thing left in my life, Ally. The only reason I want to survive this. I won't watch Malfor take you away from me again."

Her expression softens, reading the fear beneath my protective instincts. The terror that losing her would complete my destruction, leave me with nothing but revenge and empty spaces.

"Then come back to me." She steps closer, frames my face with hands that shake slightly. "Kill that bastard and come home to me."

"I will."

"Promise me."

"I promise."

The lie tastes bitter on my tongue, but some promises are made to be broken if it means keeping the people we love safe.

THE AIRFIELD SITS DARK AND EMPTY UNDER OVERCAST SKIES, runways cutting black lines through scrub grass that hasn't seen rain in weeks. A single hangar glows with muted light, large enough to hide aircraft and activities from prying eyes.

I arrive early, habit and paranoia keeping me sharp despite the grief that threatens to dull every edge.

Twin turboprops approach from the northwest—Cerberus transportation, unmarked and unregistered, carrying death in designer suits. The aircraft touches down with barely a whisper, pilots skilled enough to make heavy machinery dance.

Four figures emerge from the plane—shadows made flesh.

Ghost leads, every step honed and deliberate, violence etched into muscle and memory. Behind him, Brass hauls enough firepower to flatten a city block, each weapon handled like a trusted friend. Halo follows, smaller than the others, but with the calm focus of a man who makes buildings vanish. Whisper brings up the rear, wordless and still, knives tucked where even death wouldn't think to look.

"Martinez." Ghost clasps my hand, grip firm enough to crack bone. "You look like shit."

"Feel worse."

"Good. Angry men fight harder."

The team moves toward the hangar in lockstep precision, no wasted motion or unnecessary conversation. Inside, cases of equipment wait in neat rows—weapons, communications gear, medical supplies, everything needed to wage private war.

"Intel package." Brass drops a waterproof case at my feet. "Satellite imagery, thermal scans, structural analysis. Your mystery woman provided coordinates, but we filled in the details."

I open the case, study photographs that show Malfor's Montenegro compound in devastating detail. Cliffside location, ocean access, multiple buildings connected by covered walkways. Defensive positions. Guard towers. Everything a paranoid arms dealer needs to feel secure.

"Security assessment?" I ask.

"Heavy but predictable." Halo spreads technical drawings across a makeshift table. "Motion sensors, thermal cameras, automated weapon systems. Standard rich asshole fortress package."

"Automated systems are vulnerable to electronic interference," Whisper adds, voice barely disturbing the air. "Ten minutes with their network and I can turn their defenses against them."

"Personnel count?"

"Forty to sixty combatants," Ghost provides. "Professional contractors, not local talent. Well-armed, well-trained, probably well-paid. They'll fight."

"Good." The word comes out darker than intended. "I want them to fight."

"This is personal for you." Ghost studies my expression, reads the violence building behind my eyes.

"Very."

"Personal makes you sloppy."

"Personal makes me thorough."

He considers this; weighs my emotional state against operational requirements. Finally nods once—approval or acceptance, hard to tell the difference.

"Equipment preference?" Brass opens weapon cases, revealing an arsenal that would make arms dealers weep with envy.

"Long range first. Close quarters after." I select a precision rifle, check the scope, and feel its familiar weight settle against my shoulder. "I want to reach out and touch someone before we get intimate."

"My kind of poetry." Halo grins, expression holding just enough madness to be concerning.

"Timeline?" Ghost checks his watch, mental calculations visible behind cold eyes.

"Fourteen hours to target. Two hours for reconnaissance and final planning. Insertion immediately following."

"Tight."

"Tight is what we have."

The hangar hums with organized chaos as Cerberus gears up for war. Weapons click into readiness. Comms crackle to life. Gear is handed out; each piece matched to its master. It's not just preparation—it's ritual. A mechanical ballet of destruction.

My phone buzzes with an encrypted message. A single line of text that makes my blood run cold.

Charlie team en route to your location. Ethan.

"Son of a bitch." I look up to find Ghost watching me, expression unreadable. "You leaked this to Ethan."

"Might have mentioned you were planning something stupid." He shrugs, completely unrepentant. "Professional courtesy."

"This was supposed to be off the books."

"Still is. But Hank was their brother too. You really think they'd let you hunt his killer alone?"

Before I can respond, engines roar through the night—multiple vehicles, moving fast, chewing up gravel with no attempt at stealth. Charlie team, making their entrance with all the subtlety of a battering ram.

Three black SUVs roll onto the tarmac, doors flying open before the engines die. Ethan climbs out first, jaw set, storm in his eyes. Jeb is right behind him, silent and steady, the kind of calm that follows a decision already made. Carter stalks forward like he's hunting something, rage barely leashed. Blake and Walt exit opposite sides, scanning the perimeter, movements tight with purpose. Rigel brings up the rear, eyes cold, expression unreadable—but his fists clench like he's holding back the urge to tear something apart.

The team's intact—minus the dead. And their silence says more than any words ever could. They don't walk—they advance. Purpose in every step, boots striking asphalt like a countdown.

They cross the distance to the hangar like an advancing army, purpose written in every step. When Ethan reaches the threshold, he stops, surveys the assembled firepower, then fixes me with eyes that hold zero tolerance for argument.

Steel meets steel. No questions. No room for negotiation.

"Going somewhere without us?" His voice carries command authority that brooks no dissent.

Not a suggestion. A line drawn in the sand.

"This isn't Guardian business."

"Fuck Guardian business." Carter's voice slices through the dark, jagged and bleeding. "This is family."

"He was our anchor—" Walt starts.

"Our brother," Blake finishes.

"Our friend," Rigel adds, voice steady despite emotion bleeding through.

They fan out, a wall of muscle and conviction, forming a semicircle between me and the exit. No need for threats. Their bodies say everything—*You're not doing this alone.*

Ethan steps in, close enough I can see it—the grief threatening to crack him wide open, the fury welded over it like armor.

"You really think we'd let you honor him without us?" His voice doesn't shake. It hits like impact. "You think we'd let you carry this weight alone?"

The gesture hits harder than expected. Because despite everything—the fight with Hank, the guilt, the isolation of grief—they still consider me family. Still want to stand beside me when it matters most.

The ground shifts beneath me.

For days, I've been drowning in guilt, in silence. Hank's voice gone. His laugh. His steady hand. I kept breathing, but nothing felt alive. Now, standing in the eye of this storm of loyalty, everything inside me stirs.

Breaks.

"This could go sideways fast," I warn. "No official support. No extraction backup. No guarantees any of us come home."

"We know," Ethan responds without hesitation.

"Malfor's got forty to sixty professional contractors defending that compound."

"We know."

"This is pure revenge. Blood for blood. Nothing noble or patriotic about it."

"We know." His tone softens, just enough to crack the shield he wears. "Yet, we're still here."

It slams into me—this moment. The loyalty. The love. The brothers who choose to stand in fire with me, not because they have to, but because they won't let me go alone.

The support staggers me. After days of feeling isolated in grief, of believing I had to carry this burden alone, discovering my brothers are willing to walk into hell beside me …

There are no words.

"Gear up." My voice barely works. "We've got a war to win."

Charlie team surges into the hangar like a force of nature, integrating with Cerberus like they've always belonged here.

We're ready to descend on Montenegro like the wrath of God. The hand of vengeance itself.

For Hank.

Ghost appears at my shoulder, voice pitched low enough that only I can hear.

"Still think this is suicide?"

"Probably."

"Good thing you won't be doing it alone."

I watch my team—my family—transform into instruments of violence, and for the first time since Hank died, I believe we might actually survive this.

More importantly, I believe we're going to make Malfor regret the day he decided to make it personal.

FORTY-EIGHT

Blood Debt

GABE

THE AIRCRAFT CUTS THROUGH MONTENEGRO AIRSPACE LIKE A blade through flesh, engines muffled by modifications that make us invisible to radar and nearly silent to the mountain peaks below. Cold air seeps through the hull, carrying the metallic taste of violence about to be unleashed.

We sit in tactical formation, weapons checked and rechecked, gear secured with the obsessive care of men who know that a loose strap or forgotten magazine can mean the difference between going home and going into the ground. The aircraft's cabin reeks of gun oil, sweat, and something darker—the collective rage of brothers who've come to collect a blood debt.

Death comes to Malfor tonight. And I'm going to be the one to deliver it.

I stare out the small porthole at mountains carved black against a star-drunk sky, breathing in recycled air that tastes like metal and fury. The peaks below rise like ancient teeth, jagged and unforgiving, the same mountains where we extracted Sophia and the kids from Malfor before. That operation ended with explosions and narrow escapes, but we all made it out alive.

Tonight feels different. Tonight carries the weight of promises made to the dead, of justice delayed but not denied. Tonight, I paint these mountains red with the blood of the man who killed my partner.

My finger traces the trigger guard of my rifle—custom work, precision barrel, rounds designed to punch through body armor like it's tissue paper. Each bullet in the magazine carries Hank's name, carries the memory of his last breath rattling in his chest while I held his cooling hand.

"Five minutes to drop zone." The pilot's voice crackles through our comms, professional calm masking the fact that he's flying an unlawful combat mission into hostile airspace.

Ethan checks his gear one final time, movements precise despite the aircraft's subtle vibration. Magazine seated. Safety on. Knife positioned for rapid deployment. His face holds the carved-stone expression he wears before we go to work—the look that tells enemies they're about to meet something that doesn't negotiate, doesn't retreat, doesn't show mercy.

Across from him, Carter stares at nothing, jaw working silently like he's chewing broken glass. Still processing Jenna's kidnapping. Still carrying rage that hasn't found a proper outlet. His hands flex around his weapon's grip, knuckles white with pressure that speaks to violence barely contained.

Walt and Blake exchange final equipment checks while Rigel reviews building schematics on his tablet, memorizing room layouts and defensive positions. These men have bled with me, killed beside me, and watched Hank die with me.

Now, they're here to help me balance scales that death tilted too far in the wrong direction.

Cerberus occupies the aircraft's rear section with the kind of professional calm that speaks to decades of off-the-books operations. Ghost studies satellite imagery, memorizing approach routes and defensive positions with the patience of a hunter who's tracked prey across continents. His face holds no emotion, but I catch the way his thumb caresses his weapon's selector switch—muscle memory from a hundred similar operations.

Brass arranges demolition charges with loving care, each explosive device positioned for maximum psychological impact. C-4 molded like clay, timers, and enough destructive power to turn concrete and steel into rubble and memory. He hums under his breath while he works—some half-remembered tune that turns preparation for mass destruction into a lullaby.

Halo tests electronic countermeasures, fingers dancing across devices that will turn Malfor's defensive systems against him. His boyish face holds anticipation that borders on hunger—the look of a man who genuinely enjoys watching technology bend to his will. Small and unassuming until you see him work, then you understand why Ghost keeps him around.

Whisper sharpens knives with a meditative focus. The sound of steel against whetstone fills spaces between engine noise— rhythmic, hypnotic, the cadence of death being honed to razor precision. He doesn't speak, doesn't need to. The knives do his talking, and they're fluent in terminal conversation.

The aircraft banks sharply, beginning its final approach to a mountain meadow that barely qualifies as a landing zone. Trees whip past the windows as we descend, the pilot threading the needle between peaks that could turn aircraft into scrap metal with one miscalculation.

G-forces press us into seats as engines whine with effort.

"Intel confirms Malfor's in the primary structure," Ghost announces, consulting encrypted communications that glow green against his face. "Thermal imaging shows approximately fifty heat signatures scattered throughout the compound."

"Defensive positions?" Ethan asks, voice carrying the flat affect that means he's already shifting into combat mode.

"Guard towers at compass points. Automated weapon

systems covering approaches. Patrol routes follow predictable patterns." Ghost's smile holds predatory satisfaction, lips peeling back from teeth that look sharp in the cabin's dim light.

"Rules of engagement?" Carter's question carries steel wrapped in velvet, dangerous gentleness that makes smart people step away.

"No prisoners," I answer before anyone else can speak, tasting copper and cordite on my tongue. "No mercy. No quarter. No one walks away from this compound except us."

The words carry the weight of divine judgment, a final verdict on men who chose to serve evil for money. Tonight, we're not Guardian HRS operators following protocol and engagement parameters. Tonight we're avenging angels delivering retribution with automatic weapons and high explosives.

"Copy that," Ethan confirms.

Eleven confirmations sound off.

The aircraft shudders as the landing gear deploys, the pilot fighting crosswinds that try to slam us into granite walls. Mountain air leaks through hull seams, carrying the scent of ozone that speaks to storm fronts moving in from the Adriatic. Weather that will cover our insertion and muffle the sounds of systematic slaughter.

"Thirty seconds," comes the warning.

I close my eyes, breathe deep, and let Hank's memory settle into my bones like armor plating. His voice in the medical bay, using his dying breath to forgive sins I didn't deserve absolution for. His faith that Ally and I could build something beautiful from tragedy.

His certainty that love doesn't diminish when shared but grows stronger, becomes something larger than the sum of its parts.

Tonight, I honor that faith by destroying the man who took

him from us. Tonight, I water these mountains with blood and call it justice.

The aircraft touches down with barely a shudder, props winding down as the pilot maintains engine readiness for rapid extraction. Cargo doors slide open with a hydraulic hiss, admitting mountain air that tastes like the approaching storm.

"Time on target: forty minutes," Ghost announces as we disembark onto rocky soil that crunches under tactical boots. "Synchronized watches. Kill everything that moves except us."

We move into Montenegro darkness like shadows given lethal purpose, twelve men who've come to collect what's owed.

It's time to hunt, and we're out for blood.

FORTY-NINE

No Mercy, No survivors

GABE

THE COMPOUND SITS ON A CLIFF FACE OVERLOOKING THE Adriatic like a concrete cancer growing from living rock. Lights glitter behind reinforced windows while guard towers sweep searchlight patterns across approaches that seem impossible to breach undetected.

The architecture screams paranoid wealth—walls thick enough to stop artillery, windows bulletproof, defensive positions that could hold off small armies.

Could. Past tense. Because tonight, those defenses face something they weren't designed to stop.

Cold wind carries salt spray from waves that crash against cliffs two hundred feet below, mixing ocean scent with the sharp ozone of approaching weather. Storm clouds gather on the horizon, promising rain, wind, and darkness that will swallow gunfire and screams.

Perfect conditions for murder.

We belly-crawl through scrub brush and granite outcroppings, each man invisible against terrain that's trying to kill us through exposure and elevation. The compound's lights create pools of visibility that we navigate around, flowing like water between illuminated zones.

My rifle's scope shows guard positions in crystalline detail—two men in the north tower, sharing cigarettes and conversation. Three more walking patrol routes. Sentry posts at critical choke points, each manned by professionals who know their business.

They're about to learn that knowing and surviving are different skills entirely.

"Overwatch positions," Ethan whispers into comms, his breath visible in the mountain air that's dropped twenty degrees since we landed.

Blake and Walt ghost toward elevated positions with sniper rifles slung across their shoulders, moving through terrain that would challenge mountain goats. They'll provide overwatch and eliminate sentries when the dance begins—death delivered from distances that turn men into memories before they hear the shot.

They disappear into granite and shadow, two predators who've learned to make mountains their hunting ground. Walt's bulk seems impossible to hide until he simply vanishes behind a boulder and scrub. Blake flows between rock formations like smoke; there one moment and gone the next.

"Electronic warfare," Ghost directs Whisper toward the compound's communication hub.

Whisper emerges from the shadows, carrying devices that will turn Malfor's defensive systems against him. Electronic warfare specialist, communications expert, the man who makes billion-dollar defense networks commit suicide on command. He moves through darkness with the grace of someone who's learned to make technology his weapon.

Ten minutes with their network and every automated gun becomes our ally instead of an enemy.

"Assault teams, standby for signal."

I check my weapon for the hundredth time, as muscle

memory takes over, rendering conscious thought a liability. The magazine is seated with a metallic click. Safety engaged. My backup pistol is secured in a shoulder holster, knife positioned for rapid deployment.

I carry everything needed to paint this compound red with the blood of men who thought money could protect them from consequences.

The wind shifts, carrying new scents—diesel fuel from generators, gun oil from weapon maintenance, fear-sweat from guards who know something's wrong but can't identify the threat. Smart money says they're professionals, experienced contractors who've survived conflicts most people can't imagine.

Smart money's about to lose its shirt.

Through my scope, the north tower's lights flicker and die as Blake's rifle speaks twice with suppressed authority. Muzzle flashes are invisible at this distance, sound muffled to whispers that won't carry past the next ridge. Two soldiers who'll never see another sunrise, courtesy of precision marksmanship and right-eous fury.

"Guards eliminated," Blake's voice whispers through comms like death's own lullaby. "Tower one clear. Two targets down."

"Tower two down," Walt confirms, his voice carrying satisfaction. "Patrol route alpha neutralized. Three more for the collection."

More lights die as Walt works his magic from an overwatch position that turns him into God's own sniper. Professional contractors who thought themselves safe behind walls and weapons discover that distance is just another word for tempo-rary safety.

"Security grid compromised," Whisper reports, voice barely disturbing air that tastes of ozone and approaching violence. "Automated defenses offline. Motion sensors are feeding false data. Thermal imaging shows what I want it to show. We own their eyes and ears."

Electronic warfare at its finest—turning billion-dollar defensive systems into elaborate decoration. Cameras that see nothing, sensors that report all clear, and automated weapons that won't fire when targets appear.

Our technology serves justice instead of greed.

"Phase one complete," Ghost announces with satisfaction that sounds like anticipation wrapped in professional calm. "All teams, you are clear to engage. Remember—no survivors. No witnesses. No mercy."

We flow toward the compound like death given form, moving through defensive positions that no longer defend anything. The main building looms ahead through darkness and storm clouds, a concrete and steel monument to Malfor's paranoia and accumulated wealth.

Tonight it becomes his tomb, and I'm going to be the one who seals it.

The entry point Halo selects allows access through a maintenance corridor that bypasses primary defensive chokepoints. It's smart tactical thinking—avoid the kill zones, find the soft spots, get inside before anyone knows you're there.

Explosive charges eliminate locks and barriers, each explosion muffled by storm wind and careful placement. C-4 shaped to focus blast energy inward, turning steel doors into twisted metal and concrete barriers into rubble. The sound carries no further than the next corridor, swallowed by the mountain wind and approaching thunder.

Our first significant resistance comes from two guards in the corridor—professional contractors in tactical gear who recognize our threat and react. They're combat veterans who've survived wars in places most people can't pronounce, carrying weapons that could stop armored vehicles.

But, they die anyway.

Carter's rifle speaks twice; each shot a decree of authority. The first guard spins with his chest blown open, arterial spray painting white walls red as his heart pumps its last beat. The second manages to bring his weapon to bear before Walt puts two rounds center mass, body armor useless against tungsten-core penetrators that punch through Kevlar like tissue paper.

We reduce the threat to cooling meat in less than three seconds.

"Contact eliminated," Carter reports, already advancing past bodies that twitch with final neural impulses.

The corridor reeks of cordite and copper, blood pooling on industrial carpeting that will never come clean. Emergency lighting casts everything in red relief. It's an appropriate atmosphere for the slaughter we're about to unleash.

We clear rooms methodically, stacking on doors with the expertise that comes from years of elite operations. Fatal funnels become killing fields as we flow through chokepoints like smoke, each movement dictated by experience and muscle memory.

Ethan takes point, rifle at ready, eyes scanning for threats that might survive long enough to matter. Behind him, Rigel covers angles while Blake watches our six.

The first room holds three contractors playing cards around a table covered with weapons and ammunition. They look up as the door explodes inward, reaching for rifles that might as well be decorative for all the good they do.

Ghost puts them down—two rounds each, center mass. The smell of gunpowder mingles with the copper tang of blood painting playing cards red.

"Clear," he announces, already moving toward the next door.

We advance through luxury that belongs in corporate board-rooms, not military compounds.

Brass plants explosive charges as we advance, each device

designed to collapse the structure behind us and deny retreat to anyone foolish enough to follow. No withdrawal, no second chances, no option except total victory or glorious death.

The way Hank would have wanted it.

"Second floor," Ethan announces as we reach the stairwell.

More resistance here—four contractors in a defensive position that should hold this chokepoint indefinitely. Sandbags and automatic weapons, overlapping fields of fire, a professional setup that could stop a conventional assault.

We're not conventional.

Halo produces something small and round, a timer already counting down. The grenade bounces once, twice.

The explosion turns sandbags into confetti and contractors into abstract art, blood and tissue painting walls in patterns that would make Jackson Pollock weep. Concrete craters exist where professional soldiers used to stand, their weapons twisted into modern sculpture by high explosives and righteous fury.

"Clear," someone calls through smoke and debris.

We advance through devastation, boots crunching on rubble and bone fragments—the stairwell reeks of death that tastes of victory and approaching storm.

Another defensive position ahead—professional setup with interlocking fields of fire that should stop anything short of an armored assault. Five contractors with weapons that could ventilate tanks, and training that cost governments millions to provide.

They don't stand a chance.

Walt flanks left while Blake takes right. The pincer movement turns their stronger position into a killing ground. Crossfire erupts as they engage from unexpected angles, muzzle flashes strobing in confined space like demonic photography.

Blood slicks the marble under our boots.

The higher we climb, the harder they push back—more

contractors, better weapons, more desperate. But desperation without precision is just noise. We're here to silence it.

A machine gun nest waits at the next landing—dug in tight, with overlapping fields of fire. Suppressive rounds chew through the stairwell, turning it into a kill box. They're dug in like they mean to hold this floor until the world ends.

But Whisper steps forward, calm as a surgeon.

He unpacks a small case, fingers flying across a matte-black interface. No shouting. No orders. Just code and intent.

The gun hesitates. Then pivots.

It opens fire on its own. Controlled bursts, pinpoint accuracy—rounds chewing through the men who trusted it to protect them. They scream, panic, and scramble.

Doesn't matter.

They're already dead.

The walls catch it all. Bone. Blood. Shreds of flesh. Reinforced steel painted red. Whisper watches without blinking, already packing away his gear like he's folding laundry.

We move on.

"Saferoom," Ethan mutters as we reach the final door.

It's a beast—reinforced steel, triple-lock mechanisms, facial recognition scanner, and military-grade blast resistance. Designed to withstand sieges.

Designed to keep people like us out.

But it's just a door. And all doors eventually open.

Especially when justice is pounding on the other side.

Whisper produces devices that make locks irrelevant—electronic warfare tools that turn billion-dollar security into elaborate decoration. Sparks cascade as circuits overload, steel barriers becoming no more effective than paper against a focused electromagnetic pulse.

Trigger under my finger. Muscles coiled. Breath steady. Every thought narrowed to a single name.

Alexei Malfor.

Terrorist. Arms dealer. The man who built empires from blood and ruin. The man who took Hank from me. Thought a fortress would make him untouchable.

He's about to learn how wrong dead men can be.

Wind shrieks against the reinforced glass behind us, driving rain sideways, electricity crackling in the air. Ozone and smoke. Gunpowder and vengeance. The mountain peaks flash with lightning—serrated stone fangs looming like ancient gods come to witness a reckoning.

"Breach, breach, breach!"

The blast punches the world sideways. Steel screams. Fire and smoke bloom outward, choking heat surging with it. We pour through the gap like a tidal surge made of flesh, fury, and loaded weapons.

The penthouse sprawls in opulence—floor-to-ceiling glass framing the black sea beyond, marble veined like bone, artifacts mounted like trophies. Power layered in every object. The cold kind. The purchased kind.

And behind a monolithic obsidian desk, sits Alexei Malfor.

FIFTY

Debt Collected

GABE

HE'S SOFTER THAN I IMAGINED. PALE SKIN, RECEDING HAIRLINE, jowls tucked into a bespoke suit. No armor. No weapon. No dignity. Just a twitch in one manicured hand and eyes struggling to keep up with how fast death is arriving.

A dozen rifles raise in silent chorus.

His mouth works. He tries to fix his face into calm, into control, but the tremor in his voice betrays him. He clears his throat like a man used to commanding rooms.

Not this one.

"Gabriel Martinez." My name rolls off his tongue, wrapped in an accent and feigned serenity that doesn't reach his eyes. "I wondered when you would find me."

"Found you." My rifle stays locked on his chest. Finger tightens on the trigger, tension singing through tendons.

"Your friend—Henry, yes?—he died well. Fought to the end. Very brave. You should be proud."

The words detonate in my chest like white phosphorus, rage flooding my system with the kind of intensity that turns my vision red and makes my hands steady as surgical instruments.

He dares speak Hank's name.

Dares reduce his death to casual conversation.

"His name," I say, voice dropping to whisper that carries more menace than shouting, "was Hank."

"Tell me—does his death haunt your dreams? Do you see his face when you close your eyes?" Malfor smiles. That smug, smirking kind that dares me to break.

I don't answer. Don't need to. The weapon in my hands speaks fluent death, and I'm about to provide simultaneous translation.

"Wait…" He lifts his hands higher, panic leaking like blood through gauze. "We can negotiate. I have resources—money—information—anything—"

"You killed my partner."

"Business. Nothing personal. Professional necessity."

"Everything about this is personal."

The first shot takes him in the shoulder. 7.62mm of truth rips him into a grotesque spin. Arterial spray spatters priceless art. He goes down hard, screaming. Hands scrambling at slick marble as if they can claw him out of his fate.

"That's for using our women as bait." I advance around the desk.

Thunder crashes outside reinforced windows as the storm front arrives with divine timing. Rain begins pattering against bulletproof glass, nature providing percussion for the symphony of justice about to reach its crescendo.

The second shot shatters his kneecap, bone fragments and cartilage decorating marble like grotesque confetti. His scream rises in pitch and volume, agony given voice in language that transcends cultural barriers.

"That's for making Ally watch him die."

Malfor writhes on expensive carpet, his thousand-dollar suit soaked with blood and other fluids, as his body processes the reality of its approaching termination. Fear replaces arrogance in eyes that no longer hold calculation, just animal terror facing a predator that won't be negotiated with.

"Please," he gasps, voice breaking like adolescent pleading for reprieve from inevitable consequences. "I can pay—anything you want—money, information, whatever—"

"Give me back my friend." I kneel beside him, press the rifle barrel against his forehead with pressure that dents the skin. "Give me back the man who died because you're a coward who hides behind walls and weapons."

"I can't …"

"Then you have nothing I want."

The third shot destroys his other knee. The joint explodes like an overripe fruit under hydraulic pressure. Blood pools around shattered bone while he screams with a voice that's lost all pretense of dignity or control.

"That's for every nightmare she'll have because of you."

I set the rifle aside and draw my knife—seven inches of steel honed to surgical sharpness. The blade catches the light streaming through reinforced windows, casting razor shadows across expensive carpet now soaked with blood and terror.

"Now we get personal," my voice drops to a whisper that carries more menace than screaming.

His eyes widen with fresh terror as understanding dawns. This isn't just an execution—it's itemized retribution for every specific horror he inflicted. A reckoning measured in blood and pain; each drop earned through the suffering of innocents.

But before I can continue, Ethan steps forward.

Silent. Cold.

Controlled fury simmers behind every precise movement like a nuclear reactor operating at critical temperatures.

"My turn." His voice carries authority that makes even Ghost step back.

Ethan lifts his combat boot and drives it down into Malfor's ribs. Once. Twice. The sound of bone cracking echoes through the office like gunshots—sharp, final, irreversible.

"You shattered Rebel's ribs." Ethan's voice never rises above a conversational level. Another calculated blow, higher this time, targeting the floating ribs that protect vital organs. "Left her gasping like a landed fish, unable to breathe without agony."

Wet crunch. Malfor's howl reaches frequencies that suggest something primal and animal, all pretense of civilized behavior stripped away by pain that transcends rational thought.

"You broke her arm." Ethan seizes Malfor's wrist—the one still functional—and slams it down against the marble desk edge.

The bone snaps like brittle wood, a compound fracture sending white fragments through the skin, already slick with blood. "Made her watch it heal wrong in that cell, knowing it would never be right again."

The scream that follows is high and thin, almost inhuman. Malfor's face has gone chalk white, shock and blood loss combining to shut down non-essential systems as his body prioritizes survival over consciousness.

"You sliced her face." Ethan draws his combat knife—seven inches of blackened steel designed for killing, not surgery. "Temple to jaw. Left her beautiful face looking like a roadmap of your sadism."

The blade traces the same path Malfor carved into Rebel, parting skin as blood runs in a straight line from temple to jawbone, mirroring exactly the scar that will mark Rebel for the rest of her life.

Ethan steps back without another word, his rage spent like ammunition from a perfectly maintained weapon. Hands steady. Eyes clear. The team leader who carried them all home, exacting justice with the same methodical precision he brings to everything else.

Jeb moves next, and something in his face makes the air itself seem colder. Rage distilled into something purer than fury, more focused than hatred. This is the wrath of a man who's seen his woman tortured and found it unforgivable.

"My turn." His voice cuts deeper than any blade, carrying harmonics of violence that make the storm outside sound like a lullaby.

He doesn't reach for weapons. Instead, he lifts the heavy crystal paperweight from Malfor's desk—three pounds of cut glass. Light refracts through its faceted surface, casting rainbow patterns across walls painted with blood and justice.

The first blow lands between Malfor's shoulder blades. The sound—wet impact of crystal against flesh and bone echoes like hammer strikes in a cathedral of pain. Ribs crack. Vertebrae compress. Muscle tissue pulps under crystalline edges.

"You beat Stitch like she was an animal." Jeb's voice remains conversational, each word measured and deliberate. "Cane. Fists. Whatever was convenient when you felt like inflicting pain."

The second blow targets the small of Malfor's back. The crystal shatters against bone, leaving glass fragments embedded in tissue that will never heal. Malfor's scream dies in his throat, replaced by gurgling sounds that suggest internal bleeding.

"You caned her. Whipped her. Tore her skin like you were decorating a canvas." Jeb draws his combat knife—not the surgical precision of Ethan's blade, but something cruder, designed for utility rather than elegance. "Left scars she'll carry forever."

The knife traces deliberate lines across Malfor's back, cutting through expensive silk and flesh with equal ease. Not deep enough to kill, but deep enough to leave permanent reminders. Each line represents hours of Stitch's suffering, payment extracted in skin and screaming.

"She still bleeds when she showers," Jeb adds quietly, almost conversationally. "Wounds that won't heal properly because of what you did to her."

He straightens, knife dripping, and steps away. Professional distance is maintained even in righteous vengeance. The mountain of a man who could break Malfor in half with his bare hands, choosing instead to extract payment in precise measurements.

Rigel approaches next, loose-limbed and deceptively casual, like he's strolling through a park rather than a slaughterhouse. His hands shake—not with fear, but with restraint. Fury held on such a tight leash that the effort makes his entire frame vibrate with barely contained violence.

"You gave Mia a concussion." Rigel's voice carries the lazy drawl of a man discussing weather patterns. "Threw her into a wall like she was a rag doll. Left her half-conscious on cold stone."

He doesn't use weapons. His rifle butt comes down like a sledgehammer, impacting Malfor's temple with enough force to crater bone. Blood streams down the side of Malfor's face as his head snaps sideways, eyes rolling back to show white.

"She still wakes up dizzy. Can't look at bright lights without feeling sick." The second blow targets the opposite temple. "You used the love of my life as target practice."

The third blow isn't to the head. Rigel drives the rifle butt into Malfor's solar plexus, right where nerves cluster like electrical junction boxes. The impact steals breath and consciousness, leaving Malfor gasping like a fish drowning in air.

Rigel steps back, weapon still steady, eyes never leaving his target. The sniper who can kill at impossible distances, delivering justice at point-blank range with the same methodical precision that made him a legend.

Walt moves forward next, and there's something different about his approach: less fury, more grief. The medic, who has spent his career saving lives, finally faces one that doesn't deserve saving.

"You laid hands on Malia." Walt's voice breaks slightly, emotion bleeding through professional composure. "Bruised her. Hurt her. Made her afraid to be touched."

He doesn't hesitate. A single knee strike to Malfor's gut, delivered with enough force to lift the broken man off the carpet. Malfor folds like origami, retching blood and bile onto expensive marble that will never come clean.

"She flinches when I try to hold her." Walt grabs Malfor by what's left of his hair, dragging his face up to meet eyes that burn with quiet fury. "She can't let me touch her without panicking."

The combat knife appears in Walt's hand like magic, sliding between ribs. Not fatal—Walt's too good of a medic to make killing mistakes. But agonizing. The blade finds nerve clusters and twists, painting new colors on the canvas of Malfor's suffering.

"That's for every time she woke up screaming," Walt says quietly, twisting the knife one final time before stepping back.

Carter approaches last, and everyone in the room feels the temperature drop. Dead-eyed fury radiating like heat signature from a man who's seen too much, lost too much, forgiven too little. The detective who's spent his career finding justice for victims finally faces a monster who deserves none.

"You cut off Jenna's fingers." Carter's voice carries no emotion whatsoever—flat, professional, matter-of-fact. "Two of them. Made her watch while you did it."

He lifts Malfor's trembling right hand, almost tenderly. Places it carefully on the blood-slicked marble desk, fingers splayed like a pianist preparing for a performance.

"You took two. I'm taking four." Carter draws his blade—not a combat knife, but a surgical scalpel. Precision instrument for precision work.

The first finger separates cleanly at the knuckle. Blood arcs across white marble like abstract art painted in arterial spray. Malfor's scream rises to frequencies that shatter what's left of his dignity.

Second finger. Same joint. Same precision. Same arterial spray painting walls with the crimson evidence of justice served one digit at a time.

"She can't write anymore," Carter continues conversationally, working with the precision of a craftsman. "Can't hold a coffee cup properly. Can't type without pain."

Third finger. Fourth finger.

By now, Malfor is incoherent with shock. Blood loss is combining to shut down everything except the capacity for suffering. He sobs without dignity, teeth chattering like broken machinery as pain detonates through neural pathways designed to process far less trauma.

Carter steps back, blade clean, expression unchanged. The cop who's seen every variety of human evil, finally getting to balance scales that have been tilted toward injustice for too long.

"Your turn," Ethan says to me, stepping aside.

The storm outside reaches crescendo as I approach what's left of Alexei Malfor. Lightning illuminates mountain peaks while thunder provides a soundtrack for the final movement of this symphony of vengeance.

"Hank died because of you." My fourth shot takes him in the chest, puncturing lung tissue and sending arterial blood splashing across expensive art that will never be worth cleaning. "You shot him and made me watch him die."

The fifth shot shatters his shoulder, bone fragments mixing with his blood. Malfor's breath comes in ragged gasps as his body begins the final shutdown sequence, systems failing one by one like lights going out in a dying city.

"And now you get to experience what he did," I continue, watching life leak from eyes that no longer hold calculation or malice—just animal terror facing inevitable extinction. "Bleeding out. Knowing death is coming. Having time to think about every evil choice that brought you here."

His expensive watch still ticks on his wrist, marking time he no longer has. Swiss precision counting down to justice delivered in full.

"The difference between you and him," I add, standing slowly and looking down at the wreckage of a man who thought himself untouchable, "is that Hank died surrounded by people who loved him. While those who hate you, will watch you take your final breaths and be damn happy about it."

The light slowly fades from his eyes as arterial pressure drops below sustainable levels. Blood pools around his body while his heartbeat grows weaker, fainter, counting down to the moment when Alexei Malfor becomes nothing more than expensive meat cooling on expensive carpet.

Justice served.

Blood debt paid.

Every injury avenged in full.

Hank can rest now.

The man who thought himself untouchable bleeds out on flooring that costs more than most people's homes, surrounded by operators who've balanced scales that death tilted wrong. His eyes stare at nothing, seeing whatever waits for men who build empires on suffering and greed.

Alexei Malfor dies as he lived—alone, afraid, and drowning in the consequences of choices that seemed clever at the time.

I stand slowly, weapon lowered, breathing air that tastes of justice, or maybe it's just the absence of rage that's defined me since Hank died.

Killing Malfor should bring peace, closure, and some sense of completion. Instead, it feels like the punctuation at the end of a sentence that can't be rewritten.

But it feels right.

"Gabe?" Ethan's voice cuts through the strange calm that has settled over me.

"I'm good." I check my watch, note the time with professional detachment. "Mission complete."

"Building's wired for demolition," Brass reports. "Three minutes to clear before this place becomes history."

"Copy that."

We move toward our extraction point. Down stairwells rigged with explosives, through corridors painted with violence, past bodies of men who chose the wrong side of a war they couldn't win.

Rain pounds the mountainside as we emerge into a storm that's reached its full fury. Wind howls through peaks while lightning illuminates terrain that looks like God's own killing ground.

It's the perfect kind of weather that swallows evidence.

The aircraft engines spin up for immediate departure despite weather that would otherwise ground civilian flights. We board as exhaustion settles over operators who've spent violence like currency and found themselves wealthy beyond measure.

We came to balance the scales and deliver justice.

Mission success.

As we lift off, the charges left behind detonate throughout the compound, turning it into rubble. Malfor's Montenegro fortress becomes a crater and a cautionary tale for anyone foolish enough to threaten what we protect.

I stare at the destruction below, watching fire consume the evidence of justice served and debts paid. The compound burns like a funeral pyre, expensive furniture and priceless artwork feeding flames that reach toward storm-laden clouds.

The empty space beside me feels different now.

Not a wound that won't heal, but a memorial to the man who made me better than I ever thought I could be.

"It's done," Ghost says quietly, settling into a seat across from me while the aircraft climbs toward clearer skies.

"Yeah."

"Feel better?"

I consider the question while Montenegro disappears behind us, taking Malfor's corpse into the darkness where he belongs.

"No," I answer honestly, tasting truth that's bitter as cordite. "But it feels right."

"Sometimes that's enough."

"Sometimes." I check my weapon one final time. "Sometimes justice is what you do when peace isn't possible."

The aircraft banks toward home, carrying operators who've balanced scales that death tilted the wrong way.

Justice served through violence.

Love protected through war.

Memory honored through blood and fire and righteous fury.

Hank would understand. Hell, he'd probably approve. He always said some debts could only be paid in kind, and some threats could only be answered with superior violence.

I'm tired.

It's time to go home to the woman we both loved, and to rebuild a life from what remains.

Time to find out if revenge tastes like peace or just another kind of emptiness.

Either way, Alexei Malfor will never hurt anyone again.

That has to be enough.

FIFTY-ONE

The Waiting

ALLY

THE GUARDIAN GRIND HUMS WITH RESTLESS ENERGY AT THREE IN
the morning. The espresso machine purrs like a contented cat as
steam wands hiss and portafilters click into place.

For the first time in months, every component works
perfectly.

No temperamental pressure gauges.

No stubborn grind settings.

No mysterious electronic hiccups that plagued the machine
since my arrival.

Tonight, even the coffee gods seem to understand Charlie's
Angels need comfort.

I stand behind the familiar counter. My hands move through
the ritual of pulling shots and steaming milk while my mind stays
three thousand miles away with men who've gone to collect a
blood debt.

The grinder's burr plates sing their familiar song, beans
falling like rain into the portafilter as I dose and tamp with meditative focus.

Anything to keep my hands busy. Anything to stop them from shaking.

"Double espresso, extra shot," I announce, sliding the cup across to Jenna, who sits at the counter with her bandaged hand cradled against her chest.

"Thanks, love." Her voice carries gratitude that goes deeper than caffeine appreciation.

We're all here for the same reason—because sitting alone in empty apartments while our men hunt monsters feels impossible. Because sometimes the only way to survive waiting is to do it together.

The café feels different at this hour, stripped of its daytime energy and bustling crowd. Soft lighting creates pools of warmth while shadows gather in corners, transforming familiar space into something more intimate.

More like home.

More like a sanctuary.

Rebel occupies the corner booth, her face still bearing the healing stitches that track from temple to jaw like a roadmap of Malfor's cruelty. Her arm rests in a sling while bound ribs limit her breathing to careful, measured draws. Her eyes hold fierce determination that speaks to survival instincts stronger than any injury.

"How are you feeling?" Mia asks, settling beside her.

"Like I got hit by a truck," Rebel admits with honesty that costs her. "But alive. Breathing. Ready to see that bastard get what he deserves."

Stitch moves slowly to the window seat, back still bearing the marks of Malfor's cane and whip beneath loose clothing designed to hide healing wounds. Each step speaks to pain carefully managed but not conquered.

"Tea for you," Sophia says softly, bringing a steaming mug

that smells of chamomile and honey. "Supposed to help with healing."

"Everything helps with healing," Stitch replies, accepting the cup with hands that tremble slightly. "Time. Tea. Friends."

Sophia's smile holds understanding that comes from experience. She knows what it means to survive Malfor's attention, to carry scars that are both visible and hidden.

"How are Luke and Zephyr?" I ask, remembering the children who've already seen too much violence in their young lives.

"Violet's watching them," Sophia explains. "Thought it was better they sleep in familiar beds rather than worry about things they can't understand."

The espresso machine releases another perfect shot, dark liquid flowing like silk into waiting cups. I craft drinks with extra care tonight—perfect foam art, precise temperatures, flavor profiles that speak to love made manifest through caffeinated perfection.

"Cortado for the lady with excellent taste," I announce, sliding the cup toward Malia.

She accepts it with a smile that doesn't quite hide the lingering effects of her concussion—slightly unfocused eyes, careful movements that speak to her equilibrium still recovering from trauma. But she's here, present, contributing her warmth to our collective vigil.

"This is probably the best coffee I've ever tasted," she says after her first sip. "You've outdone yourself, Ally."

"Thanks." I smile, watching her savor the drink with appreciation that makes the late-night effort worthwhile. "I had a good teacher, and the machine's finally cooperating."

"Hey." Jenna reaches over with her good hand and squeezes Malia's. "You took a beating that would have killed most people. A little confusion is nothing compared to being alive."

The truth of it settles over our group with uneasy acceptance.

We're all alive, all here, all healing despite everything Malfor tried to take from us. Broken but not beaten, scarred but not destroyed.

The café door chimes softly as a late-night security guard does his rounds, checking that we're safe in our sanctuary. The building feels more secure knowing Guardian personnel are keeping watch while we wait for news.

"Does anyone know when they might be back?" I sip from my cup and don't voice the worry in my head. I'm afraid that if I speak my fears, one or all of them won't make it back.

"They're trained for this." Stitch's voice carries wisdom earned through surviving horrors that would break lesser people. "They know what they're doing. And they have something worth coming home to."

Our men are indeed stubborn bastards.

"Speaking of devotion," Sophia observes, studying my face with the sharp attention of someone who's learned to read subtle signs, "when's the last time you ate something that wasn't pure caffeine?"

The question forces me to think, searching for meals that blur together in an anxiety-fueled haze of grief and worry.

"I had toast this morning. Yesterday morning. Some morning recently."

"That's not an answer," Jenna scolds with authority that would make Carter proud. "Ally, you need real food."

"I'm not hungry." The lie tastes bitter on my tongue.

Truth is, I've been nauseous for days—grief sitting heavy in my stomach, making everything taste wrong. Even the smell of food makes my stomach rebel.

"Everything just—doesn't agree with me right now."

"Doesn't matter," Malia says, already moving toward the small kitchen behind the counter. "Grief and worry burn calories whether you feel them or not. Your body needs fuel."

She begins assembling ingredients—fresh bread, butter, honey, and fruit that adds color and nutrition.

"I should be doing that," I protest. "You're still recovering from—"

"Injuries that are healing," she interrupts with gentle firmness. "Not from being helpless. Let me take care of you the way you've taken care of all of us."

The offer touches something raw in my chest, emotions too close to the surface for comfort. Taking care of others has become my default response to feeling helpless—if I can't control whether our men come home safely, at least I can ensure everyone has perfect coffee while we wait.

"Besides," Jenna adds with humor that holds steel underneath, "if you collapse from malnutrition, Gabe will blame us. And frankly, I'm not sure any of us could survive his protective fury on top of everything else."

"He is rather intense about your well-being," Rebel says. It's an understatement that makes everyone smile because it's true.

"Intense like a hurricane is breezy," Stitch agrees. "That man loves you with the focused intensity of a tactical laser."

"Speaking of which," Mia glances at her phone with anxiety, "any word yet?"

"Radio silence since they left." I check my device for the hundredth time in the last hour, finding nothing but an empty screen and mounting worry. "Which means either everything's going according to plan, or ..."

"Or nothing," Sophia cuts me off with authority that allows no argument. "Everything's going according to plan. Period. End of discussion."

The certainty in her voice carries weight beyond simple optimism. She survived Malfor's attention and knows intimately what our men are capable of when properly motivated. If anyone understands the odds of tonight's mission, it's the woman who lived through his cruelty and emerged stronger.

"They're probably just having too much fun killing him to check in," Rebel adds with dark humor.

"Our men against one paranoid megalomaniac?" Jenna shakes her head with amusement. "That's not a fair fight. That's pest control."

"Poor Malfor," Mia says without a trace of sympathy. "He probably thought those walls and guards would protect him."

"Should have built higher walls," Stitch observes. "And hired better guards. And maybe not tortured the women of men who kill people professionally."

"Rookie mistake," Malia agrees with precocious wisdom that would be concerning if it weren't so accurate.

Toast appears before me, perfectly golden and spread with honey that catches the café's lighting like liquid amber. Simple food that smells like comfort.

"Thank you," I tell Malia, meaning more than just breakfast.

"Thank *you*," she replies, settling back into her seat. "For letting us wait together. For making this place feel like home when our actual homes feel too empty."

The truth of it settles over us. We're family, chosen and forged through shared trials, supporting each other through enough anxiety to overwhelm our individual strength.

But together, we're stronger. Unstoppable.

"To Charlie's Angels," Rebel raises her coffee cup in a toast that carries weight beyond a simple gesture.

"To survival," Stitch adds, lifting her tea with steady hands.

"To stubborn men who keep their promises," Jenna contributes with humor that holds steel.

"To coming home," Sophia finishes, voice carrying hope and certainty in equal measure.

"Remember when our biggest worry was whether the

espresso machine would work?" Mia asks with nostalgia for simpler times.

"I remember when my biggest worry was my thesis defense," I admit, thinking of academic concerns that feel impossibly distant from my current reality.

"Now we're all in love with professional killers who think 'normal Tuesday' includes international revenge missions," Rebel observes with accuracy that makes everyone laugh.

We have to laugh. Crying is overrated.

"Could be worse," Stitch points out. "We could all be in love with accountants who think 'dangerous' means taking lunch meetings without reservations."

"True," Sophia agrees. "At least our men are competent at the violence they choose to pursue."

"And they fight like hell to come home to us," Sophia adds with quiet determination.

"They do," I agree, tasting hope that feels as fragile as spun glass.

My phone vibrates against the counter, a sharp buzz that cuts through the café like an alarm bell. Every conversation stops as attention focuses on the device that might carry news we've been waiting for.

Gabe's name appears on screen. It's a simple text that makes my heart hammer against my ribs. I answer before the second ring, voice steadier than I feel.

"Tell me."

"It's done." His voice carries exhaustion and satisfaction in equal measure, words that taste like justice served and promises kept. "We're coming home."

Relief floods my system. Around me, faces reflect similar emotions—fear transformed into joy, anxiety giving way to celebration.

"Are you hurt?" The question comes automatically.

"Nothing that won't heal."

Our family remains intact despite the night's violence. Our men who went to war are coming home.

Justice was served, and debts were paid.

"I love you." My voice carries everything I couldn't say while he was gone.

"I love you too. See you soon."

The line goes dead, leaving a silence that holds a different quality than before. Not anxiety, but anticipation. Not fear, but preparation for a celebration that's been earned through survival and sacrifice.

"It's done," I announce to faces that already know but need to hear the confirmation.

"It's over?" Rebel asks.

"It's over. He's dead." The words hold a finality that closes too many chapters written in blood and pain.

"They're coming home," Jenna finishes with joy that transforms pain into something beautiful.

Tonight, we waited, exactly where we belong—surrounded by love, sustained by friendship, protected by men who keep their promises no matter the cost.

The waiting is over.

Our men are coming home.

FIFTY-TWO

Homecoming

ALLY

The Guardian Grind buzzes with energy at four in the afternoon, twenty-six hours after Gabe's call. The espresso machine hums while late-afternoon sunlight streams through the windows, painting everything golden.

I stand behind the counter, hands busy. Steam wands hiss and portafilters click into place, each movement keeping my mind from spinning into worry about men who should have been home hours ago.

"They're probably dealing with extraction logistics," Jenna says for the third time in an hour, her remaining fingers drumming against the counter. "International flights, customs, that sort of thing."

"Or sleeping off the adrenaline crash," Mia adds, settling beside her with careful movements. "Killing megalomaniacal psychopaths is probably exhausting work."

"Probably," I agree, though the word tastes forced.

The café feels different than during our vigil—less desperate, more anticipatory. We're no longer waiting to find out if our men are coming home.

We're waiting for them to walk through the door.

Rebel sits in the corner booth, her healing face turned toward the window with the best view of the parking lot. Her good arm rests on the table while the other stays carefully positioned. Her eyes hold fierce attention.

"Movement," she announces, straightening.

Three black SUVs roll into the parking lot. Dust kicks up from tires as vehicles park in formation.

My heart hammers as doors begin opening, men emerging who look like they've been through hell but won. Tactical gear replaced with civilian clothes that can't hide the dangerous frames underneath. Eyes that scan automatically for threats, even here.

Gabe emerges from the lead vehicle, and the sight of him—alive, whole, and moving with that lethal stride—nearly buckles my knees.

He pauses in the parking lot, eyes finding mine through the window, and something passes between us. Confirmation. Resolution. The promise that justice has been served.

Behind him, Ethan unfolds from the passenger seat. Carter follows from the second vehicle, then Walt and Blake from the passenger doors. Rigel limps slightly but moves under his own power. Jeb is there too, limping more than normal, but standing tall.

Ghost and his Cerberus team emerge from the third vehicle. Brass carries a duffel bag. Halo moves with loose-limbed ease. Whisper simply materializes from the shadow.

The café door chimes as they enter, and suddenly the space feels smaller, charged with testosterone and barely contained violence that's found its target. The scent of gunpowder and travel clings to them despite civilian clothes.

Gabe reaches me first, moving through furniture and people like obstacles. His hands frame my face.

"Hey," he says softly, thumb tracing my cheek.

"Hey, yourself." My voice comes out steadier than expected.

He kisses me then, soft and careful and tasting like justice served cold. When we break apart, his eyes hold the kind of peace I haven't seen since before Hank died—not healed, maybe never fully healed, but settled.

The weight of vengeance no longer crushes him.

Around us, similar reunions unfold.

Ethan reaches Rebel's booth in three long strides, gathering her into his arms with precision that doesn't disturb healing bones. She melts against him despite injuries, fingers digging into his shoulders like she's afraid he might disappear.

"Miss me?" he asks against her hair.

"Like missing air," she admits, voice muffled against his neck.

Carter finds Jenna at the counter, his massive frame somehow gentle as he takes her bandaged hand in both of his, examining damaged fingers.

"How are they?" he asks, voice rough.

"Better. Getting better every day." She flexes her remaining fingers. "Did you …?"

"He paid for them," Carter confirms. "Twice. Every finger. Every tear. Every nightmare. Paid in full."

Walt crosses to where Malia sits nursing her coffee, still moving carefully due to lingering concussion effects. She looks up as his shadow falls across her table, and her face transforms with relief so pure it takes my breath away.

"Walt." His name comes out like a prayer.

He doesn't speak, just pulls her to her feet and into his arms, massive frame enveloping her completely. She disappears against his chest, and I hear her muffled sob of relief.

"Shh," he murmurs, voice rough with emotion. "I'm here. I'm home."

"I was so scared," she whispers. "When my head got scrambled, I kept forgetting things, but I never forgot being afraid you wouldn't come back."

"I'll always come back to you." His hands cradle her head with infinite gentleness. "Always."

Blake finds Sophia near the pastry case, gathering her into his arms. Their reunion is quieter but no less intense, hands checking for injuries that aren't there, eyes confirming what words can't quite capture.

Rigel finds Mia, gathering her into his arms. She melts against him, fingers tracing the line of his jaw like she's memorizing features she was afraid she might never see again.

Stitch rises carefully from her window seat, moving toward Jeb. He meets her halfway, movements equally careful as they navigate the space between independence and need for comfort.

"How's the pain?" Jeb asks, studying her face.

"Manageable." She leans into his touch, allowing him to support the weight she's been carrying alone. "Better now that you're back."

"Did you—" Malia starts, then stops, shaking her head. "Never mind. I don't want details. I just want to know it's over."

"It's over," Gabe confirms, still holding me. "Malfor's dead. His operation's destroyed. It's finished."

The words settle over the café like a benediction. We're safe. Our men are home. The monster who haunted our dreams has been eliminated.

"Well, well," a familiar voice cuts through our reunions. "Looks like everyone made it back from their—*vacation*." Forest stands in the doorway, flanked by Sam and CJ, all three wearing expressions that suggest they know exactly where their operators have been and what they've been doing.

"Forest," Ethan acknowledges.

"Ethan." Forest's smile holds approval. "I trust everyone

enjoyed their time off? Heard Montenegro's lovely this time of year."

The statement hangs in the air, heavy with implications.

They know. Of course, they know.

"Very relaxing," Gabe responds with deadpan delivery that makes several people smile. "Highly recommend the local hospitality."

"I'm sure." Sam steps forward, studying faces. "Any injuries requiring medical attention? Things that might need documenting?"

"Nothing that won't heal with time and proper rest," Carter responds carefully.

"Good." CJ's massive frame fills the doorway behind the other two, arms crossed in approval rather than confrontation. "Because it would be a shame if any of our operators were hurt during their well-deserved *vacation time*."

The message comes through clearly—what happened in Montenegro stays in Montenegro, but Guardian HRS supports their people even when those people operate outside official sanction.

"Speaking of rest," CJ continues, surveying the group, "I'm declaring mandatory downtime for everyone involved in recent *vacationing* events. No missions, no training, no obligations beyond healing and spending time with the people who matter."

"How long?" Ethan asks.

"Until I'm satisfied that everyone's ready to return to duty." CJ's tone warns against contradiction. "Could be a week, could be a month. Depends on how well you take care of yourselves and each other."

"That's very generous," Ghost observes.

"We take care of our people," Forest corrects. "All of our people. Including our friends from Cerberus who happened to be *vacationing* in the same neighborhood Charlie team was chilling at, and for *assisting* what I'm sure was a completely coincidental encounter."

"Very coincidental," Brass agrees with a straight face that fools no one.

"Well then." Forest claps his hands once. "Carry on with your reunions. Take care of each other. And remember—some stories are better shared over coffee than in official reports."

He turns to leave, then pauses at the threshold. "Oh and, Ally. Harrison has been dealt with."

"He has?" I can't believe it and didn't have the courage to ask, but now, I need to know. "Did he ever say *why* he did it?"

"Malfor offered him second-in-command with promises of running Malfor's entire operation. Didn't work out for him."

"What does that mean?"

"Just to say, friends dropped him off after their little *vacay*. He's providing valuable intelligence as we speak. Griff is with him and he's being *very* cooperative, but then Griff has a way with getting people to talk."

I know Griff. Another regular of The Guardian Grind, he's a part of Alpha team and known for his excellence in interrogation procedures. Hank told me never to ask what that meant, and I won't. Some things I don't need to know.

"The intelligence community sends their regards," Forest continues. "Harrison's information is dismantling what's left of Malfor's network across three continents. Arms dealers, technology brokers, former intelligence assets gone rogue—they're all scrambling for cover now that their protection's gone."

"What happens to him now?" I ask, my voice steadier than expected.

"That's classified," Sam replies, but his slight smile suggests Harrison won't be enjoying retirement. "Let's just say, after Griff's done, he'll be transferred to a facility where people with his particular skillset and betrayals can be—properly debriefed for the next several decades."

"Without sunlight," CJ adds. "Or hope."

"Enough of that," Mitzy pushes in, approaching with her tablet and a steaming cup of coffee. "We need to talk about what Malfor told you versus what we discovered."

I straighten, my scientific mind immediately engaging. "The nanobots. He said I brought them in from Kazakhstan."

"You did," Mitzy confirms gently, settling into the chair across from us. "But not by choice. Not knowingly. They were embedded in your skin, your clothes, your USB during captivity."

Gabe's arms tighten around me. "Ally—"

"No, I need to hear this." I turn to Mitzy, my quantum physics training demanding technical understanding. "Tell me how they worked."

Mitzy pulls up holographic displays on her tablet. "You probably already know this, but individual nanobots are simple machines, but they were networked through your quantum entanglement research."

"Malfor mentioned that."

"They self-replicated, and when hundreds gathered together, they created an emergent collective intelligence, like a hive mind distributed across electronic systems."

"That's why the espresso machine kept malfunctioning," I realize, pieces clicking into place. "Every system I touched became infected."

"Exponentially," Mitzy nods. "From you to devices, from devices to other people, from people to more devices. Within three months, eighty-nine percent of Guardian HRS was compromised."

The guilt hits with soul-crushing knowledge. "I brought a surveillance network into the place I love most."

"You were weaponized against your will," Gabe says firmly. "That's on Malfor, not you."

"But my research made it possible," I whisper. "He used my quantum entanglement work to create untraceable communication networks."

"And your research helped us destroy them," Mitzy interjects. "The Trojan horse we developed used your quantum entanglement principles to cause cascade failures throughout his entire network."

"The Trojan horse worked?" I look up sharply. "Wait, how did you know about that?"

"What do you mean?" Her brows pinch together in confusion.

"I developed a quantum disruption protocol. I planted it in his system to sever the entanglement pairs."

Mitzy's eyes widen. "You did, what?"

"I used my access to his quantum control interface to introduce cascading decoherence," I explain, my scientific mind racing through the implications. "I disrupted the quantum coherence states from the master control side—essentially forcing the entangled pairs to lose their connection. If the nanobots were quantum entangled, then disrupting the coherence would cause—"

"Complete network collapse," Mitzy finishes, her grin turning predatory. "But Ally, our Trojan horse worked differently, but nearly the same. Or rather, had the same end effect. We infected nanobots themselves with corrupted instructions that made them physically destroy their quantum entanglement."

"So my disruption severed the quantum connections from the control side," I realize, "while your payload destroyed the physical entanglement nodes from the nanobot side."

"Exactly. Double cascade failure—you cut the quantum strings while we destroyed the instruments making the music.

Your decoherence protocol prevented any nanobots from reestablishing contact with the network, while our payload made sure they physically couldn't even if they tried."

"Belt and suspenders approach to quantum warfare," I murmur. "Attack the same system from both the software and hardware levels simultaneously."

"Completely obliterated," Mitzy confirms. "Every nanobot globally was hit by both attacks at once. We couldn't have planned it better if we'd actually collaborated on it. What are the odds?"

"You're certain the entanglement can't be reestablished?" I ask.

"You'd know best. I'll show you what we did in the lab, and you can tell us, but I have a feeling physics doesn't lie," Mitzy replies. "Even if Malfor survived, he'd need to rebuild everything from scratch—new nanobots, new quantum hardware, new entanglement protocols. Your disruption erased the software architecture while our payload destroyed the physical infrastructure. Complete annihilation."

"So Guardian HRS is clean?"

"Every system is verified and operational. The espresso machine working perfectly isn't a coincidence—it's proof that every trace of contamination has been eliminated."

The scientific confirmation settles something deep in my chest.

"Then it's really over."

"The technical threat is completely neutralized," Mitzy confirms. "Your unwitting role as a carrier has been permanently severed. You're free, Ally. We all are."

I lean back against Gabe, processing the information with the methodical approach of a physicist solving complex equations. Guilt transforms into understanding, and self-blame into acceptance of circumstances beyond my control.

"I should have figured it out sooner," I murmur.

"Quantum-level surveillance was theoretical before this," Mitzy replies. "Even I didn't recognize the signatures until we had intact specimens. You couldn't have known what to look for."

"Besides," Gabe adds, his voice rough with emotion, "you did figure it out. Your sabotage in captivity helped us locate you and develop countermeasures. You turned his weapons against him."

"We're a good team." Mitzy grins. "Theoretical quantum physicist meets practical systems engineer. We should publish a paper about this someday. 'Quantum Surveillance Networks: Detection, Analysis, and Destruction.'"

Despite everything, I laugh. "Think we'll get citations?"

"We'll get classified," Mitzy replies. "But yeah, definitely citations."

The conversation ends with technical satisfaction and emotional resolution I didn't know I needed. The nanobots are gone. The network is destroyed. My role as an unwitting weapon has been permanently severed.

I'm finally free to be just Ally again.

"Anyway ..." Mitzy pulls her coffee to her chest. "We, meaning leadership, have a shit ton of work to do after Charlie team's *vacation*. I'm very sorry about Hank. My deepest condolences. He will be missed."

"Thanks." My eyes mist, but I manage a small smile. He will be missed, but that just means none of us will ever forget him. He lives on in our hearts and our memories.

Gabe's arms tighten around me as Mitzy leaves.

The door closes behind Guardian HRS leadership, leaving us alone with coffee, reunions, and the knowledge that sometimes the system works exactly as it should.

I lean back against Gabe's chest, feeling his heartbeat steady and strong. Around us, conversations resume as couples reconnect and families restore themselves. The café fills with warmth that has nothing to do with coffee and everything to do with love that survived separation.

"I missed you," I tell Gabe quietly.

"I missed you more." His lips brush against my ear. "It's over, Ally. Really, and truly over."

I turn in his arms, study his face for signs of trauma or unresolved anger. What I find instead is peace, not healed, maybe never fully healed from losing Hank, but settled. The weight of vengeance no longer crushes him.

"What happens now?" I ask.

"We figure out how to be happy again." His smile holds hope alongside exhaustion. "How to build something beautiful."

The future stretches ahead like an unwritten page, full of possibility and promise. We're not the same people we were, and we will never be the same again.

Maybe this is what healing looks like—not forgetting or forgiving, but choosing to build something beautiful from the ashes of what was destroyed.

FIFTY-THREE

Learning to Live Again

ALLY

THE HOUSE STILL FEELS DIFFERENT WHEN WE WALK THROUGH THE front door—pensive somehow, as if it's holding its breath.

Gabe stops in the entryway, shoulders rigid with tension that speaks to walking into a museum of memories neither of us is ready to face.

"We could get a hotel," he says quietly. "Just for tonight. Until we figure out …"

"No." I take his hand, thread our fingers together. "This is our home. We don't run from it."

But standing here surrounded by evidence of a life that included three people, I understand his hesitation. The silence feels wrong—no deep voice calling from the kitchen about dinner plans, no sound of tactical gear being stripped and stored, no presence that filled spaces without trying.

Just emptiness where warmth used to live.

"Come on." I pull him toward the living room, past the sectional sofa arranged for three bodies that will never again pile together for movie nights. "We'll figure it out as we go."

The kitchen holds the most ghosts. Hank's protein powder

still sits beside the blender he used every morning. His vitamins arranged in precise rows that speak to military precision applied to civilian life. The coffee maker is programmed for 0600 hours, ready to brew for three people who've become two.

"I should make dinner," Gabe says, moving toward the stove.

"Since when do you cook?" I ask, settling onto one of the bar stools.

"Since someone has to." He opens the refrigerator, stares at the contents without really seeing them. "Can't live on coffee and takeout forever."

"Why not?"

He arranges ingredients with movements that lack his usual confidence.

"Hank forbade you from cooking after that grease fire, you know. Sure you want to tackle dinner?"

"Do you know how to cook?"

"No."

"Didn't think so. Besides, it was one time, and it was barely a fire. More like enthusiastic splattering."

"Enthusiastic splattering that set off every smoke alarm in the house and nearly burned down the kitchen. At least, that's what Hank told me. Said he banned you for life. That the kitchen was a weapon in your hands."

"You'll be surprised by how well I can cook." His mouth curves in a reluctant smile.

"Really?"

"Actually, I'm not half bad. Hank's cooking was just so much better than mine. I may, or may not, have not so accidentally started that grease fire."

"Gabe!" I toss a kitchen towel at him. "You manipulated Hank?"

"Worked like a charm." He doesn't even try to hide his grin. "Although I did have to take up doing the dishes."

"I guess that's my job now." I gesture to the kitchen. "Show me some of this kitchen magic."

Gabe pulls out a carton of eggs, a hunk of cheese, and the last of the cherry tomatoes. His movements are slow and uncertain, like he's navigating a minefield of memory with every cupboard he opens.

He cracks eggs into a bowl, whisking with more intensity than necessary.

I lean my elbows on the counter, watching him from the same stool I sat on that first night—the night when everything shifted between us.

When laughter turned to heat, and Hank telling Gabe to fuck me like he was orchestrating a symphony.

Gabe's hands on my thighs. Hank's voice in my ear. My body caught between theirs, gasping for more.

My breath catches.

Gabe stiffens, sensing it.

"You thinking about it too?" His gaze flicks to mine.

"It was the first time you touched me." I nod. No point pretending.

A beat of silence.

"I was so damn nervous." His mouth twists. "And so hard I thought I was going to die."

"You hid it well." I huff a broken laugh.

"Hank knew," he says, softer now. "He always knew what I needed—even before I did."

My chest aches. "He gave us that moment."

"And a hundred more after."

We fall quiet again. Gabe turns back to the skillet, but his hands tremble as he pours in the eggs. The scent of butter and garlic fills the kitchen. It should smell like comfort, like home. But tonight it's laced with longing, with all the things we've lost.

He slides scrambled eggs and toast onto two mismatched

plates and sets them on the dining table, where three chairs still sit. One untouched.

I hesitate.

So does he.

Then, wordlessly, he pulls out the chair opposite mine and lowers himself slowly, like his body's made of grief.

We eat.

Chew. Swallow. Pretend the food doesn't taste like absence.

At one point, I look up and catch him watching the empty seat between us.

"I keep expecting to hear him tease me for overcooking the eggs." Gabe's jaw tightens.

Silence stretches again.

Gabe reaches for his water, then freezes halfway. "He should be here."

"I know."

He rubs the heel of his hand across his chest like it hurts to breathe.

"We were always three," he says. "It's like trying to balance on a broken leg now. Nothing feels steady."

I push my plate away. Stand. Walk around the table and drop to my knees beside his chair. He turns toward me instinctively, hands falling to my shoulders.

"We don't have to rush this," I say. "But we also can't live in neutral. We'll learn how to stand again. Maybe not steady. Maybe not right away. But together, like a three-legged race. Our third leg is gone, so we have to work together to make a new normal."

His fingers tighten slightly.

I press my cheek to his thigh, seeking that same quiet comfort he used to give without trying.

"He'd want us to be happy," I whisper. "He'd want us to

choose each other every day, the way he chose both of us. He'd want us to fuck like we mean it."

"He'd definitely want that."

Gabe's laughter is raw and unguarded, the kind that curls warm and unexpected in my chest. The kind I haven't heard in far too long.

Something shifts between us—sharp-edged grief softening under the weight of need. Of memory. Of the hunger that never really died, only slept.

He moves first, surging forward with the kind of intent that makes my breath catch. His mouth claims mine—not a question, not a whisper of what if. Just Gabe. Fire and familiarity, lips demanding and sure, tongue sweeping into mine like he owns me.

Like he remembers exactly how I taste and wants to drown in it.

I moan into his mouth as his hands frame my face, fingers sliding into my hair like he's anchoring himself to the one thing that still feels real. I reach for him, fisting the hem of his shirt, yanking it up. He breaks the kiss just long enough to strip it off, and then I'm touching bare skin, muscle, and heat and scars I could trace blindfolded.

"Bedroom?" His voice is rough.

"No." I grip his waistband, drag him closer. "Here. Now."

The counter presses into my spine as he lifts me onto it, standing between my thighs. The same spot where he first took me. The same spot Hank stood behind him, eyes dark with approval, telling Gabe exactly how to claim me. How to ruin me beautifully.

My throat tightens. Gabe sees it.

"We don't have to—"

"I want to," I whisper. "I need this. I need you."

His hands slide under my thighs, dragging me to the edge. "Then let me give it to you."

He peels away my clothes with reverence at first—each button, each inch of skin revealed like he's unwrapping something sacred. His mouth follows the trail, lips grazing my collarbone, teeth scraping down my sternum, tongue circling a nipple until I cry out and arch for more.

But it's not enough.

"I don't want careful," I breathe. "I want you."

That's what breaks him.

His grip turns bruising, his mouth punishing as he captures my lips again, this time with the promise of heat. Fingers slide beneath my panties, finding me slick and aching. He groans into my mouth, and the sound sparks something wild in me.

"I'm going to fuck you now," he growls. "And you're going to take it. All of it."

I gasp. Yes. Yes.

He tears the rest of my clothes away in a frenzy, drops his own pants, and then he's there—thick and hard and pressing against me. He pauses just long enough to meet my eyes.

"Last chance to stop me."

"Don't you fucking dare."

And then he's inside me in one hard thrust.

I cry out, fingers clawing into his back, hips jerking to meet him. The stretch is delicious. Devastating. Perfect.

He drives into me again, deeper this time. Stronger.

And I feel it—the shift. The part of Gabe that's been buried under loss and guilt and silence is finally clawing free.

His teeth find my neck, not gentle now, biting hard enough to leave a mark. His hand wraps around the back of my neck, holding me in place as he pounds into me with the kind of force that shatters thoughts and breath and pain.

This isn't soft, sweet, or apologetic.

This is him.

Us.

My moans echo off the kitchen walls, sharp and desperate. He curses, thrusts deeper. The counter jerks beneath us with every slam of his hips.

"You're mine," he growls against my ear. "Still mine. Always fucking mine."

I can't speak. Can't do anything but feel him. Take him.

He lifts one of my legs over his shoulder, changing the angle. The next thrust hits something explosive—my back bows, a scream ripped from my throat.

He doesn't stop.

Doesn't let me come down. Just keeps driving me higher, harder, until my vision blurs and the world narrows to the man fucking me like it's the only thing keeping him alive.

His name breaks from my lips over and over.

"Gabe—oh God—don't stop, don't stop—"

"I'm not stopping till you fall apart on my cock."

And I do.

The orgasm rips through me, brutal and consuming, white-hot and endless. My muscles clamp down, pulsing around him. He groans like it's killing him, curses, then shudders with his own release, buried deep inside me.

For a moment, we just breathe.

Sweat slicks our skin. His forehead rests against mine. My legs still shake.

Then he pulls back, cups my cheek.

"That was … Fuck, Ally."

I nod. Can't speak. Still floating.

He lifts me into his arms, carries me down the hallway like I weigh nothing. Lays me in bed, pulls the sheets over us, and climbs in behind me. His body wraps around mine, strong and solid.

And when he whispers, "I love you," into the shell of my ear, I don't cry this time.

I believe it.

He doesn't stop.

Not after the kitchen. Not after I come apart in his arms.

He laid me down like I'm breakable, but the look in his eyes says I'm not. Not tonight. Tonight I'm something to be claimed. Taken. Worshipped.

"I'm not done with you," he says, voice low, rough velvet laced with grit. "Not even close."

My body aches in the best possible way, but I open for him anyway. Wanting him.

Needing to feel the way he used to take me. The way he and Hank would pass me between them, relentless and hungry and so fucking loving, it ruined me.

He presses my wrists into the mattress, settles between my thighs.

"Let me remind you who you are," he growls, and then he fucks me again.

This time is harder. Deeper. The stretch burns, and my voice is hoarse from crying out, but he doesn't stop. He chases every sound like a man starved, devours every tremble, every shudder.

He flips me onto my stomach and pulls my hips up.

"Stay," he growls, palm landing firm on my ass.

I do. Because I want to.

He sinks into me from behind, and everything else disappears. No grief. No guilt. Just heat and friction, and the sound of his breath rasping against the back of my neck as he takes what he needs.

What we need.

He fucks me like we used to—feral and focused. No soft edges. Just the savage kind of love that leaves marks and bruises and makes me feel alive.

I come again. Then again.

Each orgasm strips me down until there's nothing left but the core of who I am.

Who we are.

When we finally collapse, tangled in sheets and sweat, I think we're done.

We're not.

Hours later, I wake to find him watching me, hard again, eyes dark.

He doesn't say anything.

Just pulls me over him, guides me down onto his cock.

I ride him slow, hips rolling, his hands gripping mine as we find that rhythm again. The one we used to move in with Hank watching, Hank touching, Hank murmuring praise like a benediction.

My breath hitches. Gabe sees it.

He cups my face. "Don't stop. Don't ever stop remembering him. But don't you dare stop loving me either."

"I couldn't," I whisper. "I won't."

He grips my hips, thrusts up into me, hard enough to knock the air from my lungs. My moan is half a sob, half a scream.

We break again.

And rebuild.

And when morning comes, sunlight slicing across the bed, I wake to him spooned behind me, breath warm against my neck, hand splayed over my belly like he's still holding me together.

I turn in his arms. Kiss him slowly. Deep. Hungry again, even now.

He rolls me beneath him, sinks into me without a word.

This time is different. Reverent. Lazy and tender, bodies moving in that soft early morning rhythm, skin slick, hearts steady.

When he comes, he buries his face in my neck and breathes me in like I'm the only thing that's ever made sense.

We lie tangled in the aftermath, skin damp, muscles loose.

His voice rumbles low. "Hungry?"

I start to nod. But the thought of food curls my stomach.

"Not really." The thought of food makes my stomach clench with familiar nausea that's been my constant companion since—when?

Since the rescue?

Since Hank died?

Since some point when grief settled into my body and decided to stay.

"Everything still tastes wrong."

"You need to eat something. You've lost weight."

"I know."

My clothes fit differently.

My energy levels remain consistently low despite getting adequate sleep. Even coffee tastes off most mornings.

"I just can't seem to keep anything down. Grief, probably. Stress."

"Maybe we should see someone. Doctor. Counselor. Someone who knows about trauma and appetite and—"

"I'm fine." The lie comes automatically, a defensive response to a concern that feels overwhelming when everything else requires attention. "I just need time."

But the worried expression on his face suggests time might not be enough.

"Okay," he says finally. "But if it doesn't improve …"

"It will." Another lie, but one we both need to believe right now.

We spend the morning on the deck.

"Remember the first time we brought you here?" Gabe asks, settling beside me on the bench that spans the deck's width.

"When you and Hank tag-teamed me into agreeing to stay?" I lean against his shoulder, breathing salt air that tastes of home and possibility. "Hard to forget. I was terrified."

"Of us?"

"Of wanting you both so much it made me stupid." The confession comes easily. "I miss his laugh," I say suddenly. "The way he found everything amusing."

"I miss his coffee. He made the best coffee."

"I miss the way he smelled after training. Sweat and soap and something that was just—him."

"I miss his terrible jokes. The dad jokes that made us groan but also made us laugh despite ourselves."

We trade memories like currency, each recollection both precious and painful, necessary steps in the process of transforming loss into legacy.

"I'm scared." My admission surprises me, although it shouldn't.

"Of what?"

"Of forgetting. Of moving on so completely that he becomes just a memory instead of part of who we are." I turn to meet Gabe's eyes and see similar fears reflected back. "Of being happy without him and feeling guilty about it."

"He wants us to be happy."

"I know. But knowing and feeling are different things."

"Yeah." Gabe pulls me closer. "But maybe that's okay. Maybe guilt is just love with nowhere to go. Maybe carrying it means we're honoring what he meant to us."

The insight surprises me. Gabe usually processes emotion through action rather than analysis.

"When did you become so wise?" I ask.

His smile holds sadness alongside determination. "When I realized that the best way to honor his memory is to become the man he believed I could be."

"And who is that?"

"Someone who loves you completely without trying to own you. Someone who protects without controlling. Someone who builds instead of breaks things." He pauses, considering. "Someone who makes you happy instead of just making you come."

The observation draws unexpected laughter from my chest, bubbling up from somewhere deeper than grief. "You're good at both."

"I try."

"You succeed."

"Ready to go inside?" Gabe asks.

"Yes."

We step through the sliding door into warmth and light, but I stop just inside, my gaze drawn toward the hallway that leads to his half of the condo.

To the closed door at the end. Gabe's room—a space of dominance and submission, control and surrender, pleasure and pain.

Gabe tracks my gaze, understanding flickering across his features. "Ally …"

"I know it's there," I say quietly. "I know what's behind that door. I just … I don't know if …"

"Hey." He turns me to face him, hands gentle on my shoulders. "Look at me."

I do, seeing patience in his eyes instead of expectation, understanding instead of disappointment.

"That room, what happens in there—it's not going anywhere. The equipment, the dynamic, all of it can wait." His thumb traces my cheek. "We don't have to figure it out tonight. Or tomorrow. Or next week."

"But you need—"

"I need you. However you can give yourself to me. If that's

sex in our bedroom for the next year, then that's what we do. If it's never going back to my room, then we don't." His voice carries absolute certainty. "What I don't need is for you to force yourself into something you're not ready for because you think I can't live without it. I can and I will."

The relief that floods my system is unexpected, washing away tension I didn't realize I was carrying.

"What if I'm never ready? What if losing him changed what I can handle?"

"Then we adapt. Find new ways to connect. New things that work for us instead of what worked for us before." He leans his forehead against mine. "Everything's in flux, Ally. We're different people than we were. It's okay if what we need from each other has changed, too."

"You're really okay with that? With not knowing?"

"I'm okay with whatever lets us be together. The rest we'll figure out when we're ready to figure it out."

The acceptance in his voice provides permission I didn't know I needed—to heal at my own pace, to redefine intimacy on my own terms, to let our relationship evolve instead of forcing it back into familiar patterns.

"I love you," I tell him, meaning more than simple affection.

"I love you too," he replies, understanding everything the words carry.

We move past the closed door that holds memories of different kinds of intimacy, toward the space we shared as three and now must learn to share as two. The room feels different— larger and smaller simultaneously, familiar yet strange, ours but also empty.

Tomorrow we'll take another step forward. Today, we've done enough.

FIFTY-FOUR

Life from Love

ALLY

THE RETCHING STARTS BEFORE I'M FULLY AWAKE, MY BODY rejecting nothing with violent efficiency. Stomach acid burns my throat as I barely make it to the bathroom, knees hitting cold tile just as my body convulses again.

Gabe appears in the doorway, bare chest rising and falling with controlled breathing that doesn't hide his frustration. This is the fourth morning this week, the tenth time in two weeks, and the careful patience in his expression is cracking.

"That's it." His voice carries command authority that makes my spine straighten automatically. "You're seeing a doctor. Today."

"It's just stress—"

"Bullshit." He crouches beside me as I slump against the bathroom wall, pressing a cool washcloth to my forehead. The terry cloth smells like fabric softener and safety. "You've lost fifteen pounds, Ally. Your clothes hang off you like drapes. This isn't normal."

"I'm fine."

"You're not fine. And I'm tired of pretending otherwise." His voice drops to the tone that once made me melt with submission, now edged with worry instead of desire. "I'm calling Doc Summers. You're going. End of discussion."

The command triggers responses that run deep. My body wants to obey even as my mind rebels. "Gabe—"

"No arguments. No excuses. No dismissing this as stress or grief or anything else." He helps me to my feet, gentle despite the steel in his voice. "I won't watch you waste away because you're too stubborn to admit something's wrong."

The crack in his voice cuts through my defensive instincts. He's already lost Hank. The thought of losing me must be eating him alive.

"Okay," I whisper. "Okay, I'll go."

Skye examines me with professional thoroughness, leaving no symptom unexplored. Blood drawn, vitals checked, questions asked with enough persistence that I reveal more than I intend to share.

The examination room smells of antiseptic and latex gloves. Fluorescent lights hum overhead, casting everything in harsh relief that makes my skin look pale as old paper.

Gabe sits in the corner chair, radiating tension. His hands grip the armrests, knuckles white with pressure. The chair creaks under his weight every time he shifts, leather squeaking against tactical pants that still smell faintly of gun oil despite civilian clothes.

"Well," Skye says finally, consulting lab results with an expression I can't read. Her pen taps against the clipboard in rapid staccato. "This is unexpected."

My stomach drops. The taste of copper floods my mouth. "Is that good or bad?"

"Good, I think." She turns to face us both. "Congratulations. You're pregnant."

The words strike like lightning, coming out of nowhere, and illuminating everything while simultaneously short-circuiting my thoughts.

Pregnant.

The impossibility crashes over me in waves—relief, terror, joy, confusion all tangled together.

"That's impossible," I say automatically. "I have an IUD."

"No contraception is one hundred percent foolproof. IUDs are highly effective—ninety-nine percent—but that still leaves room for the occasional surprise." She sets down my chart with a soft thud. "The question now is what we do about it."

"What do you mean?"

"Pregnancy with an IUD in place carries risks. Increased chance of miscarriage, ectopic pregnancy, and infection. The safest course is removal, but that procedure carries risks to the fetus."

The room spins around me. The antiseptic smell intensifies, making my already sensitive stomach clench. Pregnant. With an IUD that could kill the baby. Choices that could end everything before it begins.

"What kind of risks?" Gabe's voice cuts through my mental chaos, focused on practicalities while I'm drowning in emotion.

"The procedure itself can trigger miscarriage in roughly fifteen percent of cases. Leaving it in place increases that risk to thirty percent, plus complications that could endanger Ally's life." Skye's explanation comes with clinical detachment that doesn't hide her obvious concern. "It's not an easy decision."

I look at Gabe, seeing something flickering behind his eyes.

Shock, certainly. But something else too—something that looks almost like relief mixed with profound sadness.

"I want to keep it," I say before rational thought can interfere. "The baby. I want to try."

"Even with the risks?"

"Especially with the risks." The certainty surprises me, coming from somewhere deeper than logic or careful planning. "This baby … It's a miracle. After everything we've lost, everything that's been taken from us—this is life choosing to happen anyway."

Skye nods slowly, understanding passing between us that goes beyond the scope of a medical consultation. "Then we schedule the removal for tomorrow. Sooner is better if we're going to attempt it."

Tomorrow. One day to prepare for a procedure that could end everything or give us everything. One day to hold onto hope while preparing for loss.

"What are the chances?" Gabe asks quietly.

"If the removal goes smoothly and there's no immediate trauma, roughly eighty-five percent chance the pregnancy continues normally." Skye's honesty is brutal but necessary. "Those are good odds, but not guarantees."

"Nothing's guaranteed," I say, hand moving automatically to my still-flat stomach. "But some things are worth the risk."

THE PROCEDURE TAKES THIRTY MINUTES. I LIE ON THE EXAM table while Skye works.

The gel is cold against my skin, making me shiver despite the warm room. The ultrasound wand presses against my abdomen as Skye searches for the perfect angle.

Gabe holds my hand throughout. His palm is rough with calluses, warm and solid against my suddenly cold fingers.

"There," Skye announces finally, holding up the removed IUD like a trophy. The copper gleams under examination lights. "Clean removal, no trauma."

Safe. The baby is safe.

This miraculous accident that might not be an accident at all is going to have a chance to grow, to become real, to join our broken family, and maybe help heal what trauma shattered.

"How long before we know for sure?" Gabe asks.

"Two weeks for confirmation that the pregnancy is progressing normally. Six weeks for viability assessment. Twelve weeks before we can breathe easily." Skye strips off her gloves with satisfaction. "But all the signs are positive. This little one seems determined to stick around."

Determined. Like Hank.

Eight weeks later, we're back in Skye's office for the appointment that will determine the sex of our baby. The ultrasound image shows a fully formed tiny human, fingers and toes visible, heart beating with a rhythm that fills the room like the most beautiful music ever composed.

The sound echoes off sterile walls, steady and strong and absolutely perfect.

"Do you want to know?" Skye asks, positioning the ultrasound wand for optimal viewing.

I look at Gabe, seeing anticipation mixed with something else I still can't identify. He's been different since the pregnancy was confirmed—brighter somehow, like a shadow lifted from his shoulders. But also quieter, more thoughtful, carrying some knowledge he hasn't shared.

"I want to know," he says. I smile at him and nod.

"Then I'm happy to tell you," Skye announces with a smile that transforms her face, "you're having a son."

A son. A little boy who will carry forward whatever legacy we choose to give him, who will grow up knowing he was wanted and loved even before he existed.

Gabe's smile—the first real smile I've seen since Hank died—transforms his entire face. Light returns to eyes that have been shadowed with grief, hope replacing despair with such sudden intensity it takes my breath away.

"A son," he repeats softly, voice holding wonder alongside satisfaction.

"Ally?" Skye turns to me. "How are you feeling about this news?"

"Perfect." The word comes out choked with emotion that threatens to overwhelm me. "He's perfect."

"There's something else," I say as Skye cleans gel from my stomach with warm towels. "Is there a way to determine paternity? Without risking the pregnancy?"

"Noninvasive prenatal paternity testing *after* birth." Skye's explanation comes without judgment, recognition that complicated relationships sometimes require complicated answers. "Results take about a week."

We drive home in silence, hands linked across the center console, minds processing news that changes everything while changing nothing. Pregnant. Having a son. Building a family from the ashes of loss.

Late-afternoon sunlight slants through windows, warming my skin despite the air conditioning.

The sunset paints our deck in shades of gold and orange as we settle onto the deck that's become our evening refuge. Ocean waves crash against cliffs below with a rhythm that speaks to continuity despite constant change. Salt air carries the scent of kelp and brine, mixing with the jasmine blooming in our neighbor's yard.

"I can't believe we're going to be a family." My hand rests on the small bump that's just beginning to show. "Hank would have been so excited about having a baby."

"He would have been a great father," Gabe agrees, voice carrying certainty alongside sadness.

"We don't even know if it's his baby or yours. But maybe that's beautiful—not knowing, not needing to know. Just loving him because he exists."

Gabe goes very still beside me. His hand, which had been tracing lazy patterns on my arm, stops moving entirely. When I look at him, his face has gone carefully blank—the expression he wears when he's processing something too big for immediate reaction.

"Gabe? What's wrong?"

"Nothing's wrong." His voice sounds strained, like he's forcing words past some obstruction in his throat. "Everything's … It's good. This is good."

"You're being weird." I shift to face him, studying features that have gone suspiciously neutral. "You've been weird since we found out about the pregnancy. Different. Like you know something I don't."

"I don't—"

"Don't lie to me." The words come out sharper than intended, pregnancy hormones making my emotions run closer to the surface than usual. "I can read you, Gabriel Martinez. After everything we've been through, after losing Hank, don't you dare start keeping secrets from me."

He flinches at the accusation, guilt flickering across features he's trying so hard to keep controlled.

"Ally—"

"You've been lighter. Happier. Which should be wonderful, except it started the day we found out about the baby. You smiled when Skye said we were having a son. Really smiled, for the first time since Hank died. Why?"

"Because we're having a baby—"

"That's not why." I grab his chin and force him to meet my eyes. His skin is rough with afternoon stubble, warm under my palm. "Look at me and tell me what you're not saying."

The silence stretches between us, heavy with unspoken truth. Ocean wind carries salt spray that tastes of storms approaching, weather that matches the tension building in Gabe's expression.

"It's complicated," he says finally.

"Everything about our life is complicated. That's never stopped us from talking about it before."

"This is different."

"How?"

"Because ..." He stops, runs his hands through his hair in frustration. The dark strands stick up at odd angles, making him look vulnerable. "Because it changes things. Because once I say it, we can't go back to not knowing."

"Knowing, what?"

"The truth." The words come out like a confession, weighted with implications that make my stomach clench with something that isn't morning sickness. "About the baby. About what this means."

Fear crawls up my spine with icy fingers. "What truth?"

Gabe stands and begins pacing the length of the deck. Back and forth, hands clenched at his sides, internal war playing out in every movement. His bare feet slap against warm wood with each turn.

"When you asked about paternity testing," he says finally, stopping mid-pace to face me. "I wanted to tell you then. Should have told you then. But I was being selfish."

"Selfish how?"

"Because I wanted you to want this baby for the right reasons. Not because of who his father is, but because he's ours.

Because he exists. Because he chose us despite everything stacked against him."

The fear in my stomach intensifies, twisting into something that threatens to steal my breath. "Gabe, you're scaring me."

"I'm not trying to scare you. I'm trying to figure out how to tell you something that changes everything without making you think it changes everything."

"Just say it." The words explode from me with force that surprises us both. A seagull on the railing squawks and takes flight, wings beating frantically as it disappears over the cliff edge. "Whatever it is, just say it instead of dancing around it like it's going to kill me."

He stops pacing, turns to face me fully, and I see something in his eyes that takes my breath away. Not fear or uncertainty, but peace. Deep, profound peace mixed with sadness, love, and something that resembles gratitude.

"The baby is Hank's," he says quietly.

"How can you be so sure?"

"Because I can't have children."

The second revelation follows the first like thunder after lightning, rolling over me with force that threatens to flatten everything in its path. *Can't have children?*

"What?"

"Old injury. Damaged beyond repair. I found out years ago, before I met either of you." He sits back down beside me, movements careful as if I might shatter. The bench creaks under his weight. "I'm sterile, Ally. Have been for years."

The words echo in my head, bouncing around like ricochets that can't find a safe place to land. Sterile. Can't have children. The baby is Hank's.

"How long have you known?" My voice sounds distant to my own ears, shock making everything feel unreal.

"Since the first positive test." He reaches for my hand, holds it like lifeline. "Since Skye told us you were pregnant. I knew immediately it had to be Hank's."

"All this time …" I stare at him, seeing weeks of careful restraint in a new light. "You've been carrying this alone."

"I had to."

"Why?"

"Because I needed you to fight for our baby. I needed you to choose him, to want him, to risk everything for him because he mattered to you. Not because he's Hank's son, but because he's your son." His thumb traces patterns on my skin that speak to apology and explanation intertwined. "If I'd told you right away, every decision would have been about preserving Hank's legacy instead of creating our family."

The logic makes sense even as it infuriates me. Because he's right—knowing the baby was Hank's would have changed everything. The risks would have felt different, the stakes higher, the decisions weighted with grief instead of hope.

"When were you going to tell me?"

"After you had time to bond with him as your son instead of Hank's ghost." His smile holds sadness alongside relief. "I've been carrying this for weeks, Ally. Knowing and not being able to share it. Watching you worry about paternity when I knew the answer all along."

"You bastard." The words come out without heat. I could be angry, but I'm not. I've never been happier. "You manipulative, protective, impossible bastard."

"You love that about me."

"This is huge, Gabe. This changes everything."

"Does it?" He searches my face for signs of regret or resentment. "You're still pregnant. Still having his son. Still building a family with me. The only thing that's changed is certainty about paternity."

I consider this, testing the truth of it against emotions that feel too big for my chest. He's right—the love I feel for this baby doesn't depend on DNA. The future we're building doesn't require specific chromosomes to be meaningful.

But knowing he's Hank's son …

"You're carrying Hank's baby," Gabe continues, voice soft with wonder that's been building for weeks. "Part of him that death can't touch, a legacy that will outlive all of us. He's not really gone, Ally. He's going to live on in our memories, in our hearts, and in our family."

The truth of it hits like sunrise after the longest night, illuminating everything with sudden joy. Hank's baby. Hank's son. A piece of the man we lost, growing inside me, preparing to join a world that needs his father's steadiness and strength.

"Oh my God." The words come out as a whisper; my hands move automatically to my stomach, where Hank's son grows safely. "We're having Hank's baby."

"We're having Hank's baby," Gabe confirms, a smile breaking across features that have carried too much shadow for too long.

Tears fall without permission, hot against skin that's suddenly too sensitive. Hank's baby. Hank's son. A piece of the man we lost, growing inside me, preparing to join a world that needs his father's steadiness and strength.

"We get to raise Hank's son together. We get to tell him about his father—how brave he was, how much he loved us, how he died protecting the people who mattered the most to him." Gabe's voice breaks on the words as the emotion he's been containing finally finds an outlet.

"I love you," I tell Gabe, meaning more than simple affection.

"I love you too. Both of you." His hand covers mine where it rests on my stomach. "All three of us, actually. Because he's still here. Still a part of us."

The sun disappears behind the horizon, painting the sky in colors that would have made Hank smile.

Love creates its own kind of immortality.

We're going to be a family. Different from what we planned, shaped by loss but strengthened by love, carrying forward with the best of what we've been given.

Sometimes, that's not just enough.

It's everything.

FIFTY-FIVE

Carry Her Home

GABE

I watch her sleeping in the early morning light, her body curved protectively around the small bump that holds Hank's son. Our son. Her breathing comes deep and even, face relaxed in sleep like it rarely is in waking hours anymore. Dawn paints her skin gold, catching in her hair and turning ordinary brown to burnished copper.

Some mornings, I just watch her breathe. Count the inhales and exhales like they're miracles. Because they are.

Telling her about the baby was the right call. Watching her process that revelation—that Hank's legacy will continue in flesh and blood—broke something loose in both of us. A tension we'd been carrying without realizing it.

Now our grief and our hope tangle together in this messy, beautiful aftermath of loving a man who isn't here anymore.

I ease out of bed, careful not to wake her. Morning sickness has finally started to ease, but she needs every minute of rest she can get. The hardwood is cool against my bare feet as I pad into the kitchen, the familiar ritual of making coffee giving my hands something to do while my mind wanders.

It's been five months since we lost him. Five months of relearning how to exist in a world where Hank's laugh doesn't fill our home, where his steady presence doesn't anchor us in moments of chaos. Five months of Ally and me circling each other like survivors of a shipwreck, both desperate to keep the other afloat.

And now a baby. Hank's son growing stronger every day.

The doorbell rings, jarring me from thoughts that have turned melancholy despite the good news we're still processing. It's early—barely 6 a.m. Nobody visits at this hour unless something's wrong.

I check the security feed before opening the door. Forest stands on our porch, looking uncomfortable. His face is grim, the expression of a man carrying weight he'd rather set down.

"Forest." I open the door, anxiety spiking despite his nod of reassurance. "Everything okay?"

"Yeah." He clears his throat, not quite concealing his obvious discomfort. "Can I come in?"

I step aside, letting him enter our home. He looks around, taking in the changes since his last visit. The walls Ally painted pale blue last weekend. The crib parts stacked in the corner, waiting for assembly. The ultrasound photos magnetized to the refrigerator.

"Heard the news," he says, nodding toward the evidence of impending fatherhood. "Congratulations."

"Thanks." The word comes out rough, emotion still raw when people acknowledge what's happening. What's real.

"Coffee?"

"No." He shifts his weight, hand going to the pocket of his jacket. "I'm not staying. Just needed to deliver something."

An envelope appears from his pocket, thick cream-colored paper with my name written in familiar handwriting. The sight of it stops my breath, punches a hole straight through my chest.

Hank's handwriting.

"What the hell is this?" My voice comes out strangled, barely audible over the sudden roaring in my ears.

"He asked me to give it to you. If he didn't make it back." Forest holds the envelope like it might detonate. Maybe it will. "Said to wait until you'd had time to grieve properly. Until things were …" he gestures vaguely at the ultrasound photos, "settled."

My hand shakes as I take it from him. The paper feels heavy, weighted with words Hank wrote before he died. Words meant for me to read in exactly this moment, when life has found its new shape around the hole he left behind.

"He knew, didn't he?" I ask, already knowing the answer. "He knew he wasn't coming back from that island."

Forest's silence is confirmation enough.

"Not for certain," he says finally. "But he felt it. The way we sometimes do before a mission goes sideways."

The coffee machine beeps, announcing the completion of its cycle. The ordinary sound feels obscene next to the letter in my hand.

"Thanks for bringing this," I manage, throat tight with emotion I can't afford to release. Not yet. Not until Forest leaves and I can fall apart in private.

He nods, understanding passing between us. Then his hand lands on my shoulder, heavy and solid. "He was proud to serve with you. Proud to call you brother."

"Yeah." It's all I can say without breaking.

Then he's gone, leaving me alone with Hank's final words burning a hole in my palm.

I stand frozen in the kitchen, caught between wanting to tear the envelope open and wanting to burn it unread. Part of me can't bear the thought of hearing Hank's voice again, even through paper and ink. The other part is desperate for it, for one last connection to the man who was my other half for so long.

"Gabe?" Ally's voice comes from the bedroom doorway. She stands there in one of Hank's old T-shirts, fabric stretched slightly over her growing bump. "Who was at the door?"

I hold up the envelope, unable to find words to explain what it is. She moves closer, squinting in the early morning light, then freezes as recognition hits.

"Is that—"

"Yeah." I swallow hard, emotions threatening to overflow. "Forest just delivered it. From Hank."

Her eyes widen, one hand going instinctively to her stomach, the other reaching for the envelope like she can't help herself. "What does it say?"

"I don't know. I haven't opened it yet."

We stand there, both staring at Hank's handwriting like it might spring to life, might somehow bring him back to us if we just look at it long enough.

"Do you want to be alone?" she asks, understanding even in this moment how complicated my relationship with Hank was, how some things between us were just ours.

"No." I reach for her hand, needing her solid presence beside me. "Whatever he wrote, it's for both of us now."

We move to the couch, settling into the same spot we've spent countless evenings since moving in. Ally curls against my side, her head on my shoulder, both of us bracing for whatever comes next.

My finger breaks the seal, careful not to tear what feels sacred. The letter inside is several pages, folded precisely the way Hank always folded important documents. Methodical to the end.

I unfold the paper, and his voice fills my head with the first words:

. . .

Gabe,

If you're reading this, it means I didn't make it home.

The sob comes without warning, ripping from my chest with enough force to shake Ally where she presses against me. Her hand tightens on mine, anchoring me as Hank's words swim before my eyes.

Don't waste a second blaming yourself. This was always how I was meant to go—first in, last out, heart wide open. You know me. You knew this was coming long before I did.

He's right. I did know. Had always known on some level that Hank would die this way—protecting others, putting himself between danger and the people he loved. It was written into his DNA, this selfless courage that made him both magnificent and doomed.

But she's still breathing. And so are you.
So now I need you to do something for me.
Carry her home.

Ally's tears soak through my T-shirt, her body trembling against mine. I read the next lines aloud, voice breaking on words that pierce straight through every defense I've built.

. . .

Hold her when she breaks, like I would've. Wipe her tears with those rough hands of yours. Make her feel safe again, even when the world's burning down around you. She doesn't need a hero—she needs you. Solid. Steady. There.

Ally's breath catches, a sound between a laugh and a sob escaping her. "He knew you so well," she whispers.

She cried the night I left. Tried to hide it, but I saw. You did too. She bends, but she never breaks. Not really. She still believes in us—in you. So don't make her go the rest of the way alone.

I remember the night he died. The way she cried, shoulders shaking, sobbing with endless tears.

You know her better than most. That laughter like sunrise. The way she bites her lip when she's trying to lie. She gave us both more than we deserved—fire and fury, softness and steel. She wasn't mine. She wasn't yours. She was ours. In a way that never fit inside clean lines.

My voice gives out completely on "ours." Because he's right. She was never just his or just mine. She belonged to both of us in a way that defied conventional relationships, that created something whole from three separate people.

Ally takes the letter from my trembling hands, continues

reading where I left off, her voice steady despite the tears streaming down her face.

So don't you dare carry guilt. Carry her.

Breathe her in. Love her fully, recklessly, tenderly. Love her loud. Love her soft. Love her like you do, in all the ways I won't get to anymore.

Guard her.

Trace her scars like they're battle maps. Let her sleep safely in your arms. Make her coffee just right. Leave the light on when she needs it. Keep her warm. Keep her laughing. Let her cry into your chest when she needs to fall apart. Then hold her tighter than the fear.

Her voice breaks on "fear," the word dissolving into a sob that seems to come from somewhere deeper than her lungs. I pull her closer, one hand moving to rest on the small swell of her stomach, where Hank's son grows stronger every day.

When she can't continue, I take the letter back and read the final lines that Hank left for me. For us.

Tell her I didn't leave—not really. I'm still here. In your blood. In her breath.

I loved her to the end.

You're my brother. My best. My last. My always.

Now you lead.

Carry her home for me.

She's yours now.

．　．　．

– Hank

T HE FINAL WORDS HANG IN THE AIR BETWEEN US, H ANK'S VOICE so clear I can almost hear him speaking them. The grief I've been carrying these past months shifts, transforming into something different. Not lighter, exactly, but more purposeful.

Grief with direction.

Ally's hand covers mine where it rests on her stomach. "He knew," she whispers. "Somehow, he knew about the baby."

"No." I shake my head, certain on this point. "He couldn't have known. But he knew us. Knew what we'd need to hear exactly when we'd need to hear it."

That was Hank—always three steps ahead, planning for contingencies none of us wanted to face.

"He's right," I continue, voice steadier now. "He's still here. In the way we love each other. In the family we're building. In his son."

Ally's eyes meet mine, wet with tears but bright with something that looks like peace. "His son," she repeats, wonder in her voice. "Our son."

"Our son," I agree, the truth of it settling into my bones.

We sit in silence as dawn breaks fully outside our windows, painting the room in golden light that feels like benediction. Like Hank's approval washing over us as we find our way forward without him.

The grief doesn't disappear. It never will. But beside it now grows something else—a future taking shape from the ashes of what we've lost. A family built from love that transcends death, that continues in the child growing beneath my palm.

Hank's final mission for me—carry her home for me—is one I'll spend the rest of my life fulfilling. Not because he asked, but because it's who we are now. Who we've always been. Three souls so intertwined that even death couldn't fully separate us.

I press a kiss to Ally's temple, breathing in the scent of her hair, feeling the solid warmth of her against me. In this moment, I make a silent promise to Hank, to Ally, to the son we'll raise together:

We'll carry each other home. Every day. For all the days we have left.

And somewhere, Hank is watching.

Approving. At peace.

First in, last out, heart wide open.

Just like he taught us.

My dear reader...Just breathe,

Thank you for walking this journey with me. I never expected the story to take this path—or for Hank's voice to demand such an ending. Writing his death and the grief that followed broke me. His voice refused to be silenced, and in following it, I felt every ounce of the grief that Gabe, Ally, the men of Charlie Team, and the women of Charlie's Angels endured.

It broke me to write it, and it still hurts. But I hope this story delivered on the promise I've always tried to keep—that even in the deepest shadows, there is always light in the darkness. Brotherhood, love, and hope remain at the heart of every page.

With gratitude,
Ellie Masters

SO NOW WHAT? *YOU TURNED THE LAST PAGE, BUT YOU'RE NOT ready to walk away. The Guardians don't let go of the people they love—and neither will you.*

Where *one mission ends, another begins. Are you ready to keep up?*

YOU SURVIVED CHARLIE TEAM'S LAST MISSION...

RIGHT NOW, YOU'VE GOT **THREE WAYS TO KEEP THE ADRENALINE pumping and the heat burning**:

1. DIVE INTO THE GUARDIANS FROM THE VERY BEGINNING.

If you're new here, start with **Alpha Team**—then tear through Bravo and Delta teams. Fierce, protective, unapologetically alpha men. The women who bring them to their knees. Every mission is more dangerous, every romance is more unforgettable.

2. GO BACK TO WHERE IT ALL BEGAN.

Before the missions. Before the rescues. Before Guardian HRS existed.

It began with **Heart's Insanity**—Book One in the *Angel Fire* rock star romance series. Meet Skye as she falls in love with Ash,

Angel Fire's lead singer. In Heart's Insanity, you will also meet Skye's foster brother, Forest.

See the raw, emotional love story that built the foundation for everything the Guardians have become. Once you know Forest's past, you'll never see him the same way again.

3. STEP INTO THE NEXT EXPLOSIVE CHAPTER.

Already caught up on *Angel Fire and the Guardians?* Then it's time for **Cerberus Personal Security**—the brand-new spinoff series that takes the danger beyond the Guardians.

New men. New missions. Same heart-pounding mix of passion and peril. Book One will drag you in and won't let you go.

THE HEAT ONLY GETS HOTTER.
The danger only gets deadlier.
The mission isn't over—it's just getting started.

YOUR NEXT MISSION? **CHOOSE WHERE TO GO NEXT.**
Angel Fire Rockstar Romance
Guardian HRS
Cerberus Personal Security

WHEREVER YOU START, ONE THING'S CERTAIN—
You won't want to stop.

Ellie Masters Romantic Suspense and Steamy Contemporary Romance by series.

Angel Fire Rock Romance
Guardian HRS: Alpha Team
Guardian HRS: Bravo Team
Guardian HRS: Charlie Team
Guardian HRS: Delta Team
Cerberus Personal Security
The LaRouge Triplets
The One I Want Series
Angel's Peak Series
Billionaire Boy's Club
The Lovers
Changing Roles

ELLZ BELLZ

ELLIE'S FACEBOOK READER GROUP

If you are interested in joining the ELLZ BELLZ, Ellie's Facebook reader group, we'd love to have you.

Join Ellie's ELLZ BELLZ.
The ELLZ BELLZ Facebook Reader Group

Sign up for Ellie's Newsletter.
Elliemasters.com/newslettersignup

Also by Ellie Masters

The LIGHTER SIDE

Ellie Masters is the lighter side of the Jet & Ellie Masters writing duo! You will find Contemporary Romance, Military Romance, Romantic Suspense, Billionaire Romance, and Rock Star Romance in Ellie's Works.

YOU CAN FIND ELLIE'S BOOKS HERE:

ELLIEMASTERS.COM/BOOKS

Shop Ellie Masters Romantic Suspense and Steamy Contemporary Romance by series.

Angel Fire Rock Romance

Guardian HRS: Alpha Team

Guardian HRS: Bravo Team

Guardian HRS: Charlie Team

Guardian HRS: Delta Team

Cerberus Personal Security

The LaRouge Triplets

The One I Want Series

Angel's Peak Series

Billionaire Boy's Club

The Lovers

Changing Roles

Rescuing Eve

Rescuing Lily

Rescuing Jinx

Rescuing Maria

Bravo Team

Rescuing Angie

Rescuing Isabelle

Rescuing Carmen

Rescuing Rosalie

Rescuing Kaye

Cara's Protector

Rescuing Barbi

Charlie Team

Rescuing Rebel

Rescuing Stitch

Rescuing Mia

Jenna's Protector

Rescuing Sophia

Rescuing Malia

Rescuing Ally (Part 1)

Rescuing Ally (Part 2)

Delta Team

Rescuing Ember

Rescuing Aria

STANDALONES IN THE GUARDIAN HOSTAGE RESCUE

The Ties that Bind

HOT READS

Becoming His Series

Dark Captive Romance

About the Author

Ellie Masters is a USA Today Bestselling author and Amazon Top 15 Author who writes Angsty, Steamy, Heart-Stopping, Pulse-Pounding, Can't-Stop-Reading Romantic Suspense. In addition, she's a wife, military mom, doctor, and retired Colonel. She writes romantic suspense filled with all your sexy, swoon-worthy alpha men. Her writing will tug at your heartstrings and leave your heart racing.

Born in the South, raised under the Hawaiian sun, Ellie has traveled the globe while in service to her country. The love of her life, her amazing husband, is her number one fan and biggest supporter. And yes! He's read every word she's written.

She has lived all over the United States—east, west, north, south and central—but grew up under the Hawaiian sun. She's also been privileged to have lived overseas, experiencing other cultures and making lifelong friends. Now, Ellie is proud to call herself a Southern transplant, learning to say y'all and "bless her heart" with the best of them.

Ellie's favorite way to spend an evening is curled up on a couch, laptop in place, watching a fire, drinking a good wine, and bringing forth all the characters from her mind to the page and hopefully into the hearts of her readers.

FOR MORE INFORMATION
elliemasters.com

Connect with Ellie Masters

Website:
elliemasters.com
Purchase Direct:
elliemasters.com/shopify
Amazon Author Page:
elliemasters.com/amazon
Facebook:
elliemasters.com/Facebook
Goodreads:
elliemasters.com/Goodreads
Bookbub:
elliemasters.com/Bookbub
Instagram:
elliemasters.com/Instagram

Final Thoughts

I hope you enjoyed this book as much as I enjoyed writing it. If you enjoyed reading this story, please consider leaving a review on Amazon and Goodreads, and please let other people know. A sentence is all it takes. Friend recommendations are the strongest catalyst for readers' purchase decisions! And I'd love to be able to continue bringing the characters and stories from My-Mind-to-the-Page.

Second, call or e-mail a friend and tell them about this book. If you really want them to read it, gift it to them. If you prefer digital friends, please use the "Recommend" feature of Goodreads to spread the word.

Or visit my blog https://elliemasters.com, where you can find out more about my writing process and personal life.

Come visit The EDGE: Dark Discussions where we'll have a chance to talk about my works, their creation, and maybe what the future has in store for my writing.

Facebook Reader Group: Ellz Bellz

Thank you so much for your support!

Love,
Ellie

Dedication

This book is dedicated to you, my reader. Thank you for spending a few hours of your time with me. I wouldn't be able to write without you to cheer me on. Your wonderful words, your support, and your willingness to join me on this journey is a gift beyond measure.

Whether this is the first book of mine you've read, or if you've been with me since the very beginning, thank you for believing in me as I bring these characters 'from my mind to the page and into your hearts.'

Love,
Ellie

THE END